# Into the Mountains

Also by
Thomas H. Williams

*Greenbrier: Valley of Hope*
*A History of Bonafield School, Preston County, WV*

# Into the Mountains

A Novel

Thomas H. Williams

Copyright © 2015 by Thomas H. Williams.

Library of Congress Control Number: 2015903115
ISBN: Hardcover 978-1-5035-4775-9
Softcover 978-1-5035-4776-6
eBook 978-1-5035-4777-3

All rights reserved. No part of this book may be reproduced or transmitted in any form or by any means, electronic or mechanical, including photocopying, recording, or by any information storage and retrieval system, without permission in writing from the copyright owner.

This is a work of fiction. Names, characters, places and incidents either are the product of the author's imagination or are used fictitiously, and any resemblance to any actual persons, living or dead, events, or locales is entirely coincidental.

Scripture quotations marked KJV are from the Holy Bible, King James Version (Authorized Version). First published in 1611. Quoted from the KJV Classic Reference Bible, Copyright © 1983 by The HYPERLINK "http://www.zondervan.com/" Zondervan Corporation.

Any people depicted in stock imagery provided by Thinkstock are models, and such images are being used for illustrative purposes only.
Certain stock imagery © Thinkstock.

Print information available on the last page.

Rev. date: 03/05/2015

**To order additional copies of this book, contact:**
Xlibris
1-888-795-4274
www.Xlibris.com
Orders@Xlibris.com
703540

Nothing lives long. Only the earth and the mountains.

>Death song of White Antelope,
>Cheyenne chief killed at
>Sand Creek massacre, Colorado, 1864

One generation passeth away, and another generation cometh, but the earth abideth forever.

>Ecclesiastes 1:4

For my grandchildren, Katherine and Alexandra of the next generation, carriers of the torch.

# ACKNOWLEDGEMENTS

I AM INDEBTED TO many people who helped me write this book. My appreciation goes to those who gave me encouragement and graciously agreed to read early drafts. I would not have been able to complete this project without them.

I am grateful to Janet Myers and T. M. Bautista who made suggestions for the improvement of the storyline and helped me keep the characters straight. I thank Danny Miller for answering my questions about railroads during our early morning walks. Thanks to Clyde Cale, Jr, who helped clarify the section on "swabbing." An extra special nod goes to Anita Craig who provided invaluable assistance with editing. Appreciation goes to the staff at Xlibris for their expertise in the publication of this book.

I am especially grateful to Lucille Grimm and the Rowlesburg Historical Society who took time to advise me regarding historical accuracy. Thank you for the work you do and your valiant efforts to keep our local history alive.

Any errors or discrepancies from the historical record that have found their way into this book are solely my responsibility.

# AUTHOR'S NOTES

THE READER SHOULD be aware that I make no claim of being an historian. There are many excellent references available for the local history enthusiast, some of which are listed below. Although this is a work of fiction, I have attempted to remain faithful to the historical record. However, I claim "novelist's privilege" by altering certain timelines, names, dates and events.

Many of the names of towns, roads, mountains, rivers and streams were taken from Lloyd's map of Virginia published in 1862. Other than historical persons, all characters are products of my imagination, and any resemblance to real persons or their names is entirely coincidental.

With one exception, all towns and locales are real but used fictitiously–Conley's Knob is fictitious. Marling Bottom is now the site of the town of Marlinton. Both Beverly and St. George were county seats early in their histories. Leedsville was a small community near present day Elkins. I have used the name "Cannon Hill" to describe the mountaintop where "guns" were placed by Union forces overlooking Rowlesburg, although that name may have only become widely used after the Civil War. Cranberry and Mount Carmel were early names for Terra Alta and Aurora. The town of Tunnelton was not incorporated until the late 1890s–Lloyd used that name on his 1862 map and I have followed suit. Albrightsville was an early name for Albright as noted in Wiley's work.

The Northwestern Turnpike, mentioned frequently in the story, is now U.S. Route 50. The B&O Railroad was completed prior to the Civil War, and I have attempted to describe it faithfully. Commanders of Union forces, as described, are real, although some may have been moved in time and place to simplify the timeline.

In addition to a variety of web-sites, I have drawn from the following sources:

*A Dublin Student Doctor*, Patrick Taylor, 2011; *Flora of West Virginia*, Second Edition, P.D. Strausbaugh and Earl L. Core, 1970; *A History of Bonafield School, Preston County*, WV, Thomas H. Williams, 2000; *A History of Greenbrier County*, Otis Rice, 1986; *History of Preston County (West Virginia)*, S. T. Wiley, 1882; *A History of Randolph County*, A.S. Bosworth, 1916; *History of Randolph County, WV*, Hu Maxwell, 1898; *History of Tucker County*, West Virginia, Homer Fansler, 1962; *Lloyd's Official Map of the State of Virginia*, J. T. Lloyd, Publisher, 1862; Our Place in History: *Southern Preston County, West Virginia,* Connie Loraine Cox, 2005; "Swabbing for Fish in the Cheat", Clyde Cale, Jr., *Preston County Journal*, March 7, 2012; *Randolph 200: a Bicentennial History of Randolph County, West Virginia,* Donald Rice, 1987; *The Sibley Guide to Birds*, David Allen Sibley, 2000; *West End; Cumberland to Grafton, 1848 – 1991,* 1991,Charles S. Roberts; *West Virginia Atlas, & Gazetteer,* Second Edition, Yarmouth, Maine, 1997*;* "Worth to Us an Army," *Rowlesburg in the Civil War,* Rowlesburg Printing, 2008, from work by Michael E. Workman, PhD.

# PART ONE

# CHAPTER ONE

THE WEARY HORSE tossed its head, pranced in place, and then plunged into the cold, swift-flowing mountain stream. Boyd Houston encouraged the animal by clucking softly and brushing its flanks with his heels. The water rose up to the horse's belly before they made the other side. It clambered up the rock-strewn bank with its rider clinging to the saddle horn; water splashed into the air, sparkling in the dim light, dripping onto the hard-packed road. The horse trotted along, shaking its head and snorting, although both horse and rider were exhausted. They had traveled from the coastal plains of South Carolina to the Appalachian Mountains.

The road was lined with magnificent oaks and maples. A long row of sycamores flanked the stream behind them and along the river up ahead. Their silvery branches reached for the blue sky as dusk quickly settled in. Somewhere off in the brush a towhee sang—*drink your tea, drink your teeeee.*

Soon after crossing the creek, they approached a heavily rutted turnpike that ran from Richmond westward through Lewisburg, now a part of the newly formed state of West Virginia. This was the highway over which Union and Confederate forces had skirmished for the last several years as the Civil War raged on. The horse shuffled along the road to the sound of creaking leather and jingling bridle. Boyd looked for the place where only a few years before, a young Union picket had died at his hands. He couldn't find the exact spot, but a flood of emotion swept over him. Death had been his companion that day.

Soon, they came to a large house with white columns and further on the road crossed the Greenbrier River. The house looked deserted, and someone had used parts of the split-rail fence surrounding the yard for firewood. The remnants of the covered bridge that had spanned the river could still be seen. Dark, charred timbers canted crazily down into the clear water, and limestone pillars stood as lone sentinels in the river. One day, he thought, when all of this madness is done, they'll rebuild the bridge. The horse dutifully entered the swiftly moving water and began wading across. Although no deeper than the creek they had crossed earlier, the river was more than a hundred yards wide. Luckily it had been a dry spring—otherwise they would have had to swim across the river. Dark water swirled around the horse's legs, and Boyd could see the silvery flash of fish scattering before their approach.

Once they had reached solid ground again, they turned upstream away from the turnpike and looked for a place to sleep for the night. It was only a few miles further to Lewisburg, but it was all uphill. Both Boyd and the horse were about spent. Besides, he didn't know what kind of sleeping quarters would be available there. He'd find out tomorrow. A quarter-mile upstream he found a spot to camp that had been used often before. It had a circle of stones for a fire and a pile of pine boughs someone had recently used for a bed. He dismounted stiffly and stretched. The horse stomped its hooves and rolled its eyes at him.

"Okay boy, I'll get you unsaddled. Hold your horses," he said, smiling. He stripped off the saddle and the sweat-stained blanket and tossed them into a heap near the bed site. He piled his saddle bags and bedroll on top of them and began to rub the horse down with an old rag. The horse shied away, circling at the end of the reins. Boyd pulled the horse nearer, talking quietly to it and then resumed grooming. The horse stomped its hooves and snorted, but it finally stood still while Boyd finished the task. With it tethered on a long rope, he allowed it to feed on the lush grass that bordered the river.

Later that evening, as fireflies flashed over the field, Boyd sat on a rock and looked out over the moonlit river. Steep, heavily wooded mountains rose on the east side of the stream, and a broad field bordered the near side. Weeds grew in the field where crops once had been planted. The air was cool and sweet. He ate mechanically from a cloth sack and sorted through its contents hoping for an overlooked morsel and drank occasionally from a canteen of water that rested at his feet. The horse stomped nearby shifting sleepily from leg to leg. A whip-or-will called from the darkness filling him with a deep melancholy. Memories of good friends and death rose like hooded spirits crowding in around him. He blinked them away, refusing to succumb to their spell.

He reached into his pants pocket and withdrew a folded, thumb-worn envelope addressed to Mr. Boyd Houston, General Delivery, Charleston, South Carolina. He removed the single sheet of coarse paper, and turning it toward the flickering fire, read it again.

> *Dear Boyd Houston,*
> *I am not very good at writing letters. I find this one to be especially trying since I must ask you for help. I know that we didn't part as best friends, but I don't know who else to turn to. It seems that everyone that I depended on is either dead, fighting in this terrible war, or has left to seek their fortunes out west. Both Mother and Daddy have passed away. Daddy died last winter of cholera, and Mother grieved so that I fear that she died of a broken heart. Doctor Franklin*

*said that it was consumption, but I know otherwise. I miss them both terribly and without relatives close by, I am alone.*

*Everyone says that the war will one day be over and life will return to normal. A few of the men who fought in this awful conflict have returned home, many with terrible wounds, and others we fear are dead and will never be heard from again. From time to time, I think of you and wonder if you survived. And at times, I fear for my life. Oh, how I wish that you were here to come to my rescue. But I ramble. If you could feel it in your heart to assist me, I will pay you what I can. Please correspond at your soonest convenience if you are so inclined.*

*Your obedient servant,*

*Miss Lexus Saunders*
*Lewisburg, West Virginia*

He leaned back against his saddle and quietly watched the dark stream flow by. There were quiet croaks and splashes along the water's edge while insects sounded noisily in the trees around him. Smoke from the campfire floated on the still air to form a hazy mantle over the water.

What, he wondered for the hundredth time, did the letter mean? Was she in danger? Why had she written that she feared for her life? What was it with which she needed help? He absently rubbed the ugly rope scar–the result of an accident when he worked on his father's boat–that crossed the back of his right hand. At times, it itched and when his hand was cold, it became stiff and ached.

He remembered Lexus vividly; ash blond hair, blue eyes, and a straight back, fire in her eyes, too, when they'd had words. She was a spirited woman with a mind of her own–their relationship had been tumultuous. It seemed that he just couldn't do anything to please her. No matter how good his intentions, things just didn't seem to turn out right. But that was all in the past. When he received her letter, he had written a brief reply and immediately prepared to leave. The journey had been long and arduous but was almost complete. Tomorrow he would ride into town and find her, and if he could, he would help her.

He made a bed of pine boughs and covered himself with his bedroll. He slept fitfully through the night reliving battles past. At one point, he sat up abruptly and looked wildly about, unsure of where he was, fending off imagined horrors that approached him with outstretched arms. He sank back down slowly and pulled the dew-dampened bedclothes around him.

Morning light came slowly, creeping over the mountains and piercing the haunting fog that fell like a cloak around him. He awoke as the sun topped the mountains to the east. A wind had picked up during the night, and a thin layer of clouds approached from the west. "Storm's coming, boy," Boyd said to the horse. "My daddy could always tell when a storm was brewing. First there'll be thin clouds like that," he nodded toward the mountain rim, "then, there'll be dark ones following. You wait and see." The horse looked at him and snorted.

He dug into the food sack and found a hard biscuit which he dipped in the river to soften. He sat on the rock again, watched as the river slid by and gnawed on the biscuit. A bass jumped from the water attempting to catch a dragonfly that flitted by. Ripples spread in a broad circle across the placid water. What was he doing here? He'd help Lexus if he could, but he would be in deep trouble if the Union soldiers were in Lewisburg again. He was on parole from the war, but a renegade soldier had taken his papers. He'd have a hard time explaining things if they caught up with him. They'd shoot him for a spy if he couldn't prove he had been paroled. He didn't know if they kept records of soldiers who were paroled so that he might get a copy or not. He shook his head and tossed the last bit of the biscuit into the river.

He saddled the horse, and tied on his saddle bags and bedroll, mounted and rode back down along the river to the turnpike where he turned west. The horse pranced, trying to grab mouths full of grass as they moved along. They soon came to the foot of the mountain and began the long ascent. The pike followed the path of least resistance up the mountainside, roughly following a small stream, and crossing frequently. Boyd could see low, white waterfalls here and there. The thick forest pushed in around him. Dense clumps of ferns grew along the road with their fronds tumbling down the steep bank. Mosses and other deep green plants covered the rocks along the stream and boulders that crept down the mountain's flank. Birds of a wild assortment trilled from the forest's depths, and he once saw a large hawk glide away among the tall trees. The air was heavy with moisture, and both man and horse soon were covered with sweat.

The pike was deserted–they hadn't seen a soul since crossing the river the evening before. Boyd stopped to let the horse rest and sat on a rock. He remembered the night before the battle almost two years ago; scrambling up the mountainside with cursing men, struggling horses pulling cannon, officers shouting encouragement. It had taken an hour to reach the summit only to be soundly defeated by an inferior force. The Confederate army had been routed. They had run, leaving their dead and wounded behind. Boyd and his friend Charlie were among them. He shook his head and mounted the horse again. He clucked gently and the animal tackled the steep road.

At the top of the mountain, he left the forest behind and saw Lewisburg spread before him in a shallow sink that spread away to the west. Most of the trees had been cut away leaving an open savanna-like terrain surrounding the town. Only a few cattle grazed where once there had been many. It was from this vantage point that the Confederates had launched their attack. The Union camp had been on the hill across the valley, and they had fought most of the battle within the town. Boyd could see the Methodist church that had been hit with a cannon ball.

Now, he didn't see any sign of the Union troops. The pike passed through the middle of town, intersecting a north-south road in the town's center. It then rose in a serpentine path up the other side of the valley and continued on to Charleston. Somewhere, he could hear the clang of the blacksmith's hammer. Stately brick houses flanked the pike. There had been money here once, but now with the war, folks were just trying to hang on, he supposed.

He encouraged his mount gently with his heels and began the short descent into town. The horse stepped smartly along, likely expecting a cool barn and a dollop of grain. Boyd pulled the brim of his hat down over his eyes as they moved along. A plump woman in a dark dress stopped sweeping her porch to watch him ride by. Further along, he could see a few wagons and buggies moving along the street and people going about their business. Most stopped what they were doing to look at him as he passed. He wondered if they would recognize him. They probably would if they got a good look at him. There had been quite a stir in town when he was here before. He pulled his hat brim closer over his eyes.

He passed the house where he had lain wounded after the battle. Its windows were boarded up, and weeds grew in profusion in the side yard. A weathered for sale sign, nailed to one of the columns, flapped in the cool morning breeze. A sale was not likely to be forthcoming since no one had enough money to buy such a grand home. He rode on. When he reached the middle of town, he turned onto a side street and stopped in front of the blacksmith's shop. He dismounted and followed the sound of hammering to the smith's forge where a large, muscular man beat fiercely on a glowing horseshoe. He wore a leather apron over a dark, sweat-stained shirt and moved about with a pronounced limp. A skinny black man in tattered clothing pumped the billows of the forge.

The smith thrust the horseshoe into a barrel of oily water, and a cloud of steam erupted. "What can I do for you?" he asked not unpleasantly. "You need to board your horse?"

"Yes. He'll need some grain. You have any?"

"Yeah, there isn't much around, but I got a bit I can let you have. I hate to ask, but are you plannin' to pay with paper or coin? Paper money's shaky right now."

"I can pay with coin," Boyd said.

The smith grinned. "Well now, that's what I like to hear. Most everybody wants to give me paper. Precious metal's a bit hard to come by. My name's Smith. John Smith. Folks laugh, but that's my birth name and I can't help it." He grinned again, and stuck out a grimy hand after wiping it on his pants. They shook solemnly, and Boyd thought it was like shaking hands with a grizzly bear.

"This here is Moses," he said nodding toward the black man. "He helps me out now and then. It's hard to get good help now with most of the able bodied men off fighting the war and all. Not that he ain't a big help or nothin." The smith seemed to be unsure of how to go about introducing Moses and how Boyd would react to being introduced to a black man.

"I'm pleased to meet you, Moses." When Boyd extended his hand, the man looked confused but shook it briefly, his eyes downcast. His hand was hard and callous-covered. "How about taking my horse and seeing to him? He'll need rubbed down, too," Boyd said.

As Moses left to care for the horse, a brief silence settled in on the two men. "Moses is a good feller. It's just that no one knows to how to treat them now, nigras I mean. Since Mr. Lincoln set 'em free, nobody seems to know just how things are to work out," John said. "Nothing much has changed except that now we pay 'em for the work they do. I never owned slaves to start with but it sure is a mess. Moses works hard, is never late to work, and I can trust him." Another silence followed, so John decided to change the subject. "Where y'all from?"

"South Carolina," Boyd said. "Down on the coast. I was a fisherman there with my father before the war. I'll be here for a few days. Is there a place in town to sleep?" It was obvious that John didn't recognize him.

"Yeah, almost everyone has an empty room or two that they'll let out, but I'd try the boarding house just off Washington Street. The rooms are clean, and the food's pretty good."

Boyd thanked him and turned to leave and then turned back to ask, "There was a battle some time ago here in town. Were you around when it happened?"

"Yeah, over a hundred men died, and quite a number were captured. Colonel Crook's troops sent the rebels a'runnin'. They burnt the bridge down on the river when they ran so's the yanks couldn't foller 'em." He looked at Boyd anew. "You fight in the battle, did you?"

"Yeah, I was captured, but I'm on parole now. How about you? I can't help but notice you've got quite a limp. That from the war?"

"Naw," the smith laughed, "I was born this way. They wouldn't let me fight. Said I couldn't march good enough."

"Well, I'm sorry I asked. Didn't mean to pry."

"Oh, that's all right. Everybody in town knows."

"Have the Union forces been back in town lately?" Boyd asked casually.

"No, not for quite a spell now. I reckon they'll show up some time or another though. They always have before. I don't mean to be nosey, but I don't reckon I need to ask which side you were on, you bein' from South Carolina and all. But it don't make no matter to me. Most of the men from town are fightin' with the Confederacy. I just hope that this danged mess'll be over soon. Too many good men have been lost," he said. "My brother included."

"I'm sorry to hear that. Yeah, I fought with the South. But, I'm out of it now," Boyd said.

He thanked the smith again and walked back toward the pike. Boyd knew that where it passed through the center of town it was called Washington Street. He'd find a place to stay, and get something to eat. Then, he'd go talk to Lexus.

\* \* \* \*

The boarding house was a converted residence of hand-formed brick located on a side street. Boyd entered the foyer and spoke to the middle-aged woman working the desk. She was small with graying hair drawn up in a severe bun at the back of her head. She wore a dark dress covered by a striped apron. Boyd entered the dining room and sat at a table in the corner. A girl of ten or twelve served his food on cracked and chipped dishes. It was good, but the servings were small. As he ate, he watched the foot traffic on the street outside the window. People went about their business, speaking to each other in a friendly fashion. An occasional wagon loaded with rusty farm equipment or sacks of grain passed by with a swirl of red dust. He paid the woman at the desk for his meal and asked about a room.

"Yes, we have rooms to let," the woman said. "How long you plannin' to stay?"

"Just for a few days. I have business in town, and when it's done I'll be on my way," Boyd said pleasantly.

"You'll need to sign the register an' I'll need the first two night's payment in advance," she said with a frown. "Don't I know you? You ever been in town before?" She was breaking the cardinal rule not to ask strangers about their business, but she just couldn't stifle her curiosity.

"Yes, I was here some time back," he said as he signed the register.

The woman's eyes grew large when she read his name. "You're that Houston fellow that stirred up all that stink about the nigras aren't you? Well, I swan you've got some nerve…"

"Look," Boyd said pleasantly. "I don't want to cause any trouble. All I need is a place to sleep. I'll stay out of your way, and I don't plan to stir up any trouble."

"Well, I don't know. What'll folks think?"

Boyd placed some coins on the desk top. "Here, I'll pay for the week. What do you say?" Boyd asked with his best smile.

"Well," she hesitated, "I suppose it will be all right. Just don't go stirrin' up trouble." The coins disappeared into her apron.

"Take the first room on the right at the top of the stairs. It faces the street."

"Thank you. And, your name is?"

"Mary Ann Smith. You can call me Mrs. Smith."

"Thanks, Mrs. Smith. You can call me Boyd." He picked up his saddle bags and climbed the stairs before she could change her mind. The room was large with a high ceiling. A four-poster bed stood in one corner, and a pitcher and bowl had been placed on a stand along a wall. A faded oriental rug covered the hardwood floor, and the room was well trimmed with dark wood. Boyd pulled the window curtains aside and looked out onto the town. A few blocks away, he could see the courthouse. Dark memories rushed back.

After washing up, Boyd walked along Washington Street nodding to passersby, not really caring now if they recognized him. The word was out that he had returned. Mrs. Smith would see to that. But, as long as the Union Army didn't return he'd be all right. Folks may not like him, but there wasn't anything they could do about his return. Besides, he'd only be here for a few days, and then he'd be on his way back to South Carolina.

He turned onto the street where Lexus lived and stopped dead in his tracks. All that was left of her house was two tall, brick chimneys and a pile of charred rubble in between. Boyd stood on the sidewalk in front of the house site and stared. Lexus' house was gone. Was this the trouble she had written about? Was she destitute and needed help? Or was there a more sinister problem? Has someone intentionally burned the house? And, where was she? Had she perished in the fire? He looked again carefully at the ruin. It appeared that the house had burned sometime recently. A brown ring was burned in the grass around the house, and weeds had not had time to reclaim the scorched soil.

A screen door banged at the house across the street, and Boyd turned to see a thin woman standing on the porch with her hands on her hips. She wore a long dress that fell to her ankles over which she wore a brightly colored apron. She was old with long, gray hair, a wrinkled face and gnarly hands.

"The house burned," she said. "I looked out the window one night and it was all full of flames. It scared me half to death, I can tell you. I was afraid it'd set the other houses on that side of the street on fire too. There wasn't anything that could be done. It was all burned down in just a little while."

"What about Miss Saunders?" Boyd asked quickly. "Was she here when it burned?"

"No, she wasn't. As a matter of fact, I don't know where she is. I haven't seen her since the fire. Someone said she'd just disappeared. Nobody's seen hide nor hair of her."

"Do you know where she's likely to have gone?"

The old woman looked suspiciously at Boyd and asked, "Why'd you want to know?"

"Well, I used to be a friend of hers a while back. I just thought I'd look her up. See how she's doing. I heard that her folks died."

"You aren't foolin' me, mister. I know who you are. You're Boyd Houston. You stuck your nose in where it doesn't belong and got all the town folk stirred up. You an' that bunch of nigras."

"Yeah, that's who I am all right," Boyd said angrily, "but I'm not here to argue why I did what I did. I'm here to see if I can help Lexus. Do you have any idea how I might find her?"

Ignoring his question, she replied, "You're a friend of Charlie Taylor's, aren't you?"

"Yes, as a matter of fact I am. What about it?"

"Charlie's a good man, and his wife, Kate, is a fine woman. They don't come to town often but when they do, they always stop by to check on me. So, if you're a friend of theirs, I reckon you're all right. To answer your question, I don't know where Lexus could have gone, and I'm really worried about her. Come on in the house, and I'll tell you what I know."

Boyd was impressed. Here was a woman who wasn't very fond of him but was willing to take him into her home if she could help Lexus. "I'd be much obliged, ma'am," he said.

The house was a two story brick in the Federal style like most along the street. Huge sugar maples shaded the yard, and a rickety picket fence, badly in need of paint, surrounded the yard. The house boasted white columns in front and matching shutters on the windows. At one time this had been a beautiful home. They sat in the parlor on over-stuffed, formal furniture, just off the main entrance. The house was spotless but a subtle aura of disrepair had crept in. The rugs on the floor were threadbare, and here and there discrete repairs on the furnishings could be seen.

"Would you care for something, Mr. Houston? I don't have any tea or coffee but I made some cookies just this morning. Took the last of my sugar though," she said, a sad look on her face.

"You're very kind to offer, but no thank you, Mrs…" He didn't know her name.

"Howard. Ada Howard's my name."

"Howard," Boyd said thoughtfully. "Isn't Charlie's middle name Howard? I seem to remember that he used to introduce himself with his full name, Charlie Howard Taylor."

"Yes, it is. We're distant relatives by marriage. His great grand-daddy and my husband's great grand-daddy were brothers. Howard is a family name. But, you didn't come here to sort out my pedigree, did you?"

"No, but that explains things a bit," Boyd said, grinning. "Charlie is a good person, and so are Kate and their children. How are they doing by the way? Have they been getting along all right?"

"Oh my, yes! I don't get to see them as often as I'd like, but as I said before, they always drop by to see me when they're in town." She dropped her eyes to her hands in her lap. "As a matter of fact, I don't know what I'd do without their help. They bring me food, and Charlie patched the roof just the last time they came to town. It was beginnin' to leak somethin' awful. My husband died more than ten years back. He was killed in a wagon accident goin' down the mountain to the river. That hill is really steep, you know. Somehow, the horses got away from him and..." Her voice trailed off.

Boyd knew about the mountain first hand. He remembered that dark night, climbing the mountain road, the struggling horses that pulled the cannon and the heavy burdens all of them carried. "I'm really sorry, Mrs. Howard," he said.

"The folks in town have been wonderful to help me, too. I know that you didn't get along with them very well when you were here before, but they're really good people, you know."

"Yes ma'am. I know they are. Most of them, at least," Boyd said. "I don't bear them any hard feelings. It's just that we always seemed to end up on the opposite side of things."

"Well now," Mrs. Howard said brightly, changing the subject, "what can I do to help you find Lexus?"

"Honestly, I don't know where to begin. Does she have friends or relatives she might be staying with? Or, does she own any other property where she might be staying?"

"I don't know of anybody other than them I've already asked. Far as I know, all of her relatives have either died or moved away. Her daddy did own other property, though. But, I don't know much about that, only that he bought some land up on Conley's Knob. I always figured that he was fixin' to make a place where he could go with his cronies an' play poker an' smoke those stinkin' cigars an' have a good time. But, maybe I was mistaken," she said, but it was obvious she didn't think she was.

"Do you know how I could find the place?"

"No, but I'm sure you could find it in the land records down at the courthouse. You know where that is, don't you?" she asked.

"Oh yes, only too well," Boyd said, giving her a rueful grin. He would never forget the time he had spent there, and he wasn't looking forward to running into Sheriff Brown who had an office there. "I'll not take any more of your time, Mrs. Howard. If you think of anything that could help me find Lexus, please let me know. I'm staying at Mrs. Smith's boarding house."

Mrs. Howard rose unsteadily from her chair and walked him out onto the front porch. The wind had picked up and a mass of dark clouds approached from the west. "Gonna rain," she said. "I can always feel it in my bones."

Boyd walked back toward the center of town. Before he had gone two blocks, the skies opened and the rain beat down on his broad-brimmed hat, soaking him. He hunched his shoulders and walked swiftly on.

* * * *

Boyd sat in his room in a ladder-backed chair and looked out the window onto Washington Street. An occasional buggy and half empty shipping wagon passed by. Only a few men and women dressed in dark clothing walked along the muddy streets. The storm had passed, and the last of the rain dripped away from the eaves of the house. A thin ray of sunshine broke through the clouds and highlighted the cupola on the courthouse three blocks away. His shirt and trousers hung over the backs of chairs to dry and his hat balanced on the window ledge to catch any drying breeze that might come along. He wore his only change of clothing, a dark gray pair of trousers and a somewhat wrinkled, blue cotton shirt. His muddy boots sat side-by-side on a folded newspaper beside the door.

How was he going to find Lexus? Where could she have gone? Was she in danger? She had asked for his help, but what help did she need? And, why had her house burned? Had someone set the fire, or had it been an accident? These questions swirled around inside his head. As far as he could see, there were three things he could do to begin the search. First he would ask questions in town. He knew that many of the town's people wouldn't want to help him, but he would try anyway. He wasn't sure he wanted to face the sheriff, but he may have some useful information. Boyd would have to start there. Second, he'd search the courthouse records to see if Mr. Saunders had actually bought other property. Last, he'd visit Charlie up on Muddy Creek Mountain. Maybe he would know something that would help in his search. He usually knew what was going on in the county.

He rose from the chair and stretched, absent-mindedly rubbing his aching shoulder. The old wound didn't cause him a lot of trouble except when the weather changed. Then it ached dully. The wound in his leg had healed perfectly, and he walked without any sign of injury. He carefully felt his drying shirt and trousers. They were still damp and would probably take all night to dry out since the air was still heavy from the day's rain. He stretched his arms high above his head and yawned. It had been a long time since he had slept in a bed. It had taken him many days to travel from South Carolina to this remote town high up in the mountains. He had slept on the ground rolled in his bedroll wherever he had ended each day. He had bathed in the rivers and streams along the way. Although it was only an hour before dark and he hadn't eaten, he pulled off his clothes and crawled under the blankets.

He awoke later, confused and disoriented, drenched with sweat. Morning had come, and birds trilled noisily in the trees outside. He could hear wagon traffic on the street below his window. He sat up and rubbed his eyes. He had slept through the night, and it now appeared to be late morning. Although he had been very tired, he had tossed and turned, dreaming about the battle here in this town that had taken the lives of over one hundred men and wounded many more. He vividly remembered dreaming about the short, but vicious fight; guns and knives, and bayonets, and blood everywhere. Involuntarily, his fingers went to his shoulder and traced the jagged outline of the wound where the Minnie ball had entered. He signed and fell back onto the pillow. Returning to the site of the battle had awakened old horrors best left forgotten.

Boyd stumbled from the bed and looked into the cracked mirror over the wash stand. His hair was matted and tangled, and there was a dark shadow of beard on his jaw. His eyes were clear, but a slight tracing of crow's feet had appeared at the corners of his eyes. He felt as if time were passing him by. In a few years he would be thirty. He had never been married and had no family, since his father had died some years ago. His mother had died when he was only a child. Stop pitying yourself, he admonished. You have work to do.

Without warning, his thoughts turned to his stint in the army. As a young man, he had been caught up in the excitement of going to war. With his mother and father gone, he had no other family and no real ties to the community. Many of the young men his age were enlisting, and he'd just drifted along with them. He had no particular political affiliation, and the issue of slavery didn't really apply to him—neither he nor father had been slaveholders although some of his acquaintances had been. Slavery was just something that everyone took for granted. To his discredit, he had been blind to the issue. We all are captives of our cultures, he thought. What is abhorrent to some is easily accepted as the norm by others. It wasn't until he saw the issue first-hand that he realized the error of his ways.

His enlistment in the army had just happened. Before he knew it, he was given a uniform, a musket and was on his way to battle. He had been assigned to Colonel George Patton's 22$^{nd}$ Virginia Infantry. How a man from South Carolina ended up in a Virginia Infantry was a roundabout story in itself, but that's what had happened to him. They had marched north through western Virginia and had ended up here in Lewisburg, fighting the Yankees and being soundly defeated. He and his friend, Charlie, had been wounded and captured. When they were given the choice of being pardoned or sent to a miserable prison, they had chosen parole. Charlie had a family to take care of, and Boyd had had a bellyful of violence. Because of their wounds, neither would have survived in prison—they had barely survived as it was.

During his convalescence, he had been cared for by Nellie, a slave woman, whom he learned to respect and to genuinely care for. As their relationship deepened, it was she who had taught him the meaning of one man owning another. She had helped him understand the profound injustice of a political system that put profit above morality. In the end, she had taught him that she had to be free, not only from slavery, but from a relationship that was bound to stifle the freedom she so deserved. He had wanted to have a future with her, but in the end, he had realized she was right. She needed to be utterly free.

He sat on the edge of the bed and stared out the window. He remembered the sounds of the battle; the thud of cannon, the screams of wounded men, the incessant fire from muskets, the shouted commands of officers, the death cries of horses. He remembered the smell of gun smoke and fear as the Yankees had charged his position. He had fired his musket, his revolver, fought desperately with his bayonet, and then his bare hands. He knew the grunt and cry of men fighting hand-to-hand to the death. He remembered the searing pain as bullets struck his body. The Yankees had overrun their position, leaving death and destruction in their wake. His comrades had fled leaving the dead and dying behind, and he and Charlie had been among them. He didn't know how many men he had killed or wounded that day, but it had been many, and sometimes, without warning, he thought about them and the looks of terror on their faces. He thought about the lives he had taken, and cut short for a reason he couldn't put into words. Why do men fight? Was it braver to conform and fight, or to refuse? He didn't know. He only knew that good men were dead, better men than he, and their families would never see them again. Men very much like him. It was only a stroke of luck that had spared him their fate.

After their parole, Charlie's sons had loaded them into the back of a wagon and had taken them to Charlie's home on Muddy Creek Mountain. There, Kate, Charlie's wife, had nursed him back to life and had aided Boyd in his recovery.

Boyd returned to the window and looked outside again as he straightened his back and rubbed away the tension in his shoulders and neck. He opened his rucksack and took out his razor and a thin remnant of a bar of soap. Using the tepid water in the pitcher and the soap, he rubbed up a lather and began to scrape the stubble from his jaw. It was a hell of a thing, he thought as he shaved, a man his age sleeping away the night and half of the day. He finished and gave himself a quick sponge bath, drying his hard body with the rough towel hanging from a peg beside the mirror. Then dressed in his almost-dry clothing, he left the boardinghouse.

\* \* \* \*

The sheriff rocked back in his chair and stared with amazement at Boyd as he entered the office. "Houston, I thought I told you to stay out of my town," he said gruffly. It seemed that the sheriff was going to start again just where they had left off.

"Now look here Sheriff. Just take it easy. I'm only here for a day or two and there's no need to be so feisty."

"That's easy for you to say, Houston. You stirred up a lot of trouble when you were here before and almost got yourself lynched if I remember rightly. What are you doin' back here anyway?"

"I'm looking for Lexus Saunders. Have you seen her? I was by her house yesterday, and it's burned to the ground."

"Yes, the house burned. We had a hell of a time keepin' the rest of the houses on the street from goin' up in flames, too." The sheriff looked darkly at Boyd. "You didn't have anything to do with that, did you? If so, I'll see you in my jail for sure, and this time, you won't be talkin' your way out!"

"No, Sheriff. I just got to town. Her house burned several days ago, didn't it?"

"Yeah, I reckon. But, all I need is for you to start folks talkin' again. Where's that nigra girl you left town with? Lincoln signed the Proclamation, but there's a question about whether we're included or not, since we separated from Virginia. Anyway, a lot of the nigras have scattered, some are still around, but nobody seems to know what to do now. It's a mess."

Boyd ignored the sheriff's question. "I know, but I received a letter from Lexus saying that she needed help and that she was afraid for her life. You know anything about that?"

"No. Her folks died some while back, and she's on her own. Nobody seems to know where she went, and nobody knows who burnt her house."

"You sure someone set her house on fire? It didn't get struck by lightning or something?"

"Yep. When we got there, you could smell the coal oil. Someone doused the house good and struck a match to it. I've asked around, but nobody seems to know anything. You gonna try to find her?"

"Yes, I wrote back to her and said I'd help her, but when I got here yesterday, all I found was her burned house," Boyd said.

The two men looked warily at each other, and then the sheriff nodded to a visitor's chair by his desk. "Have a seat, Houston. Maybe we should talk about this."

* * * *

The military wagon bounced along the rutted road, slinging gobs of mud from its iron-rimmed wheels. The sun had come out after the downpour, and the still air was stifling. Lexus watched from the dense forest that framed the road. Branches arched over the narrow road forming an emerald canopy. A short column of Yankee soldiers followed the wagon on exhausted horses. Some slept in the saddle, and others rode along as if in a trance. Only the sergeant leading the motley band seemed to be alert and watchful. Lexus drew back involuntarily as they passed. She held her breath, fearful that they could hear her frantic gasping or her racing heart. They must not catch her again, they just must not! She knew that she had been lucky.

It had all started when Sergeant Brown spotted her on the street in town. The renegade soldiers had been camped on the hill above town, and the men prowled the streets looking for entertainment and hungrily ogled any passing female. The Sergeant had eyed her as she walked by on the way to the general store, approached her and then attempted to start a conversation. She had dropped her eyes and tried to step around him.

"Aren't you goin' to speak to me, Missy?" he had asked with mocking eyes. "What's the matter, don't you fancy Yankees? I'll bet you don't treat the Rebs this way." Lexus looked up at him with guarded eyes. He was big and rough with dark brown hair that cascaded over his ears and forehead, and his heavy jaws were covered with dark stubble. He wore a dirty Union uniform with sergeant's stripes on its sleeves and a campaign hat that perched on the top of his head like a crow on a fence post. He smelled of horses, sweat and dirt.

"Excuse me, sir," Lexus said firmly, "I'm on my way to the store." She tried again to step around him, but, grinning broadly, he blocked her way.

"Not so fast, Missy. I only want to talk to you. No harm in that is there?"

"Please, sir, don't..."

"Don't what, Missy? I'm only trying to introduce myself. I'm Sergeant Brown, Union Army, at your service, madam." He bowed stiffly and grinned briefly at his men watching along the street. "And what is your name, Missy?"

"Well," Lexus said angrily, "it isn't Missy."

Sergeant Brown roared with laughter as his men grinned at their leader's good humor.

"That's more like it, Missy. Just what I like, a spirited woman. Same qualities I look for in a fine horse."

"I really don't like to be compared to a horse, Sergeant. Now, if you'll excuse me, I have to go." She quickly stepped around him and began walking rapidly up the sidewalk. He strode quickly behind her, grabbed her arm and spun her around.

"Now look here, you..."

"Yes, Sergeant? Just what is it you want?" Lexus asked, looking him full in the face, her back straight. Passersby stopped to stare.

"And, take your hand from my arm. I don't take kindly to being grabbed like this."

He leaned down and quietly said to her, "This ain't the time or the place, but believe me, we'll get to know one another sooner or later." In a louder voice for all to hear he said, "Sorry ma'am, but I mistook you for someone else. Excuse me." With a red face, he dropped her arm and began to walk away. The soldiers, who had witnessed the Sergeant's embarrassment, laughed and hooted at him. He wheeled around and stepped threateningly toward them making them scatter.

Lexus leaned against a building and tried to get her breath. Her heart beat like a trip-hammer, and her palms were sweaty. That was a close one, she thought. Several women approached her and asked if she were all right, tittering among themselves and looking up the street in the direction the Sergeant had disappeared.

"I'm just fine now," she said, even though she was deeply frightened, not so much by the confrontation on the street but by what he had whispered to her. She had not seen the last of the Sergeant, she had thought to herself.

Lexus was abruptly brought back to the present by a stirring in the underbrush behind her. She slowly turned to see an opossum snuffling along through the woods with its nose to the ground. It was silver gray, fat and round with a long tail like a rat. Its hideous grin showed rows of pointed teeth. Lexus let out a sigh of relief. She knew it was harmless, having seen them often around her house in town.

Thinking of her home in town brought a wave of sadness over her. She remembered the house as it had been before the war and fondly, her mother and father. Her life had been good then. Sure, she had argued with them from time to time, but she missed them terribly. Life would never be the same. Would she ever be happy again? Would the war ever end, and would life ever return to normal? And, what about Boyd? She was surprised that he had so suddenly popped into her mind. She had tried to push him from her thoughts, but try as she might, he always returned. She smiled to herself thinking about him and then frowned when she thought about him with that nigra woman. To think that he had chosen *her*. Rumor had it that they had gotten married and gone back to Charleston. Imagine that! Boyd married to a nigra. Why, what would their children look like? She felt a twinge of guilt when she had thought that. Oh, why had she written that letter to him? He would never come back to the valley to help her. She must have been crazy to ask. She had agonized over the letter and made numerous trips to the post office before she had finally gotten up enough nerve to drop it into the mail slot, and then she had cried all night thinking about what she had done. She had returned the next day and asked the postmaster for the letter back, but he had said it was already on its way. He had said that it would take weeks to get there, if it arrived at all.

The incident with the Sergeant had frightened her, but she was too embarrassed to go to the sheriff for help. Besides, she wasn't sure anything would come of it, and he would have just laughed at her. That was when she had written the letter. Then, within a few days the Yankees had left, disappearing up the pike toward Meadow Bridge, and she had forgotten all about her troubles. That had been a big mistake.

Lexus sat on the ground and rested her head against a log. Soft spike-like hairs rising from a bed of diminutive moss plants tickled her cheek, and a shaft of light shone down through an opening in the heavy canopy above. It was just like in the bucolic paintings she used to see in a gallery in Lexington when she and her parents had visited friends there. A small gray bird with a black cap landed on a branch within hand's reach and twitched back and forth. It canted its head from side to side as it inspected her and sang–*chickadee dee dee dee*. It was cool and pleasant in the forest beside the road, and soon her eyelids drooped.

\* \* \* \*

"So, Sheriff, you haven't heard anything that might help us find Lexus?" Boyd asked as they sat in the office. The room was small, plain and stuffy and furnished with a rack of guns on one wall with a desk and chair along another. The desktop was littered with papers. Boyd sat in the only visitor's chair.

"Nothin.' I haven't heard a thing that would give me a clue where she is. When her house burned, I asked everyone in town that I could corner where she had gone, but didn't learn a thing. No one saw nothing. I even talked to Missus Howard, she lives across the street from Lexus' house, but she said that one day Lexus was there, then her house burned, and then she was gone. Didn't see a durned thing."

"Yeah, I know, I talked to her, too. I hate to bring this up, Sheriff, but did you poke around in the ashes of her house. You know…"

"I know what you're getting at, Houston, and I looked to see if anyone was in the house when it burned. Didn't find nothin' there neither."

An expression of relief crossed Boyd's face. "I'm at a loss where to go from here except that Mrs. Howard said something about Lexus' father buying property up on some mountain. She seemed to think that he was going to build some sort of cabin up there. You know anything about that?"

"No," the sheriff said thoughtfully," but I don't know everything that goes on in this town."

Boyd laughed. "That'll be the day. Everybody knows what everybody else is doing here. You especially." He leaned back in his chair. "Can we check it out in the court records?"

"Sure. Come on," he said, waving for Boyd to follow.

They walked down a short hallway to the county clerk's office. "Howdy, there Leona," the sheriff greeted a tall lady behind the counter who wore a pair of granny glasses perched on the end of her nose. "This feller needs to know if he can look up a purchase of property by Lexus Saunders' daddy a couple of years ago. Can you help him?"

"Sure thing, Sheriff, but I don't have to look it up. What do you need to know?" she asked, looking at Boyd with a frown.

"Did Mr. Saunders buy a piece of property up in the mountains on Conley's Knob, and if so, where is it located?"

"Yes, he bought almost thirty acres of scrub forest up on the knob. I don't know what he would want with it; there's nothing but scrub trees on the very top of that knob. Nothing up there but rocks, snakes, and wind."

"How can I get there?" Boyd asked.

"Why in the world would you want to go up there?" she asked indignantly.

"Just you never mind, Leona," the sheriff said patiently. "I'll help you out there, Houston, I know where it is."

At the mention of Boyd's name, the clerk's eyebrows shot up. "I thought I recognized you, young man," she huffed. "You're that man that…"

"Yeah, yeah," the sheriff said, holding up his hand. "That'll be all we need, Leona, thank you kindly."

Leona frowned at Boyd as he and the sheriff left her office and walked back down the hall. "You sure don't have many friends here, do you Houston?" the sheriff asked with a grin. "Seems your reputation has preceded your good looks."

"Yeah, Sheriff, I guess I earned that. But the past is just that; it's the past. Let's just move on."

"Yeah, okay. What are you planning to do now? Go up on Conley's Knob and see if Lexus is up there? We don't even know if Mr. Saunders ever built that cabin, you know."

"Yes, that's about the only thing I can think to do. You want to come with me, just in case we run into trouble?"

"Hell no! That's a fool's errand if you ask me. But on the other hand, maybe we'll get lucky."

"What do you mean 'we', Sheriff?" Boyd asked good-naturedly.

* * * *

## INTO THE MOUNTAINS

Sergeant Brown and his small band of soldiers lounged around a smoky campfire. The wind blew the acrid smoke first one way then another. Occasionally a soldier would have to move away from the fire to catch his breath. They all watched the blackened pot that hung over the fire on a chain and hook. Hank stirred its contents with a wooden spoon darkened with years of use.

"Damn, Hank" the Sergeant said, "when will supper be ready? I'm about starved to death." Hank was a thin man with a pocked face. His uniform hung on his tall frame like a burlap sack on a fence post.

"Hold your horses. It'll be ready when it's ready," Hank said curtly.

The Sergeant was becoming concerned with the troop's lack of discipline. They were ill-tempered and had started talking back to him. He'd have to do something about that before it got out of hand. They weren't regular army–they were renegade soldiers who had deserted to form this loose group of thieves and killers. While in the army, the Sergeant had reached the highest rank of any of them and thought that by rights he was their leader. They wore Union uniforms, tattered by hard use and patched together from parts scavenged from the bodies of soldiers they had found or killed.

The wood, damp from the recent downpour, smoked and sizzled. The Sergeant coughed and waved a dirty hand before his face to ward off the worst of the smoke. "You men get the tents set up. It'll be dark soon, and I want a dry place to sleep tonight," he said loudly. No one moved. "Go on, do what I tell you," he shouted. "I'll whip your asses good. Go on now, do what I say." The men stared at him briefly, but one by one they dropped their eyes to the leaf covered forest floor.

They got up with exaggerated casualness and moved sullenly toward the wagon, muttering and swearing under their breaths. He looked into the fire and shook his head. Things weren't going very well for him lately. Only a couple of weeks ago they had gotten into a brief skirmish with a Confederate patrol. They were riding along a peaceful lane and had come face to face with a dozen men. Everyone had started shooting, and before he knew it, they were running for their lives. Two of his men were killed and left behind and another mortally wounded. He'd had to put him out of his misery two days later. That hadn't gone over very well with his men, but that was war. What did they expect?

For the last couple of years, they had stolen horses and cattle, looted the farmers and merchants in the valley, and sold their plunder to one army or the other. Food was in short supply, and the soldiers responsible for procurement were always happy to see them. Whiskey was the most valuable commodity, but they'd just about wiped out the local supply. His men had thought they'd become rich, but no such thing had happened. Sure, they had stolen some money and silverware but not as much as they'd hoped. And to make things worse, the Rebs wanted to pay in paper money that was worthless. At least the Yanks paid with coin or at worst paper currency that still had some value. No, the men weren't happy, but he didn't know what he'd be able to do about it. One good haul would surely be helpful.

But, that wasn't the worst of it. The men still laughed behind his back about that incident with the woman. First, she'd told him off in front of his men, and then when they grabbed her to take along with them, she'd escaped. What rotten luck! He'd have to find her, and quick and when he did… He frowned with the thought of what she'd done to him.

He'd planned it perfectly. He'd been very patient, waiting several weeks after their run-in in town so that she'd let down her defenses. They'd even left town and ridden down the river for a couple of weeks, and then they'd slipped back to the edge of town and waited for nightfall. He'd taken Hank along, just in case he'd need help, approached the back of her house and waited until Lexus had taken a lamp upstairs to her bedroom. After a few minutes the light went out and they waited another half hour until she was asleep.

He remembered that night vividly. He could hardly wait until he had her. He'd give that snooty woman what she had coming.

He'd become excited just thinking about her soft, round figure. Oh, she was all woman, that was for sure. He could still smell her perfume from when he'd gotten close to her on the street.

The two men had crept up onto the back porch and tried the door. It was locked, but Hank quickly opened it with a metal pick he carried. They entered the dark house and paused at the bottom of the stairs. Somewhere toward the back of the house the Sergeant could hear a clock ticking, and down the street, a dog began to bark. Had it smelled them? Would it alert her? They'd have to move quickly. To be caught trying to kidnap a woman would not set well with the town's folks, not to mention the sheriff. He shuddered to think what he'd do to them if they were caught.

They quietly crept up the stairs, occasionally flinching when they stepped on a squeaky tread. They were just outside the bedroom door, when Hank knocked a vase off a hall stand. It shattered on the wooden floor, suddenly breaking the quiet of the sleeping house.

"Who's there," Lexus' yelled with a quake in her voice. "I know you're out there. I've got a gun and I'll shoot."

The flimsy door splintered and crashed on its hinges against the wall as Hank hit it with his shoulder, and the men rushed into the room. Lexus leaped from the bed and cowered against the wall, clutching the bedclothes to her breast. Her eyes were wide with fright. She was dressed in a long, thin nightshirt, and her hair cascaded down over her shoulders. Her bare feet peeked from beneath the hem of her nightshirt. The two men momentarily froze in the doorway at the sight of her, giving her enough time to drop the bedclothes and snatch a gun from the nightstand. She pointed it with both hands at the two startled men. The barrel of the gun wavered as she gripped it, her knuckles white. Pale moonlight streamed through the window to form a lopsided square on the floor, dimly lighting the room.

The Sergeant grinned and slowly raised his hands. "Now take it easy, Missy. We're not going to hurt you. You wouldn't want to shoot two brave soldiers now would you?"

"Stay away from me, Sergeant. I'll shoot."

"Yeah, I know you will, Missy. But, we're not going to hurt you," he said soothingly. "Light a lamp there Hank, would ya," he said. "I kin hardly see my hand in front of my face." Hank fumbled with a match and then lit a kerosene lamp on the nightstand. He began to edge away from the Sergeant. If she started shooting, he knew she'd shoot the Sergeant first and that would give him his chance, so he wanted to put some distance between them.

"Just relax, Missy. You don't want to shoot two innocent men do you?" The Sergeant looked carefully at the pistol she held. The gun was cocked, and he knew she was just an instant away from pulling the trigger. As Hank slid along the wall away from the Sergeant, he bumped into a chair and almost fell over it. By reflex, Lexus turned the gun toward him. That was all that the Sergeant needed to get a good look at the gun. It was an old, percussion type service revolver, and when he saw that there were no caps on the cylinder nipples, he realized with some satisfaction that the gun would not fire. He calmly stepped toward her as she pulled the trigger, the hammer falling with a dull clack. Hank flinched as if he'd been struck in the face. The Sergeant reached forward and violently jerked the gun from her hand and with a smooth, practiced motion, struck her across the cheek with his open hand.

Lexus fell against the edge of the bed then down on the floor where she landed in a heap. The Sergeant stepped forward quickly and kicked her once in the back. Her breath left her with a sudden swoosh, taking with it all ability to resist. He grabbed her hair and held her face up close to his.

"Now, you're mine, Missy. I'm going to show you what's what and who's in charge," he said through clinched teeth. He roughly pulled her to her feet. "Don't even think about screaming. I'll kill you right here and now." He produced an evil looking knife from a sheath on his belt and held it under her chin. "You won't draw another breath." Hank began to approach with an evil gleam in his eyes.

"We need to get out of here right now, Hank. Grab up some of her clothes and put them in a pillow case." To Lexus he said,

"Get dressed for the trail. You'll be ridin' hard with us, and I don't think that little shimmy you're wearing will stave off the cold mountain air."

Lexus' face blushed red with embarrassment and rage as she was forced to change her clothes as these two horrible men looked on. Both the Sergeant and Hank stared at her lustfully as she exchanged her nightclothes for a dress. The Sergeant twisted her arms behind her back and tied them with a short piece of rope he took from his belt. He forced a wad of smelly cloth into her mouth, holding it in place with a strip of cloth around her head. She could hardly breathe.

They dragged her from the room and down the stairs, pausing in the parlor. "Burn it to the ground, Hank. That'll give the sheriff something to do while we're slipping away," the Sergeant said. Lexus shook her head and pleaded with her eyes but to no avail. Hank poured kerosene from lamps onto the furniture and rugs then splashed it onto the drapes and wall. He lit a match and casually held it under one of the curtains. It began to burn immediately, and Hank grinned at her. With a mocking smirk, he tossed the match onto the floor.

They walked swiftly down side streets and alleyways to the edge of town where the other men waited. Lexus was roughly shoved up on a horse, and her hands were tied to the saddle horn. As the rogue soldiers climbed onto their horses, they could hear dogs barking and shouts of alarm coming from the town. The Sergeant swept up the reins to Lexus's horse and kicked his into a trot, leading Lexus along behind.

The Sergeant started suddenly, waking from his musings and looked into the smoky fire and at the silent forest pressing in around him. He could hear his men cursing and bickering as they set up camp. Yeah, everything had gone like he had planned, but she still had the best of him. She had escaped, but he'd find her. She couldn't have gone far, and he and his men would hunt her down like a rabbit before the hounds.

# CHAPTER TWO

LEXUS AWOKE TO the twittering of birds and from the angle of the sun filtering down through the trees, she could tell that it was late afternoon. She had slept for hours. She pulled herself up from the ground and brushed away the twigs and leaves that clung to her dress. She was unsure of where she was or the direction of the town.

She thought back on what had happened to her. After leaving town, the soldiers had picked up the wagon and team along the way. When they stopped to let the horses rest, the Sergeant pulled her down from her horse, tied her ankles together, blindfolded her and tossed her into the back. The wagon had bounced along the rough pike, and she was thankful that she had landed on the smoke-darkened canvas of one of their tents. Sometime in the night, clouds moved in to cover the moon and what little light that had filtered through the cloth over her eyes was gone. It had been dark and ominous.

The best she could tell they had traveled west along the pike for several hours. Being gagged and blindfolded had effectively confused her sense of direction, so after she'd escaped, she wasn't sure what direction to take. She was afraid to try to go back to town–the soldiers would be watching the roads and trails, sure to catch her. She'd have to fool them by walking away from the security of the town and its people.

She stretched and arched her back and tried to rub out some of the soreness. She touched her raw, red wrists carefully checking for serious breaks in the skin. As best she could tell they were rubbed raw, but the skin was more or less intact. Lexus unbuttoned her dress in an attempt to see the result of the Sergeant's kick to her back but couldn't twist around far enough to see well. It hurt badly, and she could only hope that she wasn't bleeding inside.

She sat on the log again to take stock of her situation. How was she going to get home? She could not risk being recaptured by those dangerous men. She had been unlucky to be kidnapped, but she blessed her stars that she had been able to get away from them without serious injury. Her brow knitted as she thought. What direction should she take? As best she could tell, the soldiers had moved away to the west. She could try to make a run for town, but this was a case where close was not good enough. Even if she got close to town and was intercepted, she was in serious trouble. Her only hope would be to meet travelers along the way, but that would put them in serious jeopardy. Unless they were well armed and outnumbered the soldiers, they would be quickly killed. No, she couldn't risk other's lives. She'd have to get back home by herself.

She arose stiffly from the log and set out north through the forest. This would take her farther from town, but maybe she'd be able to circle around to the east and intersect the road that led northward from Lewisburg toward Hillsboro, a small village many miles away. She had visited there with her mother and father when she was only five or six years old. From Hillsboro they had traveled on through the forest and mountains to Rowlesburg on the Cheat River where her aunt, uncle and their daughter, Rachel, lived. She vaguely remembered playing in the creek with her when they were children. It was a long journey, and it was several weeks before they had returned home.

Once she had made up her mind, she felt better and began walking briskly through the dense forest. Hugh trees, whose names were unknown to her, rose on stately trunks toward the sky. At first it was easy going, but as the slope gradually increased she grew tired quickly and leaned occasionally against a tree to catch her breath. She had learned a little about maps and directions from a teacher she'd had in school. He claimed to have been out to the western frontier and had floated on the Ohio River down from Pittsburgh like the early settlers had done.

Luckily, he had transmitted his interest in maps and travel to his eager students. Even though she didn't know exactly where she was, she had a fairly clear map of the area around town in her head. Lexus knew that if she kept the fast-setting sun to her left as she walked, she would be traveling north. Although it was not always easy to see the exact location of the sun because of the heavy forest canopy, she was confident that she was traveling in the right direction.

She caught a tawny flash of movement in the thick brush. She caught her breath, thinking that it could be a mountain lion or even a wolf, but she was relieved when a deer stepped into a patch of light. It was quickly followed by a tiny spotted fawn that twitched its tail and nosed its mother's flank. Then another appeared that bucked and kicked while shaking its head from side to side. The doe ignored her offspring and tested the air with her nose as she stared at Lexus with head raised high, both ears cupped toward her. All were frozen in place, mesmerized by the chance encounter. The doe stomped her feet and snorted. The fawns froze in place, unsure of the reason for their mother's strange behavior. A waft of air carried Lexus' scent to the doe. It reacted violently, turning suddenly and bounding away through the thin underbrush with its white tail flashing in the dim light. The fawns trotted unconcernedly after her. One stopped briefly and looked over its shoulder at Lexus with soft, dark eyes and then disappeared into the gloom of the forest. Lexus smiled to herself.

Eventually she found a faint trail made by forest animals and followed it as it meandered through the forest in a northerly direction. She struggled on for another hour, until the light was almost gone, then decided it was time to stop before total darkness set in. It was dangerous traveling in the forest at night. One could easily poke out an eye with a sharp twig, or step on a loose stone and twist an ankle, not to mention that she would have no way to tell in which direction she was traveling.

She stopped beside a small stream that tumbled down from the hill above her. Lying on her stomach, Lexus drank deeply from the pristine pool. Sunshine dappled the stream bed and she could see a small, orange-brown crayfish walking on the sandy bottom, searching for food with its claws outstretched before it, feelers waiving. The water tasted cool and wonderful, slightly acrid but not at all unpleasant. Moss-covered rocks and fallen limbs littered the stream with water swirling around them on the way down the mountain. She removed her clothing, folded her dress and underthings neatly and stacked them on the bank. She placed her shoes on top of the pile and slid gratefully into the cool water. Oh, what I would give for a bar of soap she thought, as she rubbed hands-full of water over her body. Goosebumps arose immediately on her pale skin. She didn't wet her hair for fear the cool evening air would make her sick. Never go to bed with wet hair, she remembered her mother telling her. You could catch your death…

Lexus stood thigh deep in the cold stream and checked her skin for scratches and bruises. She felt her ribs carefully with her fingers, flinching from the pain. She rotated her arm carefully to see how much damage had been done. Her ribs were not broken, she concluded, but the contusion on her back throbbed dully. Clambering up the bank, she inspected her legs, cautiously picking a tick from her shivering skin, being careful to determine that it had not yet attached itself. She tossed it away into the water. Her dress was dirty and torn, and she shook it out vigorously, picked bits of grass and dirt from it and then dressed carefully. She combed her hair with her fingers, pulled out tangles and knots and used a strip of cloth from the hem of her dress to tie it up behind her head. She felt much better now; if only she had a place to sleep for the night.

With a sigh, she walked along the stream until she came to a windfall. It was an ancient tree that had succumbed to the winds of a recent windstorm. It had been uprooted and now rested on its side. Its leaves had turned brown and would soon drop off, and its branches formed a cave-like shelter into which she crawled. Once inside, she soon made a bed of leaves and twigs and listened to the forest sounds as night settled around her. Somewhere, off to the south, she heard the muffled hooting of an owl, *hoo hoodoo hoooo hoo,* and was startled to hear the higher-pitched answer of the female nearby, *guwaay! guwaay!*

Lexus was not afraid. Not so long ago, when she was a spoiled child of wealthy parents, she might have been, blaming her parents for any discomfort she experienced, afraid of her own shadow. But now, she realized that she was responsible for her own actions and for her own safety. If she was going to get out of this mess, it would be up to her. She smiled to herself–she *would* be successful.

As she lay in her cozy shelter, she could hear the rustling and scurrying of night animals and soon drifted off to sleep only to be awakened hours later by her throbbing, bruised back. She rolled onto her side and snuggled deeper into her nest. During the night, the wind picked up, and the dead, brown leaves on the deadfall rattled and whispered to her. Barely awake, she listened intently to their message. She closed her eyes and for the first time since her sudden abduction, prayed to God to help her.

She awoke the next morning to the cheerful chatter of the forest's residents and crawled out of the deadfall. She stretched her fists high above her head feeling the pull and hurt of the bruise on her back. Her stomach grumbled. She knew that she would have to find food soon but didn't have the slightest idea which plants were edible. She drank again from the stream, relieved herself in the bushes and resumed her march along the trail.

Within minutes, the trail rose sharply up the steep hill before her, and soon she was scrambling up the rough terrain, grasping saplings and limbs to help her ascent. The vegetation changed abruptly as she rounded the western face of a knob where the afternoon sun would soon beat down, drying the sparse soil. The soft, spongy soil of the forest below had given way to dry shale as she clawed her way upward. A small lizard with a bright blue tail and parallel stripes down its back scurried away and climbed onto the trunk of a gnarled pine, moving with jerky motion around to the far side of the tree and out of sight. Soon, her dress was damp with sweat.

The view from the crest of the ridge was worth the climb. Through breaks in the sparse branches of the scrub pine, she could see the valley below. She drew a quick breath and stared mesmerized at the sight. A slight breeze ruffled the leaves of a nearby shrub, and the refreshing air cooled her moist brow. What a beautiful place, she thought. She had never appreciated the mountains before, but for the first time, she was aware–really aware–of the beauty of these highlands in which she lived.

Lexus followed the faint trail around the knob and began the descent into the valley. As she moved along she caught glimpses of the valley and noticed a clearing to the east, nestled in the headwaters of a tumbling stream. The light wind continued to swirl around her and suddenly, like the doe she had seen the day before, she tested the air with her nose. Was that wood smoke she smelled?

\* \* \* \*

Boyd sat comfortably in the hard saddle as the horse plodded along stopping occasionally to browse on the leaves of nearby bushes. Boyd jerked its head up and clucked to it. The sheriff had given him directions to Conley's Knob. Ride north, up through a couple of small settlements and over the mountain, then turn off to the left, he had said. Just follow the dirt track until he could see the steep knob rising toward the sky. Boyd surveyed the mountains around him. Their rounded tops rose to meet the bright blue sky, and huge trees of every type bordered the dusty road. Here and there he could see small clearings that had been hacked out of the forest by hardscrabble farmers. They were the latecomers to the valley, relegated to a life of backbreaking toil because they could only claim the roughest land for their life's work. It was all they could afford. Unlike the flat, limestone fields below, these steep hillsides barely yielded a meager living.

The man and horse soon came to a sturdy house nestled along a swift-flowing stream. A large black dog barked enthusiastically from the porch as a woman in a faded dress watched him carefully as he rode up. He sat with one hand on the saddle horn, removed his hat with the other and smiled. "Hello, my name is Houston. I'm trying to find my way to Conley's Knob," he said. "Am I on the right track?"

"Yeah, you are. Just follow the road there," she nodded with her head, "and once you get on top of the mountain it isn't but a couple of miles on from there. You'll see it once you top the mountain. You can't miss it." She was a young woman, not more than twenty-five years old, Boyd guessed, with a pretty smile and slim build. She was probably waiting for her man to come home from the war–if he ever did.

"I'm in need of some help. Would you know if a Mr. Saunders from down in Lewisburg ever built a cabin up on the knob? I'm looking for his daughter, she's gone missing, and I thought maybe she'd be up there."

"No, I can't rightly say that I ever seen Mr. Saunders or his daughter." She looked wistfully at Boyd and then suddenly asked, "Would you like to come inside for a bite to eat? I just finished cooking a big pot of brown beans and could whip up a bit of cornbread." She twisted a corner of her apron that covered her clean but threadbare gingham dress. Her piercing dark eyes enlivened her slim face.

"Thank you, but no, I'd better get along. I want to be up on the knob by dark." Boyd was always impressed with the friendliness of these mountain people, but the troubled look in the woman's eyes told of a deeper story.

"Well, I don't think you'll make it by dark. It's a ways yet, and it's all up hill," she grinned. The dog trotted over to Boyd and sniffed his boot in the stirrup. The horse shied away, prancing and snorting. Boyd brought it back alongside the woman as she spoke sharply to the dog, "You get there, Sampson! Get on back there on the porch!" The dog obediently trotted back to the porch and sat, watching Boyd with curious eyes.

"He ever bite anybody?" Boyd asked.

"Naw, not 'less you get too close to his food bowl. He's a pretty good dog, but he eats like a horse. Don't know how I can keep on feedin' him. You want him, you can have him."

"No." Boyd laughed. "That's all I need is a dog to take care of. I can hardly take care of myself let alone a dog that size. He's a big one."

"Yep. You sure you don't want to come in for some supper?"

"No, I'd better get along. Thanks for the directions and all." He tipped his hat and spurred the horse along the road. She watched him ride out of sight and then resumed hanging clothes out to dry.

Boyd rode silently along, pondering the conversation with the woman. Throughout these hills and across the nation, women waited anxiously for their men to return from the war. Some would be lucky and their husbands, brothers, and friends would return, but others would never hear from them again. Many were buried in shallow, unmarked graves never to be identified. In other cases letters written by officers would be lost, never to arrive home. Like all wars, it was terrible.

An hour before dusk, Boyd and the tired horse topped the mountain. He sat briefly on its summit surveying the surrounding land. Off to the north-east he could see one mountaintop that rose higher than the others. That must be the knob, he thought. Even farther on he could see a large mountain rising up, dwarfing all the rest. That had to be Droop Mountain, the one the sheriff had told him about. Maybe one day he'd go up there to see what he could see. Little did he know that a fierce battle would be fought there leaving many Union and Confederate soldiers dead.

He kicked the horse gently with his heels and clucked him along. It was almost dark when he reached the valley floor. The land lay in low rolling hills up to the foot of the knob and was spotted here and there with open fields. Clear waters flowing from hillside springs wound in cool branches among the hills then disappeared into sinkholes that pocked the land. A deep layer of limestone spread beneath the fields and woods producing a deep, rich soil. The trees were big and healthy with towering trunks and spreading limbs. Many of the old fields showed corn stubble interspersed with weeds and occasional red-cedar saplings. If the men didn't return soon, the farms would soon revert to brush, greenbriers, and then to forest.

Boyd dismounted long enough for the horse to drink. He looked carefully around again searching the trail he had just ridden for signs of life. He could see nothing untoward. Songbirds added their melodies to the whistling of the wind from among the dark branches of the trees, and far in the distance he could hear a crow call. The gloomy songs of mourning doves deepened his unrest—*ooaah cooo coo coo*. He shook his head and mounted the horse, urged it into a trot and soon found a suitable place to stop for the night. He quickly removed the saddle from the horse, hobbled its front legs and released it to graze on the lush grass along the track. A small, smokeless fire was soon built, and he dug into his saddlebags for his staples. Supper was a simple affair—a slab of cornbread and some thin slices of ham purchased from Mrs. Smith at the boarding house and a couple of cups hot, black coffee heavily laced with chicory. Boyd spread his bedroll under a tree and then sat on a nearby log. Weeks of trail life had accustomed him to simple living. He watched the horse as it cropped grass with enthusiasm and could hear the crunch of strong jaws on the coarse food. The horse kept its tail in constant motion, swishing away the flies that persistently attacked its thick hide. Its skin jerked and twitched to rid it of the annoying pests.

As darkness fell silently around him, Boyd found the quiet solitude pleasant and relaxing, but his mind began to wander back to Lexus. Where was she? Would she be in the cabin–if there was one–at the top of the knob? If so, would she be safe and well? He remembered her flashing eyes as they had first met on the street in town. She was outgoing and had seemed to be interested in him, but nothing had worked out well. First one thing and then another had caused them not to see eye to eye. And then there was Nellie. He knew that had been the straw that broke the camel's back. But, that was all water under the bridge.

He rose and stretched, working the kinks out of his back, moving stiffly from the day's ride. He knew that as far as Lexus was concerned, he was only a convenient source of help in a time of need, but he'd help her if he could. Then he'd be on his way back to Charleston, the ocean and the life he was trying to reestablish there. But first he had to find her. He wondered where she had gone off to. Had something bad happened to her? He was struck with a sudden sense of urgency and wished he could ride immediately to the top of the knob and find her, but the darkness was complete save for a pale twinkle of stars overhead and the yellow flicker of his fire. He'd have to be patient, wait until dawn arrived, and then he'd soon have some answers to his questions. The horse chewed and stomped in the darkness.

Dawn arrived slowly, and he tossed and turned in his dew-damp blanket. He sat up and rubbed the sleep from his eyes. The horse stood at a distance, its head drooping and its tail still. The flies that had tormented it unmercifully yesterday were absent, stilled by the cool night air. Boyd rolled his blanket, attached it to the back of the saddle and picked up the saddlebags that had been stacked on a nearby rock. A flap was open, and the bags were strangely light, and when he peered inside he realized that the bundle of food that had been wrapped in an old, faded napkin was gone. He looked around the campsite thinking that maybe it had dropped out as he prepared for sleep in the dark last night, but it was nowhere to be seen. Now, that's strange, he thought. After dumping the contents of both saddlebags onto the ground to check again, he confirmed that the food was indeed gone. He scanned the forest around him and watched the horse for signs of danger—horses have very good senses of smell, he knew—but it looked like it was asleep. A worried frown creased his brow as he caught up the horse and prepared to leave.

The road, nothing more than a wagon track, coiled around the mountain as it led up to Conley's Knob. The horse stepped along, its head bobbing up and down as it dug into the road. Boyd leaned forward slightly and grasped the horn to keep his seat. Up and up they went, following the track that switched back frequently as they approached the summit. The road ended in a copse of trees, and he could see three piles of dark lumber neatly stacked in a row, covered with leaves and twigs, and here and there, a layer of moss. The lumber had obviously been there for years. He dismounted, tied the horse to a sapling and begun the short climb to the top following a faint, gravel-covered path. He was breathing hard when he reached the summit. There was no cabin to be seen, but as he walked around the narrow ridge-top he soon found piles of rocks neatly stacked in a large square—the beginnings of a foundation. Mr. Saunders, or someone, had begun the cabin but had not completed the work. Boyd sat down on the stones of the foundation and looked around as disappointment rushed in upon him. Lexus was not here. No one had been here for years. A familiar fear settled upon his heart. Where was she, and was she safe?

After resting for a few minutes, Boyd retraced his steps to the road and his horse. He was getting a drink from a canteen he kept tied to the saddle when the horse perked up its ears and stared down the road into the dim shadows under the trees. The horse snorted, startling him, and he slowly drew his pistol from his belt.

He cocked the gun and yelled, "Come on out of there so I can see you." The horse stepped away, and he had to catch up the reins to keep it from running off. "I won't tell you again," he yelled, trying to calm the horse at the same time. A dark shadow moved onto the edge of the wagon track. It was the black dog from the house down below. It stepped into a patch of light, sat on its haunches and looked at him.

\* \* \* \*

Lexus walked hesitantly into the clearing, taking in the sight before her. A crude camp with a half dozen tent shelters, made up of bits and pieces of patched canvas, stood on the far side of the field. Smoke rose lazily from a fire pit surrounded with limestone rocks upon which a smoke-blackened sheet of metal provided a rough cooking surface. A coffee pot simmered cheerfully allowing a thin tendril of steam to escape from its spout. A huge pot of stew gave off a tantalizing aroma causing her stomach to growl and grumble. An odd assortment of mismatched dishes and eating utensils were neatly stacked on a neighboring rock used as a table.

Whoever was camped here had left washing hanging on a rope tied between two trees and she could see men's pants, shirts and underthings alongside women's dresses and other feminine garments. Although the clothing was well used, it was carefully mended. The tents' dark interiors gave no clue whether they were occupied or not. Personal belongings were neatly stacked in individual piles nearby. Evidently, whoever these people were, they were well organized and lived in an orderly fashion.

This was no army camp, she thought. Maybe whoever was camped here could help her. Lexus stepped tentatively toward the camp, cupped her hands around her mouth and called out, "Hello, the camp! Is there anybody here?" Her voice echoed off the surrounding hills, but there was no other answer. She moved closer to the fire. The food smelled delicious, and she wanted nothing more than to dig in and help herself, but that wouldn't be right, would it? Maybe a few years ago she'd have just helped herself, but the loss of her parents and the hard times she'd endured had matured her. Now, she knew what was right and what was not.

She sat on a nearby rock and waited, calling out occasionally without success. Sooner or later they'd return, and she'd ask them for help. The morning sun was pleasant on her face and hair, but smoke from the fire blew toward her causing her to cough and her eyes to water. She moved away and sat down again, brushing the twigs and leaves from her dress, smoothing the wrinkles, listening to the sounds of the morning. She tilted her head back allowing her hair to fall onto her shoulders and back. She closed her eyes and soon drifted off into a light sleep with her head nodding occasionally.

Her eyes snapped open. Was that a child she had heard crying? No, that wasn't possible, not out here in this forest. In the fog of sleep, she must have been dreaming. She dozed again, still trying to sit upright on her rough perch–her chin drooped to touch her chest. The snap of a twig brought her awake with a start. Standing before her was the largest, darkest nigra she had ever seen. He peered closely at her, his dark eyes squinting in the sunlight. He wore a patched work shirt and dark brown trousers held up with red suspenders. His closely cropped hair formed a tight helmet on his round head, and his calloused hands rested on his slim hips. He frowned at her.

"What you doin' here?" he asked, his voice a rough rumble from deep inside his massive chest.

She shrank back from him, her eyes huge and her mouth open. "Oh, oh," she said, stammering, "I...I, was just waiting for someone to return. I don't mean any harm."

"What you want here, anyhow? This is our camp. No whites allowed here." His frown deepened, and he leaned toward her threateningly.

"I just need a place to rest and something to eat. I'll pay you," she said. Then she realized that she didn't have any money. "At least, I'll pay you as soon as I can get back to town."

"What you doing out here all alone anyway?" he asked, softening somewhat. "It isn't safe here for anyone, let alone a girl all by herself. They're some bad men hereabouts; soldiers, raidin' and killin' an' takin' anything they want."

"Yes, I know. They took me from my home and dragged me off into the woods. I got away from them and now they're searching for me. Can you help me?"

"Help you? Why should we help you? Y'all kept us as slaves an' now you want us to help you. We're on our own now, 'mancipated by President Lincoln. Tell me, ma'am, why should we risk our necks to help you?"

There was considerable confusion in the valley about whether the slaves were emancipated or not. The President's decree freed the slaves in all of the states that had seceded from the Union, but not those that remained. Because West Virginia was newly formed from Virginia, a seceded state, some folks said they were free. Others said they were still slaves since the newly formed state had voted to phase out slavery over time. Many slaves had simply left their owners, taking the matter into their own hands. Lexus didn't argue the point.

Other nigras began to materialize from the darkness of the forest behind the camps; three women, one with a small child on her hip, another with a toddler clinging to her dress. Two other men stood by, staring at Lexus with deep concern stamped on their faces.

Lexus dropped her head. He had a valid point. Indeed, why should they help her, taking considerable risk, especially if the rogue soldiers found her here being sheltered by nigras? "I understand. I'll just be on my way," she replied as she rose and began to walk away.

"Hold on there," the woman with the child on her hip said. She looked at the big man, a question on the attractive features of her face. "Kin I speak wit you, Jacob? We better talk 'bout this, don't you think?"

The man's face softened when he looked at her and the child. "Yeah, I reckon, Sally." It was obvious that he was concerned about their safety if they became involved with a white woman. The group huddled near one of the tents whispering seriously among themselves, occasionally glancing at Lexus. Their voices grew louder, but Lexus couldn't make out what they were saying. After several minutes they walked toward her.

"You kin can stay, but only fer a little while," Jacob said. "They're some food on the fire an' you kin eat some an' then you gotta be on your way. We can't be helpin' ever one who comes by lookin' fer a handout." He jerked his head toward a rock near the fire, and Lexus sat down. Sally handed her child off to another woman, spooned a generous portion of stew into a plate and handed it to her. She produced a loaf of rough bread, broke off a chunk and gave it to Lexus, along with a cup of weak coffee. Lexus ate in silence, glancing with embarrassment toward the group. They stood in a circle around her, staring at her unabashedly. Lexus felt as welcome as a roach on a dinner plate.

Gradually her audience began to disburse, moving about the camp, doing various chores. In all, there were six men, four women and two children in the group. Sally was tall and thin with calloused hands and a graceful bearing. Her hair was done up in a knot on the back of her head, and her dark, piercing eyes followed Lexus' movements. She was dressed in a simple cotton shift with a bright sash tied around her waist. Her shoes were old and cracked, and Lexus could see her toes peeking through holes in the worn leather. She sat down beside Lexus.

"What you doin' out here in the woods?" she asked. Her frank stare unnerved Lexus. She didn't know what to expect from these people.

"Like I said, I was taken from my house by a bunch of renegade soldiers." Lexus said. She shivered as she thought about it. "They tied my hands and blindfolded me and threw me in a wagon, and we drove all night. I got away and ran into the woods. I'm sure they're looking for me."

"How'd you get away from them?"

"When they made camp, some of the men went for water, and others went into the woods to get firewood. They left one man to guard me. They didn't seem to be afraid that I'd get away because they had untied me. When the guard turned his back, I hit him on the head with a frying pan. I'd have killed him if I could have."

Sally laughed. Her brown eyes twinkled, and then she laughed again. "I'd a split his skull if I's you. Hope you brained him good," she said. She laughed again, throwing her head back, her white teeth flashing. Lexus grinned and began to feel proud herself. Sally's face darkened as she looked frankly at Lexus. "They mess wit you?" she asked.

"What do you mean?" Lexus asked, dropping her eyes to the ground.

"You know, messed wit' you. Did they take their pleasure wit' you? That what men like that do, you know."

"Oh no, they didn't," Lexus said, relief evident in her voice. "They didn't have time to, but I know by the way they looked at me that it was going to happen sooner or later. That's why I took the first opportunity to get away from them. I don't know how I'm going to get back to town without them catching me, but I'll find a way."

"Don't let 'em ketch you. They'll kill you. They can't 'low you to go back to town an' tell on 'em. They'll kill you and throw your dead body in a sinkhole." Sally became pensive. "My master took his pleasure wit me when I's only a little bitty girl. I'd a kilt him ifin I could have, but he sold me before I was old enough to know what to do." Sally folded her dark hands in her lap and became quiet. She bit her lip and looked away into the forest. "But, that's water under the bridge, isn't it? You bein' white, you don't understan' nothing, if you excuse me for sayin' so."

Sally stood and quickly walked away, leaving Lexus to finish her meal and ponder what the life of a slave must be like, but her privileged life didn't give her a foundation to begin to understand. She was a victim of her culture. Until the war, she had been a member of the upper crust—a beautiful young, white woman living in a society dominated by whites. What did she know about being black, enslaved by a culture that lacked empathy? She realized that she would never be able to understand completely and sadly until of late, it hadn't entered her mind.

* * * *

Boyd was half asleep as the horse plodded down the gravel road toward town. As they rounded a bend, the horse jerked its head and snorted at the dappled shadows from the sparse branches hanging overhead—a breeze caused them to dance and gyrate on the road. Without warning, it arched its back and crow-hopped away, leaving Boyd clutching at the saddle horn, but he was too late. He tumbled into the brush and brambles, coming to rest with his feet above his head. The horse trotted back up the road, stopped and then started to graze.

Boyd climbed out of the brush and retrieved his hat. His arms were scratched, and he had a large scrape on his neck. He wasn't seriously hurt, except for his ego. He looked up and down the road to see if anyone was looking. It wouldn't do to have been seen flying through the air from his horse. He was a fisherman but that wasn't an excuse for poor horsemanship. He caught the horse's reins and spoke sharply to it. "Here now, there's no need to go acting like a spring colt. What got into you? It was only some shadows on the road. Behave yourself, now." He led the horse across the shadows as it pranced sideways.

That's what I get for having my head in the clouds, he thought. He was worried about Lexus and didn't know how to find her. Where had she gone? Was she safe or was she dead in a ditch somewhere? The thought unsettled him.

He admitted that he wasn't the greatest when it came to talking to women. Somehow, things just didn't seem to come out right. He remembered her big eyes and blond hair. He was pleased that she thought enough of him to ask for his help, and he was glad to give it, whatever it might be. And, once she *had* asked him to a dance at her house. Unfortunately he hadn't been able to attend. He'd been unavoidably detained.

From immediately around a bend in the road, Boyd heard the bleating of sheep. He was soon surrounded by a herd of white, wooly animals that flowed around him like the current of a river. His horse pranced nervously. Two elderly men herded the animals with long curved staffs, assisted by a young boy of eight or ten years. The animals bleated pitifully, and one made a dash for freedom, but the boy turned it back into the fold. When the herd had passed, one of the men lingered to talk to Boyd. He said they were taking the sheep to summer pasture up in the mountains.

"Folks around here aren't too happy to have sheep grazing near their cattle. They say the sheep eat the grass too close to the ground, so's it has trouble growing back. But, it isn't any worse than those farmers that overgraze their land–put too many head on their pastures. The trick is to move them often enough so's the grass has a chance to recover. You from around here? I don't think I've ever seen you before."

Boyd grinned and said, "I'm just passing through. I'm looking for a friend, a young woman by the name of Lexus Saunders. She's gone missing. Have you seen her?"

"Naw, I don't think I know her. I don't get into town very often. She's missing, you say?"

"Yes, and I'm afraid something bad might have happened to her. She's been gone for quite a while, and the sheriff's out looking for her too." He described Lexus to the man.

"What would she be doin' out here all alone, a woman like that?"

"I don't know. Her house was burned, and we're afraid something has happened to her."

"Well, we'll keep our eyes peeled for her, but I don't think you're going to find her wanderin' around out here."

The two men talked as the sounds of the herd disappeared up the road. The sheepherder said, "Both of my sons are off fighting in the war. They joined up with the Rebs and have been gone near to two years now. We get a letter now and then, but it's always a worry that they'll get killed or wounded bad. There's just me and my brother left to take care of the farm, but the boy with us is gettin' to be a big help. He can work as hard as a man already, but it's a shame that the young'uns have to grow up so fast. We try to see that he gets to school, but sometimes we have to keep him home to help out. The war's been hard on everyone."

"Do you have anyone else at home?" Boyd asked.

"Yes, there're two more children, younger than the boy there, a boy and a girl. Their mamma died a couple of years back, so's it's just us old men tryin' to take care of 'em. Only one of my boys was married. Now, I don't know what will come of 'em. If it weren't for the neighbors, I don't know what we'd do. One of the women comes by to take care of the youngest ones while we're workin' the farm. I wish we had some money to pay her, but the best we can do is give her some mutton now an' then. It's a mess."

"Yes, the war has been hard on everyone," Boyd agreed. "Homes are broken up when the men go off to fight. A lot of them will never come back." He changed the subject back to Lexus. "I heard that Lexus had a run-in with a renegade soldier on the street some time back. I don't know if that has anything to do with her disappearance, but if she got tangled up with him and the others that ran with him, she's in big trouble. Have you seen them around here?"

"No, not recently. They've been stealing an' causin' trouble for months, but from what I'm hearing, they haven't been around for several weeks. They were camped on the hill above town fer a while, but not for some time now. Don't know why the sheriff didn't put them in jail or at least run them off. You think they might have got her?"

"Oh, I hope not," Boyd said. "I'm just hoping that she's somewhere safe with friends or something. I'm checking everywhere I think she may be. The sheriff's stumped too."

"We'll keep an eye out fer her. If we see her, we'll try to send a message to the sheriff, but since we'll be way up on the mountain, it isn't likely that we'll see much of anything. It's a fur piece up there."

The sheepherder left to catch up with the herd, and Boyd decided to go to see his friend, Charlie, who lived on Muddy Creek Mountain with his family. He had spent most of a summer with them recuperating from a couple of serious gunshot wounds from his short, but eventful, stint in the army. Maybe he'd have some idea of where Lexus might be.

The sky darkened as he rode along and off in the distance, the wind picked up, carrying the smell of rain. The horse looked at him and snorted. "You behave yourself," Boyd said sternly. "You throw me off again and you and I will come to serious violence. In all the time we've been together, that's the first time you have ever thrown me. You've bucked a time or two—what good horse hasn't felt its oats, time and again, especially early of the morning?" Boyd grinned, thinking he'd been alone too long, talking to his horse!

As they neared town, rain that had begun as a drizzle, soon changed into a deluge. His slicker was rolled up in his saddle bags, and by the time he got it out and put it on, he was drenched. His wet shirt stuck to him, his hair was plastered to his head, and water had run into his boots. The rain settled the dust on the road, and he could hear a rooster crowing. Somewhere, far ahead, he could hear the clang of the blacksmith's hammer.

The streets were deserted when he rode through Lewisburg and turned west along the pike. As he climbed the knoll just out of town, he could see the trampled fields and dead campfire pits left by the Yankees. Trash, and the leftovers of an army on the move, littered the countryside. He caught the whiff of latrines on the westward wind. No one said that an army had to be neat, he thought. At least they were gone. Ahead to the west, he could see a misty-blue line of mountains extending like a column of marching soldiers with a backdrop of clouds—Muddy Creek Mountain. The sun broke through the clouds and lit up the sky.

He sat on the horse, hands crossed on the saddle horn, and took in the sight. He liked these mountains, so unlike the seawaters upon which he had sailed. Unlike the gray and blue of the ocean, here he saw greens and blues and all shades in between. Wisps of steam rose from the mountainsides as if from a forest on fire. The slanting sunlight highlighted the layers of ridges falling away to the west. Here and there the green of the forest was broken by the foamy white of dogwoods and serviceberry in bloom. The smell of wet earth and ozone wafted on the breeze.

The horse turned to look at him then violently shook itself like a dog, jangling its bridle and making the leather of the saddle squeak and complain. He clucked to the horse, and it stepped away along the pike. When they reached the shallow stream that flanked the base of the mountain, Boyd and the horse crossed the tiny, wooden covered bridge, making hollow sounds that reverberated inside the enclosed place. A gristmill squatted along the stream, its waterwheel turning slowly as clear water flowed over it. A man waved to him then turned and resumed his work.

Just past the bridge the road turned sharply and then began the climb up the mountainside. Half way up, the horse slowed, blew loudly and strained to climb the steep, serpentine road. Boyd stopped to let it rest and sat against a towering tree along the road. The horse stood with its head down, its flanks heaving, darkened with sweat. The air was heavy and moist after the rain, and he could hear a woodpecker working on a hollow tree deep in the forest. Several small gray birds with white undersides and sharp pointed beaks worked up and down the sides of trees. Through a gap in the trees, he could see half a dozen turkey vultures high above the valley floor riding on a thermal. They rocked gently on the upwelling air, the feathers on the tips of their wings like the fingers of an outspread hand. The longer he sat quietly against the tree the more the forest came alive. He could see birds of many other kinds, hear insects creaking and clicking in the litter on the forest floor, and in the trees, see squirrels chasing each other along the grapevines that draped across their tops. Maidenhair and Christmas ferns cascaded down the bank along the road. Diminutive, three-lobed hepatica and foam flowers bloomed in the fecund earth. He closed his eyes and was about to nod off when the horse snorted and stomped, pinned its ears against its head and looked intently up the road.

Shortly, two horses and a wagon took shape in the gloom of the understory as they made their way down the steep grade toward him. The brake squealed loudly as it was applied to keep the wagon from running up on the horse's legs. The driver was hunched forward, intently working the brake to bring the rig to a stop beside Boyd. He was an old man with a long pointed beard and a big head of wild gray hair. He looked at Boyd curiously.

"Howdy," he said. "You lost?"

"No," Boyd said. "I'm just letting the horse blow. This is a very steep road."

"Yep. I reckon it is that. Kinda makes your nithers pucker up when you're comin' down. If your wagon gets away from you, you're a gonner. It's happened more than once on this terrible hill." He squinted at Boyd, scratched under an armpit and said, "You're a stranger here, ain't you? Never seen you before. You look like a soldier but where's yer uniform?"

"I'm not a soldier any more. Used to be, though. I'm on my way to see Charlie Taylor. Is he still living up there on the mountain?"

The old man brightened, smiled, worked his stubble-covered jaw and squirted a dark stream of tobacco juice into the ditch. His strong hands—the color of old saddle leather—held the reins confidently.

"You're a friend of Charlie's? Ain't you the one that fought with him? What was your name?" he asked, mumbling to himself. His eyes brightened and he shook a gnarled finger at Boyd's chest. "Houston. That's your name. Houston." He seemed to be pleased that he could summon the name from the depths of his aging mind. "Charlie speaks highly of you. You just here for a visit or somethin'? Oh, sorry. It ain't none of my business. Where's my manners? When you get to be my age, sometimes things just pop out when you think you're only thinkin' them."

"That's all right." Boyd chuckled at the man's friendly manner. "I don't mind telling you that I need to talk to him but would like to visit some too. Mostly, I'm trying to find a friend from town who has gone missing, and I thought maybe Charlie would know where she's gone."

"What's her name? Maybe I can help." The man's bushy eyebrows rose when Boyd indicated he was looking for a woman.

"Lexus Saunders. Her house was burned and now she's missing. I'd like to find her and help her if I can."

"Lexus?" She's missing is she? She's a fine girl. Knew her folks. I hadn't heard that she's gone, though. I haven't been to town for a spell. But I can tell you this much; one of those rogue soldiers that's been stealin' and plunderin' the valley had eyes fer her. The gossip in town is that he got right fresh with her on the street one day, and she kinda poked a stick in his eye, so to speak." He chuckled. "Got her back up, she did."

"Do you think he could be responsible for her disappearance?"

"Don't know. Could be. That was a nasty bunch. We don't get much news up here on the mountain, but if anyone knows, it'll be Charlie and Kate."

They talked briefly about the battle and of Charlie and his family, the old man anxious for news. When they parted, the old man, mules and wagon proceeded on down the mountain, the brake squealing like a stuck hog. Boyd mounted his horse and continued upward.

The valley looked just as it had when he was here before except that the house and barns had a prosperous look to them. The pasture fields were green and verdant, and across the valley, Boyd could see a man with a team of horses plowing a long narrow field that hugged the contours of the mountain's base. He trotted the horse down the twisting road and approached the house. From horseback he called out, "Hello the house!" He couldn't have created any more turmoil if he'd fired a round through a window.

A large dog erupted from the door barking furiously followed by a slim girl of eight years with an open book in her hand. Her flaming hair was pulled over her ears and tied in a loose braid behind. She hooked a finger under the dog's collar and told it to be quiet and sit, which it obediently did. A slim woman, a more mature version of the girl, stepped out onto the porch with a big smile.

"Well I'll be," she said, "if it isn't Boyd Houston. Colleen, you remember Mr. Houston, don't you?" Kate asked.

Colleen frowned and looked at her feet. Then she smiled and said, "Yes ma'am, I remember. He's the one that had that pretty nigra girlfriend, ain't he?"

"Colleen! Mind your manners now and you know better than to say ain't. Say hello to Mr. Houston." Then, to Boyd she said, "Well don't just sit there grinnin' like a possum. Get on down and come in the house. Have you eaten yet?"

Inside the tidy log house, Boyd and Kate sat at the table and drank steaming mugs of black coffee. The house hadn't changed since his last visit. Kate had moved books, tablets and stacks of graded papers from the table to make room for them. The blackened fireplace was cold now; the windows open to let in the cool mountain air. The home was filled with the detritus of an active family, but a sense of organization prevailed. There was a loft above and sleeping rooms toward the back. Colleen was sent for Charlie who was plowing the corn field for spring planting.

Kate questioned Boyd unmercifully about his life over the last months, asking where Nellie was and if they had gotten married.

"No, we didn't, but not because of me. She decided that she wanted to be on her own and I can't say I blame her. She got a job as a seamstress in Charleston, and I went back to the coast and took up fishing again." He looked wistfully out the open front door. The big dog sprawled on the fireplace rug, snoring softly. "I don't seem to have much luck with women," he said.

Thankfully for Boyd, Charlie stepped through the door with a huge grin on his face. The two men solemnly shook hands and pounded each other on the back. It was obvious they were delighted to see each other. Charlie was a tall man with a high forehead and a large hooked nose, but his most compelling feature was a pair of piercing eyes. He wore tattered coveralls and tossed his hat onto the table. Colleen stood near her father with one finger hooked into his pants pocket, bright eyes following the conversation back and forth between the adults.

"Hot damn, boy, it's good to see you. Where you been?" he asked. "You're a sight for sore eyes. Where's that good lookin' woman of yours?" Kate quickly stepped in, sparing Boyd the need to rehash the unhappy story, quickly summarized for Charlie, then deftly steered the conversation in another direction. She told Boyd that Jacob, now sixteen, and Matt, their twelve-year-old, had gone to town to the store and should return soon. Jacob was seeing a young woman who lived down the valley, and Charlie and Kate were beginning to think about grand-children sometime in the future.

Soon, the two boys returned and greeted Boyd enthusiastically, asking a flood of questions which he answered patiently. They were especially interested in his life as a fisherman, remembering what he had told them before about his life on the sea. They asked about the ocean and what it was like since neither of them had ever seen one.

After supper, as the sun slid behind the green mountains, the two men sat on the front porch and talked with quiet voices. From inside they could hear the clatter and clank of dishes and pots being washed and stored away. The voices of the two boys drifted down from the loft, and Colleen chattered pleasantly away. Cool air drifted down from the knob and pooled in the lower reaches of the valley. Out near the barns a cow bawled for its calf, and a mule brayed in answer. They quickly established the old rapport that had been the hallmark of their acquaintance before. They had been through a lot together.

"So, Boyd, tell me what brought you back to this part of the country. Not that we aren't tickled to see you, but you look like you've got something on your mind," Charlie said.

"Yes I have. You remember the Saunders' who lived in town with their daughter Lexus?"

"Yes, of course. I've known them all my life. Mr. Saunders was a pompous sort, not to speak ill of the dead. He and the missus died some time back."

"Have you heard that their house burned, and Lexus is missing?"

"Yeah, I heard. I talked to the sheriff about it, but he doesn't know anything. It isn't like him to not have heard something, but he's been gone a lot, seein' to his ailing momma over to Meadow Bridge. He was an only child, you know."

"Lexus wrote a letter to me asking me to come back here and help her but didn't say why. I was a bit surprised that she'd ask me, what with that thing with Nellie," Boyd said with down-cast eyes.

Charlie grinned to himself at Boyd's description of his relationship with Nellie as "that thing." "Somethin' else, Boyd, the gossip in town is that Lexus had a run-in with some Yankee soldiers in town. Turns out they were the same bunch that caught you and threw you into Grapevine Cave. A bunch of renegades. Seems there are about a half dozen of 'em left, and they're getting desperate. The Yankees have been after them, and they'll either find 'em and wipe 'em out or run 'em clean out of the country."

Boyd frowned. "I heard that too, and yeah, I remember them. How could I forget? The one called Hank put me in that cave. It was only blind luck that he didn't kill me. I'd have thought they'd have been long gone."

"Well, me too, but I think they've been out of the valley for a while and just recently drifted back this way."

"Charlie, I need to find Lexus and quick. You don't suppose they've taken her away or maybe killed her? It could have been them that burned the house."

"I was thinkin' the same thing. I'd hate to think what they'd do to her if they have her."

"How can I find her?" Boyd asked. "I've looked everywhere I can think of. I even went up on the knob that her father owns to see if she was there, but without luck."

"One other thing," Charlie said, ignoring his question, moving around on his creaking chair, "old man Smythe and his missus brought me a couple of bushel of seed potatoes a week or so back, and said that he thought that he'd seen that Yankee gang along the pike between here and Meadow Bridge. Said he'd of missed them except that he'd smelled wood smoke, and he crept down through the brush to see who was camped there. He's a nosey ol' so and so. He didn't get too close for fear of bein' seen, but he recognized a couple of their horses. We were talkin' that we should get a few of the fellers together and run them plumb out of the country, but right now, everybody's trying to get their fields planted and don't have time to go gallivantin' around on what would probably turn out to be a wild goose chase."

The two men fell silent, each trying to sort out what had happened to Lexus. Kate came out of the house and placed a hand on Charlie's shoulder looking inquisitively at Boyd. She had been listening to their conversation and was concerned that Boyd would do something rash.

She said, "When Mrs. Smythe was here, we had a chance to talk a while. She said there're all kinds of rumors flying around the valley about Lexus and that bunch of Yankees. Said she'd heard that they'd killed her, and another woman said that Lexus had been, you know, been raped or something."

With a shake to his voice, Boyd said, "I hope she's all right. I'll kill those…"

"Take it easy," Charlie said. "It won't do any good to get all riled up at gossip. Who knows what has happened, and it isn't any use to worry until we know exactly what. I know how you feel, Boyd. I remember Kate helping you buy clothes for Lexus' party that you never got to attend. She's a nice girl, especially after she grew up some."

Their talk began to go in circles, repeating what they'd said earlier; they were getting nowhere. Boyd shook his head and said, "I guess the only thing left to do is to go see where those Yankees are and find out if they have Lexus."

"Tell you what," Charlie said. "Why don't you do that, but you'll have to be careful. If they catch you, you're a dead man. If you find them, come on back and get me and the sheriff. We'll rustle up some others, and we'll go sort this out. Don't you try to take 'em on by yourself. You're only one man, you know, even if you are a war hero." Charlie grinned at him, a teasing look in his eyes.

"Yeah, I suppose." Boyd became serious and said, "Do you ever think about the war?"

"Yeah, sometimes I do. I was in the army for several years and we fought in a lot of skirmishes and some pretty big battles. Mostly I remember all of the marching we did, first one place then another. We were hungry most of the time, and some of us didn't have decent shoes or uniforms, just bits and pieces we picked up here and there."

"Do you ever think of the men we killed? I mean, sometimes they just pop into my mind without rhyme or reason."

Charlie's eyes darkened and he admitted, "Sometimes I wake up Kate, late in the night, yellin' and thrashin' about, dreamin' about fighting. It scares her. She doesn't know what to make of it. Oh, she understands, but then, she really doesn't know what it was like. Sometimes, some of the men I've killed come to me in my dreams, and they line up in formation and point their fingers at me. I'd wake up, and sweat would be pouring off me."

Boyd said, "It's like that for me too, sometimes. Being back here where the battle was has stirred up memories best left alone. I remember the men I shot, too. Especially that young picket down on the river. He was just a boy. Sometimes I think about what his life would have been like if I hadn't come along."

"You can't think that way, Boyd. Thinking 'what if' won't get you anywhere. I know it's easy to say, but I reckon we just have to let it go, let the memories go and get on with our lives."

The two men sat on the porch as dusk fell around them, each lost in his thoughts, and then Boyd said, "Sometimes I think about her, wondering where she is and what's become of her." Charlie knew that he was talking about Nellie. "She was a good person and if anyone deserved freedom, it was her."

"Yes, I have to agree with that. She was a good woman. It makes me wonder just what this war is all about. We can say it's about not bein' told what to do by some distant government, but like most things, it all boils down to the almighty dollar. I don't know how it will all end, but I hope someday we can all live together, and in peace. But, it will be a long time before that happens. The war has been hard on everyone. Kate and me and the kids are lucky to live up here on the mountain where life just goes on pretty much as usual. Oh, it's hard to get building materials and coffee an' sugar and such, but we're pretty much self-sufficient. If we can't grow it or make it ourselves, we just do without. But, the ones that suffer most are the widows whose husbands aren't ever coming back. There are kids who won't ever know their daddies because they won't be comin' home. Who is goin' to feed and provide for them?" Charlie looked down at his shoes. "An' then there's them that won't ever know what happened to their menfolk—mothers and fathers and wives and children. They'll be buried in some dark grave somewhere and won't have anybody to grieve for them 'cause nobody will know where they are. This war can't be over too soon for me, but I'm afraid it will drag on for years."

Boyd sat quietly, watching the fireflies begin to flash and the stars twinkle overhead, as his thoughts turned to Lexus. Where was she? Would he be able to find her in time?

\* \* \* \*

## INTO THE MOUNTAINS

Lexus left the camp carrying a bundle of food she had been given by the nigras. She didn't know what to do, where to go. After the relative safety of the camp, she began to worry, her confidence slipping. She was afraid to go directly back to town for fear of being intercepted along the way. She looked at the morning sun just topping the eastern mountains and made a quick decision. She headed east, into the sun, toward the river. She felt that was the best choice but didn't know how far away it was. One way or another she'd get there. Once she reached the river, she could travel downstream until she hit the pike and then back up the mountain and into the town. She walked briskly along, skirting a huge mass of wind-blown trees only to have to crawl through a patch of rhododendron. The brush and brambles plucked at her dress, but after an hour of frantic scrambling, she came to the road that led north out of Lewisburg. She knew that being anywhere near it was dangerous. The soldiers could be anywhere, searching for her. Looking each way carefully, she made a mad dash across, her skirt whipping around her legs, hair flying. But, just as she entered the woods, just as she thought she'd made it, she heard the clamor of hoof beats.

# CHAPTER THREE

**B**OYD SADDLED THE horse and led it from the barn as dawn was breaking. The sun peeked over the mountains, staining the sky ruby red. A large red rooster strutted out of the chicken coop and crowed lustily. It shook its head and extended the feathers on its neck to form an intimidating ruff. The hens ignored him, scratching and pecking in the grass.

He said goodbye to Kate and Charlie while the children still slept and then rode down the road that led up and over the ridge. The trip down the mountain and across the covered bridge was uneventful. He turned west toward Meadow Bridge when he reached the pike, cautiously moving along, stopping frequently to look for sign of the renegades. He paid special attention to the horse's ears and demeanor. The road was well-traveled and marked with wagon-wheel ruts and the tracks of horses. Yesterday's rain had softened and partially erased the sign. Cattle dotted the fields that spread toward the mountains

By mid-morning he found the renegade's vacated camp just off the pike; trampled grass, trash strewn about, discarded clothing, horse droppings and a crude latrine in the edge of the woods. In the center of the camp he saw the remains of a campfire, placed his palm on one of the blackened logs and found it was still warm. He stirred the ashes with a stick and saw a curl of smoke rise into the still morning air. They hadn't been gone long, he concluded. Maybe they'd left during the night. He walked back to the edge of the pike and studied the ground carefully. He wasn't much of a tracker, but it was easy to see that the heavy wagon and horses had turned back toward town. He climbed onto his horse and they trotted along following the tracks as best he could. He took special notice of the edges of the road to see if they had turned off anywhere along the way.

Within the hour, he was back in town. The streets were busy with pedestrians, and two men unloaded a large freight wagon that sat before a store, its team of horses standing patiently. Boyd heard the ever present clang of the blacksmith's hammer. He approached the men, dismounted and wiped his forehead with the sleeve of his shirt. The men looked at him suspiciously. One was tall and muscular and wore heavy boots and rough clothes. His hat was pulled down over his forehead and hooded eyes peered from beneath. The other appeared to be a clerk or store keeper and wore a vest over an expensive shirt with a string tie pushed up close to his neck. A pair of spectacles hung from a chain around his neck. His hair was short and appeared to be recently barbered, and his shoes were polished to a high shine.

"Hello," Boyd said and using his best smile. He introduced himself.

"Yeah, I know who you are. I heard you were back in town," the clerk said. "Someone said you're lookin' for Lexus Saunders. That right?" The other man stood mutely, shuffling his feet in the dirt. The clerk didn't seem to be particularly unfriendly.

"Yes. She's a friend and I'm worried that something bad might have happened to her. You have any idea where I could find her?"

"No I don't." He turned to the worker beside him and said, "You have any ideas?"

The man was startled that he had been asked a question. "Naw, I don't know nothin' about her. I don't get to travel in her crowd, you know."

"Have you talked to the sheriff? Maybe he knows what happened to her," the clerk said.

"Yes I have, but I'll go see him again. Maybe he's heard something new."

"He's not here. Went to take care of his mother. Nobody knows when he'll be back. I heard she's very ill and is not likely to make it through the summer," the clerk said.

"Thanks, I'd heard something about that, too. One other thing, did you see that bunch of renegade soldiers go through town recently? I'm worried that they may have something to do with Lexus' disappearance."

The clerk said, "I didn't see them myself but sometime in the middle of the night, they came through town. Mr. McCoy's dog ran out barking at them, and one of the soldiers knocked it in the head with his gun barrel. It crawled under his porch and died. Mr. McCoy saw the whole thing because he was on his way to the outhouse, but he didn't say anything about seeing Lexus with them. They didn't even stop–went right on through town and were gone. Something needs to be done about them. They've caused a lot of grief in the valley."

"Did they continue east on the pike?"

"No, McCoy said they turned the corner in town and went north toward Falling Spring. You don't think they really have Lexus do you? She won't have a chance if they do. They'll stop at nothing."

"I don't know. I'm going to follow them, and if I can catch up with them, I'll try to find out what they're up to. I plan to come back and get some men to help. Charlie Taylor said he'd help and maybe the sheriff will be back by then."

"Yeah, I heard that you and Taylor were friends. He'd be a good one to have with you if it comes to a fight. I'd not like to be in the sights of his rifle. Me, I wouldn't know one end of a gun from the other."

Boyd left the two men to their work and turned up Court Street, past the courthouse, and found the wagon road that led north out of town.

\* \* \* \*

Lexus was terrified. She ran through the trees and brush, mindless of the scratches and bruises she was suffering. She lost one shoe and stumbled across a log, sprawling headfirst into the rough ground. She jumped to her feet, fleeing through the woods. She could hear the men behind her whooping and hollering in mad pursuit. To them it was great fun chasing their defenseless prey. She wasn't sure how many there were but judging from the noise, at least three. Now she knew what it was like for a coon being chased by a pack of dogs. Her breath came in great gasps, and her heart raced like a trip hammer.

How could she get away from them? They'd surely catch her, and she knew what they'd do to her when they did. Death would be a welcome reprieve from their torture. She remembered their lustful stares as they sullenly sat around the campfire when they had her before. She bunched her skirts with her hands and ran on through the forest, dodging tree trunks and fallen timbers. The land suddenly sloped away into a large sink hole, and using trees and saplings to slow her descent, she made her way to the bottom. It was quiet there in the wooded hole in the ground. In the distance she could hear the men calling to each other, searching for her. It wouldn't be long until they found the tracks and scuffs she had made in the leaf-covered forest floor, and then they'd run her down. She ran across the bottom of the sink, stepping across a tiny stream that meandered around rocks and debris and into a narrow hole that opened into the darkness of a cave below.

An explosion of sound caused her heart to leap into her throat. Huge wings beat the air frantically as turkeys took sudden flight all around her. Others ran, necks outstretched, into the brush, their bronze feathers flashing in the dim forest light. The leaves on the forest floor were raked, as if by some mad yardman, into piles and windrows where they had been searching for food. Within seconds they were gone, and the forest was quiet save for a light breeze that rustled and tossed the leaves on the trees around her. Surely the soldiers had seen the turkeys flying away and would quickly descend upon her. She ran up out of the sink and on through the woods.

She soon came to an opening in the forest—a pasture with two skinny cows standing in the middle, chewing their cuds in the hot sun. They lazily stomped their hooves to set into motion a huge swarm of flies that crawled over them, only to have them settle again. Their tails were in constant motion, flipping up over their backs at the tormenting pests. The pasture was dotted with thistles and red cedar saplings and was slowly reverting to forest untended by an absent farmer. Lexus dashed across the field, jumped over the brush and brambles, and fled into the woods beyond.

"There she is!" a soldier yelled. "She just crossed the field." He gave pursuit, and Lexus could hear him crashing through the brush behind her. She ran on, mindless of the cuts and abrasions her bare feet were suffering. Somewhere along the way she had lost her other shoe. If only she could get away from them long enough to find a place to hide, she could rest and maybe bind up the scrapes and wounds that were seeping blood. Frantically, she ran with a strength born only from fright, but now she could hear a man's ragged breath behind her as he sucked air into his lungs, and his running feet beat a constant tattoo. For her, time slowed down. She felt as if she were running through water, slowing her until she could hardly get one foot in front of another. The muscles in her legs burned with a crimson fire, and her arms pumped like the pistons of a locomotive as she strained to run even faster. Air rushed into her breast in great gulps, burning down into her lungs.

Branches whipped by, clawing at her clothing as a deep, visceral groan escaped her lips.

Without warning, a rough hand grasped the collar on the back of her dress and dragged her viciously over backward and onto the ground, her legs bent beneath her. The shock of the impact with the ground knocked the breath from her, stunning her into nothingness. The man's heavy body fell on her without mercy and pinned her motionless to the rough forest floor.

Lexus awoke minutes later to see the soldier sitting on a log, staring at her. She was prone on her back with her hands tied with strips of dirty cloth. Her dress was thrown up over her waist, and he stared at her, clad only in her undergarments. She pushed her dress down as best she could, and the man laughed. His head was bound with a bloody rag, and his jaw bulged with chewing tobacco. Stubble covered his chin, and a droopy mustache covered his upper lip. His uniform was dirty and wrinkled and had tobacco stains down the front. A large revolver was tucked under his belt. As Lexus looked at him, she realized that he was not an old man, but years of living in the sun had burned his skin a deep brown, and crow's feet spread from the corners of his eyes. He dipped his head to spit a stream of tobacco juice onto the leaves between his feet, keeping his rheumy eyes on her.

"Well now, I gotcha," he said. "You run purty good fer a woman. Thought I'd never catch you. Where you made your mistake was crossin' that field back there. You mighta got plumb away if you hadn't done that. That was when I seen you." He chuckled. "Them other fellers are still lookin' for you, but let 'em look. You're mine. After what you done to my poor head, you'll have everything comin' that I give you."

Lexus squirmed and tried to sit up, but he pushed her back with his foot. "Yer not goin' nowhere, Missy," he said. "When I get done with you there weren't be much left fer them others. They don't deserve none since they couldn't find a woman in a whorehouse." He chuckled at his own cleverness.

"Let me go! I haven't done anything to you. You're some kind of big strong man, aren't you, beating up a woman?" Lexus taunted him knowing it was useless to try to reason with the man. She couldn't think of anything else to do.

"You hesh up now," he said. "I don't want to hear nothing more from you." He grabbed her by the hair and roughly brought her to her feet, pulling her close and looking into her eyes. Lexus twisted and screamed, tried to knee him in the groin, her teeth clinched together and her face in a wild grimace. "Well now, you're a wildcat, ain't you?" His face was so close that she could smell his fetid, tobacco breath. She struggled again, trying to break free. He laughed, a high braying sound, and shook her like a rag doll. Lexus was disoriented, and her teeth rattled like dice in a cup. With her last strength, she twisted around and sank her teeth into his arm. With his reddened face contorted into a frightful mask, he jerked his offended arm away and slammed his fist into the side of her head.

\* \* \* \*

The Sergeant sat on the wagon waiting for his men to return. He knew it was only a matter of time before they caught her. He looked up and down the road expecting someone to come along at any time. They needed to get moving. He knew that sooner or later the sheriff would round up some men and come after them. Either that or the Yankee army would return and although they bought plunder from him, they wouldn't stand for kidnapping and mistreating women. There were some things even the Yanks wouldn't stand for. Colonel Crook would put all of them before a firing squad. Deserters and rapists weren't tolerated. His face twisted in a grimace at the thought.

Before long, he could hear the men coming through the woods, laughing and talking. As they drew near, he could see that they had the woman. Two of the men carried her between them, her arms draped over their shoulders. Her head hung down and swung lifelessly as they walked—blood dripped from her nose and streamed down her neck onto her chest. Her hair was a tangled mess, and her dress was ripped. They tossed her in a lifeless heap on the ground at the Sergeant's feet.

"Is she still alive?" he asked. He poked her with the toe of his boot.

"Yeah, she's alive," Hank said. His pocked face broke into a nasty grin. "But no thanks to Joe there. He had her down on the ground when we found 'em. Took two of us to pull him off her. He clubbed her on the head and might near kilt her."

"I caught her. By rights I otta get first dibs," Joe said with a whining voice. "I'm the one she brained with a frying pan." The other men sniggered and laughed.

"You ain't got no dibs on nothing," the Sergeant said. He glared at Joe who wouldn't look him in the eye. "I see you messin' around with her, and I'll cut out your eyeballs."

Joe decided to cut his losses and avoid a confrontation with the Sergeant, for now. But sooner or later he'd settle with the girl *and* the Sergeant. He's get his chance. All he had to do was bide his time. But one way or another, he'd satisfy himself and in more ways than one. He gave the Sergeant an insolent salute and said "Yessiree, Captain!" He turned on his heel and sulked away.

"Hank, you and Luke pick her up an' get her in the wagon. Make sure she's tied and gagged. Cover her with some canvas or something." He had to be careful. Sooner or later they'd meet some farmer going to town, and he didn't want anyone to see the girl. He was in enough trouble as it was. His gang had slowly diminished until he was left with only three men. Only days ago, two of them had slipped away in the night taking a couple of horses and a good part of their food. He'd kill them if he ever saw them again, which was doubtful. He knew it was time to get out of the valley. He had decided to go north, maybe to Beverly or even as far as Clarksburg.

They dumped Lexus in the wagon and covered her, noticing that she had not stirred. Luke drove the wagon with his horse tied behind. The Sergeant rode in front with the other two as a rear guard. The wagon rattled over the rough road. The men rode in silence, turning occasionally to look back down the road.

They soon came to Falling Spring, a community situated on a hill above the Greenbrier River. The men wanted to stop and find something to eat, maybe stop at a house and try to buy a ham or something, but the Sergeant would have none of it. They still had an hour of daylight left and he meant to make the most of it. They trotted casually through the small collection of houses and kept their eyes straight ahead. Just on the north side of town, they passed a house perched on a knoll overlooking the road. An old man, smoking a pipe, sat in a rocking chair on the porch. He watched them silently as they passed. He used his toe to roust a yellow dog sleeping at his feet that jumped up and began barking. As he passed, Joe pointed his finger at the dog then made a cocking motion with his thumb as if to shoot it. The old man puffed on his pipe, a blue cloud of smoke circling his head. The yellow dog soon lost interest and flopped down on its side and went to back to sleep.

Once through town, the road rose sharply up the mountain, but their horses had little trouble climbing the grade. They traveled on a couple of miles then pulled the wagon off the road and into the woods. They found a spring flowing from the mountainside, scooped out a trough large enough to water the horses and began to set up camp. They tied the horses on long tethers so they could graze and left them saddled in case they had to leave in a hurry. They dragged Lexus out of the back of the wagon and dumped her inert form onto the ground. Joe stood by looking down at her crumpled body. Blood still seeped from her nose, and a large bruise had swelled up on the side of her face. Her eyelids fluttered as she began to stir. Well now, Joe thought, that's more like it. Maybe she'd live and be of some use after all. He picked up a stick and used it to pull aside the front of her torn dress.

"You get away from her, Joe. I'll beat you senseless if you so much as lay a hand on 'er. I thought we had all that settled back yonder," the Sergeant said. Joe glared at him then turned without a word and walked away. Insolent bastard, the Sergeant thought. I'm going to have to put a bullet in his head before it's all over.

They struck a fire and began to make supper. They didn't have much to eat and would have to raid a farm soon, but for now they'd make do. They didn't dare attack a farm this close to a town, especially now since they were down to only the four of them. Most men in the area knew how to shoot even if they were past draft age. Half a dozen angry men could make their lives miserable, and they weren't anxious to tangle with the sheriff. No, they'd wait until they found a farm back away from the main road and raid it. Maybe tomorrow.

After they had eaten, they strung up their tents and tossed their bedrolls into them. Much to the consternation of the men, the Sergeant made them put out the fire so as not to attract undue attention. As dusk fell, the men began to bed down. The Sergeant took Lexus by the arm and dragged her to her feet. She was awake now, and her eyes grew large when she saw where she was and who had her. Her knees shook with fear and fatigue, and her head throbbed unmercifully. She felt as if she had been run over by a team and wagon. He took the gag from her mouth and growled into her ear, "Scream and I'll break yer arm."

She recoiled in fear at the appalling look in the man's bloodshot eyes. "Why are you doing this?" she asked through bloody lips. "I want to go home."

"Not likely, Missy! I got you and I ain't going to ever let you go. You're mine now and I won't make the same mistake twice, letting you slip away. You pert near cracked ole Joe's head. You ain't never going back to your mammy and daddy."

Lexus tilted her head back, her chin rising, "I don't have a mother or father. They're both dead. I only have an aunt and uncle left–they live in Rowlesburg, but you wouldn't know where that is, you being an ignorant moron." She knew she was treading on dangerous ground by talking back to this man, but as long as she could distract him by talking, she could postpone the inevitable. Oh, how was she going to get out of this?

"I ain't ignorant," he shouted, twisting her arm painfully behind her back. "You watch your mouth or I'll close that other eye for you." This was even better than he could have hoped for. If she didn't have parents or other relatives in town, no one would likely come looking for her. People disappeared all the time as the war dragged on. Oh, the sheriff would search all right, but after a few days, he'd give up. As soon as they got out of his jurisdiction, they'd have smooth sailing. It was only a few miles more until they'd cross the county line and they'd be home free.

Lexus twisted violently from his grasp, raked her fingernails across his face and turned to run when he grabbed her dress from behind. He twirled her around like a fish on a line and hit her on the jaw with his fist. She was flung to the ground like a rag doll, her arms spread wide. Her eyes rolled up into her head and darkness swept over her.

\* \* \* \*

Boyd urged the horse on. He had found where a wagon had been pulled off the road into the brush and had found tracks and scuffs where several men had milled around it. Tracks led from the woods, and if he wasn't mistaken, someone or something had been dragged to the wagon. He'd found blood on the leaves. Did they have Lexus? Was that her blood on the ground back there? If so, what had they done to her? He was worried and urged the horse to move even faster.

When he arrived at Falling Spring, he began looking for someone who might have seen the renegades. He saw a scattering of houses, but no one was around. He was almost through the village when a yellow dog stood up on the porch of a nearby house and began to bark at him. The front door stood open but otherwise the house looked empty. Boyd didn't know what to do. Surely someone had seen them pass through town and might be able to tell him if Lexus was with them. Just when he was about ready to go on, an old man stepped out on the porch with a smoking pipe in his hand and told the dog to be quiet.

"What can I do for you, young fellow?" the man asked. "You look like you're lost."

"No, I just need some information."

"I'll help you if I can. I'm always willing to help my fellow man," he said.

Boyd could tell from his speech that he was well educated. "I'm looking for a woman."

"Well now, I don't think I can help you there. As a matter of fact I'm looking for one, too, but I'm not having much luck either," he said, chuckling at his joke.

"No, what I mean is that a woman from Lewisburg has gone missing, and I'm looking for her."

"Oh, you mean Miss Lexus?"

"Yes. Do you know her?"

"Oh sure, I've known her since she was a tiny thing. I've eaten many a meal at her daddy's table. We were college mates at Virginia Military Institute over in Lexington. I heard that she's missing and had thought I'd go look for her myself, but I'm not as steady as I used to be."

"Have you seen some soldiers, a half dozen or so of them, ride through here today?"

"Yes, not more than an hour ago. There were four of them. They went on north, up the mountain."

"Could you see if a woman was with them? They may have kidnapped Lexus"

"What makes you think that? Oh!" the man said, "There was that nasty run-in she had with them in town a month or two ago. I had forgotten about that. If they have her, may God have mercy upon her soul. They were a rough looking bunch. They had a wagon with a canvas over the stuff in the back. I guess she could have been under it, but if she was I didn't hear a peep from her."

"That's what I'm thinking," Boyd said. He quickly told the old man what he had found back down the road.

Boyd thanked him and had turned his horse to leave when the old man said, "What are you planning to do? Surely you can't be thinking of going after them alone. They looked like they would just as soon kill a man as blink."

"I don't see that I have much choice. You know what they'll do to her as soon as they have a chance."

"Yeah, I know," The old man sighed. "Wait a minute, and I'll go with you. I may be slow, but I can still shoot straight."

Before Boyd could object, he hurried back in the house. Within a few minutes, the old man came around the house leading a large, black mule. It stood quietly, twitched its ears one at a time and rippled its hide. Boyd's horse looked at it and laid its ears back. As the man cinched the saddle and got ready to leave, Boyd asked him what his name was.

"Perkins," he said. "Nathaniel Perkins, but you can call me Nate. I was a professor at VMI until I got too old, and they put me out to pasture, so I came back home here to Greenbrier County. I was born in this house."

"I thought you said you were a student there."

"I was, but after I graduated I went to school for a while at Virginia Polytechnic Institute and then returned to VMI to teach."

"I have to admit that I'm not familiar with either of those schools."

He smiled. "Don't feel bad, most people aren't either and couldn't care less."

The old man went back in the house and returned with one of the new repeating rifles over his arm. He stiffly climbed onto the mule, and they rode up the road together.

"I haven't seen one of those rifles before. It looks like it's brand new," Boyd said as they rode along.

"It is. One of my former colleagues at the Institute sent it to me for my seventy-fifth birthday. It's a dandy."

"Oh, by the way, my name's Boyd Houston."

"Yeah, I know," the old man said. "Your reputation precedes you."

They paused at the top of the hill to let the animals rest. The two men talked quietly, discussing what strategy to use when they caught up with the renegades. The road had wound up and around the undulating ridges, having been cut into the hillside here and there to make it as level as possible, but it was not much more than a track with rutted lanes where wagon wheels had sunk into the rain-softened soil. Red oaks and maples arched overhead forming a green tunnel broken here and there with puddles of light. In a tree near the road, a red squirrel chattered at them, cranking its thin tail in indignation. Darkness began to settle in around them as the sun set over the nearby mountains, and over in the southwest sky a lone star sparkled.

"Do you smell that?" Boyd asked. "Smells like smoke."

"No, I can't smell anything. The sense of smell is the first thing to go as you get older. Well, maybe not *the* first," he said with a rueful smile.

"I think I can hear voices, too. Let's leave the horses here and creep up a bit to see if it's them."

"All right, just give me a minute to get down from this infernal animal and stretch my legs." He dismounted, stretched and rubbed his legs and back.

They tied the horses and hoped that they wouldn't nicker if they smelled the renegade's animals. It was just a chance they'd have to take. Boyd's horse began to stomp and whirl around when he tried to tie it close to the mule. He moved it across the road and tied it there. It seemed to calm down and began to eat some of the tree leaves within reach. I hope it doesn't make itself sick, Boyd thought.

The two men walked up the road, keeping to the shadows as best they could. It was getting dark under the tree's canopy, but here and there where the road had opened a channel to the sky, dim light filtered down. As they drew nearer, they heard the rumble of men's voices, and they could just make out the outline of horses tethered nearby. A struggle seemed to be taking place in one of the tents and they heard a fist hitting flesh. The smell of wood smoke grew stronger. They crept closer but were still thirty yards away when a shift in the wind took their scent to the horses and one of them nickered loudly. Back down the road, Boyd's horse answered immediately, and the mule brayed loudly. Boyd and the old man were caught in the open with a dim sliver of the setting sun backlighting them. Later, the old man would say that what happened next was just like poking a stick in a big hornet's nest.

Gunfire erupted from the camp; spears of red flames from the renegade's guns darted out at them. The old man returned fire, and they heard a startled yip as someone was hit. One of the renegades swore violently. There was pandemonium in the camp as the men scrambled to find cover. Boyd fired his pistol, aiming high, and he was soon fumbling to replace the empty cylinder. Clouds of gun smoke hung in the air. A tin cup that had been sitting on a rock near the fire was hit with a bullet and went spinning away into the forest. Twigs and leaves rained down on both sides. The night seemed to be full of flying lead as the guns roared.

"Aim high," Boyd yelled to the old man, "Lexus might be with them," but he didn't seem to pay much attention to Boyd's suggestion. They fired several more rounds and another man screamed–the renegades had had enough. Soon, their horses burst from the gloom, the men clinging to saddle horns, leaning low over their horse's necks frantically kicking their flanks. They pounded away up the road, swearing and yelling at each other. The old man watched carefully, his eyes alert, and when the fleeing men rode through a shaft of light he fired. A rider slumped in the saddle but was able to stay aboard. Soon, all that could be heard was a whisper of wind and a whip-or-will singing somewhere far in the distance. Otherwise the forest creatures had fallen silent.

Nate slumped to the ground like a deflated hot air balloon. He rubbed his shoulder and looked at Boyd, a grim look on his face. "So that's what it's like. I have never fired a weapon at another person in my life but always wondered what it'd be like. I didn't serve in an army, at least not a real one. Can't say I care much for it. You all right, Boyd?"

"Yeah, I'm not hit or anything." His hands were trembling as the adrenaline left his bloodstream. "That was quite a shot when they were riding up the road. You must be pretty good with that thing," nodding at the rifle in Nate's hands.

"Thanks, but you never did ask me what I taught at the Institute." Without waiting for Boyd to reply, he continued, "Among other things, I taught the cadets marksmanship!" He laughed and slapped his knee. "First time I ever had to use it for real."

The two men reloaded and then cautiously approached the camp. Gear and odds and ends of clothing were scattered around on the ground. The little light that was left from the setting sun was quickly disappearing. As they used their gun barrels to carefully lift the canvas flaps of the tents to peer inside, looking for they knew not what, maybe a wounded man, they heard a soft groan. It came from a tent that had been set aside from the others. As Boyd drew the flap away he saw what he thought was a rumpled pile of rags and an old blanket wadded up in a ball. It was so dark under the canvas that he couldn't make out what it was. He struck a match, and it was then he saw a swirl of ash-blond hair. The match burned out and he tossed it aside. He knelt quickly beside her, throwing the blanket aside, drawing her to him in the darkness.

"What is it?" Nate asked. "Is it Lexus?" He tried to see over Boyd's shoulder.

"It's her. Light another match," Boyd said. "She isn't conscious." Boyd was surprised at the emotion in his voice. He didn't know this woman well, but there was still something about her.

Nate struck another match and then they could see Lexus' pale face, battered into an almost unrecognizable mess. Her left eye was swollen shut, and a bruise covered the side of her face. Then she opened her good eye, looked at them, frowned and squinted against the light of the match. She shrank away from Boyd, pushing at him with her hands, shaking her head from side to side. She turned her face away from him, and her eyes closed slowly as she passed out.

The men scrambled to get a fire built more for the light than the heat. When it was blazing high enough to see well, they placed her on a couple of bedrolls and began to examine her. She had scratches and bruises on her arms and legs and a large gouge on the side of her neck. Her nose was clotted with blood and was bruised and swollen. They wanted to wipe away some of the dirt and grime to get a better look at her wounds, but they didn't have water with which to work. Lexus began to shake and tremble, her teeth chattering. They wrapped her in several blankets in an attempt to keep her warm.

"We have to get her to a doctor. I think she's going into shock. I've seen it before when people were badly injured," Nate said.

"Yes, I agree. If you'll stay with her, I'll try to find the team for the wagon. I don't think they took them with them."

It took Boyd half an hour, thrashing around in the dark, to find the team and get it hitched to the wagon. He looked frequently at Lexus, lying motionless beside the fire. The old man seemed smaller, somehow, as he crouched beside her. He touched her tenderly, checking her pulse, placing his palm on her forehead. He looked exhausted. That was the way fighting was, Boyd thought. One minute you were fighting for your life with the strength of a Titan, and then when it was over, you felt deflated, used up. At any age, you just wanted to rest.

They loaded her carefully into the back of the wagon on some bedrolls, covered her with blankets, and the old man climbed in beside her and cradled her in his arms. Boyd tied the horse and mule to the back of the wagon and began the trek back down the mountain. He couldn't see very well in the dark but trusted the horses to find their way. Once he stopped to check on Lexus and then went on. Soon, they came to the old man's house. The old man limped up onto the porch, went inside, and soon the yellow glow of a lamp lit the windows and doorway.

"Bring her in here, and put her in my bed, there in the back," he said, giving orders like a general. Gingerly, Boyd lifted her from the wagon and carried her inside. He placed her in the bed and pulled the blankets up to her chin. The old man lit another lamp on a bedside stand, and Boyd drew in a sharp breath when he got a closer look at her face. It was far worse than he had feared. She was a terrible sight to his eyes. The old man started a fire in the kitchen stove and soon had warm water to use to bathe her.

"I'll clean her up, Boyd. How about going to get Nettie Lightfoot? She lives down over the hill near the river."

"Is she a doctor?"

"Well, no but she's about the closest thing to one we have. The nearest real doctor is all the way back in Lewisburg. At best, it'll take you hours to get there and back. Nettie's, well, Nettie's the one who takes care of our animals," he said softly. "She has never had formal training, but she seems to know what she's doing, and sometimes she takes care of us when we can't get to the doctor. A couple of times she delivered babies. She uses a combination of medicines–with some herbs and roots thrown in. Usually gets good results."

"I don't know, Nate. Maybe I'd better go get a real doctor."

"Tell you what. Why don't you ask Nettie to come take a look, then go to town and see if you can get ole Doc Franklin to ride all the way up here? I don't think we can risk taking Lexus to town until she's feeling a little better, you know, stabilized some."

Boyd reluctantly agreed, and after Nate had given him directions, he rode down to the river to find her. It turned out to be quite easy. As Nate had described, hers was the only house perched on stilts along the edge of the river. As he approached he could hear singing in the house and someone dancing, twirling around and passing in front of first one window then another in the front room. The dancer's shadow flicked and danced on the ground amid golden pools of lamplight. Fascinated, Boyd sat on the horse and watched. The dancer was a woman who held a large yellow cat at arm's length, its tail swinging back and forth as she twirled and sang a waltz that Boyd didn't recognize. She sang with a strong voice, slightly off key, that echoed off the water. The cat yowled occasionally to add to the surreal performance.

"Hello the house," Boyd shouted. Immediately the singing stopped, and seconds later the lamp was blown out. The house sat in silence on the riverbank, the river flowing, murmuring in the night.

"I got a gun," the woman shouted. "Who are you and what do you want?"

"Nate Perkins sent me. We've got a hurt woman who needs some help."

"You've told me what you want, but you haven't told me who you are."

"You don't know me. I'm Boyd Houston from down in South Carolina."

"What you doin' here, Houston? I thought they ran you out of town long ago. What is it with you, can't you take a hint?" The woman cackled and re-lit the lamps. "Come on up on the porch where I can get a look at you. I want to be sure you're who you say you are."

Boyd tied his horse and climbed a steep set of steps that led to a long porch that spanned the front of the house. Boyd was no longer surprised that people knew who he was. His reputation had, indeed, preceded him and people had long memories. He stepped through the door into the front room. He wasn't prepared for the vision that faced him. A tall, slim woman, maybe thirty years old, stared back at him with bright, black eyes and black, shiny hair that cascaded over her shoulders, glistening like coal. She wore a wrinkled, pale-green gown with a neckline that plunged lower than was currently acceptable in fashionable circles. The dress, elegant at some time in the past, was accented with a garish red sash that she had wrapped around her neck and had thrown one end over a soft, tawny-brown shoulder. On her head she wore a sparkling tiara. Her lips, painted with vermillion makeup, had smeared to form a clown's mouth. Rouge illuminated her high cheekbones and on her feet, she wore a pair of men's work boots.

"What are you looking at, Houston? Haven't you ever seen a woman before?"

Boyd closed his mouth and smiled uncertainly. "Uh, well, certainly," he said, stammering. "Can you come and help? She's pretty sick. Someone beat her badly."

"Did you hit her? That's what men do, you know. I'd kill any man who did that to me." The cat rubbed against her legs and then hissed at Boyd.

"Oh, no," Boyd said quickly. "Nate will vouch for that. Can you come now and help? She's really hurt."

"Yeah, lemme get my stuff." She went into a back room and closed the door. Minutes later, she emerged dressed in a pair of baggy men's pants and an oversized work shirt with red banker's garters on each arm. She had removed the makeup and tied her hair back in a long braid. Around her neck she wore a heavy necklace of bright beads and baubles. She carried a burlap bag like a purse, filled halfway and tied with a silk ribbon. She wore an elegantly beaded pair of high-top moccasins on her feet.

To Boyd's surprise, she climbed up on the horse behind him and wrapped her arms around him. Within minutes they were back at Nate's house where she quickly took charge, shooed the men out of the bedroom and closed the door. A few minutes later she emerged to tell them what she needed; more hot water, some strips of cloth for bandages, a large bowl and some of Nate's wine. Boyd frowned and asked her how Lexus was doing, but she just shook her head and returned to the room.

*****

The Sergeant looked at the three men sprawled on the leaf-covered ground. They were in sorry shape. Luke was bleeding from a bullet graze on his arm, and Buck had lost part of his right ear. But Joe was the worse off–he had taken a bullet in his side, and it had exited from his belly. He writhed and groaned, pleading with the men to help him. He sat against a tree holding a bloody rag over his stomach, his face pale and drawn. Blood covered his hands and seeped from under the rag. Being gut shot is a death warrant, the Sergeant thought. And we can't waste time dawdling while whoever attacked them caught up. He didn't know who they were, but there must have been a passel of them judging by the amount of gunfire. They were pretty good shots even in the dark. He knew that in battle the vast majority of shots went wild and hit nothing. These men, whoever they were, had hit all three of his men. He was lucky he hadn't been shot too. He knew that Joe was doomed to die. The only question was what to do with him. Should he finish him off? It wasn't like he hadn't done it before. Or should they just leave him here to die? They couldn't afford to leave him for the followers to find. He didn't want to leave a witness behind.

"Hank, you and Luke are all right to travel, aren't you? You've only got a scratch or two. Joe there is another story."

"Yeah, we can travel. What you goin' to do with him?" Hank nodded toward Joe.

The Sergeant didn't answer. "You an' Luke take the horses up the road a ways. I'll be right there."

Hank and Luke knew the fate that awaited Joe. They couldn't meet his pleading eyes, and they were relieved that it wasn't them lying there with their blood all over the ground. They took Joe's weapons and led the horses up the road. Hank's arm throbbed where the bullet had taken a chunk of flesh away. The rag tied around it would have to be changed soon and the wound cleaned or gangrene would set in. He didn't want to lose the arm. Luke stumbled along, feeling the ragged edge of his ear gingerly with his dirty fingers. About half of it was missing, and a dribble of blood ran down his neck. He fumbled in his pocket for a rag he used for a handkerchief and pressed it over what was left of the ear.

"What we goin' to do now, Hank? The Sergeant gets meaner ever day. Next time it'll be one of us back there waiting for a bullet between the eyes," Luke said. His voice shook as he spoke.

"Shush. If he hears us talking 'bout him he'd just as soon shoot us as not. We'll stick with 'im fer a few more days, then the first chance we get we'll skip out. Just keep yer mouth shut."

A shot rang out behind them, the sound reverberating off the surrounding hills, and they both flinched as if the bullet had hit them, too. The horses snorted and stomped. A few minutes later the Sergeant caught up with them, and they mounted up and rode up the mountain road leading Joe's horse, its saddle empty.

The Sergeant talked as they rode. "We need to get out of these uniforms. First chance we get, we'll raid a farm and get some different clothes an' food. We ain't got nothing but our horses an' guns an' the clothes on our backs. We'll ride out of here. Go on up north." They walked their horses briskly along, each pondering his dismal future.

* * * *

Boyd and Nate sat on the porch and watched the sun rise. Roosters crowed in the village, and mourning doves hooted their mating calls. A huge flock of crows passed overhead and settled in the trees just north of town, noisily calling and bantering with each other. During the night, Mattie had said that Lexus would survive, but it would take time for her to fully recover. Upon Nate's urging, Boyd decided not to go for the doctor but to wait a couple of days and then take her back to town when she was stronger. Then, they'd have the doctor look at her. Mattie wouldn't allow them to enter the bedroom to see Lexus but said that she had a fierce headache–the bruises and scrapes would heal with time, but the emotional distress she had endured would last a lifetime. Neither Boyd nor Nate had asked the question they most wanted to ask.

The two men talked quietly. "Nate, what do you think we need to do with the team and wagon we took from the renegades? They aren't ours to keep," Boyd said.

"Far as I'm concerned, they're yours. I don't have any use for them. After this is over, I'm just going to sit on this porch with that old yellow dog and mind my own business. Not that I wasn't happy to jump in and lend Lexus a hand, but I'm getting too old for this."

"But, I don't have a bill of sale. The sheriff would probably arrest me for stealing them."

"Well, I'll have something to say to him about that. I've known him since he was a little boy. His daddy and I used to play chess whenever I was in town. The sheriff is a pretty good fellow once you get to know him. I don't guess you two had much chance to get together socially," he said, grinning.

"Don't remind me, Nate," Boyd said. "We'll use the team and wagon to take Lexus back to town when she's ready, and then I'll go to the sheriff and see what he wants to do with them. It'll be his problem to deal with. The horses aren't in the best shape I've ever seen. I suppose they've been used hard over the last couple of years."

"Yes, I noticed that too. They're back there in the barn with the mule eating hay to beat the band. They acted like they hadn't had grain for a month of Sundays judging by the way they were putting it away, the poor things."

Boyd said, "Tell me about Nettie. She's a strange one. Seems nice enough but there's something about her that I just can't put my finger on."

"It's an interesting story. She just showed up one day and took up residence in the stilt house by the river. The owner was a bachelor man who went away to the war, and no one's heard from him since. He's probably dead. She told me once that she's part Indian, Cherokee I believe she said. She has the features of one. Folks in town don't want to have much to do with her except when their animals get sick, and then they want her help. I've always kinda liked her."

"What do folks have against her?"

"You know how it is. Anyone who is different is always looked at with suspicion. She refuses to go to church like everyone else. She says her beliefs aren't anyone's business but her own. People say she's a witch because she uses those magic potions to cure their animals. I know for a fact they aren't magic, just herbal remedies handed down to her by her momma. I recently read a book in which the author said that if a man doesn't keep pace with his friends, it may be because he hears a different drummer. Nettie certainly must be hearing something that the folks around here aren't."

"When I went to fetch her last night, I saw her through the window, dancing with her cat, singing at the top of her voice. She was all dressed up in a ball gown. It made the hackles stand up on the back of my neck."

"You see? Just because she's different we want to make her evil or something. That's just not the case. Other people have said they'd seen her doing that, too. I think at one time she must have been a socialite somewhere. Judging by her speech, she must have had at least some education. There's a story behind all that, but I've never been able to get it out of her."

"Yeah, I see what you mean, but I have to admit that she put me ill at ease," Boyd said.

"You watch. She'll do wonders for Lexus. You need not worry."

The yellow dog, sprawled on the porch between them, groaned in its sleep. Nate scratched it behind its ear. The morning passed slowly with the men alternately caring for the horses–brushing them down, checking their hooves, carrying water for them–and sitting on the porch.

As it was nearing noontime, Nettie came out of the door and stood with her hands on her hips. Boyd couldn't help but notice how attractive she was. "You two going to sit there all day or are you going to make yourselves useful? I'm hungry, and I think Lexus could use something to eat, too. She has to keep her strength up."

Nate went into the house and began building a fire in the cook stove. He soon had food warmed and made a thin broth for Lexus with some beef he'd cooked the day before. Boyd stood around not knowing just what to do. Nettie took the broth into the bedroom but left the door ajar. Boyd could see Lexus reclined in the bed, her bruised face turned away from him. The poor girl, he thought, what more does she have to endure? But at least she's safe now. He would see that she wasn't hurt like this again. Nettie saw him looking into the room and pushed the door closed with her foot.

The next morning, Nettie said that it would be all right for Boyd to see Lexus for a few minutes. He stood by her bedside and looked at her with a concerned expression on his face. The blankets were pulled up to her chest, and he could see that Nettie had combed her hair carefully. Her eye was still badly swollen, her lip was split, and her nose was puffy and red. She would have black eyes for some time. She opened her eyes, catching her breath when she saw him.

"You came," she whispered. "I didn't think you would. I...I'm sorry," she said. "I didn't mean to get you involved in my problems, but I didn't know what else to do. Thank you."

"I know. I'm pleased that you wrote to me. Now you need to rest and get better. We'll get you back to town in a day or two, just as soon as Nettie says you can travel." He touched his fingertips to the back of her hand, and she gasped, tears in her eyes.

"They caught me in the woods. I tried to get away, but they ran me down. I was trying to get back home after they took me away. Oh, it was terrible. I got away once, but they caught me again. I can't remember where they took me or when you came for me. I guess I was passed out most of the time."

Boyd quickly told her about catching up with the renegades, and how he and Nate had run them off. They talked quietly for a few more minutes until her eyes drooped and slowly closed. In seconds she was fast asleep. Boyd stepped into the other room where Nate and Nettie sat at the table talking. He asked Nettie how long it would be before she could travel.

"Maybe tomorrow. She still has violent headaches and nausea. She was beaten very badly, but I don't think there will be permanent damage. She should recover quickly. She's young and that'll go a long ways to help her get better," Nettie said.

"Will you go with us when we take her home? I'll pay you to take care of her until we can turn her over to a doctor."

Nettie laughed at him. "Yeah, you can pay me the same as I charge for taking care of a horse." She giggled and poked Boyd on the arm. "You got a deal. I haven't been to town for weeks. I may even buy a new dress or something with all that money you're going to pay me."

Nate said, "Didn't Lexus' house burn down? Where's she going to stay?"

"Oh, I didn't think of that. I guess she'll have to stay at the boarding house. Or, maybe Mrs. Howard could take her in until we can figure out something else."

"That's a great idea, Boyd. And, Nate here can make all the arrangements. Didn't you tell me once that you and Ada used to go to the dances together before she married that other man?" Nettie asked with a devilish grin.

Nate's ears turned red and he frowned at her. "That's the last time I'll tell you anything in confidence, young lady," he said. Nettie laughed and went back into the bedroom with Lexus.

"What about your cat, Nettie?" Boyd asked, calling through the door. "Who'll take care of it?"

Nettie cackled and said. "Oh, it'll take care of itself. It stays out most nights anyway. Its half wild, just like the old man there."

Nate frowned again and shook his head.

Late the next morning, they helped Lexus into the back of the wagon where they had prepared a bed for her. Nettie climbed in beside her, and they set off down the road. Boyd's horse trailed along behind, and Nate rode the mule. The yellow dog sat on the porch and watched them leave.

88

They reached town shortly after noon and drove the wagon directly to Mrs. Howard's house. She was pleased to see Lexus but was concerned about her condition. They carried Lexus into the house and upstairs to the spare bedroom. Mrs. Howard looked Nettie over carefully, unsure of what to make of her but seemed pleased to have help caring for Lexus. Nate left to find the doctor, and Boyd took the team and wagon and their other animals around the corner to the blacksmith's shop. Then, he walked across town to the courthouse looking for the sheriff. When he entered the vestibule, the usual group of old men were seated on the benches in the lobby. I might as well get this over, he thought. What better way was there to let the town know that Lexus had been found than to tell these old gossips? They were full of questions, and he briefly answered them and then went into the sheriff's office.

Boyd found him seated behind his desk, frowning at a ledger that contained the meager budget the county gave him. His clothing was rumpled, and there were worry lines around his eyes. Boyd asked about his mother and was told that she had passed away. He expressed his condolences to the sheriff, and they talked about the inevitability of the Grim Reaper's visit.

"Sheriff, I found Lexus," Boyd said.

"The hell you say! How's she doing?"

"Not so well. Those renegade soldiers had her and just about beat her to death." Boyd said. "She'll recover, but they almost killed her."

"You mean they're still hanging around here? I thought they'd left the country."

"Evidently not. They came to town and grabbed her and then burned her house. I was lucky to find them when I did. They were on their way out of the valley."

"How'd you get her away from them?"

Boyd told him about meeting Nate and their encounter with the soldiers. "I was surprised that they ran from us, being soldiers and all, but Nate thinks that in the near darkness they didn't know how many of us there were. There was a lot of confusion, and with my pistol and Nate's repeating rifle we threw a lot of rounds at them."

"What about Lexus? Is she all right?"

"She's in pretty bad shape, but Nettie says she'll recover."

"Nettie? What's that witch doing caring for her? I thought she only took care of animals," the sheriff said.

"Well, she does, but she was the only choice we had. She seemed to do a pretty good job. It was good to have a woman there with her."

"They didn't mess with Lexus, did they? I wouldn't put it past that bunch to bother a woman. Why else would they kidnap her?"

"Frankly, I don't know. Nettie didn't say, and I just couldn't bring myself to ask Lexus."

"I hope they didn't. It would be terrible if she got in a family way. How long ago did all this happen?"

"A couple of days. With any luck they're long gone," Boyd said.

"I reckon I'll get a few men first thing in the morning and go up there and see if they're really gone. You want to go with us?"

"Sorry sheriff, I think I've seen enough of them. Besides I want to stay here and see how Lexus gets along."

"Can't say I blame you, Boyd. I'll let you know what we find out."

"What do you want to do with their wagon and team? I took them over to the blacksmith shop, and he said he'd board them until you decide what to do with them."

"As far as I'm concerned, they're yours. You took them fair and square," the sheriff said.

"I don't know, Sheriff. I don't have a bill of sale for them, and I'd need one if I tried to sell them."

"That's not a problem. I'll write you one that will explain how you came by them. No one here will argue with that, but I don't know how you'll be able to sell them with money bein' so scarce."

"Thanks Sheriff. If I can find a buyer, the money should go to Lexus. She's probably going to need it."

Boyd left the sheriff's office and walked back toward the boarding house, but he was stopped by several people asking about Lexus. Evidently, the old gossips had wasted no time spreading the word. Lexus was well liked in town, and everyone wished her well. He entered the boarding house, being careful to remove his hat. Mrs. Smith stood behind the desk, and Boyd approached her with a smile.

"Hello, Mrs. Smith. I need a room for a few days. Do you have one available?"

"As a matter of fact, Mr. Houston, the room you were in before is available, and I believe you have a couple of days left on the money you gave me," she said. She actually smiled at him. "And you can call me Mary. I heard what you did for Lexus, and I want to thank you. I think I misjudged you before. How is she getting along?"

"Why thank you Mary. Lexus is going to be all right. She's pretty banged up, but we think she'll recover."

They chatted pleasantly for a few minutes and then Boyd returned to Mrs. Howard's house, surprised at Mrs. Smith's turnabout. News spread fast in this town. As he mounted the porch, a short stocky man with a bowler hat on his round head was leaving. He was well dressed in a frock coat and vest with a gold watch chain stretching across his ample belly. He carried a black doctor's bag.

"Excuse me doctor," Boyd said. "Did you just examine Lexus? How is she? I mean, is she going to be all right?"

"Who are you? I can't give out private information to just anybody."

"I'm Boyd Houston, Lexus' friend."

"Oh, now I recognize you. Thank you for helping her. She told me what you did, so maybe you're not so bad after all. I guess I can tell you about her. She has a severe concussion. The other bruises and scrapes aren't so serious, but I'm concerned about her head. She still has headaches and feels like throwing up. Classic signs of a crack on the head. But, I believe that with a few day's rest, she'll be as good as new. She's a spunky girl, you know."

"Thank you, doctor. Yes, I know she has a lot of spirit. She fought them until they overpowered her. One more question. Did they mess with her. You know…"

"I don't know. That quack of a horse doctor wouldn't let me examine her that way, and Lexus didn't say. Unless she's hurt down there, it's none of my business. But, if I were you, I'd get that witch away from her."

"We'll see. Thank you for all you've done for her."

"Mark my word, no good will come of letting that woman hang around here. Before you know it she'll be hanging out a shingle in town, wanting to act like a real doctor. Now, I have to go. I'll be back tomorrow." He stomped down the steps and waddled down the street.

Boyd knocked on the front door, and Ada let him in. "Boyd, Lexus is asking for you. You can go on up. Just knock on the door before going in."

Boyd did as he was told, and the door was opened by Nettie. She was still dressed in men's clothing, and he could smell the faint aroma of herbs and spices coming from her. She chucked his chin playfully as she swirled out the door.

Boyd drew a chair close to the bed and sat down. Lexus opened her eyes and sighed. The bruises on her face were tinged in yellow, and the gouge on her neck had scabbed over. She reached for his hand and pulled it close. He bent toward her, as she fought to stay awake.

"The doctor gave me some laudanum, and I can hardly keep my eyes open. But I wanted to talk to you, Boyd, and thank you for all you did for me," she said in a voice that was barely audible.

"You don't have to thank me, Lexus. Besides you already did."

"I did? I can't remember. Things are a swirl in my head right now, and it still hurts, especially when I move around, and sometimes it feels as if the bed is rocking like a boat."

"You lie still now and sleep. We'll have time to talk later."

"No, I need to talk to you now." She shifted restlessly, her breasts rising and falling beneath the blankets. "Something has been on my mind for some time now, and I'm embarrassed to ask, but I need to know. What happened to you and Nellie? I don't understand. If you got married, why did you come all the way here to help me?"

Boyd looked away, and then said quietly, "We didn't get married. I took her to Charleston and set her free. Actually that's not entirely accurate. She claimed her freedom from me." Boyd gulped, and his face began to redden. "It was what she wanted—to be on her own and not be beholding to anyone. I went back home to South Carolina, and then I received your letter."

Lexus' once beautiful face softened. She closed her eyes, but moments later opened them slowly, looked at him and nodded.

"Was there something else you wanted to ask me?"

She pulled him closer yet and looked into his eyes. "I don't want to impose, but I'm afraid I must ask you for another favor. You've done so much for me already."

"What is it Lexus? I'll do anything I can to help you."

"Boyd, I can't stay here. There's nothing left for me. My life, as I knew it before, is over. All of my family is gone, my home is gone—burned to the ground—and everything I owned was in it. My friends are either dead or have moved away." She smoothed the blanket with her free hand, and he could see that she was struggling to keep tears from welling up in her eyes. "People will be kind at first, but then they'll begin to whisper. They're good people, but I know them. They don't really know what happened to me out there in the woods, but will fill in the gaps with their gossip. It's just human nature. I want to go away. Will you take me?"

"Where is it you want to go?" Boyd asked.

"North," she whispered, "into the mountains."

# CHAPTER FOUR

NATE LEFT FOR home early in the morning, and Boyd sat in the sun on Ada's front porch talking to the sheriff who had just returned from the mountain above Falling Spring where the encounter with the renegades had occurred. His clothing was dirty, and his jaw sported a couple of day's stubble. The dust flew when he slapped his leg with his hat. At a house nearby, three children ran and giggled, stopping occasionally to pull their dog's ears. A large, striped cat sat high up on the porch banister watching them with yellow eyes, its tail twitching. The children's laughter was a pleasant addition to the morning.

"We didn't find much at their camp, just some ole worn out tents an' a bunch of clothes an' rags an' some old cooking pots and such. The camp was much as you told me," the sheriff said. He stretched and rubbed a knot out of his shoulder. "But, there was one thing you might find interestin,'" the sheriff said. "We found a packet of papers in an old canvas bag. I suppose they left in such a rush they just plumb left it behind. The bag's down at the courthouse where we're tryin' to figger out who the stuff belongs to."

"What kinds of papers?" Boyd asked.

"Old deeds to property, wills, tax papers, death certificates, and one marriage certificate. I guess they just picked up anything they could find when they were raidin' and couldn't read well enough to know what they were or if they were valuable." And then with a big grin he said, "An' this here paper." He withdrew a folded sheet from his pocket and handed it to Boyd.

When he unfolded it, Boyd knew immediately that it was his parole papers. His shoulders slumped with relief as he held the precious document with unsteady hands. "You don't know what a relief this is, Sheriff. I've been dodging one bunch of soldiers or another for the last year. I've been looking over my shoulder every day, thinking I'd be captured and shot for a spy. There're conscription gangs out working to fill rosters, and I'd be a prime candidate."

"Well now, I'd not put too much faith in that piece of paper. You lost it once. It'd be mighty easy for them to lose it for you again if they need able bodied men, but I reckon it's better than nothin.'"

"I'll keep that in mind, but thank you kindly," Boyd said sincerely, relief evident in his voice.

"You don't owe me any thanks. Just doin' my job," the sheriff said, his voice gruff.

"Was there any sign of the soldiers up there? Anything to indicate where they went?" Boyd asked.

"Well, I was just gettin' ready to tell you. We were 'bout ready to come back to town when we saw some turkey vultures in the sky just up ahead on the mountain. When we rode up there to see what they were after, we found one of 'em. He was mostly dressed in a ragged Yankee uniform an' had a bandage around his head. His eyes had that bruised look when you're just getting over a knock on the head or something, an' he had teeth marks on his arm."

"You mean an animal had got to him or something?" Boyd asked, his eyebrows knitting together.

"Well, you could say that, but the bite was made by human teeth. Peers like he was bit by a child…or a woman."

"I don't recall Lexus saying anything about biting the man who attacked her, but anything's possible. I can imagine what kind of a fight she put up," Boyd said. The troubled look on his face revealed the concern he had for her. It made him angry just thinking about what they had done to her.

"But, that weren't all. He was gut shot and then someone had finished him off. There was blood everywhere. What I figger is that one of you hit him first, and then one of them renegades shot him in the head like a hog on butchering day. Reckon they didn't want to leave a witness behind, but he'd not lasted more 'an a day or two anyway. Cold hearted bunch! If they've left the valley, it'll be good riddance."

"Did they go on up over the mountain or what?"

"Yep, their trail led up the road toward Droop Mountain. They were plumb out of the county by the time we got to the line."

"Could you tell how many of them there are? In the dark, Nate and I couldn't tell, but there're probably not more than four or five of them."

"Yeah, we could make out tracks for four horses. We figger there're three of 'em left and one extra horse from the dead man."

"Even if there're only three of them, I hope I never see them again," Boyd said with feeling.

"Well, you're not likely to have reason to run into 'em again. I think they're gone from the valley for good."

"You never know, Sheriff," Boyd said.

\* \* \* \*

As the days crept by, Lexus slowly gained strength and with Nettie's help was able to walk down the street to the center of town. She chatted pleasantly with people who stopped to wish her well and glance curiously at Nettie, who hung back not wanting to intrude. They entered the dry goods store and began browsing through the women's clothing. Nettie held a gaudy dress up to herself, looking in a long mirror, turning one way and then another.

"What do you think of this one, Lexus?" she asked. "I like the bright ones."

"Yes, I can see," Lexus said, laughing. "It's bright and cheerful, all right."

The storekeeper, a pretty, middle-aged woman with auburn hair, approached. "May I help you find something?" she asked, smiling. She looked Nettie up and down.

"Oh, we're just looking right now. I need a new dress, and you have a better selection than I expected with the war and all," Nettie said. "How much does this one cost?"

"You probably can't afford that one," the storekeeper said. "It came from Lexington on the last supply wagon. It's store bought, you know," she said, tilting her nose upward just the slightest bit.

"What makes you think I can't afford it?" Nettie asked, bristling.

"What she means is that it's well made and will last a long time. That's why its cost is so high," Lexus said quickly, but she knew that Nettie would not let this drop.

"I'll take it. Why don't you wrap it up for me?" Nettie asked. "And if you..."

"Could I speak to you, Lexus?" the storekeeper asked, drawing her aside, looking over her shoulder at Nettie's work shirt and men's pants.

When they were alone she said, "You know, that woman has a very bad reputation. She's a...well let's just say that she's *unusual*, living up there by herself, doctorin' animals and all, men comin' and goin' at all hours. That's no occupation for a lady! And, everyone says she's got Indian blood. I'm surprised that you associate with her."

"Thank you for your concern, but I've found her to be a perfect lady. And, I have her to thank for helping me recover. I don't know what I would have done without her," she said evenly, her teeth clinched.

"Well! I was just trying to be helpful," the woman said indignantly. "After what happened to you, your reputation needs all the help it can get."

Lexus talked to her a few minutes more, trying to smooth out the confrontation. She returned to Nettie and helped her complete the purchase and then they continued down the street to the hardware store. Wistfully, Lexus looked at the modestly priced clothing the store sold. She didn't have *any* money. What little she had before was gone in the fire. Although her parents had been well off before the war, all of that was gone. She didn't know how she was going to survive. She picked a pretty hat and tried it on, remembering the dances and balls she had attended before everything had fallen apart.

Blunt as ever, Nettie asked, "Aren't you going to buy a new dress, Lexus? You've been wearing the same one since I've known you. You only take it off to wash it and stay in your room until it has dried."

"Oh, Nettie, I'd love to buy one, but frankly I just can't afford it. You don't know how difficult it is not having any money at all. I don't need much, but somehow I need to get a job or something."

Nettie's eyes softened. "I'm sorry, Lexus, I just thought you were wealthy, living in town and all."

"No, not at all. We lost everything. And, I'm embarrassed to tell you, I've asked Boyd to take me to stay with my relatives in Rowlesburg–that's up in the northern part of the state–because I don't have anywhere else to go," she said matter-of-factly. "I'm not feeling sorry for myself, but those are the cards that life has dealt me, and I'll just have to play them."

"Have you ever been there before? That's a long way off."

Lexus tried on another hat. "Yes, long ago when I was just a child. My family and I visited them. I have an aunt, uncle and one cousin, a girl, about my age. If I can't stay with them, I don't know what I'll do."

"What's it like up there? I mean, is it a big city?"

Lexus laughed. "No, it's just a small village in a deep valley along a river, but the thing I remember most was the trains. The B & O Railroad crosses the river there, and the trains are huge, belching smoke and cinders. My cousin and I used to put bits of metal on the tracks, and after the train passed we'd have a flattened piece like a penny."

"I'm sure it'll work out for you, and Boyd will help you." Nettie looked at Lexus wisely. "He's sweet on you, isn't he? I can tell by the way he looks at you when you're not lookin.'"

"Oh, I…I don't think so," Lexus said. "And, I think he cares for another woman."

"Well now, I've been around men all my life, and I have to say I know when a man's interested and when he's not. I was married once, and…" Her voice trailed off and a small frown creased her brow. "An' we all have a past, a lot of baggage we drag along behind us like a sack of coal." Then, her face brightened. "I'll tell you what. I'll loan you enough money to buy a dress and maybe a new pair of shoes. You can pay me back sometime when you get settled and all. What do you say?"

"Oh, I couldn't do that. I've never taken charity before in my life."

"Well, who said anything about charity? I fully expect my money back, with interest," Nettie said, grinning. "Which one do you like?"

Lexus was embarrassed but reluctantly agreed to take the loan. The two women spent a long time picking out the clothing, and Lexus chose a modest dress made of dark blue cloth and a pair of sturdy shoes. They put their purchases, wrapped in brown paper and done up with string, under their arms and walked back to Ada's house, chatting and laughing.

\* \* \* \*

Boyd took the bill of sale for the team and wagon with him when he walked over to the livery at the blacksmith shop. The horses were doing well, and John stopped work long enough to talk to him.

"I hope you have a pocket full of money, Mr. Houston. Those horses are eating me out of house and home," he said chuckling. "It won't be long before they're ready to work again. That Nettie has been here a couple of times checkin' on 'em. She seems to think they'll be just fine."

"Thanks for taking care of them for me. I don't have a lot of money, although I do have enough to pay their feed bill, but I'm not planning to keep them for long. Do you know anyone who would buy them and the wagon, or maybe trade for a horse and light wagon? They're draft horses and just too big for what I need," Boyd said.

"Selling them could be a problem. Most folk are just makin' do with what they have, and everyone worries that the Yanks will take their horses. Most of the farmers hide 'em in the hills when the Army's around. Most folk around here don't have much free money."

"How about a trade? What I really need is a small wagon, something easy riding with enough room for a few supplies and such in the bed. Wouldn't take much room."

"I have an old wagon out back that might work. You wanna take a look at it?"

They walked around the shop to find a rickety old wagon standing on wobbly wheels against the side of a shed. The seat was attached to a pair of steel springs that softened out the bumps, and it had a short bed in back. Although it was in poor shape, it had been well made, and sometime in the past it undoubtedly had been someone's pride and joy. Boyd walked around it checking for needed repairs.

"It looks like it's been over the hill and back, John. It'll take some work to get it fit."

John removed his hat and ran his fingers through his hair. He squinted his eyes and said, "I reckon it will at that. Tell you what. I'll make the repairs if you can pay for it in coin."

They haggled back and forth until they arrived at a price, and Boyd paid him. John suggested that Boyd talk to the owners of the lumber yard just outside of town to see if they wanted to buy the wagon and team.

"They're the only ones I can think of who might want a team and wagon that size that is most likely to have some spare cash," John said. "And, I'll have that wagon back in shape in no time, Mr. Houston."

"You need to call me Boyd. Everyone else does."

Boyd walked into the lumber yard to see two men standing toe to toe arguing. He was afraid they'd come to blows. When he walked up to them, they stopped and turned to glare at him, their faces red. One was tall and thin and the other of medium height and thick through the middle. They both had wide-brimmed hats pulled down to their ears.

"John, over at the livery, said you might be interested in buying a team of horses and a wagon," Boyd said.

"John? You mean that cripple? He don't know nothin,'" the tall one said. "We don't want to buy nothing. We're goin' under. Ain't nobody building anything since the war started an' nobody's buying anything. We're going to sell out if we can find a buyer," he said. "But, Steve, down at the dry goods store, said something about needin' another wagon to haul supplies in."

Boyd thanked them and started down the street just as the two men resumed their argument. What that was all about? Boyd wondered. When he got to the dry goods store, he found the owner in back unloading a wagon. It was the same man he had talked to on the street in front of the store a few days ago. The men recognized each other.

"Yeah, I'm interested in another team and wagon, but I'm just a bit short on cash right now. Most of the folks in town are too, and they charge much of what they buy. What do you have in mind?" the man asked.

Boyd described the team and wagon, and then they walked together to the livery where Steve examined them thoroughly. After dickering back and forth for a half hour, they finally came to an agreement with Boyd giving considerable concession in the price. He traded them for some cash, a selection of dry goods, and the balance in trade at the store for Ada. In all, Boyd felt he was lucky to get that much for them. Steve looked askance at the bill of sale, but accepted it when he saw the sheriff's signature at the bottom. When Steve had left, Boyd found John who was pounding vigorously on a hot horseshoe as Moses pumped the forge. Sweat streaked his face and darkened his work shirt. When he stopped to take a break, Boyd told him about the sale.

"Yer lucky to strike up a deal like that. How did you end up talking to Steve?"

"The two men at the lumber yard sent me to him. They said they didn't want to buy a team because they're going out of business, but that Steve had been talking about buying another one."

"You don't say, now. Going out of business, huh? Well, it's happening to a lot of folks."

"They were arguing something fierce when I got there. I thought they were going to get in a fight any time," Boyd said.

John laughed. "They've been arguin' like that since they were little boys. They're twins, you know. They fight tooth and nail, but if folks say a bad thing 'bout one of 'em they'll stand up for each other, and they'd as soon fight you as not," he said chortling and shaking his head.

"Twins? They sure don't look like it."

"Yeah, they hardly look like two peas in a pod, do they?"

Boyd changed the subject. "John, now that I sold the team and wagon, and bought a wagon from you, I'll need another horse, one that's broken to harness and is strong enough to travel."

"I don't know of one fer sale right off hand, but I'll ask around. But if you're payin' with coin, you shouldn't have a problem. Come to think of it, they's a man over at Blue Sulfur Springs who breeds some fine horses though he tends toward expensive ones. He sold one to General Lee, I heard. But, I 'spect that you're just wantin' a good dependable horse, a mare maybe."

The two men talked comfortably with each other, weighing the benefits of first one breed of horse then another. When Boyd left, he felt confident that John would find what he needed.

* * * *

The horse trotted along on the road leading north away from town with the newly refurbished wagon bouncing along behind it. Nettie expertly drove the chestnut mare John had found for them, sweet talking it. Lexus sat beside her in her new dress and shoes while Boyd rode his horse alongside them, occasionally glancing at the two pretty women. The bed of the wagon was laden with supplies, an old army tent and two sturdy camp cots that Boyd had bartered for in town. They were taking only enough food to last a few days, but Boyd was confident that they could purchase more along the way. Nettie had agreed to ride along as far as Falling Spring where they would drop her off at her house and then Boyd and Lexus would travel on to Rowlesburg.

Earlier that morning as they prepared to leave, the women had shared a tearful moment on Ada's porch, hugging each other and promising to write. Ada had said she'd miss them after having them in her house for so long, and she had cried and hugged Boyd when he told her about her line of credit at the dry goods store. She was already making plans to buy paint for the house and a little sugar for cookies. Boyd and Lexus had a lively discussion when he insisted that she take the money he had gotten for the team and wagon. Boyd had told her that she—more than anyone after what she'd been through—deserved it. It wasn't a lot, but at least she'd have a few dollars of her own. After a long discussion, and at Nettie's insistence, Lexus had tearfully relented and accepted the money.

"Besides," Nettie had said, laughing, "you owe me for the dress and shoes, and you can repay me now."

By late afternoon they arrived at Nettie's stilt house on the river. Her yellow cat sat on the porch banister with its long tail wrapped around its feet. It licked its paws and groomed its face, ignoring them all. "He's mad that I've been gone so long, but he'll come around," she said laughing. The cat jumped down, trotted down the steps and disappeared around the house.

They had hardly settled in the kitchen around the table drinking coffee when they heard the clip-clop of horse's hooves. A small, wizened man sat on the buggy's seat. He wore a pair of pants pulled up to mid-chest held in place with a belt cinched tightly around him. He wore an old, flannel shirt with long-johns peeking out of the cuffs even though it was a hot evening. On his head he wore a rumpled wide brimmed hat that shaded his face and lantern jaw. He looked first at Boyd and then Lexus.

"You're finally back," he said to Nettie. "I been waitin' fer a couple of days fer you. Mr. Nate said you'd be along directly."

"Yes, I've been in town with these folks. How can I help you?"

"Well, you remember that sow I bought from Mr. McCord up on Butler Mountain? Well, she got in the family way and had a litter of shoats an' a couple of 'em ain't doin' too good. I was wonderin' if you could whip up some of that potion that you gave me last time." He rubbed his face with both hands, looking as if he bore the weight of the world on his skinny shoulders.

"What do you think is wrong with them? Are they nursing all right?" Nettie asked.

"I don't know. They seem to be eatin' well enough, but they're just lookin' poorly."

"Maybe I'd better go take a look at them."

His face lit up in a toothless grin. "That's a grand idee, Nettie. Kin you come along right now?"

Nettie made her excuses to Boyd and Lexus as she gathered up the needed herbs and roots and placed them in a burlap bag and tied the top of the bag securely with a bright ribbon. She climbed into the buggy with the old man. Soon, the sounds of the horse and buggy faded as they rounded a bend in the rutted track that led to the main road.

Boyd and Lexus sat on the porch idly listening to the sounds of the river as it slid by. As dusk slowly approached, they heard a chorus of frogs and toads as they trilled in the river's margins, laying eggs in gelatinous clumps and long strings. A beaver swam across the river, its dark head leaving a vee of ripples in its wake. When it reached the far side, it climbed onto the bank and began gnawing on a river birch sapling. The call of wood ducks from somewhere far up the river wafted on the still air to them, and a flock of mallards, quacking loudly, swept across the rooftop and away with whistling wings. Fireflies flashed in an ancient conglomeration low to the ground and down to the water's edge.

Boyd noted Lexus' bruised eyes, even darker in the gloominess of the porch, and reflected on the terror she must have experienced as she fought for her life. He liked the strong line of her jaw, high cheekbones and soft hair as she sat comfortably in the chair. She used the tip of one toe to rock back and forth, her hands clasped in her lap. Her dress was buttoned high near her throat, but it did little to hide her alluring shape.

Boyd cleared his throat and said, "Have you thought what you want to do when you get to Rowlesburg?"

"No, not exactly. I'll have to find a way to support myself. Maybe I can become a store clerk or teach a subscription school. I could teach children how to read and write and do sums."

"I'm sure you will be successful at any employment you choose," Boyd said.

"Oh, I don't know. I liked school when I was a student, especially math and science. Most of the other girls liked reading stories, and I liked that too, but I liked math and the sciences best."

"You could attend a normal school that would prepare you to teach," Boyd said.

"Perhaps, if there're one nearby. But, mostly the only requirement to be a teacher for young children is to have been a student yourself. I'll see what's available and decide what to do when we get there." As they spoke quietly of what could be, her eyes sparkled, and the lilt in her voice said that she was looking forward to whatever came in the future.

Nettie returned late that evening, and they settled for the night. The two women slept in a back bedroom and Boyd on an old couch on the porch. He awoke the next morning with the cat, its yellow eyes staring at him, perched on his chest. Its claws gently kneaded his shirt, and it purred loudly.

After a breakfast of bacon and biscuits they said goodbye to Nettie and, sitting on the seat side by side, drove the wagon back to the main road and turned north. Boyd's horse trailed along behind. They stopped to visit briefly with Nate who was sitting on his porch and then continued up the mountain. They passed the renegade's abandoned camp with hardly a glance, choosing to avoid the distress it was sure to cause. They entered a long valley where the road wound around low knolls. The forest pressed in, and they finally arrived at the foot of Droop Mountain. After stopping to let the horses rest, they began the climb up the mountain and clung to the sides of the seat as the wagon lurched and swayed. As they ascended the mountain the vegetation changed from maples, oaks, and white pines to spruce and hemlock. At the lip of the mountain, they passed fractured rock formations–many larger than houses–that crept century by century down the mountainside, leaving passageways as wide as roads between them.

When they finally reached the top, the road passed across a vast flattened expanse interspersed with narrow glades, open fields and farmland. The horses trotted easily along the mountaintop and then were allowed to stop to graze. Boyd and Lexus rested under a large tree and ate biscuits and ham washing it down with water from Boyd's canteen. A mild breeze wafted through the forest, sighing pleasantly as the warm sun filtered down through the trees. A comfortable silence enveloped them, each deep in thought, contemplating their lot. When they moved on, they soon came to a steep promontory. The road twisted down and away to the north, and in the blue distance they could see smoke rising from the chimneys of houses in a small town, nestled in a vast valley.

It was on Droop Mountain that, not too far in the future, Brigadier General W. W. Averell, commanding 5,000 Union soldiers, would meet in battle Brigadier General John Echols with more than 2,000 men. The Union forces would suffer 119 casualties and losses and the Confederates, 275. When the Confederate forces were soundly defeated, resistance in the area would essentially collapse.

But today, the wagon speeded up as they descended into the valley, and Boyd had to apply the brake frequently. Halfway down they stopped at a spring that arose from an opening alongside the mountain and allowed the horses to drink and rest. They entered Hillsboro just as the sun began to set behind Greenbrier Mountain.

\* \* \* \*

They found a place to stay for the night—recommended earlier by Nate—with Hiram O'Donnell and his wife, Hilda. Their house was a two-story, wooden structure with a limestone chimney. There were several rooms upstairs that were rented to overnight guests.

"How's that ole bog trotter, Perkins, doin' down there in the land o' the Greenbrier?" Hiram asked. "I've known the ole highheejin fer ever, an' he sold me a spavined horse once; but to be fair, it may have been because we were both half cut. Och, 'an he was a lord muck from clabber hill!"

"Now, Hiram, don't get your dander up. It's been ten years since he sold you that horse." Leaning toward Boyd and Lexus, Hilda said, "He has never forgotten. And, don't mind him, he just givin' you some paddywhackery."

They sat in the parlor just off the main entryway on large, comfortable chairs stuffed with horsehair. Hiram, an Irishman of medium height and build, had reddish hair streaked with gray. His green eyes peered at them from under bushy eyebrows. Hilda, thin as a reed, told them she was originally from Kington in northern Wales. Her dark, mahogany hair was tied in a severe bun on the back of her head. She spoke with a pleasant, musical accent.

"Yes, Nate's doing fine. We saw him just this morning on the way up here. He suggested that we stay for the night with you folks," Boyd said.

"Where're you heading? If you don't mind my askin'," Hiram said.

Boyd explained where they were going and why they had decided to make the trip. Lexus chimed in occasionally clarifying details. Boyd briefly told them about Lexus' abduction, and Hilda clucked sympathetically and patted Lexus' hand when he described her injuries.

"Yer a strappin' sound man to not be fightin' in the war. You plannin' on signing up when you get up there? They'd like to have a fine gosson like you," Hiram said.

"No, I'm on parole, and I plan to honor that pledge," Boyd said. "I have papers that should satisfy any questions that I'm asked."

"Who signed the papers? If it was a Confederate, it won't hold much stead with the Yankees."

"I was paroled by Colonel Crook after the battle in Lewisburg."

"Well, that's good 'cause from here on north, yer most likely to run into Yankees an' them town peelers, but the rebels could show up anywhere. The Yanks have taken over Beverly, have a big camp up there, and I've heard that the people living there must have passes just to go in and out of town," Hiram said. "They're like bees on a hot rock up there, 'an folks hereabouts think there'll soon be a battle. There've been skirmishes here and there since the beginning. In fact, the first land battle of the war was in Philippi, just over the mountains there to the west."

They talked about what roads Boyd and Lexus should take and where they could camp along the way. Hiram described the mountain ranges and the passes through the mountains they would have to use and told them what he had heard about troop locations and numbers. He knew very little about Rowlesburg since he had never been there.

"Your best bet is to take the road up through Marling Bottom and on up thonder over Elk Mountain. Yer horse will be banjaxed by the time you get to the top. Then, you'll have one more mountain to cross and then you'll be on the Tygart Valley River. It's maybe a day's ride to Beverly from there. If you can get through the guards and sodger men there, ya can take the road over to the Cheat River and down through St. George. If you stay on Cheat River, it'll take you right to Rowlesburg, or so I've heard. You'll know you're on the right river when you notice it flowin' north. The water down here in the Little Levels flows south into the Greenbrier."

The next morning, Boyd bought a sack of grain for the horses from Hiram and stowed it in the back of the wagon. He told him about the renegade soldiers and the possibility that they were headed his way. Hiram said he hadn't heard of any problems with them in the area.

"They're bad men, Hiram, and likely to be desperate. The sheriff and I thought that maybe one or more of them was injured," Boyd said.

"I'll spread the word so's folks can be on the lookout. Thanks fer lettin' us know."

Boyd and Lexus said their goodbyes and, as the sun was topping the mountain, trotted the horse down the road until they came to the river. Before long they passed through Marling Bottom and a cluster of houses at the confluence of Naps Creek and the Greenbrier River. North of town, the road paralleled the south-flowing river for a ways then curved sharply away from it and turned upward. The horses labored up the steep incline, and they had to stop frequently to let them rest. The mare pulled the wagon along gamely, yet Boyd considered replacing her with his horse, but he knew that the horse would throw a fit if he tried to harness it. He got down and rode the horse while Lexus drove the wagon. It was early afternoon before they reached the summit of Elk Mountain where they stopped to eat and stretch. Rows of high mountain peaks marched away to the north and south, their tops capped with dark spruce trees. Before them, through narrow openings between the trees, they saw only more mountains—green, dark and respiring in the warm sun.

By evening they had traversed a winding, narrow valley with a whispering stream flowing away from them along its bottom. They crossed frequently through muddy fords. Occasionally, they saw small homesteads hugging the mountain bases, away from the road, and once they passed a lone farmer following two large horses with a plow. He waved and then returned to his task, the reins tied together and looped over his head. They could hear him shouting commands to the team.

Their horses moved down along the road easily, and before long they saw where the stream turned sharply to the west and passed through a narrow gap in the hills. They turned north, along a rushing branch, leaving the main stream behind. Curiously, the stream disappeared briefly into the ground only to emerge some time later from the limestone rock. Soon, they came to the base of another mountain and decided to stop for the night. They would tackle the ascent the next day with rested horses.

Boyd watered the horses, fed them some grain, hobbled them in a patch of grass, and then unloaded the tent and began setting it up in a level spot under a tree. As she was preparing their supper, Lexus looked at the two cots, the tent and then at Boyd, a troubled look on her face. I like this man, she thought, with his broad shoulders and handsome face, but we can't share a tent together, not yet anyway. If anyone found out, my reputation would be worse than it is now. She remembered her mother's admonishment that the most valuable asset a woman had was her reputation. Besides, what would Boyd think of her afterward? Even if nothing happened, and it certainly wouldn't, he'd think poorly of her later. That's just the way things happened.

Boyd saw her looking at the tent and cots and grinned. When the tent was pitched, he put one cot and bedroll in it. Then, he set up the second cot and placed it a short distance away. He rummaged in the back of the wagon and came away with a bedroll and a piece of canvas which he tossed onto the cot.

"There," he said, "we're all set for the night. I'll be close by in case you need anything."

"Oh Boyd, thank you," she said blushing, "you knew just what I was thinking, didn't you?"

"Well, I never had a sister, but if I had, I'd want to know that she was taken care of and respected. I couldn't do anything less for you," he said awkwardly, shuffling his feet.

"But what if it rains? You'll get all wet."

"Oh, I'll be all right. I have a piece of canvas to use to turn the wet, and besides I can see that the stars are beginning to shine. It'll be a clear night."

"That's right. You were a sailor and can forecast the weather," she said, teasing.

"Yes, but I have to admit these mountains have weather patterns I've never seen before. I'm wrong as often as not," he said.

"Tell me about the ocean. I've never seen it. Is it as big as they say?"

"Oh, it's big all right," he said. "Most of the world is covered with water you know."

"Yes, I read that in a book somewhere, and it's salty, too."

"Yes, it wouldn't do to drink it. That's why ships carry large barrels of fresh water, and if they run out, the men die of thirst if they can't replenish their supply."

"Did you like living there near the ocean and being a fisherman?" she asked.

"Oh yes," he brightened, "but then it's the only place I have lived for any length of time just like, I'm sure, you like living in the mountains. Fishing is the only occupation I've ever known."

"Yes, I like the mountains. With four seasons, we get a little of each; cold and snowy in the winter, hot and muggy in the summers. But, my favorite time of year is the fall with all the bright colors," she said.

They ate their supper of bread and cold meat and drank cool spring water from a glass jar that they passed back and forth. Their small fire cast ghostly reflections off the trees, and burning embers flew briefly up into the dark night–the smell of wood smoke permeated their hair and clothes, providing a pleasant fragrance. Bobwhite quail whistled in the evening air and a screech owl trilled back in the forest. A chill ran down Boyd's spine at the sorrowful sound.

\* \* \* \*

The Sergeant sat alone on his horse, hidden by a copse of trees on a hill away from the road and watched Lexus and Boyd as they sat by their fire. He and the two other men had raided a farmstead earlier and were now dressed in civilian clothing. The pants and shirt he wore were a poor fit, but they were far better than the filthy uniforms they had discarded. Luckily, the farmer and his wife had been away, probably having ridden into town for supplies, so they hadn't had to kill them, not that he would have cared one way or the other. He recognized Lexus and was determined to get her back. He didn't know the man, but somewhere in the back of his mind, he thought he'd seen him before. He was well armed with a pistol under his belt, and the Sergeant could see the stock of a rifle sticking out of the bundle in the bed of the wagon, within easy reach. He turned the horse and quietly walked it back up the road.

When the sergeant rode into their crude camp, Luke and Hank were hunkered over a small fire roasting shriveled potatoes and carrots they had found in the farmer's root cellar. They had stolen a ham and were slicing off thick chunks to cook in an old frying pan, and because they hadn't had much to eat over the last few days, the smell from the sizzling ham caused their stomachs to growl.

"Hot damn, I'm so hungry I could eat a polecat," the Sergeant said, rubbing his hands together. He looked at the two bedraggled men with contempt. Hank's arm was swollen and red; they'd washed the wound and sloshed some whiskey on it, and he'd squealed like a stuck pig. Luke's ear was also swollen and capped with a large scab which he constantly felt with his fingertips.

"You'd better leave that ear alone, Luke, or it'll rot off," the Sergeant said unkindly.

"But it hurts something awful, Serge," he said, whining. Luke and Hank had tried to steer clear of the Sergeant and were still wary of him, fearing the same fate as Joe. They sat on logs and rocks around the fire and ate with their dirty fingers. They talked about what their next move would be, and the Sergeant told them about seeing Lexus and Boyd.

"I'm goin' to get that girl back. I don' know who that man with her is, but they's three of us an' only one of him. I'll shoot him from the bushes if I have to," the Sergeant said.

"I think we'd better just let her be. Look how much trouble she got us in the last time. Poor ole' Joe got hisself kilt, and me and Luke here came within a whisker's breadth of the same fate," Hank said. He looked at Luke for support.

"I agree," Luke said guardedly. "Ain't no woman worth that kind of trouble." He looked carefully at the Sergeant, trying to judge the extent of the wrath that was sure to come.

"Well, we ain't votin' on it," the Sergeant said menacingly. "You two yellow dogs are goin' to help out whether you want to or not. They're camped just up the valley there, and it won't be no trouble at all to go get her. First light in the morning, we'll sneak up on 'em and take care of business, an' that man with her will be the first to go."

The two men cowered from the Sergeant and suddenly became busy eating, shifting their eyes away.

"After we get the girl, we'll go on to Beverly. There're bound to be some soldiers there, but we'll skirt 'round 'em. I'd like to trade Joe's horse for some food an' get a new set of clothes and such. Then we'll go on to Grafton. We could catch a train there if we'd a mind to, an' go anywhere we like. Out west maybe. We could probably get back in the army once we get out there far enough. They'll be fighting Injuns long after the war is over an' will need good men with experience."

"What we goin' do with the girl? We can't take her to Beverly with us. We get caught with her, an' we're gonna get shot or hung," Hank said. This fool is going to get us killed, he thought. At first chance he'd light out, maybe taking Luke with him.

The Sergeant laughed and said, "After we get done with her, there won't be much left. We'll just throw her in a hole somewhere."

The renegades threw some more wood on the fire and rolled themselves in blankets on the ground. Soon, all three were snoring loudly and when they awoke the next morning, the sun was well up in the sky.

\* \* \* \*

Lexus had awakened just as the morning's light was creeping into their camp. As she left the tent, she tossed a stick on the canvas covered hump on the cot outside. Boyd drew the canvas aside enough to expose his face and rumpled hair and said, "Couldn't sleep, huh?"

"No. Too much noise with the birds and all, but it's wonderful. They sound so cheerful. And all night, I heard something scrambling up and down the tent. Do you have any idea what it could have been?" she asked.

"I had something crawling around on me, too. I think they were flying squirrels because I saw one swoop over the fire last night. I hope it didn't' get its tail burned."

Lexus laughed and stretched, her bright eyes sparkling. "I'm about ready to go, how about you?" He could tell that she was recovering from her ordeal and was pleased to see it.

Boyd laughed and threw the canvas and bedclothes aside. "We might as well start up the mountain. I'm already awake."

They quickly ate a cold breakfast, struck the tent, and loaded the wagon. Soon, they were on their way up the mountain, and within an hour had reached the summit. As they rested the horses, they took in the view–layer after layer of mountains reaching as far as they could see to the horizon. Pigeons, thousands of them, swooped past them in an immense flock, their gray-blue backs and reddish-fawn breasts flashing in the sun. They flew on long, pointed wings that supported tapered bodies of almost a foot and a half. They called to each other, adjusting their flight to keep up with their neighbors. Within minutes the flock had passed leaving the travelers gawking.

"Passenger pigeons," Lexus said. "We see them occasionally here in the mountains, but their numbers are dwindling. They're more common up north."

"We have sea gulls where I live, but I've never seen anything like that before," Boyd said. "Are they good to eat?"

"Oh yes. They're hunted and shipped all over the country. Squabs mostly."

As they prepared to leave, Boyd looked back down the mountain the way they'd come. Riding toward them, appearing no bigger than ants, were three riders, coming fast. He took a small brass spyglass from his saddlebags and extended it to its full length. He studied the riders carefully as they first passed behind a clump of trees then into the open again. He handed the spyglass to Lexus, showing her how to use it, steadying it on the back of the wagon.

She caught her breath when she saw them. "Oh my God," she said, her voice shaking. "It's them, the men who kidnapped me."

"You're sure?"

"I'll never forget. Never! Oh, they can't do that to me again. I'd rather die," she said, her breath coming in great gulps, a terrified look in her eyes.

They scrambled onto the wagon and Boyd slapped the reins on the mare's rump. Startled, she bolted down the road with Boyd's horse jerking along behind. The wagon jolted and thumped, the load in the back making a clatter, as they flew down the steep grade. They rounded a sharp bend with the wagon sliding sideways and then straightening. Boyd used the brake sparingly, narrowly avoiding running up on the mare's flashing hooves. Before long, they heard the distant rumbling of hooves and the whoop of the renegades as they crested the mountaintop in wild pursuit. The wagon, with its load and trailing horse, was no match for the speed of the pursuers on horseback.

Boyd stomped on the footbrake and drew back violently on the reins bringing the wagon to a grinding stop. A cook pot, dislodged from the wild ride, rolled past the wagon and down over the hill. Boyd jumped to the ground and grabbed the reins of his horse, bringing it alongside the wagon.

"Quick," he yelled. "Get on the horse and ride. I can't risk you being captured."

"I...I, can't leave you. They'll kill you for sure–there're three of them."

"Don't argue. They'll be here in seconds." He threw an arm around her and dragged her roughly from the wagon and onto the horse. "Go now. I'll catch up. Just ride!" He slapped the horse on the rump, and it crow-hopped a couple of times and then flattened its ears and ran. Lexus clung to the saddle horn, her skirts flying, and they were quickly gone, down the winding road.

The renegades rounded a bend in the road and spurred their horses toward Boyd. He crouched behind the wagon, taking aim with his pistol. The men saw him and automatically spread out as best they could on the narrow road, but two of them lagged behind. They fired at Boyd with bursts of smoke whipping from their weapons and flying away behind them. Their horses pounded on toward Boyd with wild, flaring nostrils.

With Boyd's first shot, two of the men swerved their horses and disappeared into the brush leaving their leader to shift for himself. Boyd fired again, causing the rider's hat to fly away behind him. The renegade pulled his horse to a stop as it pranced and twirled around, spoiling his aim. He fired a couple of wild shots at Boyd and then spurred his horse back up the road, swearing foully. Boyd could hear them arguing; the leader, shouting and swearing, berating them, trying to get them to charge again.

While the renegades argued, Boyd jumped into the wagon and whipped the mare into a gallop down the mountain. The mare, game as she was, could not outpace the riders behind them, but twice more they were rebuffed as Boyd fired at them. They fell back, waiting for a chance to get a good shot at Boyd. Again, he slapped the mare's rump with the reins, encouraging her to run, but soon, lathered with sweat, she began to slow. Boyd was frantically trying to drive the horse and at the same time, reach behind in the wagon's bed for his rifle when a round struck the seat beside him, sending a splinter flying and lodging in his leg. It stung, blood running onto the seat, but he hardly noticed with his body charged with adrenaline. He turned to fire at them again, but the hammer of his pistol fell on an empty cylinder. The men behind him whooped with glee and spurred their horses toward him, gaining quickly.

Boyd rounded a sharp bend just at the bottom of the mountain and ran into a Yankee patrol that was dismounted along the road. Soldiers scattered and ran to control their horses. In the confusion, Boyd saw a soldier doggedly holding onto the reins of his horse which bucked and pitched having already thrown Lexus to the ground. Alerted by the gunfire, a brace of soldiers leveled their muskets at Boyd. He pulled the mare to a sliding stop, and the blue-clad soldiers moved in around him. Upon seeing the patrol, the renegades roughly turned their horses and fled back up the mountain.

A captain stepped forward and ordered Boyd to get down from the wagon. He slid to the ground and limped to Lexus' side

"Are you all right?" he asked. Her dress was rumpled and somewhere in her wild ride she'd lost her bonnet.

"Yes, but that horse of yours needs some discipline. It was determined to unseat me," she said. "I was scared. I was afraid those men had caught you, or worse yet, shot you dead." She placed her hand on his arm and smiled with relief.

"It's all over now."

The captain nodded toward a couple of his men and they stepped to each side of Boyd and escorted him over to him. "What's this all about?" he asked. "Why were those men chasing you?"

"It's a long story. The short of it is that they were trying to take Lexus there," he said nodding toward her. "We had a run-in with them before."

"Who are you and what are you doing here?" the captain asked. "You could be arrested and shot as a spy, you know. You're not in uniform. For all we know, you're scouting for the Confederates."

"No, no," Boyd said quickly. "It's nothing like that. I was a soldier for the Confederacy but I'm out of it now."

The captain raised his eyebrows. "You're a Reb? What do you mean, you're out of it?"

Boyd took his parole papers out of his pocket and handed them to the captain who read them carefully and then looked at Boyd. He read them again.

"You mean Colonel Crook pardoned you? You fought in that battle at Lewisburg?"

"Yes. I was wounded, and when he offered me and my friend parole, we took it." The captain snorted, obviously not impressed with Boyd's lack of dedication to the cause. "It was either that or go to prison," Boyd said, trying to explain.

"Huh!" the captain said. He looked Lexus up and down, and then turned to Boyd and said, "I reckon we'll have to let the general decide what to do with you." He gave the order for his men to mount up, and with Lexus and Boyd riding the wagon they set out down the valley to Beverly, the mounted patrol spread out in a ragged line behind them.

# CHAPTER FIVE

BOYD ROSE FROM his bed in the jail and looked out the window at Rich Mountain that rose high above the valley. The rounded mountain had been worried away by uncounted eons of erosion, and he could see that headwater streams had cut waterways into the slopes like the branches of a tree. The sun crept like a familiar lover over the peaks, streaking the sky and flooding the dirty jail floor with rose-colored light. The smell of unwashed bodies assailed his nostrils, and a soldier with a large gash on his forehead and two black eyes snored loudly in the adjacent cell. A few other cells were occupied by sleeping men who tossed and turned restlessly, and he could hear the rumble of voices somewhere toward the front of the building. He reclined again on the hard pallet where he had spent the night, his hands behind his head, staring at the cobweb-draped ceiling, recalling how he had ended up here.

After being seized by the Yankee patrol they had been escorted to Beverly, a mountain town on the Tygart Valley River—it had taken them all day, and they arrived as dusk was falling. They had followed the road, in places little more than a buggy track, down the river, past Salt Lick, to Huttonsville where it intersected the Staunton-Parkersburg Turnpike. Cheat Mountain rose to the east behind a formidable line of rounded foothills and faded into the distance in each direction. Travel became easier on the improved road, and the assembly of mounted soldiers escorting the solitary wagon had moved rapidly along. The turnpike was much used. Beverly stood at a crossroads and was a flourishing town with hotels, stores, blacksmith shops, and schools, and it was the county seat with an impressive courthouse. The jail that now housed Boyd had been completed a couple of decades earlier.

A layer of wood smoke from scores of cooking fires covered the town. The Union encampment spread away to the cemetery and academy grounds. Other fires flickered on Butcher Hill where rough cabins had been built from construction materials taken from buildings in town. After routing the Confederates in the Battle of Rich Mountain in 1861, the Union Army had maintained a strong presence in Beverly. The approaching roads were heavily guarded, and they'd had to pass through a barricade manned by wary soldiers to get to the town.

Although Confederate sympathies held a majority among the local population and most able-bodied men had joined the rebel army, the valley was nonetheless held firmly by Union forces. Boyd was no longer in an area where most would sympathize with his former alliance with the Confederacy—the locals maybe—but not the Army. He would have to tread carefully, and he wondered if they would honor his pledge to lay down his arms.

Toward the middle of the morning, the prisoners were fed a breakfast of brown beans and stale bread. They sat on their bunks and used their fingers to sop up the runny mess with chunks of bread and washed it all down with cups of weak coffee. The prisoner with the black eyes studied Boyd suspiciously.

"You're not from these parts, are you? Haven't seen you around before," he said, looking through the bars at Boyd. He was a frail looking kid with large teeth, an untidy mustache, and freckled hands. His blue uniform was wrinkled and stained and missing a couple of buttons on the front.

"No, I haven't been here before. I'm just passing through," Boyd said, a friendly smile on his face.

"Didn't think so. You that Reb they caught up on the mountain with that good lookin' woman?" he asked. "All the others are talking about youins."

"Yeah, that was me."

"Where's your uniform? You a spy or something?" he asked, curious.

Boyd told him about the battle in Lewisburg and being wounded and captured. The soldier nodded occasionally as if he agreed with him. "How about you? Where are you from?" Boyd asked, trying to shift the focus away from him.

"I'm from Pennsylvania. Joined up just about a year ago and first thing I know, here I am in these godforsaken mountains. It was colder than a mother-in-law's heart here last winter. I almost froze to death," he said. He went on to tell Boyd about his home and why he'd decided to join the Army. He'd been a store clerk and just couldn't wait until he was old enough to enlist.

Boyd said, "If you don't mind my asking, how did you end up in jail?"

He laughed and shook his head ruefully. "I've always said that my mother didn't raise any fools, but I might have been mistaken. I was playing cards with a bunch of men from the cavalry when we got in a big ruckus. I said they were cheating, and one thing led to another." He shook his head again, grinning. "First thing you know, they were all pounding on me, and the next thing I remember is waking up here. I don't know what happened to them, but they're not here in jail. Wherever they are, I hope they feel as bad as I do. My head's about to bust."

The jail doors banged out front and soon a soldier came toward Boyd, swinging a set of large keys. He opened the cell door and nodded at him. "Come on, Reb, the major wants to see you," he said. "And lickety-split."

Boyd, guarded on each side by armed soldiers, was marched down the street to a large house. Men in officers' uniforms bustled in and out of the front door, barely looking at him. They entered an expansive foyer, and Boyd was told to sit on a bench against the wall. His guards stepped out on the porch but remained in sight. Boyd looked around at the impressive home that been commandeered as headquarters. A sprawling set of stairs swept from the foyer to the second floor and was trimmed in stained and varnished hardwood. The walls were covered with wallpaper of an elaborate design, and an elegant chandelier was suspended from the ceiling on a golden chain. Toward the back of the house, he could smell food cooking that made his mouth water.

An hour later an orderly came for him and led him up the stairs to a room set up as an office. "Sit," the soldier said curtly and nodded at an uncomfortable-looking wooden chair. "The major will be with you in a minute." Boyd heard the man's footfalls recede down the hallway, and a door banged shut. Moments later, the major entered abruptly and Boyd jumped to his feet, coming to attention without thinking.

"At ease, soldier. You're not in uniform," the major said. He was a tall man in an immaculate uniform that bristled with brass buttons and ribbons. His sandy hair was of medium length, and his upper lip was covered with a drooping moustache. A long, thin scar ran from the corner of his mouth to his ear, and he walked with a slight limp. Boyd remained standing as the major sat behind his desk.

"General Harris asked me to gather the facts about your case, and then he'll make a decision about what to do with you." He picked up Boyd's parole papers from the stack in front of him and studied them thoughtfully. "Myself, I think you're a spy. Why else would you be out on your own traipsing around the country like you own it. The woman with you is probably one too," he said, frowning at Boyd. "The captain said you were being chased by some men. What was that about?"

Boyd cleared his throat and shifted his feet. "Sir, those men were trying to take Lexus, and…"

The Major interrupted, "What do you mean they were trying to *take* her?"

"If I could start from the beginning, sir?" Boyd quickly told the major about Lexus being abducted by renegade soldiers and how they had beaten her. He frowned when Boyd told of the injuries she had received.

"Yes, yes, I understand that part, but what are you doing all the way up here in Beverly? We're a long way from Lewisburg."

"I agreed to escort Lexus to her family's home in Rowlesburg." Boyd was getting a little annoyed at having to tell their sad story so many times.

"I've talked to Miss Saunders and her story matches yours pretty well, but you could have hatched this story together."

"May I ask, sir, where is she?" Boyd had been worrying all morning about her.

"She's staying in the boarding house down the street. You can be assured she's being cared for." The major's eyes softened a little.

"Thank you, sir. I appreciate anything you can do for her. She's had a hard enough time already."

The major picked up the parole papers and waved them at Boyd. "Tell me about these. I've heard of men being paroled before, but this is the first time I've seen it myself. You swore not to fight against us?" He waved the papers at Boyd again.

"Yes sir. I gave my word when I signed them, and I mean to honor it," he said solemnly.

"I can't say I think highly of you, mister. I think I'd of fought to the bitter end."

Boyd stood mutely, returning the major's glare.

Without another word to Boyd, the major shouted for the orderly down the hall who appeared as if by magic. "Take this man back to his escort. Tell them to put him back in jail."

* * * *

Lexus sat in her upstairs room in the boarding house and watched the traffic go by on the busy street below. She was fretting because she had been to the jail twice but had been denied permission to see Boyd. Two soldiers had been detailed to escort her everywhere she went. They were pleasant enough, just young boys, but it annoyed her to have them trailing along behind her.

The major had told her that when General Harris returned, they'd get an answer about Boyd's fate. She was worried—it was her fault that he had landed in jail. If she hadn't asked him to escort her to her relatives' home, he'd be on his way back to the coast by now. How was she going to get him out of that jail? Breaking him out was out of the question. There were soldiers everywhere, and all roads out of town were heavily guarded. Besides, she didn't know what had been done with the wagon and horses. They'd have no way to travel even if he could escape.

On a whim, she stomped out of the house, her guards trailing along behind, and went to see the major. She waited in the foyer, tapping her foot, and soon the orderly came for her and escorted her to his office. He looked up, startled to see her standing before him with a determined look on her face.

"Major, what have you heard about the general's return? How much longer will you keep Boyd in jail? He hasn't done anything wrong."

The major stood behind his desk, resting his fingertips on its top. He nodded to the visitor's chair and said, "Please have a seat, Miss Saunders. Would you care for some coffee?"

Lexus flounced onto the chair and then sat rigidly, her lovely face a study in frustration.

"No thank you, major. All I want is some answers. When are you going to let Boyd out of prison?"

"The general should be back late tomorrow. He's gone to Buckhannon to meet with some of our commanders."

"Well, I should think that someone could make a decision while he's gone. Who's in command now?"

The major ignored her question. "The general said to wait until he got back, and I'll follow his orders. Besides, your friend can cool his heels in jail for a day or two. Won't hurt him any."

"That's easy for you to say. We need to be on our way, and I need to find my relatives in Rowlesburg."

They sat in silence for a few seconds, the major looking frankly at Lexus, taking her measure. The house throbbed with activity; doors slammed, hollow footsteps sounded in the hallway. Somewhere deep in the house two men laughed at some unknown joke. Outside, a heavy wagon passed by, the team grunting with effort. The driver shouted and swore at them.

The major's tone softened. "I'll tell you what. I'll let him out for a couple of hours this afternoon, under guard of course. But he'll have to spend the night in jail, and you will continue to have an escort. I can't have you two getting away from us. The general would have my commission." He liked this attractive woman sitting there, looking unabashedly at him with fire in her eyes.

"Thank you, Major," she said simply. "I'll see that he gets back in time for supper."

The major took her by the elbow as she descended the stairs and walked her to the front door. "What happened to your parents, if I may ask? Did your father serve in the army?"

"No, he didn't serve. I guess he was too old. Then, he died of cholera and my mother followed soon after. I've no one left in this world except for my aunt, uncle and cousin. That's why it's so important to find them. Family is important, don't you think?"

"Yes, very important. I have a big family back in Ohio. I hope that I survive this war to rejoin them. But it looks like it won't be over for a long time. Both sides seem to have settled in."

"Well Major, I hope you're able to get back home in one piece, too" she said sincerely.

"What do you know about Rowlesburg? Have you been there before?" he asked.

"Only as a very young child. All I remember is playing in the creek with my cousin and the trains that roared through town."

"The railroad is critical to us. It's a main transport route for all points from Baltimore to Ohio. I'm sure the Confederates would like to cut the line, and the most likely place to do that is where it crosses the river. They tried once without success, but they'll probably be back."

\* \* \* \*

The three renegades sat on their horses and regarded the farmer who stood on the front porch of his log house. He was a sturdy, elderly man with muscular arms and big calloused hands. A crumpled hat covered gray-streaked hair that reached down over his ears. He held a double barreled shotgun over one arm, and he looked like he'd be more than willing to use it. His prominent Adam's apple bobbed up and down as he spoke.

"You say you're wantin' to go to Grafton? That's a fur piece from here."

"Yeah," the Sergeant said. "We've got business there, and we need to know the best way to get there."

"There ain't a best way, fur as I know. You could go through Beverly on the turnpike but the Yanks have that whole valley plugged up. They're checkpoints and patrols everwhere. You fellers don't look like you'd want to have any truck with them."

"You got that right, friend. We've had a few run-ins with 'em, and I can't say we want anything else to do with 'em. We just want to pass through and get about our business," he said, remembering how they had been chased up the mountain by the cavalry. They'd had to take to the brush to escape them. The soldiers had been reluctant to leave the road. They'd been lucky that their commanding officer had only sent a few of them.

The farmer looked at the bandages on Hank's arm and Luke's scab-covered ear and said, sniggering, "Looks like y'all came out on the short end of the stick."

"Ain't there no way to get around Beverly?" the Sergeant asked, ignoring the insult.

"Yeah, there is. What you do is, go on down the valley 'til you get to the pike at Huttonsville. You'll have to be careful 'cause that road is patrolled and there's a lot of wagon traffic on it. Then, you take the road to the west over Rich Mountain. That way you won't have to go through Beverly. That's where the Union camp is at."

"Won't there be pickets on the mountain pass?" Hank asked, looking doubtfully at Luke.

"Yeah, there likely will be. You'll just have to take to the woods to get around 'em. Once on the other side, you should have a clear road fer a while. You turn north at Frenchtown, then on up across French Crick and on to Buckhannon and then Philippi. Grafton ain't too fur from there. They'll be Yankees in them towns an' y'all will have to skirt around 'em."

"How long you reckon it'll take us to get there, to Grafton, I mean?" Hank asked.

"I don't rightly know. Several days, I reckon. Depends on how long it'll take you to skirt the towns. Once you're through Philippi it ain't too fer to Webster an' the railroad, then you can foller it east to Grafton."

"Mind if I ask why you're being so helpful? Most folk around here ain't too anxious to talk to strangers. You're not goin' to tell the Yanks where we're goin' are you?" the Sergeant asked, placing his hand on his pistol.

"Naw, why would I want to help the Yanks?" the farmer asked, spitting on the ground beside the porch. "They've taken over the whole county. A man can't go nowhere without 'em stopping you, askin' questons an' searchin' your wagon an' such. Besides, I got two young'uns fightin' fer the south."

The renegades talked to the farmer for a while longer, trying to bring to light as much information about the soldiers as they could. The Sergeant tried to sell him their extra horse but the farmer didn't want it. Said he had all the livestock he needed. They returned to the road and headed north.

Their horses plodded along as darkness settled in around them, and when they reached the turnpike they turned toward

Huttonsville, the small town that had grown up there. Here and there lantern light showed in windows, yet the pike was deserted. The town was quiet, and there was no sign of the soldiers. A large dog streaked out from behind a house and barked furiously at the men. Luke cursed and kicked at it when it lunged at his stirrup, and their horses gamboled and snorted. When they trotted their horses up the dusty road the dog lost interest and then returned to the house. The men looked behind them, back toward the house to see if anyone would come out to investigate, but no one stirred. After passing through the town, they found the road leading west up through the mountains. They rode on a few miles and then turned off the road to bed down in the brush. They'd have a cold camp tonight, Hank thought.

They spent a miserable night rolled up in damp blankets, trying to fight off the mosquitoes. They awoke early, and before daylight rode quietly up the road toward Rich Mountain. Long before they reached the summit, they could smell the encampment—the odor of wood smoke, sweat, urine and horses. The Sergeant dismounted and cautiously walked along the edge of the road, leaving the two men holding the horses, scouting for the pickets sure to be there. Before long, he spotted a sleepy sentry leaning against a tree with his musket thrown casually over his shoulder. He stamped his feet and hunched his shoulders against the morning chill. The Sergeant backed quietly away and trotted back to the waiting men.

"We can't get through here. We'll be caught for sure. I reckon we'll have to ride around through the woods."

They left the road and circled around the encampment, leading their horses through the brush. They scrambled up the steep, wooded mountainside, sliding and cursing, and had to stop frequently to rest and let the horses blow. They finally found a low gap over the mountain and made their way to a small draft that flowed west through a narrow valley. They stopped to let the horses drink and then continued on. They soon came back to the road, mounted up and trotted their horses away from the encampment. By noon, they reached Frenchtown which was little more than a cluster of log cabins and outbuildings. An old man and woman, both gray-haired and stooped, wordlessly watched them from their garden patch as the renegades passed.

The Sergeant talked as they rode along three abreast. "Once we get to Grafton, we'll sell the horses. We won't have any use fer 'em because we kin ride the train to Rowlesburg. That's where I figger that woman is headed. That's what she told me when we had her before." The Sergeant assumed that Hank and Luke would be going with him and would continue to do his bidding.

He said, "Then, when we get done with her, we kin ride the train out west and join the cavalry, 'an they'll provide us with mounts. Room and board too, an' a decent wage. If it gets too bad, we can always light out for Texas or somethin,' I ain't too anxious to get my hair lifted by an Injun."

Hank and Luke had decided that they'd not be going out west with the Sergeant or anywhere else for that matter. They'd had enough of being yelled at, taking his orders, and doing all of the work. They'd knock him in the head in his sleep if they had to. No, once they got out of these infernal mountains they'd part company with him. When they got to the railroad, they'd get away from him before he got them killed.

They forded French Creek and began the climb up a steep incline when the Sergeant called them to a halt. He pointed to a cabin nestled in the trees away from the road and said, "Let's take a look at that cabin. It looks like it'd have some extra food and maybe some better clothes, an' I'm not anxious to spend another night sleepin' in the woods with the chiggers 'an skeeters. Come on. Let's see what we can find." They turned their horses onto the grassy lane leading to the house and approached cautiously.

"Hello the house. Anybody home?" the Sergeant yelled.

* * * *

Boyd and Lexus strolled down the dusty street, her hand lightly on his arm. Civilians bustled along the rough sidewalks, what there were of them, and children tagged along behind, chattering and laughing. Most stared at the tall, handsome man dressed in rough trousers and shirt and a broad-brimmed hat and the petite, well-dressed woman. It was unusual to see a young man out of uniform and a woman who was obviously not from Beverly. They walked along taking in the hustle and bustle of the busy mountain town. Wagons heaped with military gear, food, and other supplies rumbled down the street. Soldiers loafed in small groups on the street corners, looking enviously at them. Away in the fields surrounding the town, they could see a vista of tawny, canvas tents and blue uniforms stretching into the distance. They found a bench in front of the courthouse and sat down.

"Oh Boyd, I'm so sorry you're being kept in jail. It's my fault. You would be safe and sound back home if I'd not asked you to help me," Lexus said. She had a serious look on her face, and she kept her eyes downcast.

Boyd laughed. "It isn't all that bad, Lexus. At least I have a roof over my head and food to eat, such as it is. I'm used to being confined in a small space. My fishing boat is quite small, so I've spent many a night sleeping in a narrow berth."

"I know, but it's my fault," she said again and then suddenly brightened. "Maybe when the general finally returns he'll let you go, but I don't know why the major couldn't just let us go now," she said, dismay clouding her pretty face. "He actually accused us of being spies."

"I'm not surprised. I guess it's natural for them to be suspicious of a man out of uniform. In all fairness, I'd probably be suspicious, too, if I were them, but all we can do is wait. Sooner or later, they'll make a decision about us."

"I suppose. At least, I don't have to pay for the room myself. The major said the army is obligated to pay since they have forcibly detained us." Lexus sighed and smiled at Boyd.

They talked pleasantly and watched the happenings on the street as the sun set behind the hills. Boyd gazed at her, noticing a wisp of hair that had escaped her bonnet, curling and twisting in the slight summer breeze. Her skin was soft and smooth, and the bruises that had darkened her eyes and cheek were almost gone. Her eyes were deep blue, almost violet, with long curving lashes. She looked briefly into his eyes and then turned away with blushing cheeks. Boyd could not help but be attracted to this vibrant young woman beside him.

They were startled to see the major standing before them, his hand resting comfortably on the grip of the service revolver in his belt. "I see you finally got him out of jail," he said, regarding Lexus with a friendly smile and a curt nod at Boyd. "I saw you sitting here and thought I'd let you know that a courier came in from Buckhannon late last night. The general will be back sometime tomorrow. Then, we'll find out what he's going to do with you two."

"Thanks for letting us know, Major," Boyd said. "We need to be on our way."

"Yes, I understand. But, you have to admit, Mr. Houston, it's mighty suspicious, you running around loose after being captured."

"That's true, Major, but my parole papers are pretty clear. I have agreed to lay down arms for the duration of the war, and I mean to do just that," Boyd said heatedly.

"Take it easy, Reb. You don't have to convince me of anything. It's the general who will make the final decision. This time tomorrow you could be on your way, or facing a firing squad. The general won't hesitate to dispatch you quickly if he thinks you're anything but what you claim to be." He looked unwaveringly at Boyd with intense eyes as he stroked the ends of his moustache.

"I understand," Boyd said, calming a bit. "But, you have to look at this from my point of view. I haven't done anything wrong. I've upheld my end of the bargain, and I expect you to uphold yours. I fully expect to be released and on the way to Rowlesburg shortly. Nothing else is acceptable," he said firmly.

"We'll see, Reb, we'll see," he said grimly. He tipped his hat at Lexus, turned on his heel and walked away.

# INTO THE MOUNTAINS

\* \* \* \*

General Harris was a tall man of middle age who sat on a folding camp chair behind a portable field desk. His blue uniform was dusty and rumpled from a day's ride from the neighboring town, and a shock of dark hair stood in disarray on his bare head. Because of the day's heat he had chosen not to use a room as his office but had set up shop in the shade of the front porch of the commandeered house. Officers and aides came and went with fists full of requisitions and orders for him to sign. He read each carefully before affixing his signature.

Boyd stood under guard awaiting his fate on the front lawn as an unmerciful summer sun beat down on them all. Sweat ran down his back and stained his shirt as he shuffled his feet impatiently, wanting to get this over with one way or the other. He was seriously concerned, but could not convince himself that the general would choose to ignore the parole issued by one of his comrades-in-arms.

The three soldiers who guarded Boyd were friendly, joked and laughed with each other and casually held their muskets in the crooks of their arms. One, taller than the others, wore sergeant's stripes on his sleeves and was the one to whom the others deferred. Boyd had struck up an easy conversation with them and found that they, like the black-eyed man in the jail, were from Pennsylvania. All three had volunteered for duty in the Union Army at first opportunity. The sergeant was a young man, no more than twenty, and the other two were in their late teens. They had seen only limited battle and were anxious to prove themselves as soldiers. Each admitted to being a bit homesick. They liked the camaraderie of the men but disliked forced marches and the lack of good food.

"Hey, Reb," one of the recruits said, "weren't you in that battle in Lewisburg? What's it like, getting whipped like that?" He asked the question without rancor, curious to hear Boyd's answer.

"Well, to tell you the truth I didn't like it at all. We had you Yankees outnumbered almost two to one, but when our ranks broke and ran, it was all over."

"So, you ran. How did you get yourself captured?"

"My friend and I were wounded. Our men left us behind, and we were taken prisoner," Boyd said, remembering the battle and the time it took to recover from their wounds. "We didn't have much choice in the matter."

Their discussion was interrupted when an orderly approached and told Boyd to step up on the porch and wait for the general to acknowledge him. The guards stayed close by as he approached the general and stood obediently waiting to be noticed. A dark cloud abruptly obscured the sun, casting a gloom over the house and yard as if a harbinger of ill tidings. Thunder rumbled to the west over the mountains, and a cool breeze lifted the leaves of the maple trees in the yard causing their silvery undersides to flash.

The general noticed Boyd and motioned for him to approach his desk. Boyd stood at attention, not knowing whether to salute or not, but decided that since he wasn't in uniform he probably shouldn't. Besides, he wasn't a Union soldier. The general looked weary to the bone. His creased, weather-burned face held a perpetual frown, and piercing eyes looked Boyd over from under shaggy eyebrows. He was clean shaven except for a drooping moustache and goatee. He leaned back in his chair and released an exaggerated sigh.

"What in tarnation am I supposed to do with you?" he asked Boyd rhetorically. "I hadn't heard that ole Crook was handing out paroles. What in the world got into him? I haven't met the Confederate yet whose word was worth a tinker's damn."

The two men took each other's measure as an uneasy silence fell over them. To the west, thunder rolled again and the breeze, freshening now, brought the scent of dust and wood smoke.

"Well, what do you have to say for yourself, soldier?" the general asked.

At least the general viewed Boyd as a soldier rather than a civilian, or worse yet a spy. He was encouraged. "As the major probably told you, I was wounded and captured at Lewisburg. General Crook gave some of us parole papers rather than taking us to prison. I probably wouldn't have survived otherwise, and neither would my friend."

"Yes, the major told me all that. What's that woman doing traveling with you? Who is she and where are you taking her?" the general asked.

Boyd patiently told the story of Lexus' capture by renegade soldiers. When he mentioned that the soldiers were in Union uniforms the general frowned.

"You sure they were Union soldiers? What makes you think they're not Confederates raiding the countryside, blaming everything on us?"

"All I'm saying, General, is that they had on Union uniforms. They could have been anyone, even a bunch of civilians. All I know is what I saw. You can draw any conclusion you want to," Boyd said. "No offense intended, general."

"The major said that you're a fisherman from South Carolina." He shuffled through the papers on his desk and withdrew a report. "Charleston, if I'm not mistaken. What in the world are you doing up here in these mountains?"

"I've been asking myself the same thing, General, but when Lexus wrote to me and asked for help, I came as fast as I could. She's a good woman."

The general looked at Boyd with softer eyes and said, "If I have you shot as a spy, I don't know what'll happen to her. These are hard times, soldier. The Rebs will make another try to take this valley soon, and there will be blood let. There are marauding forces raiding and killing at will on both sides. It's not safe for a woman to be wandering around here unchaperoned, but on the other hand it wouldn't be the first time a woman served as a spy in this war." He looked again at Boyd with sharp, calculating eyes.

"General, if I may speak? As I told the major, I thought long and hard before I signed those parole papers. I pledged that I'd not fight in this war again, and I mean to keep my word. I'm out of it and God help those of you who remain in this fight," Boyd said sincerely. "And, I give you my word that I'll take Miss Saunders to her relatives and nowhere else. I'll do nothing that will make you regret your decision if you choose to release me. Other than that, you'll just have to decide one way or the other." Boyd was finished with his plea and stood mutely as the general made up his mind.

"The major said he'd thought at first that you and Miss Saunders were involved in some sort of an elaborate hoax to gather intelligence for the Confederates but had later changed his mind. Don't ask me why." The general, accustomed to making quick decisions, looked again at Boyd and said, "Against my better judgment, I'm going to release you two. I'll give you a pass to use to get out of town and past the pickets—as long as you go on north. If you're caught trying to travel back to the south, or if you come back this way at all, you'll both be shot as spies. No questions asked. You understand what I'm saying, soldier?"

Boyd grinned and snapped to attention. "Yes sir, General. You won't be sorry. I'm good for my word."

The general scribbled a pass on a pad of paper, tore off the sheet and handed it to Boyd. "And, just for good measure, your escort will stick with you until you leave first thing in the morning."

"Thank you sir," Boyd said, trying unsuccessfully to keep a grin off his face.

As he turned to leave, the general said, "And one more thing. Don't think you're going to sleep in the jail and eat our rations tonight. You'll have to find somewhere else to stay."

Boyd left quickly before the general thought of any more conditions to his release. His escort tagged along as he walked quickly toward the boarding house. As he approached, he saw Lexus sitting in a rocking chair on the porch, and when she saw his beaming face she knew that his meeting with the general had gone well. Rain began falling just as he stepped onto the porch.

## INTO THE MOUNTAINS

Early the next morning, rain poured from the sky as Boyd and Lexus rode their wagon out of town along the bustling turnpike. A steady stream of wagons loaded with provisions to support the Union encampment moved along slowly in the rain and mud. Several times, Boyd had to drive their horse and wagon off the road to allow them to pass. Deep ruts had formed in wet areas and mud stuck to the horse's hooves and legs. When he realized that the rain had set in for the day, Boyd cut a square of canvas to serve as a poncho for Lexus and he put on his raingear, but even with this protection from the deluge, their clothing was soon wet and clammy against their skin.

Before long, they came to a toll gate manned by two civilians who charged them a fee for passage: twenty-five cents for Boyd's horse and seventy-five cents for the mare and wagon. Boyd paid the toll without complaint. He was just glad to be out of Beverly and on the road. The toll-takers explained that the turnpike—running from Staunton to Parkersburg—was funded by local businesses and the money the tolls provided, but a lot of revenue was lost when the Baltimore and Ohio railroad had been completed.

They could see Laurel Mountain to the west, long and ominous, stretching along parallel to the road. A light fog had formed, and along the mountain ridges low clouds draped the forest canopy. The dripping forest crept in on them from both sides of the road. The trees, massive and towering, cast gloomy shadows beneath.

The night before, Boyd had slept in the haymow at the livery after leaving Lexus at the boarding house. Good to his word, the general had made sure that the escort stayed with him all night. They had marched along behind him when he went to the wrangler to see if he could re-claim their horses and wagon. At first, he had thought that the army was going to requisition them, but after half an hour of negotiations, Boyd had finally paid the wrangler five dollars to release them to him. Boyd had shown him the pass signed by the general and had to only bend the truth a little to suggest that the horses and wagon were part of the deal.

Luckily, the wagon still contained their gear but all of their food was gone.

The pickets north of town had carefully examined the general's pass, but they had questioned them about who they were and where they were going. They had to wait for half an hour in the rain while one of the soldiers scribbled a hasty letter to be given to his sister when they reached Rowlesburg. They were glad to deliver the letter if only they would be allowed to pass through the checkpoint and get on their way. After much discussion and delay, they were allowed to pass.

Now, the horse pulled the wagon along as if in a trance, its head down. Mud caked the wagon's wheels. Boyd's horse walked along behind the wagon and snorted and tossed its head each time a heavily loaded wagon rolled by. Its legs and chest were covered with the yellow mud that only a few days before had been a fine, powdery dust.

Boyd said, "We'll stop in Leedsville and see if we can buy some food. Those scoundrels took all we had, but I guess we're lucky to get the horses and wagon back. I was sure the army would just take them."

"Yes, I'm surprised too. All the civilians I talked to in town said the army just commandeered whatever it wanted. Most of them have sympathies with the rebels. I'm sure it's hard for them being occupied by the Union Army," Lexus said. "They growled they felt like prisoners in their own town."

"I'm surprised that they didn't search me closely enough to find my money belt when they threw me in the jail. If they had taken that, I'd be in trouble. Did they take your money, Lexus?" he asked.

"No, I had it well hidden under my dress. They wouldn't dare search me, being a woman."

"That's good. We shouldn't have a problem buying enough food to do us. We should be in Rowlesburg in three or four days if this rain lets up. We should come to a fork in the road soon. The pike continues to Philippi, but we need to turn north past

Leedsville. We have one more, low mountain to cross, and then it's all downhill from there. The road will follow Clover Run to St. George where it empties into the Cheat River. At least that's what I was told by the soldiers in the jail. That's what Hiram said too, if I remember correctly."

Lexus smiled at him, water dripping off her bonnet and said, "At least something good came from your time there."

"Yes, I suppose. I figure one or two days to St. George and another day or two from there to Rowlesburg. I just hope we don't run into any more patrols. I'm getting tired of having to explain myself. If I have to tell our pitiful story one more time…well."

"I'm so sorry, Boyd. I caused you all of this trouble. It's my fault."

"No, get that thought out of your head," he said with feeling. "If it wasn't for the war, we'd be able to go anywhere we wanted to. But, I guess we just have to accept it for now. Sooner or later, the war will be over."

By noon they came to the fork in the road and were happy to see that most of the traffic was left behind when they turned north. The road was narrow and winding but was not as rutted and muddy as the pike. The mare was able to move at a faster clip. Even Boyd's horse seemed more settled as they left the pike behind for the quieter road. Before long they came to Leedsville—a cluster of wood-sided houses and out-buildings—where they stopped at a one-roomed store building. A covered stoop sheltered the entrance, and a horse was hitched to a metal ring set into a stone block to one side. They could hear the hum of voices inside. A cold wind picked up, and rain fell in sheets.

Boyd and Lexus shook off their ponchos and left them in a heap on the stoop. Boyd knocked on the door and then pushed it open. A young couple stopped in mid-conversation and turned to look at them. The man was tall and thin with sandy hair and sad eyes. He was supported on one side by a wooden crutch held under his arm. The woman was dark-haired and pretty. A gray light filtered in through an undraped window, casting their faces in shadow.

"What can I do for you?" the young man asked. He stepped behind a wooden counter that ran along one side of the room. Partially bare shelves stood in mute testimony to the shortages that plagued the area.

"We need to buy some food," Boyd said. "We're traveling and lost all we had. The army took it."

"Well, as you can see, we don't have much for sale. We have some dried beans, a little bit of corn meal, and we just bought a smoked ham from one of our neighbors. A little later in the summer we'll have some local produce to sell. Oh, and we have a few potatoes left over from last year, but to tell you the truth, they're all about gone to sprout," the young clerk said. "Sorry, we don't have any spare grain for your horses."

"You the owner?" Boyd asked.

"Yep, me and the missus here." He put his arm around the pretty woman at his side. "I'm just back from the war. I got shot in the leg and almost lost it. I was lucky they didn't saw it off." The woman frowned at the thought. "I reckon I'll go back when this leg is well enough for me to march." The woman looked up at her husband and frowned again. "You serve in the army?"

"Yeah, I did. Confederate. Were you a Yank or a Rebel?" Boyd asked, hoping not to get in a ruckus with this man.

"Confederate, too. Around here, some of the men went with the North but most joined up with the South. Go on up north only a little ways and the reverse is true. When the blue boys come by, I have to take to the cellar. Most of the towns around here have been occupied by first one side then the other. I heard there's a Confederate force heading for Belington, but you couldn't prove it by me. Not much news here."

Boyd was relieved that they had fought on the same side. "We're heading for Rowlesburg. Have you ever been there?" Boyd asked.

"Yep, been there several times. Rode the train to Cumberland once, looking for work. That was back before the war started."

As they made their purchases, Boyd explained why they were traveling to Rowlesburg. The young woman tallied up their bill on a scrap of brown paper. Boyd paid it and then asked about a dry place to sleep for the night.

"Well," the woman said in a pleasant voice, "we'd let you sleep in our house, but with four children and my mother staying with us, we don't have any spare room. The barn isn't fit for our cow and pigs, let alone humans. John, what about we let them sleep here in the store? At least they'd have a roof over their heads. We could move some of these barrels and make a place for them."

The young man frowned and looked at his wife questioningly. Boyd could see that he was afraid they'd steal something. She pulled him aside and with whispering voices, they talked it over. Then, they turned toward Boyd and Lexus. "My name's Sarah and this is John," she said, smiling. "You can sleep here for the night if you want. I'm sorry we can't offer you anything better, but at least it'll be dry."

Lexus said, "Thank you. We're both soaked to the skin and I'd just about taken on a chill. My name is Lexus and this is Boyd. We're grateful to be in out of the rain. I hope it stops soon".

Boyd asked if they'd seen the renegade soldiers but knew that by now they would have gotten rid of their uniforms and would be impossible to identify. John shook his head, saying that the only people they'd seen for the last several days were folks they knew. The young couple left for their house with John limping along with the crutch supporting his bad leg.

Soon, as an early dusk settled in, the rain slacked off and then stopped altogether. Boyd stripped the harness off the mare and picketed it along with his horse in the overgrown field behind the store. He stacked the harness on the stoop and brought in their bedrolls. Luckily, they were still dry, having been protected in the back of the wagon by the tent canvas. Boyd's stomach began to grumble–it had been a long day without anything to eat. They didn't have any way to cook the food they had bought, so it would be a long, hungry night.

They were startled by a sudden rapping on the door and then it swung open, and Sarah entered. She held a cloth-wrapped bundle in her hands, and Boyd could smell wonderful aromas coming from it. "I know that you're hungry, not being able to cook and all, so I brought you some ham and cornbread. We just finished up our supper and thought we'd share with you."

After Sarah had left and they had eaten, they rolled out their bedding on the hard wooden floor—a proper distance between them—and began to settle in for the night. The store lantern cast a pleasant yellow glow on them, and outside they could hear night hawks calling in the night. The drone of insects lent a comfortable background serenade. When Boyd turned off the lantern, a ray of pale moonlight fell through the window. The rain was over.

"Boyd," Lexus whispered in the darkness, "what do you think we'll find in Rowlesburg? I don't even know if my relatives are still alive. Some towns have been stricken by cholera and other diseases."

"I don't know, Lexus. We just have to hope for the best, but I sure pray they'll be all right."

"What do you plan to do once we get there? Are you going to go back to South Carolina? You could probably take the train to Baltimore and then catch a boat down the coast," she said. She wasn't sure what she felt for Boyd, but she knew that she didn't want him to leave.

"I hadn't thought about it. I had been leasing a fishing skiff and cottage so I don't have any real ties there. My mother and father died long ago, and since I am an only child, I don't have family to return to. You were an only child, too, weren't you?"

"Yes. I always thought I'd like to have had brothers and sisters, but that wasn't to be."

"I've also wondered what it'd be like to be a part of a big family."

"I have to admit that I'm a little nervous about going to a new town where I don't know anyone and having to start over. When you're planning and making decisions about a move like this, it's easy. But, when it comes down to actually doing it, it's not easy at all," she said.

"I know what you mean. Planning's the easy part, but doing is much harder. But, you'll have blood relatives, and I'm sure they'll be a big help to you."

"I hope so," she said sadly. "I don't want to be a burden to them, though."

"You won't be. They'll likely need your help if times are as tough in Rowlesburg as they are everywhere else."

Lexus sighed and stirred in her bed. "I wonder where those renegades are. From what that Union patrol said, they could be headed in this direction too."

"Don't worry, Lexus. They're probably long gone by now. It's not easy for able-bodied men to move around without being noticed."

Lexus sighed again and turned on her side, trying to find a comfortable spot on the hard floor. Soon, Boyd could hear her rhythmic breathing as she drifted off to sleep. He folded his arms across his chest and looked out the moonlit window. Somewhere, off to the south, he could see a bright constellation of stars twinkling in the night sky. A sudden gloom swept over him, taking him back to his father's cottage by the sea where he had spent his youth. He remembered the hot, sweaty summers working on a pitching boat, hauling nets and sorting fish to sell on the docks. He thought about his father shouting commands over the whine of the wind through the boat's rigging. He remembered the night his father had been lost, and the void it had left. Lexus was right. It would have been good to have been a member of a large family with brothers and sisters and cousins coming and going: people upon whom you could depend and they depend upon you, people who could fill any void.

He gathered his hands behind his head and stared at the ceiling, lit only by the feeble moonlight. It was at times like these—quiet minutes in the darkness—that he thought about the men he had killed. The young picket, the men he had shot as they charged the Confederate lines, and others who had died at his hands in the frantic hand-to-hand battle for survival behind the split-rail fence. He remembered Charlie telling him about killing his neighbor's son and that he would have to go tell him he had done it. How, he wondered, did mankind arrive at such a dreadful place where men could commit such deeds on principle? Brothers killing brothers, cousins killing cousins, friends killing friends.

Lexus whimpered and twitched in her sleep. She, too, fought demons best left alone. Demons that came creeping in the dark of night, seeking her out, wanted or not. She had been through some terrible times, and in a way, she and Boyd were kindred spirits, each with night-stalking demons to be kept at bay. He wasn't sure what he felt for this woman, but he knew that he'd stay by her side as long as he was needed. Maybe one day he'd go back to his fishing village but not until he was convinced that Lexus was safe and settled into whatever life she chose.

Lexus turned toward him in her sleep, an awful moan escaping her lips, her hands pushing unseen apparitions away. She struggled, tearing at the blankets and shaking like a leaf in the wind. Boyd took her in his arms, holding her tight, speaking soothing words into her ear. She struggled against his chest, writhing to escape his embrace, her body rigid and stiff with fear.

"Sssshh. It's all right," he said, whispering to her. "It's all right." Responding to his voice, her body relaxed, and he could feel her tears on his cheek. She placed her arms around his neck and drew him close against her. He could see the shine of her hair in the moonlight and feel her breathing against him, her breasts pressing against his chest. He stroked her hair and held her tight, taking in the smell of her and her warm breath on his face. Gradually she relaxed and sank back on her bed, her breathing steady and strong. Boyd watched her as she slept. He watched the rise and fall of her chest, the fluttering of her eyes beneath pale lids, and wondered where his emotions were taking him. He brushed a tendril of moon-streaked hair away from her face and leaned over to place his lips on her smooth cheek, causing her to stir, a tiny smile gracing her features. They slept the night away, accepting the gift of dreamless sleep, and morning came with a rush. Sunlight streaked into the store and lit them with a brilliance that signaled a new day.

Boyd harnessed the horse amid a riot of bird sounds—robins, tufted titmice, cardinals, mourning doves, chickadees, passenger pigeons—all singing as if their lives depended on it. Far off, along the margin of the farmer's field, a turkey gobbled. The morning sun filtered down through the forest canopy, and the scented breeze made dappled shadows and sunny spots dance on the forest floor. His horse snorted and stomped, eager to be on its way. He hadn't ridden it for days, yet it looked at him expectantly, swishing its tail.

They loaded the wagon, said goodbye to Sarah and John and then began the trek up the road paralleling Leading Creek. Laurel Mountain marched away to the north, rising to the sky. By noon, they had passed through a low gap and entered a north-flowing watershed. They had reached Clover Run. Boyd noted the change of direction of the water flow and was confident that they had at last entered the Cheat River basin. As they moved along, the creek became larger as side rivulets entered the main stream. They repeatedly crossed the stream as the road meandered back and forth. They stopped in the late morning to allow the horses to rest and graze.

Boyd jerked a long hair from his horse's tail, causing it to dance and snort. He fashioned a noose with it and attached it to the end of a long hickory wand allowing him to pull the noose tight when he pulled on the end of the hair. He carefully approached the stream and soon found several good-sized trout finning in the current. After several unsuccessful attempts, he was able to get the noose over one of the fish's heads, jerked the noose tight and tossed the fish onto the bank. Using this primitive method, he soon had a nice mess of trout for lunch. Lexus laughed when he said this method of fishing was called "noosing" and that his father had taught him how to do it.

They took time to build a small fire and fry the fish in tallow. Lexus mixed corn meal batter and dropped spoonsful into the grease to make corn dodgers, watching them splatter and pop. They ate their simple meal, leaning against the trunks of towering hemlocks and talked quietly, enjoying each other's company. The horses stomped, and strong teeth cropped the rough grass. A family of crows, black and sleek, called to each other in the branches of large oaks and red maple trees. The roar and splash of the creek lulled them into noontime listlessness. Their heads drooped, and soon they dozed, content in the warm summer sun, a pleasant respite after the chilling rain of the day before.

\* \* \* \*

It was late that afternoon when they reached the Cheat River. They stood on the shore and looked across the flat expanse of the swift-flowing river. An elderly man approached them gesturing toward an old rowboat tied to a tree.

"I kin row you across fer a quarter. You won't even have to get your feet wet. It's shallow enough for yer horses to wade, but I figger your stuff in the wagon will risk getting' wet, and I'll bet you'd not want this pretty lady gettin' dunked."

Boyd looked at the swirling water and said, "Tell you what. I'll drive the horse and wagon across and Lexus can ride in the boat with you."

The old man grinned and said, "That's probably a good idee. The river's up a little with the rain and all. You might get a dunking, an' I'd not want to see this young lady get an unexpected baptizing."

The man helped Lexus into the boat and began rowing vigorously toward the other side, zigzagging erratically across the glassy water. Boyd climbed aboard the wagon and clucked the mare into the river. They all made it to the other side without incident and Boyd fished a coin out of his pocket and flipped to the man.

"Where can we find a place to stay for the night?" Boyd asked.

"Waal, there's a couple of places. There's the Saint George Inn there on the main road through town, but myself, I'd stay with Gracie. She has rooms to let in her house an' she's the best cook in these parts."

Boyd and Lexus climbed onto the wagon and made their way toward the houses spread along the broad river valley. The county courthouse rose above the homes, its white-painted copula shining in the late evening light. Their horses trotted along wearily. Wooden, two story houses lined a broad main street, and evening fires produced gray smoke that rose vertically from chimneys. To the west, over the tops of the mountains, the sun set with a yellow glow. Swallows swooped and darted around their animals, feeding on a myriad of insects disturbed by their passage. Doves sat hunched in a row on a split rail fence, dipping their heads as they passed. Diminutive frogs peeped in wet ditches along the fields.

Following the old man's directions, they soon found the rooming house. A sign with the words "Rooms to Let" hung on a post in front of the large home. Boyd knocked on the front door, and it was opened by about a nine-year old girl with large blue eyes. She wore a faded dress covered with an adult's colorful apron, folded to keep it from dragging on the floor. She smiled and looked shyly at them. "You lookin' for a room?" she asked.

Lexus responded before Boyd could answer. "Yes. My name is Lexus, and this is Boyd. We need rooms for the night, and if you have anything to eat, that would be wonderful. We're really hungry."

The girl turned on her heel and ran to the back of the house calling, "Mama, we have people wantin' a room. An' they're hungry, too."

An attractive young woman walked onto the foyer where Lexus and Boyd stood looking around the house. They saw a parlor set with formal furniture to one side and a dining room to the other. Two elderly men sat at a long, wooden table eating and casting sidelong glances at the new arrivals. The woman wiped her hands on her apron and smiled. She had hair the same color as her daughter's and wore a long, dark dress. She had crow's feet around her bright eyes and a tired look on her face.

"Welcome. Are you looking for a room? If you're hungry, I'm just serving supper. This is Becky," she said, placing a hand on her daughter's shoulder, "and I'm Grace."

Boyd quickly explained that they'd need two rooms, and yes, they were hungry. The woman said she had several rooms to let, and that if they'd take a seat at the dining table she'd prepare supper for them. As Lexus entered the dining room, the two men rose stiffly to their feet and nodded at them. One, tall and thin, held Lexus' chair as she sat down. He introduced himself as Mat Tribble.

"This here feller is Wally Dumas," he said, pointing a crooked finger at his friend. "We eat here once in a while when we get tired of doin' our own cookin.' We both lost our wives some time back." Sadness crept into his dark eyes. Wally, shorter than his friend and on the stout side nodded in agreement. "Gracie here is a mighty fine cook," he said, smiling at their hostess.

Grace left for the kitchen, but Becky hung back in the doorway as they talked. Boyd was curious about the road that led down the river to Rowlesburg. "How long do you think it will take us to get to town? Can we make it in one day, or will we have to sleep overnight?"

Wally was first to answer. "It's 'bout twenty miles. The road's in purty good shape, and you should be able to make it in one day. You'll have to ford a couple of little streams along the way, but the last time I made the trip, it weren't a problem."

"That is, if we don't get another gulley-washer tonight," Matt said, "and the Confederates raid this area from time to time. Hopefully, you won't have a problem with them."

They chatted comfortably and Lexus told them why they were traveling to Rowlesburg. "Do you know Frank and Martha Saunders? Frank's my father's brother so their daughter, Rachel, is my first cousin. I haven't seen them since I was a child. I hope they're all right after all this time."

"Yes, I think I know who they are, but I don' know them personally," Matt said. "Wally, have you ever heard of 'em?"

"Yeah, but like you, I don't think I've ever talked to 'em. As I recall, Mr. Saunders has something to do with the railroad, but it's been years since I've seen any of 'em."

"I hate to tell you this, Miss Saunders, but we had a pretty bad spell with cholera a few months back. Several folks died." He shook his head and looked knowingly at Wally.

"Oh," Lexus said, "I hope they're all right."

Grace served their meal of cornbread and beans cooked with thick slices of ham. She poured tall glasses of milk floating with chunks of cream. They ate in companionable silence, and then Wally asked about the Union forces in Beverly, eager for any news from the outside. Boyd told them about spending time in their jail, laughing now that the experience was over. He carefully told them about the pardon he had been given and was relieved as the two men nodded solemnly. They talked briefly about the war and other national events of the day.

"Folks around here have mixed opinions about us seceding from Virginia, but from what I've heard, we're a separate state now. It seems like Mr. Lincoln's in favor of anybody that wants to stay in the Union. The politicians had a time figuring out a name for the new state. Someone wanted to call us Kanawha, but they settled on West Virginia."

Wally and Matt entertained them by telling funny stories and tales. Matt told a story about the county clerk who worked in the courthouse. "He has seven daughters and he's always fretting about the young men that try to hang around his house, you know, lookin' to do some courting. Well, one of his daughters took a shine to a clerk that worked in the courthouse with her daddy, an' they tried to figure a way to do their courtin' without her father findin' out. If nothin' else, young'uns in love are ingenious. Of a morning she'd slip a love note in her daddy's hat band. He'd wear it to work and hang it on the hat rack when he got there, an' the young man would fish it out and read it an' then put his reply back in the hat. Unbeknownst to him, the clerk was carryin' the love letters back an' forth for 'em." Boyd snorted in amusement, and Lexus covered her mouth with her fingers as she smiled in delight. Wally and Matt laughed and grinned at them, thoroughly enjoying being the centers of attention.

And then Wally told a story about a farmer who made a deal with a neighbor to take two of his piglets and raise them, and when they were grown, the farmer would take one back and the neighbor would keep the other one in payment for feeding and taking care of both of them until they were of market age. A few days later, the neighbor saw the farmer in town and said that the pigs were such good looking stock; could he buy the farmer's pig?

"The farmer said he reckoned he'd sell it to him. Well, he was halfway home before he realized he'd just sold his neighbor two pigs for the price of one," Wally said laughing and wiping his eyes.

The conversation again took a more somber turn as Mat and Wally talked about what it meant to be a new state separate from Virginia. "If we're a part of the Union and the Confederates win the war and have their own nation, will we have to have papers to go to Richmond, or even Staunton?" Mat asked. "And, right now, if I read the papers right, the new state of West Virginia will gradually phase out slavery. When that happens, some folks are going to lose a lot of money. Where will all those black folks go? All these goings-on have stirred up a passel of confusion. That's what it meant when the President signed the bill for us to become a separate state."

Wally chimed in and said, "Yes, it sure is a mess. Even though we've separated from Virginia and are still a part of the Union, lots of folks 'round here are Confederates, but in Rowlesburg and the rest of Preston County, they're Union all the way. They've had union meetings all over the county for the last several years trying to drum up support for secession from the rest of the state. Some folks around here don't take kindly to bein' a part of the Union."

"Yeah, an' if the Union splits, it won't be long until we'll have a bunch of little countries scattered from here to the Pacific Ocean. You just know that sooner or later Texas will make a break to be its own country again, an' California is certain to become one too. We'll be just like Europe with all of those itty-bitty countries, all with their own languages and money," Matt said. He laughed and then said jokingly, "I reckon it won't make that much difference. Those Yankees up north speak their own language anyway. But, you have to admit it will be right inconvenient to have to change to a different kind of money when we go from one state to another or have to go through a checkpoint to cross their borders."

They sat quietly for a few minutes with each pondering what it really meant if the Union split apart. The two old men were too good humored to dwell on such serious thoughts for long and soon reverted to their storytelling.

Early the next morning Boyd and Lexus talked with their hostess over breakfast, and then they returned to the river to find the old man waiting for them with the boat. He rowed Lexus to the other side, and Boyd drove the mare and wagon across as his horse trailed docilely behind. The old man displayed a big smile when Boyd gave him another quarter.

It was a pleasant morning, and the miles slid by quickly. The mare trotted along briskly, and they were soon splashing through Licking Creek. Just to the east, Limestone Mountain formed a continuous barrier with the river hugging its base. Before long the road left the river and crossed a series of low gaps to Buffalo Creek. They followed it downward between steep hills, and long after noon they came to the Northwestern Turnpike.

As they approached, a stagecoach, decorated in vermillion and yellow, appeared from around a bend and rapidly approached in a swirl of mud and noise. The driver snapped a long whip over the horses' backs and shouted at them. Boyd's horse immediately nickered and began twirling in circles, frightened by the noise and commotion of the large vehicle. As it drew abreast of them, they could see passengers inside—soldiers and civilians—peering out of its windows. A red-headed boy no more than six or eight years old shouted and waved. Within minutes it was gone around the next turn, rumbling along into the distance on its way from Romney to Parkersburg.

When the coach had passed and Boyd's horse had settled down, they crossed the pike and continued onward until they rejoined the Cheat River. A small herd of cattle grazed in the knee-deep grass growing in a long, narrow meadow along the road. Virginia bluebells formed an azure bed under the forest canopy along with a riot of trilliums and a dozen different kinds of ferns. Then, farther down the river, they heard the mournful wail of a train's whistle and saw a plume of dark smoke billowing above the trees.

# PART TWO

# CHAPTER SIX

CHEAT RIVER FLOWED away to the north with a roar, squeezing through a constricting gap in the mountains. Whitewater showed along rocks, and boulders were strewn haphazardly in its bed. The turbulent water heaved and danced. Birds of myriad forms and colors darted among the rocks and spray seeking food, and sycamore trees leaned haphazardly over its bank. Cliffs soared skyward along the river's edge as the road squeezed through with water lapping at its edge. A formidable breastwork of logs and rocks had been thrown up restricting traffic to a narrow lane. Blue-clad soldiers with muskets at the ready barred Boyd and Lexus from passing through to the town.

"Halt there," a ruddy-faced soldier shouted. "State your business." He stared fiercely at Lexus and Boyd as men rose from makeshift stations and command points behind the logs and rocks.

"Easy soldiers," Boyd said with a friendly smile. "We've business in town, and we're not looking for trouble."

"Who are you, and what is your business?"

Boyd signed heavily, dreading having to go through his story again, but after showing his pardon papers, they grudgingly allowed them to pass. The soldier in charge assigned a detail of men to escort them to their commanding officer.

Once through the pass, the valley opened as the river formed a long, sweeping arc, an alluvial valley, allowing for the growth of the small town. Houses and businesses spread on each side of the railroad tracks that streamed out of Salt Lick valley. The tracks crossed the river on a wood and iron trestle and continued through town. Horses and cattle grazed in a patchwork of pasture fields tucked along the river's curve, and the army's camp dominated the bottomland. The main road through town was muddy and rutted with side streets spreading along the river bottom and climbing up the hillsides servicing the houses that clung precariously there. Chimney smoke joined a veil-like haze that hung over the valley.

Relieved to be at their journey's end, Boyd and Lexus sat on the wagon on a rise above the town gazing at the scene before them and were startled by the piercing scream of a locomotive's whistle. A train, pulling an assortment of cars and a brightly painted caboose, thundered across the trestle making it groan and quake and came to a grinding halt in the center of town. Steam poured from vents on the engine as it wheezed and clicked like a mechanical monster being restrained by the hand of an unseen master. Sulfurous smoke hung in the air stinging their eyes. Boyd's horse snorted and bucked, broke away from the wagon and trotted back up the road, tossing its head wildly. Far across the valley on the tallest peak overlooking the town a cannon emplacement, manned by ant sized men, guarded the trestle.

The soldiers in their escort chortled and laughed at the horse's antics, elbowing each other and slapping their knees. They leaned on their muskets and grinned at Lexus. A dark-haired soldier with stripes on his sleeve stepped forward. "Reckon it's never seen a locomotive before. You want us to fetch it up for you?" he asked with a clipped accent.

"If you would be so kind," Lexus said, smiling. "We're all tuckered out from our long ride." She chatted pleasantly with the soldiers, and soon they were falling over themselves to help her. Boyd scowled at them from his seat on the wagon.

After the horse had been tied again to the back of the wagon, the soldiers led them through town and into the Union encampment. Judging by the number of tents and the amount of equipment stacked in orderly piles, Boyd figured several hundred men were posted here. Soldiers stood in small groups talking and laughing and others seemed to be going about the business of being soldiers; relaying orders, stacking firewood, preparing the evening meal. Campfires were burned down to ashes, and wisps of smoke rose lazily from them. Some distance away, they could see a detail of men digging what appeared to be a latrine and rigging canvas shields around the opening in the dark earth.

Several tents, larger than the rest, were pitched under a clump of linden trees, their canvas yellowed and dirty from hard use. A large man, whose uniform bore a colonel's insignia, sat behind a field desk and watched their approach. Aides came and went, shuttling orders and tending to his needs.

Colonel James Irvine stood politely as Lexus and Boyd approached. Their escorts hung judiciously behind. "What have we here, sergeant?" he asked. "Who is this man?"

Boyd answered before the sergeant could reply to the colonel's question and began the re-telling of his story. The colonel took the parole papers from Boyd's hand and read them quickly. He looked up at Boyd and frowned and then swept his eyes across Lexus. He sat down heavily in his chair, motioning for an aide to bring chairs for his guests.

"How do I know you're not some sort of Confederate spy, comin' here to observe our fortifications and strengths? Ole Grumble Jones already tried to burn the trestle there." The colonel nodded toward the structure that spanned the river, "Some time back, it was."

The colonel thought back to the brief skirmish. The Confederates used a two prong attack. One force came over the mountain onto Salt Lick Creek, and the main detachment came down the river from the pike. They were all set to running and his forces were more than a match for them because they were dug in and had their sharpshooters ready. Some of the townsfolk even came running to pitch in. It hadn't been much of a contest. Major Showalter had turned them away easily.

"You saw the breastworks along the river when you came into town, didn't you?"

"Yes sir, I did," Boyd said. "Looks like it would be almost impossible to get past that."

"That's right. What with the cannon on the hill there, we can hold this valley 'til doomsday comes, but some of 'em went over to Newburg and tore up some tracks there and caused general mischief."

"I'm not a threat to you, Colonel. I'm no part of Jones' forces or any other for that matter. What'd you say his name was? Grumble?" Boyd asked.

The colonel snickered, "Yeah, W.E. "Grumble" Jones is his name. He's a general under J.D. Imboden from over in the Shenandoah Valley somewhere. His troops gave him that nickname, I suppose. Thought he'd come here and tromp all over us, but we showed him. We sent 'em back where they came from, but we have to be on the alert. They could return anytime."

"Yes sir, I understand, but I've been through all this before–several times. General Harris down there in Beverly gave me a pass through." He handed the folded document to the colonel. "All I want to do is get Lexus settled in with her relatives. Colonel Crook gave me a pardon, and I'm honor bound to abide by it." He described his part in the Battle of Lewisburg and his subsequent capture and pardon. The colonel asked for details and then questioned Boyd and Lexus closely about their trip through the mountains. He was especially interested in the troops they saw. They answered his questions patiently until he finally fell silent,

"What do you say, Colonel? Is there any problem with me being around here for a few days?" Boyd asked.

"You sound like you're telling the truth, but I'll have to run this by General Hill. He's the man in charge here. Far as I'm concerned though, your story seems to check out. I'll contact General Harris in Beverly and see if he confirms what you've told me. I have to send a messenger down there anyway. Then I'll report what I find to General Hill. His is the final say-so. Don't go too far from town in the meanwhile." The colonel turned back to his desk and began working, obviously dismissing them.

Boyd heaved a sigh of relief that he wasn't going to be rotting in a Yankee prison, at least not for a while.

Boyd and Lexus climbed back aboard the wagon and began talking as they rode back toward the center of town. "How do you suppose we can find your aunt and uncle, Lexus? Do you have any idea where they live?"

"No, I was too small to remember where their house was located. I just remember playing in their large back yard with Rachel and a spotted dog. It shouldn't be hard to find them, though. This isn't a very big town."

"Let's go by the hotel. Someone there should be able to help. Besides, I have to find a place to stay. It will be good to have a hot meal and a warm place to sleep."

\* \* \* \*

Sergeant Brown sat propped against the side of the rocking railroad car with his legs spread out in front of him. He contemplated his shabby boots. The soles were almost worn through, and they'd have to be repaired soon. Too bad he hadn't been able to find a pair that fit him in any of the houses they had raided. The car clacked and banged rhythmically over the rough rails and tossed him from side to side as the train wound its way through the mountains. He had stowed aboard as the train stopped for water and coal near Grafton.

He had awakened one morning to find that Hank and Luke had crept away like dogs in the night, leaving him without a horse or food. He was lucky to have a few coins hidden in his coat that they'd missed. He rubbed the knot on the back of his head where he'd been clubbed in his sleep. He'd kill the dirty cowards if he ever caught up with them. The sheriff in Taylor County was looking for him for robbing a farmhouse, and he'd only narrowly escaped by jumping on the first train that came along. He had no idea where Hank and Luke had gotten to.

Several years ago he had raided in the area, so he had a general idea of where the train was headed. It was travelling east, and one of the stops along the way would be in Rowlesburg. He knew that Saunders woman had gone there, and he'd sure like to have another shot at catching her alone. The thought of her, warm and soft against him, caused him to smile.

The train moved along, and dim light filtered through the cracks in the railcar. He'd have to be careful not to get caught by the railroad bulls or the soldiers who were in one of the cars just ahead. It was good that he was no longer in uniform, but he wasn't anxious to have to try to talk his way out of trouble if they caught him.

Presently, the train began to slow, and then unexpectedly all light was snuffed out as it entered a tunnel. The sound of the train was amplified and pungent smoke from the engine filtered into the car making him cough and gag. The train passed through it quickly, but soon entered a second tunnel. It was a long one, and before long, it filled with smoke, sending him into another coughing fit. The train exited the tunnel suddenly, and the bright light made him squint as it slowly ground to a halt. The Sergeant could hear car doors sliding open, and workmen began unloading freight. He slid down lower and pulled some crates around him making a place to hide. The train sat on its rails huffing and groaning as the men went about their work. A dozen soldiers in the car ahead climbed down and milled about on the depot landing. He crept to the side of the car and put his eye to a crack in its wall and took in the scene outside. A sign was attached to the side of the small depot building that read *Tunnelton*. He vaguely remembered hearing about the tunnels here and that they were prime targets of the Confederacy. If they could close them, the vital route that carried men and supplies to the Union Army would be cut. Armed soldiers patrolled the area around the tunnel opening.

The door to his car was thrown open, and bright light flooded in. He hunched lower behind his barricade. A man dressed in rough clothing with an old felt hat perched on his head climbed aboard, muttering to himself, and began looking through the crates until he found the one he was looking for. He scooted it toward the door with his foot, then jumped down and pulled it out, placing it on the ground. With a grunt, he slid the door shut with a crash. The Sergeant realized that he had been holding his breath and slowly let it out. He shook his head with relief and marveled at his good fortune of not being discovered. If he had been, there was little he could have done except try to lie himself out of it.

Presently, the soldiers climbed aboard their car again, and the train began to snort and buck and slowly gained momentum. The Sergeant climbed from his hiding place and sat on one of the boxes. That was close, he thought. He needed to get off the train as quickly as possible.

Soon, the train's wheels set up an ear-splitting screech as the brakeman slowed its progress down a grade toward the river. The Sergeant pressed his eye to the crack again and could see that the railroad clung to a cut along the side of the mountain. Far below, the river twisted through a serpentine gorge, and whitewater bounded over huge rocks strewn in its path. The faint rumble of the river reached his ears. From his vantage point it looked as if the train was suspended in the air, the river like a silver ribbon below. It passed over first one iron viaduct then another, crossing side tributaries. The train's whistle sounded, and slowly, its speed was reduced to a crawl. The Sergeant slid the door back a crack and slipped out and into the trees along the track as the train came to a lumbering halt. He kept to the shadows as he walked cautiously toward town until he could see a sign on the depot wall. *Rowlesburg.* Well, he thought, I'll just see what opportunities this little burg has to offer.

* * * *

J. Martin Tingle sat at his desk in his office and stirred a lump of sugar into a cup of black coffee. The pot had been left on the stove in the front room too long. The coffee was stale, but it was strong and black, just the way he liked it. He was lucky to have coffee at all, but figured that it was one of the perks of having a mercantile business like his. He was a tall man, in his early fifties, with thick, silver hair. His dark brown handlebar moustache was waxed and curled up at the ends. Even in the heat of the day, his expensive shirt was buttoned up to his neck. His dress jacket hung on a hook on the back of the door. He had piercing eyes, and a perpetual frown creased his brow.

He looked out a grimy window as the train pulled slowly into the depot. Soldiers disgorged from one of the cars and began moving away toward the encampment along the river. As a merchant, he was making good money providing supplies to the army and had a half-dozen men working for him. He had other holdings and interests and realized that the war would be over— one way or another—in a few years. He'd have to find another way to make money. He was proud of his accomplishments so far. He had a nice house and wife and the best buggy and team money could buy. His two children, a boy and a girl, were grown and had moved away as soon as they could. They were both married and living near Baltimore. They came to visit once or twice a year, riding the train on tickets his wife sent them.

He leaned back in his chair and folded his hands across his midriff, interlocking his fingers. He found it harder each year to keep his weight under control and only last winter had a bout with gout. Too much rich food, the doctor had said, and he still limped as a result sometimes, especially late in the day. He had grown up on a hardscrabble farm up on Salt Lick Creek, and his mother and father had died of hard work and heartbreak. At an early age, he had decided that he would never go without as they had. At first opportunity he had found a place to live in town and hadn't looked back. He had graduated from eighth grade and started work as a bookkeeper in one of the town's stores. It hadn't paid much, but he had learned how to keep books, place orders, and do payroll for the small staff. He soon realized that there was money to be made, but digging in the dirt as his parents had done wasn't the way to do it. He was proud of the fact that people in town called him *Mister* Tingle.

He had bought and sold a few pieces of property in the area, making a nice profit each time, but the war had put a stop to that. In this little town, there was little money available for buying anything but the bare necessities. His side business of selling food and clothing to the locals produced some profit, but only a trickle. Not nearly enough, but he figured he knew what the future would hold. When this war came along, he had profited from it.

He figured that after the war, all of the money now spent on rifles and cannons would be channeled into new businesses and homes. Lumber and building materials would be in great demand in a nation recovering from the ravages of war, and he meant to be among the ones supplying them.

He had his eye on a nice tract of timber on Little Wolf Creek up the river from town. It had everything he needed. The timber could be easily cut and stacked during the winter and then floated down the river to the railroad here in town or to Morgantown. When the snow melted in the spring, there'd be enough water to float the logs. There would be plenty of men available to do the work as they drifted back from the war and would be willing to work for a little bit of nothing. They'd be desperate for money. He could see it in his mind's eye. He'd be filthy rich in no time. There was only one problem. He didn't own the timber and didn't have enough money to buy it, but as someone once said, where there's a will, there's a way. He grinned to himself because he figured that he had the will and knew the way.

\* \* \* \*

As darkness settled in, the Sergeant walked boldly toward the edge of town. His stomach growled, and he needed a good meal and maybe a drink of whiskey. Rowlesburg was a small town with only a few boarding houses, but he soon came to one. He'd had to pass up the big, grand hotel that sat along the tracks. It was too rich for his blood. The boarding house had a weathered sign swinging from a bracket on a post that advertised rooms and drink. That was just what he needed. Yellow light streamed from the house's windows, and he could hear the hum of voices inside and an occasional burst of laughter.

He pushed through the front door and stepped into the dark, smoke filled room. There were half a dozen tables in one end occupied by a handful of men in dark clothing and a polished wooden bar at the other. Kerosene lamps attached to the walls provided dim, flickering light, and shelves behind the bar were filled with glasses, mugs and a meager assortment of liquor bottles. A brass foot rail ran the length of the bar, and a man leaned over it, supported by his elbows. His head nodded as he swayed slightly, and his hand cupped a shot glass. His eyes were downcast, and his foot rested on the rail.

A hush settled over the room as heads turned toward the Sergeant, and they boldly looked him over. He stepped toward an empty table near the door and sat down. Slowly, the murmur of voices resumed as the men turned back to their drinks, heads close together. He knew that they were talking about him, trying to figure out who he was and what he was doing here—a stranger—but he couldn't care less. Right now, all he wanted was something to eat and a drink. Later, he'd want a place to sleep and maybe clean up a bit. His clothing was dirty and ill-fitting, and he needed a haircut and shave.

An elderly man who wore a soiled apron around his waist approached his table. "What can I get fer you, mister? The missus made up a pot of stew. You want some of that?"

"Yeah. That'll be good. You have any whiskey?" the Sergeant asked in a growl.

"I think I have a little left. Them soldiers drink it up as fast as I get it, and it's hard to come by, I can tell you."

"What kind of stew is it?"

The man laughed and said, "Don't ask. We're lucky to have any meat and taters at all. Them soldiers are like a swarm of hungry locusts. They've just about eaten everything in the valley. I think it may be deer meat or maybe goat for all I know. You still want it. It's 'bout all we got."

"Yeah, guess it'll have to do. Whatever it is, it'll be better than what I've had recently."

The man shuffled over to the bar and returned with a shot glass full of amber liquid. "Man up the river makes this rotgut. I don't drink, so I don't know whether it's any good or not. Them soldiers would drink turpentine if they couldn't find anything else, so they've never complained. Hope you like it." On the way to the kitchen in back, the old man said, not unkindly, to the man clinging to the bar, "You go on home now, Herman, before you pass out on the floor. Mabel will have my hide if I let you get so drunk you can't find your house again. If you keep this up, you're going to have the Sons of Temperance down on me."

"Yes sir!" the man said, surging upright and saluting, swaying just a little. "I'm on my way." He strode to the door with an unsteady gait, turned and said, "See you tomorr.'"

The man shook his head and went into the kitchen, returning with a large bowl of steaming stew and a chunk of bread. "There you go, mister. Hope you enjoy it. The missus is a durn good cook, if I do say so myself."

The man said his name was Franklin and asked the Sergeant what his name was but was ignored. The Sergeant dunked the bread in the stew and wolfed it all down, chasing it with two glasses of whiskey. He paid for the meal and asked about a place to sleep and was told that there was a room available on the second floor–a traveling salesman had just left. It was the last room to be had. He climbed the stairs to the room and collapsed on the rickety bed, pulling the thin blankets over his head and was snoring within minutes.

The next morning, the Sergeant relieved himself in the privy out back and then helped himself to the razor and soap he found there, scraping the thick whiskers from his face. He washed in the tin basin and slicked his dark hair in place. He looked at himself in a piece of broken mirror attached to the wall and decided that he didn't look too bad. With a change of clothing he might even be half presentable.

He walked down the road to the center of town and entered the dry goods store. He rummaged through the piles of clothing and found a pair of pants and a shirt that he thought would fit him. None of the boots were of the right size so that would have to wait. Maybe he could put a piece of leather or something inside his boots to make do. He was trying on a felt hat when the proprietor approached.

"You goin' to be able to pay for all that stuff, mister?" the tall, silver haired man asked. "Not tryin' to be contrary or anything, but money is tight now."

The Sergeant turned to him and said, "You don't have to worry none. I got enough money to pay for this piddling bunch of stuff." He glowered at him.

"No offense mister, but as I said, money's tight here. I'll be happy to help you."

"Yeah, well all right then." He carried his stack of clothing to the counter near the door and fished his stash of coins from his pocket.

"My name's J. Martin Tingle," the storekeeper said, extending his hand. "I own this store. You just passin' through?"

"Not that it's none of your business, but I just got into town. I'm looking for work. You know anybody who's hiring?"

Tingle laughed and said, "No, there isn't any work here. The railroad's about the only place that hires people, but they haven't needed anyone for quite a while. You'd have to get in line anyway. Job comes up and every able bodied man in the county wants it." He looked at the rough looking character before him and began to think. He needed a man who wasn't too particular about what kind of work he did and wouldn't ask too many questions.

"Guess I'll have to move on then," the Sergeant said.

"Just a minute. What kind of work can you do?"

He snorted. "I can do just about anything you need done. I need the money, and right now I'm not too choosy. What do you have in mind?"

"Come on back to my office and let's talk," said J. Martin Tingle.

\* \* \* \*

Boyd and Lexus climbed down from the wagon in the center of town. Boyd's horse was tied firmly to a hitching rail while the mare stood with its head up, ears perked. Instead of going to the hotel, they decided that the post office was a good place to find where Lexus' aunt and uncle lived. The building was one of several built side by side along one side of the busy street. It had a high false front and two windows flanking the entrance. As they entered, the floor creaked and groaned under their feet. A striking, middle aged woman busily worked behind a counter laden with a mound of mail. She sorted through the letters and small packages, stacking them into piles.

She began talking before they had a chance to speak. "Sakes alive, I've never seen the like. The mail just keeps pouring in. I hate to see the train pull into town because I know I'll have a good day's work just to get it sorted and put in the mail boxes." She nodded toward a wall full of wooden mail cubicles. "Most of it's for the army. Soldiers writin' home and folks at home writin' back. Every once in a while, there's an official letter or two, but most of that kind of stuff's in their own mail bag. Keeps me on my toes, I can tell you." She looked up from her work and smiled.

Lexus stepped forward and said, "We're new in town and I wonder if you could help us."

"Well, I'll do all I can. Are you wanting to set up a mailing address?" She looked Lexus up and down and then glanced at Boyd.

"No, I don't need one just now. I'm looking for my aunt and uncle. I believe they live in town here."

"What's their names? I reckon I know just about everybody that lives here. I've only been doin' the postmaster's job since my husband went away to war. They gave me the job temporary until he comes back. I've lived here all my life."

"Saunders. Frank and Martha Saunders. They have a daughter named Rachel. I haven't seen them since I visited them here years ago."

The woman brightened and said, "Oh yes, I know them. I practically grew up with Martha. We went to school together. Frank, well I've known Frank for a long time." Her face became pink, and it lit up with a small smile. "Me and Frank used to be sweethearts when we were young, you know." She looked away, touched her hair and then frowned. "But that's water under the bridge. My, how I ramble on. I can tell you where they live. They have a nice house here in town, but let me draw you a map. It'll be easier that way. They live on a knoll above the river." She took an envelope from a stack of discarded mail and began drawing streets and houses on the back. "It's only a few blocks from here. It won't take you any time to get there."

Lexus introduced herself and Boyd. "I've lived all of my life in Lewisburg, but my mother and father died. I lost my house to a fire, and I thought I'd come here to be with my family, what's left of it," she said. "Boyd's a friend who agreed to escort me here."

"My name's Agnes Chestnut. Me and my husband live in town too, or at least we did until he decided to join the army and go gallivanting' around the country, a man his age. I took on his job here at the post office and barely can make ends meet. I've got four kids and two still at home, so it's a job trying to keep the family together. If this war isn't over soon, the whole country will go under, but I guess I shouldn't complain. Me and my girls are much better off than most folks. I only hope that Larry comes home in one piece. His name is Lawrence, but we all call him Larry."

They discussed the war and how it had changed their lives and shared the latest gossip of the town. Boyd shifted from one foot to the other as he stood awkwardly with his hat in his hand. Finally, the women said their goodbyes, and Boyd and Lexus climbed onto the wagon and started down the street with the map in hand.

The house wasn't as easy to find as Mrs. Chestnut had led them to believe. The town was more or less laid out in a grid, but the streets were poorly marked and she had left out streets and houses. After several wrong turns, they finally came to the house she had described. It was a two story structure with a sweeping porch on two sides. The house was constructed of white-painted wood with the windows and eaves decorated with gingerbread detailing. Potted plants sat on the wooden steps that led to the porch and front door. The yard was neatly tended with a variety of flowering plants, but Boyd had no idea what they were. He could see a selection of vegetables growing in beds along the house.

Lexus jumped down from the wagon and excitedly said, "This is it, Boyd. It's exactly as I remember it. Oh, I wish my mother and father could be here with me. I have such good memories of this place, of the one time I visited. I just hope they're alive and well." She climbed the steps and gave the circular doorbell a brisk twist. It sounded just as she remembered. As they waited, she said, "When I visited before, Rachel and I used to ring this doorbell, then run and hide around the corner of the house. Uncle Frank finally caught us and made us sit on chairs in the kitchen. We laughed and giggled the whole time."

The door opened and a tall woman with graying hair piled atop her head looked blankly at them. "Yes? What can I do for you," she said with a pleasant smile.

"Aunt Martha. Do you remember me? I'm Lexus."

Her aunt's face lit up. "Well for goodness sakes. It is you, isn't it? Where did you come from?" She stepped forward and embraced Lexus warmly. "I haven't seen you since you were a child. How many years has it been? But, where's my manners. Come in, come in." She stepped aside from the doorway and led them into a cool, high-ceilinged parlor just off the foyer.

"Oh, it seems forever, since I was here to visit," Lexus said. "How is everyone?" she asked, a worried frown on her face.

"We're all well. Frank had a bout with cholera a year or so ago. At least that's what I think it was, but the doctor said he wasn't sure. Whatever it was, he was sick off and on for a month or more. Otherwise, we've been well. He'll be home from work any time now."

"Mother, who is it?" a voice asked from within the house.

"Come here, Rachel. It's your cousin Lexus from Lewisburg. You remember her, don't you? She came to visit when you were just a youngster."

The young woman who appeared was about Lexus' age and was dressed in a long, fashionable dress. She had long, dark hair that fell in ringlets to her shoulders. A sprinkling of freckles spread across her nose and cheeks. She was achingly beautiful–tall and slim like her mother.

"Lexus!" she exclaimed. She rushed forward and embraced Lexus and then stepped back and beamed at her. "I'm so glad to see you. I thought I'd never see you again." She then regarded Boyd standing in a corner of the room, his hat under his arm. "And who might this young man be?" Rachel asked, eying him frankly. "Is he your man? Are you married?"

"Oh no," Lexus said quickly. "He's a good friend who agreed to help me. He escorted me through the mountains from Lewisburg. I would never have made it without his help."

"Pleased to meet you," Rachel said, looking him boldly in the eyes. She extended a delicate hand to Boyd who shook it carefully. He felt like a knot on a log and didn't know what to do with his hands. His feet shuffled about as if they had a life of their own.

Mrs. Saunders greeted Boyd warmly and then taking Lexus gently by the hand led her to a seat. She motioned Boyd to a chair with a stiff wooden back. He sat gingerly as if he were afraid it would break. The women chatted excitedly, catching up on news and family matters. Lexus explained what had happened to her parents and how her house had burned. She didn't mention her run-in with the renegade soldiers.

"Oh yes, I received your letter some time ago. Frank was saddened to hear of his brother's death. We all were, and I always liked your mother. I'm so sorry."

"I wrote you that I was coming. I guess you didn't receive the letter," Lexus said.

"No we didn't, but that's not unusual since the war is making such a mess of things. The mail is fairly reliable up north from here, but anywhere to the south, well I'm just not surprised that your letter didn't get through," Mrs. Saunders said. She turned to Boyd and asked about his background and how he'd come to know Lexus. He replied as best he could, explaining briefly the events that led to their travels through the mountains. All the while, Rachel kept her eyes on Boyd, smiling brightly whenever he looked at her. She sat up straight on the edge of her chair, her hands clasped in her lap. Lexus looked first at Boyd and then at Rachel, and a frown stitched across her forehead.

The front door banged and Frank Saunders strode confidently into the room. He was tall with gray hair that touched his ears. His upper lip was graced by a dark, bushy moustache. He was well dressed and wore expensive leather boots. His eyes brightened when he saw Lexus. He swept her into his arms. "My, my," he said, "I wondered what had become of you. I'm so glad you're here. Where in the world did you come from?"

Mrs. Saunders quickly brought him up to date on Lexus' travels. They all talked and laughed at the same time, filling in the details of the story. Mr. Saunders beamed at Lexus, and Boyd was pleased to see such obvious affection for her. Rachel nodded and smiled and then stood beside Boyd and looked up at him.

Boyd was usually at a loss when it came to women, but he was astute enough to catch the immediate current of competition that had flowed between the two young women in the room. He was amazed at how quickly the tension had arisen between them, unspoken but there nonetheless. He carefully averted his eyes from Rachel and focused on Mr. Saunders and the others in the room.

\* \* \* \*

The town's people gathered along the edge of the river, their spirits running high. Bands of children milled about in the warm summer sun as neighbors greeted one another. They all talked excitedly. Picnic baskets were placed in the shade until the swabbing was done; a grand feast waited. Although it was late in the morning, the sun had just topped the mountains that encircled the town. Children ran and jumped, threw rocks in the water and chased each other. They laughed and gamboled along the water's edge. Dogs joined the melee barking excitedly. Soldiers hung back and watched with fascination, appreciative of any distraction from the boredom of camp life.

Dozens of men and older boys selected a large pool in the river that contained schools of fish. Using rocks and logs they constructed a large vee spanning the width of the river, and then made a pot at the narrow, downstream end. The water was low enough to allow the men to work easily except for the pool that was as much as twenty feet deep. After the vee was completed, they collected wild grapevines from the mountainsides nearby and wove them into a rope long enough to span the river. To this they attached shorter vines and ropes that hung down toward the bottom and weighted them with stones, making a curtain of sorts called a swab. Men and boys grasped the rope at each end of the swab, and began to pull it downstream through the pool, herding the frantic fish into the top of the vee.

Other men and boys, their pants wet and dripping, formed a ragged line behind the swab and beat the water with sticks and branches and yelled to keep the fish from escaping around it. Water splashed into the air making brief rainbows in the morning sun. One of the beaters stepped off an underwater rock and fell in over his head. He rose to the surface sputtering and coughing and thrashed back toward the bank. The crowd laughed and talked loudly among themselves, cheering the man on. As the swab approached the vee, the fish began to panic. Some jumped into the air and sailed over the stone containment walls and others escaped over the swab. Some of the fish jumped so high they hit the beaters, and others just swam in frantic circles. One man standing in a rowboat in the middle of the pool was hit by a large jumping fish. He caught in his hands and pinned it to his chest, as the crowd called his name and cheered.

Rachel explained the process to Lexus and Boyd who watched from a safe distance. "It's so exciting! Each year, the people from town and all around gather here to catch fish, and then we divide them up. Mother and Daddy usually salt our share down in a big barrel in the cellar. Sometimes they last all winter, but more often, they're gone by Christmas," she said breathlessly.

One large fish jumped onto the bank to avoid the melee, beating the mud with its broad tail. A large spotted dog promptly grabbed it and trotted away, holding its head up high, dragging the struggling fish. The fish beat and thrashed in the dog's mouth as a rag-tag group of children chased after them, laughing and giggling. The town's people laughed and roared in amusement.

The pot was soon full of struggling fish, some with their heads above water, mouths gapping and sucking air. The crowd surged forward, waded into the river and surrounded the pot as water poured over the rocks and raced away downstream. Some caught their slimy prizes with their hands and put them in buckets, and others caught them by their tails and pulled them thrashing onto the bank. There were bass, pike, suckers, rock bass, salmon and a myriad of other species. They caught as many as they could, large and small, before the lucky ones made their escape and darted back to the safety of the deep pool.

The catch was quickly divided into piles and the leader, a tall, elderly gentleman, turned his back on them. A second man pointed to a pile of fish with a long stick and said, "Whose pile is this?" and the leader called out the name of a family who quickly picked up their pile of fish. The man pointed to a second pile and asked the leader, "Whose pile is this?" and another family name was called. Thus, the fish were randomly awarded, reducing competition and the attendant arguments that would have surely followed when one family or another felt it had been short-changed. These people could use one of the nets from his fishing boat, Boyd thought.

Picnic baskets were soon arranged on blankets and sheets, and the wet, smelly men sat on the ground with their families and ate their lunches. The children stopped only long enough to gulp down their food and then resumed their play with brothers and sisters, cousins and friends. The adults visited and talked and exchanged the news of the day.

As the crowd began to disburse, Boyd thought back to a few days earlier. He had left Lexus with her family and had taken the wagon and horses to the livery to be cared for. He had visited the various boarding houses looking for a place to stay, but had quickly found that all rooms were taken by army officials and businessmen. When asked, no one knew of anyone who had a room available. He had just about resigned himself to having to camp in the woods when he had a flash of inspiration. He walked back to the center of town and entered the post office.

"Mrs. Chestnut, I have a question for you," Boyd said. The postmistress was busily sorting mail into mailboxes.

"Oh, call me Agnes. Everyone else does. What can I do for you?"

"I'm looking for a place to rent, a room. I just thought that maybe you would know someone who needed a few extra dollars who had a room to let."

"Well, everyone needs a few extra dollars, but I can't think right off of anyone who lets out rooms who isn't full. I'd offer to help you, Lord knows that I could use the money, but all my rooms are full of kids." She looked at Boyd wistfully, clearly wishing she could help him.

"Oh well," Boyd said, "I guess I'll just have to get out the tent and pitch it somewhere. I was hoping that I'd be able to have a roof over my head for a change."

"Well now, if it's only a roof you're looking for, I just happen to have an old shed that sits near the river. It's full of tools and other junk, but I think it could be cleaned out and would make a right good place to sleep. My husband used to have a workshop there. I don't know what he did in there, but he spent a lot of hours puttering around. I think he just wanted to get out of the house and away from me and the kids. Can't imagine why," she said, grinning. "It even has an old Burnside stove in it that will keep it warm in the winter."

"That sounds perfect, Mrs., er Agnes. But, I seriously doubt that I'll be here for long, certainly not through the winter. Now that Lexus is settling in with her aunt and uncle, I'll probably be on my way, but I'd like to see that she has everything she needs before I go."

Agnes frowned, wondering if it would be worth the effort to clean out the shed if Boyd was leaving soon. "Well now, if you'll come back after I'm done with work, say about five o'clock, I'll show you the shed, but I'll have to ask you to do the cleaning-out. Then, you'll be able to set it up just about any way you want. Come to think about it, I believe there's a set of old springs and a mattress in there." She smiled, thinking that maybe she'd make a few dollars at that. Maybe she could charge him for a month in advance, squeeze a few dollars out of him before he left. Even at that, she'd have a place to rent. Any little bit of income would help.

Boyd hung around town, watching wagon traffic come and go, observing the movement of soldiers into and out of their camp. It was a busy little town, with several trains rumbling through each day. Little wonder the Confederates wanted to cut the train line and disrupt the flow of troops and war materials.

At five o'clock he was back at the post office, and Agnes walked along with him to her house and then led him to the river's edge and showed him the shed. It wasn't much, just one large room with a sagging porch on the front, but it sat on a rise facing the river, and he could hear the rush of water and see ducks flying up and down. It would do very well.

It took him most of the next day to clear out the shed and carry the usable tools and other assorted goods to the main house to be stored in the cellar. He swept out the dust and cobwebs and set up the bed in a corner. The stove was rusted and the stovepipe sagged dangerously, but with care, he was able to put it in working order. One window provided a sliver of light and was in sore need of cleaning; he'd need an oil lamp to ward off the dark of night under the giant sycamore trees. He made a mental list of things he would need to make the shed into a home; oil lamps, wicks, lamp oil, bedclothes, and maybe a cast-iron pot that he could use over a fire, and maybe even some dishes and tableware. All in all, he was pleased that he'd have a roof over his head and not have to sleep on the ground with the mosquitoes and ticks. He grinned to himself at how Agnes had deftly separated him from a month's rent. It wasn't cheap, but it was less than a room rented by the day in a boarding house. Plus, he'd have the privacy he wanted since the shed was secluded and screened from public view by big trees and a large clump of river birch.

Boyd was brought back to the present as Mrs. Saunders chatted casually with him, and Rachel and Lexus strolled along the riverbank. Soldiers loitered in small groups, watching the two slim young women, not daring to approach them. The town's people were reluctant to go back to their homes.

"Lexus is adjusting nicely to living with us," Mrs. Saunders said. "She told me all about your journey up through the mountains, and the trouble you encountered." She looked at Boyd frankly. "We'd like to thank you for helping her. We're relieved that she's here and is safely in our care. She and Rachel are becoming like sisters."

"I was happy to help her," Boyd said. "She's had a rough time of it, but that's all behind her now."

"She only told me a little about being captured and her rough treatment. I'm afraid she hasn't told me everything. She seemed to suppress the details. What do you know? I'm only asking because I want to help her and want her to be safe and happy."

"Not much. I know that she was treated roughly and that we found her pretty quickly after she was taken. She hasn't confided in me the extent of her mistreatment."

"I worry," Mrs. Saunders said. "I can hear her crying and whimpering in her sleep at night. And once she woke up screaming. Maybe one day, she'll confide in me."

Boyd looked away into the distance. He worried too, knowing what had likely taken place before they had freed her. He clinched his fists angrily, thinking what he'd do if he had a chance to meet the Sergeant alone. He talked quietly to Mrs. Saunders as the crowd dispersed around them. Mr. Saunders stood nearby talking with friends.

Boyd looked up to see Lexus rushing toward him with Rachel walking swiftly to keep up. Her face was a mask of fury and her eyes brimmed with tears. She took Boyd firmly by the arm and led him around a large tree for privacy.

"I saw him!" She hissed. "He was talking and laughing with a bunch of men just down there," she said, pointing with a shaking finger. "He wasn't in uniform, but I'm sure it was him. Oh, I hate him." She was shaking with rage.

"Who? Who did you see? Was it the Sergeant? How could that be? How could he know where you are?"

"I don't know, but it was him. I'll never forget his hateful face. Oh, what am I going to do now? I thought I was safe here." She wrung her hands and wiped her nose with her sleeve as tears streamed down her face.

\* \* \* \*

The Sergeant faded back into the crowd and then walked swiftly toward his boarding house. So she's here, he thought. He was sure it was her. How could he miss that figure and the long, blond hair? Just like I thought–she said she was going to live with her aunt and uncle in this sorry little town, and here she is. Good! I'll catch up with her one way or the other. He would never allow her to get away from him alive again. She had recognized him, he was sure, but little good that would do. He'd just deny everything if she went to the law. It would be her word against his. He'd deny that he had ever been in Lewisburg or anywhere near there. He'd make up a story about where he had been for the last couple of years, maybe living in Fairmont or somewhere like that. How would they be able to check up on him, especially if he was vague about the details? He'd say he had been working in the woods cutting railroad ties and not often in town. They'd never be able to prove he wasn't. Just deny it all. That was the ticket.

He turned on his heel and walked to the dry goods store and walked swiftly into Tingle's office without knocking.

"Here now, you can't just barge in here anytime you feel like it. I'm busy," Tingle said.

"I'm real sorry," the Sergeant said, "but I need to talk to you. What kind of work do you have for me? I need to make a few dollars before my stash runs out."

"Well now, sit down, but next time, knock before entering."

"Yeah, yeah, okay. Do you have some work for me, or don't you?" he asked shortly. "If you don't, just say so and I'll find something else."

"I don't know how much to tell you. I don't know you, and I don't know if I can trust you or not."

"Oh you can trust me. If there's money to be made, I can keep a secret with the best of 'em," the Sergeant said, looking Tingle straight in the eyes.

"Okay. Here's the deal. There's a tract of timber up on Little Wolf Creek that I have my eye on, big, tall timber just waiting to be cut and taken to market. The thing is I don't have all the free capital I need to buy it."

"Timber? What good is that going to do you? No one around here is going to buy it. Thanks to the war, there ain't no one building nothing," the Sergeant snorted. He shook his head in disgust. "An' I thought you had something good going."

Tingle laughed, and then said, "That's the problem with men like you. You can't see beyond a few coins in your pocket today. You never think about tomorr.' This war will be over in a couple of years. It doesn't matter who wins, when it's over there will be a demand for lumber, and I plan to supply it."

"Yeah, but how are you goin' to pay me? I can't wait for years to get my money."

"Oh, I have enough money to make payroll. I just don't have the money to make a purchase that big. You don't have to worry about a thing. You'll get paid, and on time."

"Well, that's more like it. Now, who do I have to kill to get that money?" the Sergeant asked.

"Good God, man, don't say that. I don't want you to kill anyone. I may want you to scare the pants off someone, but I don't want any killing. You hear?"

"Whatever you say, Tingle. Just tell me what you want done."

"It's *Mister* Tingle to you!" A silence fell over the office as the two men glared at each other and then Tingle relaxed. "Here's the deal. I paid a clerk in the courthouse to change the deed to the land. It originally belonged to Frank Saunders' grandfather. Somewhere way back, he was given the land for service in one of the wars the States waged. I don't remember which one, but it has been handed down through the generations. It's a couple thousand acres and has never been improved—no house ever built on it, and it's too steep to farm. But the timber is there for the taking. And, I'm taking it. But, here's the problem. If the clerk ever talks, I'm going to have to answer to the sheriff."

"Well now, that's a easy problem to solve. We just make the clerk disappear."

"Didn't you hear what I said? No killing, but I may want you to put the fear of God in 'im. And, sooner or later we'll have to deal with Frank Saunders. He won't give up that land easily."

"You don't have nothing to worry about, Tingle—Mr. Tingle," he corrected—"I'm just the man to solve yer problems. Now, let's talk turkey. I don't work fer nothing."

\* \* \* \*

The white clapboard church with its tall, wooden steeple sat just on the edge of town, and Sunday services had just concluded. Large, fluffy clouds sailed across the sky, occasionally casting shadows across the green land, and cardinals sang lustily in the trees—*pichew, pichew, pichew, tiw, tiw, tiw*. The congregation filed solemnly out the front door and scattered into the churchyard, grateful for the cool morning breeze after the stuffiness of the church's sanctuary. Riding horses with loosened saddles stood patiently, tied to trees and bushes, and others that pulled light wagons stood with harnesses slackly draped over their backs. An assortment of buggies, some expensive and others less so, awaited the congregation that was reluctant to disburse.

Boyd waited patiently while the Saunders family shook the preacher's hand and visited with friends and neighbors. It was obvious to him that this was the social highlight of the week. During the service, the preacher had told them all, in no uncertain terms, that they were going to hell in a hand-wagon, and that they all had better change their ways. He had worked up a pretty good head of steam, speaking rhythmically and shouting "aaaahh!" with each great, sucking breath between sentences. His face soon became red with exertion, and his shirt pulled open where a button had been lost, exposing a strip of his white belly. The congregation nodded and shouted amen when he paused to wipe the sweat from his forehead with a crumpled handkerchief. They didn't seem to be offended by the dressing down and smiled and told him what a great service it had been as they filed out. The preacher beamed at each of them and shook their hands and patted their backs. He bent low to talk to a small boy wearing short pants who promptly hid behind his mother's skirts.

Boyd watched with interest as Mr. Saunders had an animated discussion with a man about his age. He frowned and wrung his hands as the man spoke earnestly to him. When the conversation concluded, Boyd edged closer as Mr. Saunders talked to his wife. The expression on her face showed that there was something seriously wrong. He picked up parts of the conversation, something about a deed and a place called Little Wolf Creek. It wasn't any of his business so he drifted away, looking for Lexus.

Later, they all gathered in the Saunders' home for Sunday dinner. The women worked in the hot kitchen to prepare the food as Boyd and Mr. Saunders lounged in the parlor.

"Boyd, there's something I need to talk to you about. You seem to have a lot of experience in the world, and I could use your advice," Mr. Saunders said.

"I'd be happy to help, but I'm just a simple sailor. My father and I had a fishing boat in South Carolina, and until his death, we worked together on it. I sold it several years ago, and that, and a short stint in the army, is about all the experience I've had."

"Yes, but you sold property and must have some knowledge of how that works."

"Yes, but that was pretty limited," Boyd said.

"Just hear me out. Here's the problem I face. I inherited some land from my father—it has been in our family for several generations—and now I hear that there's a problem with the deed. Frankly, I haven't paid much attention to it. It' just some mountain land, not worth a lot right now, but I figured someday the timber on it might be worth a little something. I haven't been on the property for years, not since my father died, but I've been paying taxes on it every year. Now, I hear from a man, a lawyer who works in the courthouse records room occasionally, that the land has been sold to some company. I can't understand that since I haven't signed anything except the tax documents. What do you think the problem could be?" Mr. Saunders looked at Boyd in puzzlement.

"I really can't say, Mr. Saunders. I sold the boat and our cottage in South Carolina, and the laws are different in each state. My best advice to you is to hire a lawyer to help sort this out."

"I suppose so, but I really can't afford a big lawyer's fee right now. We're doing okay financially, but just barely so. Everyone is suffering from the war. I was wondering if you could go to the courthouse and see if you can sort this out. That land might be of some value to Rachel and Lexus sometime in the future."

"Yes. I'd be happy to help any way I can. I've just been sitting around trying to figure out what I want to do with my life, so I have some time on my hands. Someday I suppose I'll go back to South Carolina, but with the war and all I'm not really free to travel. I had a devil of a time getting here from Lewisburg, but I'll see what I can do. I hate to seem ignorant, but I haven't seen a courthouse in town. Just where is it?"

"Oh, Rowlesburg isn't the county seat. You'll have to go to Kingwood, about fifteen miles away. That's the county seat, and the courthouse is there. Boyd, I really appreciate your help. I'd be happy to pay you for your time."

"That won't be necessary, Mr. Saunders," Boyd said. "I can smell the odor of something really good to eat coming from the dining room, and that's payment enough. I haven't had a home-cooked meal for quite a while. And besides, maybe I can talk Lexus and Rachel into going with me."

Mr. Saunders laughed, "Oh, I'm sure they'll be happy to accompany you, especially Rachel. She's taken quite a shine to you, Boyd. Lexus, too, so I'm afraid you're in for quite a time of it. Good luck," he said, chuckling. "I'm afraid we men are always in the dark when it comes to women."

Boyd frowned. "While we're talking, there's something else you should know about. Lexus saw that rogue soldier that abducted her. He was here in town."

"Yes, Lexus told Martha, and then she told me about it. You have any idea how he found her here?"

"I think Lexus let it slip that she was coming here, so he followed. I'd like to get him in my sights for just a minute. I'd take care of the problem," Boyd said quietly.

"I understand you saying that, but you should let the sheriff handle it. You can talk to him while you're in Kingwood. He's a good man and will help you and Lexus. In the meanwhile, we'll both have to keep an eye on her."

Boyd frowned again. Yes, he'd talk to the sheriff, but given the chance, he'd even the score.

# CHAPTER SEVEN

BOYD SAT IN a dilapidated rocker on the porch of his cabin. He knew that it was stretching things to call the shed a cabin, but in his mind, that's what it was. It was much larger than the cabin of his fishing boat, so the description fit. He rocked and watched the river flow by, noting the swirls and patterns on its surface. Frogs croaked along the river's bank as evening approached. Somewhere in the clearings along the river, whip-or-wills called, reminding him of the Greenbrier Valley and his time there. A bobwhite quail vocalized its evening hymn–*bob, bob white, bob, bob white.*

A motion caught his eye, and he saw a fat dog waddling toward him. It panted heavily and stopped occasionally to scratch itself. Its long ears drooped, and its eyes were bloodshot, but its tail arched proudly into the air over its back. The dog continued toward him slowly until it sat on the leaf-strewn ground in front of the porch and looked soulfully at him.

Boyd watched as the dog waited patiently. It licked its lips and wagged its tail. "What is it you want, boy?" he asked. The dog thumped its tail on the ground and then became still. Boyd went into the cabin and returned with a scrap of meat left over from dinner. He tossed it to the dog and expecting it to catch the meat in its mouth, was surprised when the meat struck the dog on the nose and dropped to the ground. The dog sniffed the offering, looked forlornly at Boyd and then slowly picked it up and shuffled away.

Boyd was still thinking about the dog when he heard footsteps on the path leading to the cabin. He peered into the gathering gloom and saw Rachel walking toward him. Oh dear, he thought, this can only be trouble.

"Hello there," she said with a smile. "I brought you some pumpkin bread." Her extended hand held a bundle wrapped in a napkin. "Mother just made it. It's still hot from the oven, and I thought you'd like some." She looked expectantly at Boyd. Her long, raven hair was combed carefully about her face and fell in ringlets on her shapely shoulders. She batted her long lashes at him.

"Why, thank you, Rachel. That's very thoughtful. I've just had supper, and I have nothing for dessert." She stepped onto the porch and handed him the cake. Its amazing smell wafted from the napkin. The way to a man's heart… No fool this woman, he thought. He put the aromatic bundle on the porch railing and invited her to sit in his rocker. He leaned against the railing a substantial distance from her, and said, "There was a dog here just now. It was really strange. He acted as if he knew me and expected me to give him something to eat. I did, and then he went away. Most dogs trot from one place to another, but he just walked and slowly at that."

Rachel tossed back her head and laughed. "That was Abe. He's the community dog. I don't know where he sleeps, but he spends the day going from one house to another begging for food. By the looks of him, he gets more than enough to eat. He's a smelly ole thing."

"Oh, well, that explains it. He seemed like a good old dog, but he'll be lucky not to be run over by a wagon or something, no faster than he moves."

Rachel tossed her head again making her ringlets bounce and swirl, clearly bored with talk about Abe. They talked casually about the war and what life was like in a small town, and Rachel told him about Lexus' visit back when they were kids. "We used to sneak out of the house at night and come and sit on the riverbank. We talked about New York and Paris and swore to each other that one day we'd go there. It didn't work out that way. So far, I haven't even gotten to ride the train, and they pass through town every day," she said bitterly.

"You just have to be patient, Rachel. You're young yet, and the war will be over one day, and that will change everything." She looked at him doubtfully.

"Lexus tells me that you were a sailor. That true?"

"Yes. I grew up sailing and fishing. My father and grand-father were fishermen, and so was I. I loved being a fisherman, but it was hard to make a living at it."

"If you loved it so much, why'd you leave?"

Good question, Boyd thought. Just why did I leave? "Guess I thought being a soldier would be more exciting."

"You were wounded, weren't you? A hero," she said, her eyes sparkling. "The soldiers here are just boys. They haven't fought yet, at least the ones I've talked to. I suppose the older ones have. I wish I was a man. I'd go fight too."

"Well, Rachel, fighting is nasty business. Killing other men isn't as heroic as you might think."

"Oh bosh!" she said. "You sound just like my father. That's what he said." She looked at him with a challenge in her beautiful eyes.

"I suppose I do, but that's what I think. Anyway, I'm on parole, so I'm out of it for the duration of the war. I gave my word."

"Well, that's okay I suppose since you fought, and you're a hero. Are you and Lexus in love?" she asked, changing the subject without taking a breath. "I think she's all moon-eyed about you."

Boyd was taken aback and didn't know how to answer such a frank question. Besides, he didn't know the answer. Good question, he thought, just what were his feelings for her? "Well, that's between Lexus and me, isn't it?"

She tossed her head again and laughed. Her eyes became large, and she looked carefully at him, trying to read his face. "Lexus is very pretty, don't you think? Who is Nellie? Were you in love with her too?" Another abrupt change of subject.

Good Lord, he thought, has Lexus told this woman everything she knows about me? He didn't understand women at all. To him, such things were private but evidently not to them. He wondered what else about him they had discussed. "Oh yes, I love them all," he said, joking. "Young or old, it doesn't matter to me. I love them all." He stood and motioned toward the encroaching darkness. "It'll soon be dark. Don't you think you'd better be getting along home before your daddy comes looking for you? I'll walk with you, if you want."

"I can find my way home, Boyd Houston," she said, smiling, "thank you very much. I hope you enjoy your dessert. I'll bring you something more, one day." She stood before him on tiptoe with her nose an inch from his and paused to look deep into his eyes, swirled her skirts and stepped from the porch. She disappeared up the path.

Boyd sank heavily into the rocker and took in a deep breath. Women are like thunderstorms, he thought. They come suddenly into your life with a lot of noise and turmoil, disrupt everything and then leave with the smell of ozone and perfume hanging in the air, tension and confusion washing over everything like rain. He wondered what that was all about, but deep down he knew. He didn't know much about women, but he wasn't entirely clueless. The question wasn't so much what it was all about, but rather, how was he going to handle it?

He took the napkin-wrapped parcel from the porch rail and carefully opened it, drawing in the wonderful smell. He broke off a large chunk and placed it in his mouth, savoring its flavor. It was really good. A low whine caught his attention. Abe had magically appeared and was prancing in circles, licking his lips. He sat down and thumped his tail.

\* \* \* \*

Sergeant Brown hung back in the deepening shadows. He watched the man sitting on the porch of the shack, talking to a mangy dog. Who is he? He seemed vaguely familiar, but he couldn't immediately place him. Then it came to him. He was the man who had escorted Lexus here from Lewisburg.

The Sergeant had followed the girl from the big house in town thinking at first that it was Lexus, but he soon saw that she had black hair, unlike Lexus' blond tresses. He had followed her anyway, liking her looks, and she had soon led him to the man who lived in the shed. The man was tall and slim with broad shoulders, thick forearms and strong looking hands. Not someone he wanted to tangle with on an even plane, but there were always ways to get the upper hand. Fighting fair was for fools. A shot from the dark was much better. But not yet, not until he found out what he was doing here.

He returned to the big white house and sneaked behind it, stretching on his tiptoes to look in the windows, confident that the darkness gave him cover. Lamps flickered in their wall brackets, casting a warm glow over the home's interior, and a mummer of voices flowed from the open windows. He knew that he was taking a huge risk sneaking around in the dark, but he just couldn't resist seeing Lexus again. He finally caught a glimpse of her as she walked up the staircase to the second floor. Soon, a light came on in a back bedroom. Well now, he thought, it was worth the risk to find out where her bedroom was located. They'd meet again soon enough, and then after he'd had his way with her, he'd slit her throat. Just you wait and see, Lexus Saunders, just you wait and see.

\*  \*  \*  \*

The locomotive engine grunted and growled, its wheels alternately slipping and grabbing as sand poured onto the track from under the train, giving traction as it slowly gained momentum. The great beast chugged and clanged, and a billow of dark smoke rose from its stacks briefly obscuring the depot. The cars jerked and banged as the moving train took up slack between them. The racket echoed off the mountains that surrounded the town. The train was made up of a long string of coal and freight cars and two passenger gondolas. As its speed slowly increased, it headed west toward Tunnelton where it would make its first stop. It would only take half an hour since the town was only a few miles away.

Boyd, Lexus and Rachel sat in the passenger car and watched with fascination as the train left town and began the long pull up along the side of the mountain. None of the three had ever ridden in a train before, and they were excited. The women chattered constantly with the novelty of it. Rachel talked nonstop about how grand the car was and how this was the only way to travel. No more horses and carriages for her. She could go to Baltimore or even New York if she had only a little money.

Boyd sat stoically as the scenery passed by–trees and raw earth from the railroad bed had been gouged from the mountain and streamed down its side. They had unrestricted views of the river valley far below. Boyd caught his breath as the train crossed a viaduct, and the valley fell away below. They crossed a second longer one a short time later. For a flatlander like Boyd, the height was breathtaking. His knuckles were white from gripping the seat-rests. They saw an area covering several acres of woodland near the tracks that had recently burned. The conductor told them that it was caused by sparks from the engine. Soon, the train topped the summit and began to speed up. The trio was astounded with the speed with which they were traveling.

All too soon, the train began to slow with its brakes screeching and steam swirling. They laughed with the thrill of it all and walked from window to window in fear they'd miss something. The cars began bucking and jerking as the train slowed and stopped. Just outside their car they saw a small depot and a scattering of houses and buildings. The conductor deftly produced a set of portable stairs for them to use to disembark, and Rachel swept down to the platform with a swish of her skirts, a triumphant look in her eyes.

Workers swarmed around the train as they loaded and unloaded boxes and crates of goods. One man waited excitedly as a large wooden barrel was unloaded with *Baltimore Fish and Seafood Co.* stamped on its side. Boyd asked him what was inside and he said, "Why, they're oysters in there, all the way from the Chesapeake Bay, that's what. I have never et oysters before, but I'm going to try them," he said proudly. "Imagine that," he exclaimed, "fresh oysters only a couple of days out of the bay."

"Have you ever eaten oysters, Boyd? I'll bet you have, haven't you? What were they like? Did you like them?" Rachel asked breathlessly.

"Yes, I have. Often. And, yes I like them just fine, but they're an acquired taste. I hope that man likes them," he said, grinning. Lexus smiled stiffly looking askance at Rachel.

Boyd quickly hired a hack to transport them to Kingwood. It was an awfully extravagant way to get there, but Rachel had begged her father to allow her to ride the train, even if it was for a half hour each way, and it was another eight or ten miles to town. It would have been much more economical to use Mr. Saunders' horse and buggy. But, Rachel had won in the end, as she usually did, and the three had enjoyed the ride immensely. They looked forward to the return ride on the evening train.

They soon left Tunnelton behind after marveling at the tunnel's yawning mouth. The depot clerk had bragged it was the longest hand-dug tunnel in the world. Soldiers loitered at the depot and along the approach-way to the tunnel.

The rented horse trotted along easily, pulling the hack without effort. They'd be in town soon, they thought, but the pike took a sharp upward turn that soon had the horse lathered. Boyd decided to stop at a farmhouse for water and a brief rest. They knocked on the door, and it was opened by a man of middle age. Two young boys hung back in the doorway.

"And what can I be doin' for ye?" he asked with a melodious Welsh accent.

"Our horse is about winded, and we need for it to rest and maybe have a drink of water," Boyd said hopefully.

"Well and now ye have come to the right place, my friend," he said. "Bring 'im on around the house to the cowshed and he can have a drink from the trough there." He led them behind the house with a spring in his step. The boys tagged along, watching them. "Ye help yerself, now. Water 'n' rest are always to be free my daddy tol' me once upon a time."

Boyd and the two young women talked with the man, learning that he had once worked at the foundry in Mount Savage near Cumberland where they made iron railroad track. He had met his wife there, and they now had the two boys and had moved here when they bought the farm. He had immigrated from Wales more than a decade ago.

When they again climbed onto the hack, Boyd thanked him and offered to pay, but the man would have none of it. "Ye come back again and meet the missus. She pines something frightful for a woman's company." He stepped back from the hack and waved solemnly as they moved away. The boys waved to them as the horse trotted up the pike. They arrived in the county seat before lunchtime.

Kingwood was a bustling town, perched on a mountaintop far above the river. A flagpole, over a hundred feet high, displayed a long streamer with the word "Union" prominently embossed upon it. On a side street, a two-story academy building bustled with students and faculty. Store buildings with tall false fronts crowded together along Main Street and intersecting Price Street. Horses, tied to hitching posts and metal rings in the sidewalk, stood sleeping with drooping heads. The morning sun pounded down on the town, promising a hot, muggy afternoon. Three children and a dog waited impatiently for their parents in the bed of a large farm wagon. They waved merrily as Boyd and the two young women passed in their rented hack. Pedestrians paused to watch as they made their way up the street.

Boyd tied the horse under a shade tree in front of the three-story, brick courthouse and helped Lexus and Rachel down. They entered the cool interior of the building to the dank smell of old sweat and moldering paper. The county clerk's first floor office was brightly lit by a bank of windows along one side, and men and a few women, toiled at desks, sorting and filing papers into large folders. Boyd had no idea what the papers were or what purpose they served. He stepped to the counter and asked the clerk where he could find the deed to Mr. Saunders' property.

The clerk had large brown eyes behind a pair of wire-rimmed spectacles and was short and pudgy. "The Saunders property, eh? That's up on the river above Rowlesburg on Little Wolf Crick if I remember correctly. Deeds are down in the lower level. Jimmy Smith is in charge of deeds."

"Thank you," Boyd said, and turned toward the door.

"He isn't here," the man said before Boyd and the women could leave. "He hasn't been to work for over a week now. Don't know where he is." The clerk looked at Boyd without expression. "He isn't here," he said again.

"When will he be back?" Boyd asked.

"Don't know when he'll be back. He just disappeared. The county clerk's been looking for him."

"Well, is there any way I could take a look at the records down there? Is there someone else who could help me?"

"I reckon I could. Don't know as much about deeds as Jimmy, but I'll try to help." He lifted a hinged section of the counter and walked toward the door, beckoning them to follow. They made their way down a narrow set of stairs to the lower level that was lit by narrow windows. Lamps in wall holders cast a yellow light on the space, and the air was stuffy with the odor of mold and musty paper. Parallel rows of shelves held a bewildering array of large binders, each with beginning and ending dates for their contents embossed on their spines.

"You have any idea when Saunders bought the property? The deeds are arranged by the dates of their sales."

"No, I don't have any idea. Mr. Saunders said that he had inherited the property from his father."

"Well that helps. Let's look at the will books." With only a little searching, the clerk found Mr. Saunders' father's will, and from that he found a reference to the volume and page number in the deed book. He quickly found the appropriate volume and opened it, paging through it carefully.

"Well now, that's funny," the clerk mumbled to himself. "The deed's gone. It isn't here." He showed Boyd the pages, flipping them back and forth. "See here? This is the last page of the previous deed," he said, pointing the number stamped at the top of the page, "but the next three pages are missing. That's where the Saunders deed should be. It peers as if someone took the binder apart and took the deed, and then he put the binder back together. That's all I can figure." He scratched his thatch of wiry hair as he stared at the binder. Lexus and Rachel looked over his shoulder. They climbed back up the narrow stairs to the clerk's office, their footfalls and voices echoing in the closed stairwell.

"Tell me, mister, er, I don't know your name," Boyd said.

"Ed. My name's Edward, but I go by Ed."

"Okay, Ed, tell me, if the property was sold, where would the transaction be recorded?" Boyd asked.

"In the deed books downstairs, just where we come from," he said with an exasperated look on his face. "You want to go back down there and look?"

"Tell you what, Ed. Why don't you just go see if you can find it and bring it back up here?"

"Look here," the man blustered, "I got a lot of work to do."

Boyd cut him off, saying, "Okay, Ed, how about if I give you a dollar for your time? No one has to know, and we'll both be satisfied."

The clerk grinned and said, "Well, I reckon I could do that." He left the office and Boyd and the two women looked at each other and shook their heads. A few minutes later, Ed came back into the room carrying a binder with a triumphant look on his face. "Here 'tis." He tossed the heavy volume onto the counter and opened it to a dog-eared page. "It's right here. The deed says that property was sold to the Little Wolf Company. Never heard of it. No name is listed as the owner, just the company name."

"Someone must have written the deed. Who would that be?"

"Jimmy. Jimmy Smith, but he isn't here. Don't know where he is or when he'll be back."

"How about a lawyer? Don't you need one to write it up to be legal?" Boyd asked.

"No, anyone can write up a deed and file it with us. That's 'bout all there is to it."

"Wouldn't the seller have to sign the new deed?"

Ed slid his index finger down the last page of the deed to the signature line. "Right here. See? Mr. Saunders signed it, all legal and proper."

Boyd looked closely at the deed. He had never seen Mr. Saunders' signature, so he had no idea if it was his or not, but he said, "He didn't sign this. Someone must have forged his signature. Who would have received the deed?" Boyd asked, but he already knew the answer.

"Jimmy Smith!" Ed cackled. "Looks like you're at a dead end. Now, give me my dollar." The clerk extended his hand with a big grin on his face, his eyes twinkling.

Lexus, Rachel and Boyd sat on a long bench in front of the courthouse eating the lunch they had brought with them. A large oak tree shaded the lawn and cast a pleasant shadow upon them, providing a pleasant relief from the stifling heat of the day. A large wagon loaded with shelled buckwheat came up the hill on Main Street, dust rising behind it. A long-legged hound trotted along beside it with its tongue hanging out of the side of its mouth. The wagon creaked and groaned with its load and the matched pair of horses strained, their muscles bunched, to pull it up the steep hill. The Union pennant hung limply from its pole.

Lexus fanned herself with her hand and asked, "What can we do now, Boyd? Uncle Frank can't prove he owns the property if the original deed's gone and a new one written." She frowned then smiled at him. "I know it's not your responsibility, but do you have any ideas?" Rachel looked expectantly at him.

"As a matter of fact, I do. We're going to go see the sheriff. Maybe he can help us file a complaint. If we can get a judge to hear the case, whoever is behind this will have to show up to defend his claim. Besides, we need to tell the sheriff about the Sergeant and see if we can get him to arrest the man."

They reentered the courthouse and soon found the sheriff's office on the second floor. It was in a small room toward the back of the building. The door had a large rippled-glass panel in its upper half, and large letters proclaimed the tenant was sheriff of Preston County. His name was stenciled in below–Arthur Petrowski. Boyd rapped on the glass and then opened the door and stepped inside. The two women followed. The man who sat behind an oak desk toward the back of the office looked up at them expectantly. "Yes? What can I do for you?" He was a large man with huge shoulders. A sweat-stained hat hung on a peg behind him, and a large silver star was pinned to his suspenders.

"Are you the sheriff?" Boyd asked. "We need to talk to you if you have a few minutes."

"I'm the sheriff. What kind of problem do youins have?"

Boyd introduced himself and the two women. "Oh yes, I know Miss Rachel. I've known her since she was a child." He nodded at her and smiled. "I can't say I know Miss Lexus there. I've never seen you before, and I have a pretty good memory for faces and names. Guess I wouldn't be much of a lawman if I didn't."

Boyd briefly explained how he and Lexus came to be in Preston County and gave him a quick description of Frank's problem with the deed. The sheriff listened carefully, making notes on a pad of paper.

"Now, let me get this straight," the sheriff said. "Frank's deed for the property up on Little Wolf Crick is missing, and someone else has written a deed on it. What did Jimmy Smith have to say about that? He's in charge of deeds."

"He seems to have disappeared. No one in the clerk's office knows where he's got to," Boyd said. "So, we're stuck. Mr. Saunders asked me to sort this out, but I don't seem to be getting anywhere. You have any suggestions?"

The sheriff leaned back in his chair and ran his fingers through his damp hair only to make it stand up in clumps. He combed it down with his fingers and looked thoughtfully up toward a large crack running across the ceiling. A brown water stain spread from its end, and it was this that the man seemed to be studying. "Well, the only thing I can think of is for Mr. Saunders to file a suit challenging the new deed in circuit court. The prosecuting attorney might be interested, too, if there's fraud involved, but that's getting the cart before the horse. Yeah, now that I think about it, I'd file the suit and see what Judge Hannah has to say about it."

"Thanks, Sheriff. Those were my thoughts, too. How do you go about filing a suit? I assume there's a lot of paperwork to be done."

"Not so much as you would think. All you have to do is fill out a form or two, and you're in business. Unfortunately, anyone can sue anyone for just about anything, anytime. Lots of frivolous suits are filed, but they don't get very far. The judge doesn't take kindly to folks filing suits for every little ole thing. He kicks them right out of the courtroom and maybe fines them for contempt of court. He doesn't suffer fools lightly. Oh yes, besides the forms there's a five dollar filing fee. The circuit clerk can help you do the filing."

"There's another thing, Sheriff. Miss Lexus is fearful for her life," Boyd said. He quickly told the sheriff about the renegade soldiers and Lexus' abduction. The sheriff carefully questioned Lexus, his face getting redder with each answer. Lexus dabbed at the corners of her eyes with her handkerchief and Rachel frowned and wrung her hands. Boyd stood quietly as he listened to Lexus answer the sheriff's pointed questions. When the sheriff was done, he turned his note pad over on his desk and patted her on the shoulder.

"I'll send a deputy to Rowlesburg to see if he can round up this scoundrel. From your description, we should be able to locate him pretty handily. It's not that big of a town. Don't you worry now dear, we'll find him and then he'll have to face Judge Hannah. He'll put him *under* the jailhouse!"

They went to the circuit clerk's office and soon had a stack of forms to fill out for the suit. Boyd offered to pay the clerk the five dollar fee but was told that it would be due when Mr. Saunders submitted the forms for processing. They were soon in the hack and headed to the depot at Tunnelton to catch the evening train back to Rowlesburg. Rachel talked excitedly about riding the train again.

Before their hack was out of sight, a man left the circuit clerk's office and stopped in an alcove to write a quick message to J. Martin Tingle. He told him about Boyd picking up papers to file a suit against the new deed for the property. He smiled thinking about the five dollars he would be paid for the information. He stuffed the message in an envelope, affixed a stamp and walked to the post office. He handed it to the postmaster ensuring it would be in the evening mail to Rowlesburg.

* * * *

Boyd and Lexus scrambled up the steep mountainside, following the rough road to Cannon Hill. It was much used by soldiers climbing to the mountaintop from their encampment along the river. Boyd had marveled at the stories about how mountain howitzers had been hauled to the top of the mountain by a local farmer and his oxen. The artillerymen had set up a camp on the peak and erected a Union flag.

They paused to rest on a fallen log along the road. They were only halfway up the mountain, but they already had a breathtaking view of the town below. Sweat poured from their faces, and Lexus' dress had a ring of dirt around the hem. Their hands were dirty, and their faces were flushed with the exertion. Boyd removed his hat and wiped its lining and then his face with his handkerchief.

"Whew! It's hot. It's a good thing that we got an early start," Boyd said. "By afternoon, we'll have a rainstorm. You can see those big, fluffy clouds beginning to pile up already and the air is heavy with moisture."

"Yes, it's hot, but just look at that view. Everyone in town says that it's worth the climb. Rachel said that when she was just a little girl, Uncle Frank brought her up here. It was exciting for her."

"I'm sure it was. We all remember special times like that, especially when we have a parent all to ourselves for an afternoon. I remember the times I spent with my father."

"Boyd, you've never told me much about your work as a fisherman. Is that where you got that scar on the back of your hand?" She gently touched the shiny, red weal with her fingertips.

"Yes, it's a rope scar. When I was young, just learning about the boat and how to fish, I made the mistake of wrapping a line–that's what sailors call a rope–around my hand. When we swung the net full of fish into the boat, the rope slid and burned the skin off my hand. It didn't hurt much, but it left a pretty bad scar. It's just one of the many hazards of fishing, but it's not much different from other kinds of manual work."

"Did you enjoy fishing? Do you plan to return?" she asked. She watched him carefully, trying to read his features. She was fearful of his answer.

"I truly don't know. As I told you before, my father died at sea. He went out in the boat one day and never returned. I never knew how it happened, but I just knew he was gone. My mother died when I was very young, and they were all the family I had. My father never remarried, and I could tell when he was thinking about her. He'd get very quiet and go out on the porch and sit, and rock, and look out at the sea. All it would take was to see her things still hanging in the closet, or someone would mention her name, and he would be gone for days. Oh, he was still there, but he just wasn't with us. And then after a day, or sometimes several days, he'd be back to normal, just like himself again. Some folks only get one chance at finding the right person, and when they're gone, that's all there is. What do you think, Lexus? Can a person fall in love more than once?"

She turned toward him and said, "I believe so. At least some can. I think my mother died mourning for my father, but they were older. Maybe older people who have lived together for years have a harder time of it. But, yes, I believe that a person can fall in love more than once. Why, when I was a teenager, I was in love with a different boy just about every week," she said, laughing. "And, if you remember, you were one of them."

Boyd leaned back and looked at her. "I'm surprised. I thought you hated me."

"Oh, I did, and I thought I loved you too. It was all very confusing." She laughed again and then became serious. "Forgive me for asking, Boyd, but did you love Nellie? Oh! You don't have to answer if you don't want to. I didn't mean to ask that," she said, her face flushing, "but it just popped out of my mouth."

"I don't mind answering. Yes, I loved her, but she wanted her freedom and to be on her own, and like it or not, I had to agree. It was the hardest thing I ever had to do. It wasn't what I wanted at the time, but it was what fate gave me, and I had to accept it. But it's funny, when I think about her now, I can't remember her face. I try to, but I just can't. I've heard people say the same thing after losing a loved one. It's frightening, but maybe that's the way it has to happen for us to be able to move on. The memory just fades until there's room in your heart for another person. It just fades and fades until there's only a ghost left of what was there before. What about you, Lexus? Could you fall in love more than once?"

She answered quickly, almost in a whisper, "I don't know Boyd. I've never been in love before."

Although he often had trouble understanding women, this time he was listening to her answer carefully. And, in her answer he learned what he needed to know. She had said *before*. She hadn't been in love *before*. "I think that I can love again, Lexus," he said.

"Oh Boyd, I hope you can," she said. And, before they could think about it, she was in his arms. He pressed his face into her hair, drawing in the fresh smell of soap and the faintest hint of cinnamon. He closed his eyes, drew her tighter still and smiled.

They were startled by a slide of rocks and dirt from the trail above, and they heard the voices of approaching soldiers. Two young men, carrying their muskets casually, stumbled down toward them. They stopped abruptly, surprised to see Boyd and Lexus sitting on the log.

"Uh, sorry youins. We didn't mean to interrupt anything," the younger of the two said, grinning. "We got to get back to camp before those others eat everything. It's dinnertime. Our relief has already clumb up." The two soldiers stood awkwardly, shuffling their feet. Then, abruptly, they dove on down the trail. From far below, Boyd and Lexus could hear their laughter. As abruptly as they had come, they were gone.

Boyd and Lexus chuckled and resumed the climb up Cannon Hill. Soon they were on the top of the mountain. A small area had been cleared and fortified with stones and logs. The howitzers had been set up and aimed toward the town five hundred feet below. From that point, the Army could command all approaches to the town and protect the railroad trestle. It was a strategic emplacement, and the Union Army guarded it jealously.

From that elevation, they could see the town snuggled in a sweeping horseshoe bend. The railroad spilled from the narrow valley formed by Salt Lick Creek and onto the trestle that crossed the Cheat River. The depot looked like a toy, and rounded, green-clad mountains rose all around. Trees of every shade of green colored the forests clinging to the steep mountainsides, and the river was interrupted here and there by whitewater. Far below a bald eagle floated on the thermals, patrolling the river for its quarry, and they heard the *quark* of a raven.

The soldiers hung back, giving them some semblance of privacy as they stood, arm in arm, taking in the vista. Miniature people went about their business on the streets far below. Lexus leaned her head on Boyd's shoulder–an unspoken commitment bound them together, and they would not be the same again. They didn't know what the future held for them, but one thing was sure; something profound had happened to them halfway up Cannon Hill.

\* \* \* \*

J. Martin Tingle looked out the window in his office in the back of his dry goods store as robins squabbled in the mulberry tree outside. He turned away and started pacing, jingling some coins in his pocket. A light coating of cinders covered the desktop and filing cabinets, but he wasn't thinking about housekeeping. It had been two days since he received the message from the clerk in the courthouse, and he was having second thoughts about trying to steal Saunders' property. What had he been thinking? What had possessed him to think that he could get away with this ill-conceived scheme? Now, the sheriff would be after him and he'd lose everything. Worse yet, he could go to jail. The thought made him shiver. The more he thought about it the more it made his stomach ache.

His only salvation would be to fail to show up to answer the suit. His name wasn't on the deed. No one knew what he had done, except for Jimmy Smith. Maybe he could buy him off. At the worst, he'd plead ignorance, and all of this would blow over. Oh, what a mess he had gotten himself into.

He heard heavy footsteps approach his office door, and loud knocking made him flinch. He told whoever it was to come in and was startled to see the Sergeant stride into the office.

"We need to talk, *Mister* Tingle. You owe me a lot of money," he said. He sat down in Tingle's chair, placed his heavy boots on the desktop, leaned back and placed both hands behind his head, grinning broadly.

"What do you mean I owe you money? I've paid you everything you have coming. And, get your feet off my desk, and get out of my chair."

The Sergeant ignored his commands. "You owe me for that little job I did about the deed clerk. What was his name? Jimmy something?"

Tingle gasped. "What did you do? I didn't tell you to do anything to Jimmy."

"No? Well, just what do you suppose would happen when he went blabbing to the sheriff? You know he was going to, sooner or later. Even if he didn't blab, he'd be on your payroll for the rest of your life. So, I took care of 'im."

Tingle covered his ears with his hands. "Don't tell me! I don't want anything to do with you. Get out! Get out, right now! Why, I'll tell the sheriff myself." Why did he become involved with this ruffian?

The Sergeant let out a loud guffaw. "It's a little late to be thinkin' about backin' out now. We'll see this thing through to the end. I want my share of the profits from that property, and you ain't going to cheat me out of 'em. As a matter of fact, I think I should get a bigger cut, so you owe me. Right now!" He slammed his palm down on the desk, and the two men glared at each other.

Tingle's face flushed red as he suddenly sat down heavily in the spare office chair, and then he told the Sergeant about Saunders' pending lawsuit. "If he files that suit, the judge will revoke our deed unless we show up to defend it." He stared at the horrible man sitting in his chair, and then his shoulders slumped. He leaned forward and placed his elbows on his knees and hung his head in dismay. He wondered how he was ever going to get out of this mess. He took a stack of bills out of the office safe and handed them to the Sergeant. "Now, get out of here. Our business association is over."

The Sergeant laughed and said, "Not hardly, Tingle. Not hardly. Here's what we're going to do. I'll catch Saunders alone and talk some sense into 'im. He has a beautiful daughter and a right good looking niece to think about, not to mention a wife. I'll tell him in great detail what I'll do to them if he doesn't drop the suit, and he'll come right around. Or else."

"You can't go around threatening people like that," Tingle said.

"Of course I can. It happens all the time. How do you think business is done?" He got up and walked to the office door and with a smirk on his face said, "I knocked 'im in the head and threw him in the old quarry along the river. They'll never find 'im."

Tingle clasped his hands over his ears again. "Who are you talking about? Jimmy? You killed him? I didn't hear that. I didn't have anything to do with that. It's on your head." He paced around the office again, wringing his hands.

"Whatever you say, *Mister* Tingle," the Sergeant said laughing. "You just leave this to me. I'll take care of everything." He swaggered out of the office, leaving the door standing open.

Tingle sat in his chair and put his arms and head down on the desk. He was horrified at this turn of events, but was relieved nonetheless. He hadn't planned to kill anyone, but maybe this would work out. He'd get the Sergeant to do the dirty work and then pay him off. He wasn't about to split his profits with that crude man. He sat up in his chair and rubbed his throbbing temples. No, this wasn't how he had planned it, but he just might wiggle out of this yet and make a nice profit at that. He'd have to be very careful–he could lose everything he had worked for–but with a little luck, he just might be able to pull it off. He'd have to get rid of the Sergeant, but he'd wait until the dirty work was done. The Sergeant could be very useful, but eventually he'd have to be dealt with. Yes, this could work out. He'd make it work. He had to.

\* \* \* \*

A few days later, Frank drew Boyd aside. "Do you have a few minutes? I'd like to talk to you."

"Sure. What is it?" Boyd asked.

"There's a new development about the suit. A man stopped me on the street. He was big and dirty-looking, and he had a mean way about him."

"What did he want? What did he say?"

"He threatened me in no uncertain terms. He told me to forget about filing a suit, or else."

"Or else what?"

"Or else he'd kill my whole family," Frank said. "He looked like the kind of man who'd do it. You don't think he's the man who's been following Lexus, do you?"

"I don't know, but it seems unlikely. I don't see how the two things could be related. What did you tell him?"

"I told him in no uncertain terms that I'd get the sheriff after him and to leave my family alone. He just laughed and said I'd had fair warning. It sent chills up and down my spine. He left before I could get anyone to help."

"How do you suppose he knew you were going to file suit? Have you mentioned it to anyone?" Boyd asked.

"No, the only thing I can think of is that someone at the courthouse is involved somehow."

"I guess that could be," Boyd said. "It's a small community and people just seem to know everything that goes on. Maybe someone was hanging around and heard the clerks talking."

*\*\*\**

Boyd and Lexus sat in Mr. Saunders' parlor with their heads together, hands touching. They had talked for hours and now they laughed at something Boyd was saying. Mr. Saunders strode into the room, and Boyd stood to shake his hand.

"Boyd I'm glad you're here. I've been thinking about that problem with my property. I've filled out the suit papers and will post them first thing in the morning, but I think I'd better ride up on Little Wolf Creek and take a look at that land. I haven't been up there for years. Would you be willing to go along with me? I hate to ask you to do more than you already have, but for all I know, someone could be taking timber out of there."

"Yes, I'd be happy to help. When do you want to go?"

"Right now, if you're free." He looked at Lexus. "How about it young lady? Can you spare your beau for a few hours?"

Lexus smiled and said, "Of course Uncle Frank. I think I can live without him for an afternoon, but only that."

Boyd walked to the livery and saddled his horse. It had been exercised each day, but with good grain and grass to eat, it had added a few pounds. He mounted and gritted his teeth as the horse bucked stiff-legged a couple of times before trotting along to the Saunders house. By the time he arrived, Mr. Saunders was mounted and ready to start. They traveled out of town, up the river, and soon encountered the breastworks and the detachment of soldiers on guard there. The soldiers waved at Mr. Saunders as they passed, and Boyd sighed in relief that he hadn't had to present his papers again. They trotted along pleasantly until they came to the Northwestern Turnpike where they turned east. Boyd and Mr. Saunders conversed pleasantly, passing the time as they rode. Boyd told him about some of his experiences as a sailor and being wounded in the Battle of Lewisburg. He fondly told him about Charlie and his family.

As they traveled, Boyd noticed telegraph poles and wire along the pike. When asked about it, Mr. Saunders explained that the Army had a telegraph in town and one at the covered bridge just ahead. "They use it to keep in contact with the men guarding the bridge. If the Confederates return, they might decide to burn it. The Army is determined to prevent that from happening. The telegraph can also be used to warn the camp in town if the Confederates are coming to attack the railroad bridge again."

They soon came to a long, covered bridge and were challenged by the guards posted there. Mr. Saunders identified himself, and they were allowed to proceed. Boyd's horse snorted and pranced at the sudden explosion of sound made by the wings of dozens of pigeons that flew from their roost in the bridge's rafters.

The valley widened somewhat, and they passed a scattering of houses along the road. The pike paralleled the river for another mile or two and then began an abrupt, steep climb up the side of the mountain. Instead of climbing out of the valley, they turned off the pike and followed a rough trail that wound around the base of the mountain. They splashed through a small stream, and soon the trail petered out. Mr. Saunders called a halt, dismounting and tying his horse to a sapling. They could hear the river whispering nearby.

"That was Little Wolf Creek we just crossed. I know, it doesn't seem like much, but when it rains it's something to behold where it comes down out of the mountains. We're almost to a place on the river called Seven Islands. Another ten miles or so and you come to St. George."

"Lexus and I stayed overnight there when we came from Lewisburg," Boyd said, "but we crossed over to Buffalo Creek instead of following the river all the way around this big bend."

Mr. Saunders pointed to a large tree and said, "There's the blaze that marks the southern boundary of my property. The deed says it contains all of the land in Little Wolf Creek's watershed. It ranges from here to the top of the mountain, and there's more along the river. There's almost two thousand acres." He looked around them and said, "It doesn't look like anyone has been here for ages."

Boyd looked in wonder at the towering timber all around him. "Just what kind of trees are they? You have to remember that I'm a fisherman. I don't know one tree from another."

Mr. Saunders chuckled and said, "Mostly red oak, some hemlock, and chestnut. See the burrs on that chestnut tree? They're the hulls that contain the nuts. Folks around here turn their hogs out during the summer to feed on them, and deer, bear and other animals eat them, too. The lumber is strong and has a straight grain. Most of the houses around here are made of chestnut. The oak is good, strong lumber, too, and there's some hard maple in there, higher up on the mountainside. There are sycamores along the stream, but it's not worth as much as the rest. All in all, I guess this stand of trees is worth a lot of money if I can get it to market."

"I heard someone claim you can float the logs down the river. It doesn't look like there's enough water in it to float a large beaver, let alone a huge tree like this one," Boyd said.

"In late winter and spring, when the snow melts, the river gets up and will have plenty of water to float barges of logs, and maybe someday the railroad will build a branch up here. That would make it feasible to cut the timber and get it to market, but that's a pipe dream right now with the war still raging. Besides, there's hardly any market for lumber now. The Army buys some now and then, mostly railroad ties and telegraph poles, but not much else, and the B&O doesn't burn wood in their engines since they switched to coal. I wish this terrible war would end. All that senseless killing!"

It was approaching dusk as they set out for town. They crossed the covered bridge again and waved at the guards as they made their way down the river. Campfires smoked, and men lounged around them, smoking and talking. Tin plates, pots and pans were stacked on makeshift tables, and a row of tents slouched in the falling dew. Muskets were stacked like pole bean stakes within easy reach. As they passed, pickets leaned on their muskets and watched them, looking over their horses. Wind sighed through the hemlocks along the river, and pigeons roosted in the branches high above the pike. A pale, quarter moon hung low in the sky.

"We'd best be getting along, Mr. Saunders. It'll be full dark by the time we get home. That moon won't give us much light to ride by," Boyd said.

"I suppose so. I have to tell you, Boyd, I enjoy your company. I've lived with two women long enough to miss having a man to talk to, not that I'm complaining you understand. I hope you'll see fit to settle close around here."

Boyd chuckled and said, "Let's not get the cart before the horse, Mr. Saunders."

"You know, it's time for you to call me by my first name. Call me Frank."

"Why, thank you, Frank. I'd be pleased to."

They trotted their horses along the pike and then turned north on the river road to town. They passed the army pickets and guards at the barricade again without incident, but as they came out of the mouth of the canyon at the edge of town, they saw smoke and flames belching from Frank's house. They spurred the horses into a gallop and soon arrived at the burning home. Soldiers and some of the town's men ran frantically about, throwing buckets of water in the windows and the front door.

"Where're Martha and the girls?" Frank shouted to the men. "Has anyone seen Martha and the girls?"

A large, strapping man with a soot stained face approached and said solemnly, "They're at the neighbor's house, but I'm afraid Rachel's hurt pretty bad."

"What? Did she get burned?" Frank asked, worry showing on his face.

"No, not burned. Someone said she'd been beaten pretty bad."

"Beaten? How'd that happen?" Boyd asked.

"I don't know," the man said. "You'll have to ask them."

Boyd and Frank walked swiftly to the neighbor's house and mounted the front steps. They knocked, and Frank's worried-looking neighbor came to the door. "Come on in," the man said. He folded his arms across his chest and looked grimly at Frank and Boyd. "She's pretty bad, Frank. Someone jumped her and hurt her bad. She was on the way back from your shack, Boyd. Don't know what she was doing there," he said, frowning at Boyd. "The doctor's on the way, but he had a baby to deliver somewhere on the other side of town."

"I was with Frank here. We were up the river looking at his property," Boyd said, feeling it was necessary to say where he was when Rachel was attacked.

Frank and Boyd found Rachel wrapped in a quilt and laying on a bed in an upstairs bedroom. Her face was badly bruised, and one eye was swollen shut. She had a damp cloth on her forehead, and her eyes were closed. Lexus sat on the side of the bed beside her, holding her hand, and Mrs. Saunders hovered over her, trying to sooth her. The neighbor woman stood to the side with a troubled look on her face. Rachel's body shook as she sobbed, and blood leaked from her split lips, dripping onto her clothing. A washbowl of reddened water sat on a nightstand beside a pile of blood-soaked cloths.

Boyd caught Lexus' attention, a look of question on his face. She turned away from him, her gaze going back to her cousin. Lexus' face was as pale as if all blood had been drained from her, and a sob escaped from her throat. Boyd went to her and placed his hand on her shoulder, but she shook it off and averted her face from him again. "Who did this to her?" he asked.

Without looking at Boyd, she said in a guttural whisper, a catch in her voice, "It was him!"

# CHAPTER EIGHT

THE SERGEANT WATCHED the smoking house from the shadows as men scurried about dousing glowing embers with water. The house steamed and smoked and smelled like a smoldering trash heap. The windows on the first floor were broken out where the firefighters had gained access to douse the flames. The yawning openings resembled the eye sockets of a skull, and dark, sooty stains marred the wall above them where the flames had licked the white clapboard siding. The front porch sagged at one end. The men's voices echoed from the sides of the neighboring houses as a ring of curious neighbors gawked and pointed at the burned-out hulk from the surrounding darkness.

He chuckled to himself at the sight. Their response was just what he had hoped for. The more trepidation and confusion he could create, the easier it would be for him to get Saunders to knuckle under. And, catching that girl alone in the woods had been a bonus. Just thinking about her soft body caused his emotions to stir. As much as he enjoyed hearing her sob and beg, he would enjoy her cousin even more. He had let her go so that she would tell her father what had been done to her, but that other one wouldn't be so fortunate. His dark features contorted in fury, and his huge hands knotted into fists.

He faded back into the trees and was soon walking toward the town's business district. The stores and other businesses were closed for the night, and dark shadows draped the alleyways between the false-fronted buildings that lined the street. He saw a flicker of light in a back window of the dry goods store just about where the office was located. He walked down the alley between the buildings and looked in the window. Tingle was hunched over a dog-eared ledger, making entries with a stub of yellow pencil. The Sergeant pecked loudly on the window with a grubby knuckle and sniggered when the man jumped. Tingle came to the back door and waved him in.

"What are you doing out this time of night?" Tingle asked him.

"Why, I'm working, just like you. I seen you countin' up your money in that little book there."

"That's part of being a businessman. Sometimes you have to work late to get caught up. Being the owner, I don't always get to go home at the end of business hours, unlike my employees. It's part of being the boss."

"Well, *Boss*, my work is done for the night, too, and I'm goin' to go get a drink. I just thought I'd report in since you're burning the midnight oil." He looked at Tingle with disrespect.

"Report in? What do you have to report?"

"I've taken things into my own hands, *Mister* Tingle. I reckon you've heard all the commotion about the fire up the street."

"Yeah, sure. I talked to one of the soldiers who was hurrying up that way. He said Mr. Saunders' house had caught fire. Say, you didn't have anything to do with that did you?"

"Of course I did. I thought I'd soften him up a might bit more after I had my talk with him. I gave his daughter what for, too!"

Tingle sat down in his chair with a thump. "Good God, you're going to get us both strung up. You might get away with setting a fire, but you'll get folks all riled up messing with a woman. You didn't kill her, did you?"

"No, I didn't kill her," he said. "I'm not stupid. What good would a dead daughter do us? I'm just giving Saunders something to think about. He'll drop his challenge of our claim on the timberland. Just applyin' a little pressure. I'll give him a day or two to think about it, and then I'll have another heart-to-heart talk with 'im."

"Pressure is one thing. Attacking a woman is something else. If the sheriff gets involved it'll mess everything up," Tingle said. He looked at the Sergeant with a frown. Good Lord, he thought, what kind of monster have I have I got myself involved with?

* * * *

The following day, Frank stood on a stepladder that leaned against the house and used a brush to scrub the soot from the clapboards above a window. He dipped the brush in a bucket of water and scrubbed vigorously. Boyd worked to replace the glass that had been broken in a window, using a putty knife to seal it along the edges with spackling. Friends and neighbors had dragged most of the furniture from the first floor out into the yard to dry in the sun, but it would take a good scrubbing to make it usable. The rooms and furniture in the upper floor had escaped the water used to put out the fire, but they reeked of smoke. It would take weeks to put the house back in order.

"How's Rachel feeling this morning?" Boyd asked as they worked.

"She's in pretty bad shape. One eye is swollen completely shut and the other one is almost as bad. Her face is a mess, and she has deep bruises on her arms and body. Whoever did this is an animal," Frank said, his voice husky with vehemence.

"Are you going to get the sheriff involved?"

"Yeah, I sent a message to him. He should be here sometime in the next couple of days. You don't think this Sergeant fellow has anything to do with that claim on my property, do you?"

Frank asked. "I wonder if it was him who threatened me about the lawsuit."

"No, I don't see a connection. How could he know about you owning the property? Besides, it looks like it took some planning to steal the deed from the courthouse and make a new one. I don't think he's smart enough to do that, and he's only been in town for a few weeks."

"Yeah, I guess you're right," Frank said, "but if he isn't behind it, who is?"

"That's a good question. Do you have any enemies that have it in for you?"

"No, no one I can think of, but it doesn't look like a revenge thing anyway. It's more like someone is trying to make some money out of it someday and for the same reason that I think I'll be able to. They'd have to have a lot of nerve–what makes them think that I'll give up and just let them have the land? They'd have to be in it for the long haul. There's no money in it right now. It will be years before they'd see a penny."

"It looks like I'll have to make another trip to Kingwood to talk to the judge. If you haven't mailed the papers for the suit, I could take them along with me."

"No, I haven't had the time with everything that's going on. I would appreciate it if you'd take them. Boyd, you're a good man, helping me out with this. Thank you."

\* \* \* \*

It was a cool, overcast morning as Lexus walked along the street toward the center of town. Humid air hung heavily over the valley with the promise of rain, and leaves drooped languidly from the trees along the street. She wore her best dress and a hat with a colorful plume protruding from its band that Rachel had loaned her. As she walked along, she could hear the morning train grinding down the grade from Cranberry. Dark smoke billowed above the tracks while the train was still hidden by the lush foliage of the sycamores that grew along the creek and then it suddenly burst onto the trestle. Smoke curled from under the roof of the trestle, and the cars swayed back and forth on the uneven tracks. The ground shook beneath her feet with its weight and substance as it ground to a halt, blocking the road through town. Two towheaded boys stood near the locomotive, oblivious to the smoke and cinders that swirled around them and waved hopefully to the engineer, wishing for a chance to climb onto the engine. The engineer waved back to them but then went about oiling the wheels and other moving parts with a large oilcan. A man wearing bib overalls and a grimy railroad cap shoveled sand into bins above the gigantic wheels.

A group of soldiers approached the train, opened a railroad car and began unloading an assortment of boxes and crates. One wearing captain's bars on his blue uniform checked the shipment against a sheet attached to a clipboard as the soldiers bent quietly to their work.

The tall, well dressed owner of the dry goods store watched as one of his employees loaded his order onto a handcart, berating him for not moving fast enough, and then they made their way along the street to his store. A group of loafers began drifting away after the excitement of the train's arrival, and the conductor called for a group of soldiers to board. They picked up their meagre belongings and filed aboard.

Lexus waited impatiently until the train moved away and then crossed the tracks and walked into the lobby of a large square-like hotel. She approached and smiled at the stout, middle aged woman behind the desk. Her florid face was round with faintly rouge-painted cheeks. Her clothes were clean and neat.

"Can I help you?" she asked.

"I'm here to see Mr. Clawson. I have an appointment."

"Oh, you're Miss Saunders aren't you? You're the one that wants the teachin' job," she said as she wiped the surface of the desk with a rag, streaking the fine layer of black soot that spread across everything.

"Yes. Is Mr. Clawson in?"

"Yeah, he's in his office. I'll go get 'im. You can set over there by the window."

Lexus looked around the lobby. It had high, punched-tin ceilings and ornate lamps that hung from decorative brackets. A narrow staircase that led to the second floor sported a railing made of lustrous hardwood. The wooden floor was covered with an assortment of woven rugs. Upholstered chairs were arranged around the walls in informal groupings and in a formal seating arrangement in front of the large window that faced the railroad. Through the window, Lexus could see Cannon Hill rising across the river and remembered her afternoon there with Boyd.

Lexus sat at the table, her back straight, holding a tiny bag in her lap. She watched as boarders came and went; a well-dressed couple, a man with a stovepipe hat in one hand and a valise in another, a man of medium height with wiry red hair dressed in an expensive suit. She wondered who they were and why they were staying in the hotel. She speculated about where they were going and what their business was.

A man in a rumpled suit and tie approached. "Hello. I'm Charles Clawson. I assume you're Frank's niece. I understand you're interested in teaching school." He smiled warmly and sat down across the table from her. "We have a subscription school here in town that is in need of a teacher."

"Oh yes. I'm interested. I don't have a lot of experience teaching children, but I think I can do a good job." Lexus frowned and said, "Has Uncle Frank talked to you about me wanting a job? I had hoped I'd be able to be hired on my own merits."

He laughed and said, "No. People like to gossip. We know all about you." Lexus laughed nervously. I hope they don't know *everything* about me, she thought.

Mr. Clawson patted her hand and said, "Everything will be all right. As soon as the other two board members arrive, we'll ask you a few questions, and you can do the same with us. I always thought that an interview was a two-way street, and it has to be a good fit for both parties." He rose and pointed toward the door. "Here they are now." Two men walked toward them, removing their hats. They were both well dressed—one tall and lean, the other short and portly. They smiled as they approached, and Mr. Clawson introduced them.

"This is Mr. Tingle. He owns the dry goods store just around the corner. He's been on the board for years—his children completed their educations here."

Lexus rose from her seat and extended her hand. "I'm pleased to meet you Mr. Tingle. I believe I saw you at the train depot just a few minutes ago. You and another man were loading parcels onto a handcart."

"Oh yes, we have to keep the shelves stocked you know. I've owned the store for more years than I like to remember," he said.

"And this is Mr. Jefferson Knight. He owns the freight company. He's just the person you need to get to know. One never knows when one may need to have something hauled," Clawson said, chuckling.

Lexus lowered her eyes after scrutinizing the two men carefully. Tingle was the older of the two and seemed to be confident and somewhat overbearing. He had examined her from head to foot, while Mr. Knight had looked her in the eye with a bemused expression.

"It's a pleasure to meet you, Miss Saunders," Mr. Knight said. "I've heard only good things about you. My wife and I are anxious to find a competent teacher for the school. My two children attend there, you know." He clasped his hands over his belly and rocked back on his heels. "Mr. Clawson's children will be in your classroom, too, that is if you get the job. They're wonderful children. Prime examples of what youngsters from good families represent."

They seated themselves around the table, Lexus on one side and the three men on the other. The interview began with questions about her education, where she had attended school, and what her academic interests were. She replied tentatively at first but soon relaxed and warming to the subject, gave them the information they requested. Mr. Clawson and Mr. Knight seemed to take a liking to her, but Mr. Tingle frowned and seemed bothered by something.

After exhausting their questions, the men retired to Mr. Clawson's office to discuss her fate. Lexus was nervous about the outcome of the interview and sat stiffly twisting her kerchief in her hands. She needn't have worried. A half hour later, the men returned to the table with smiles, except for Mr. Tingle, who looked at her without expression.

"Miss Saunders," Knight began, "we have discussed your qualifications at some length, and we're pleased to inform you that you have been selected as the schoolmarm for the coming term that begins in mid-September. We can forgo the usual letters of reference since we know your aunt and uncle. I'll draw up a letter of agreement that will outline the conditions of your employment, and we'll all sign it. Your salary will be the same as Miss Slater, the former teacher. Of course, you won't be paid as much as a male teacher, since you don't have a family to support, and we'll expect you to resign immediately if you should marry." He continued to outline a litany of do's and don'ts as conditions of her employment. "If you need a place to live, it has been tradition for our teachers to stay with the students' parents, alternating from one to another each month, but if you choose to live with your uncle, we would agree to that. Of course we expect you to dress appropriately and abstain from the use of tobacco and alcohol, and you must be home each evening by seven. Your reputation is a valuable commodity, and we expect you to guard it judiciously. We expect to see you in church each and every Sunday." He took a deep breath and said, "Do you have any questions for us?"

"No, I think you've answered my questions before I could ask them. You've been very thorough," Lexus said.

They exchanged pleasantries for a few minutes, and then stood and shook hands. They said goodbye, and Lexus left the hotel and began walking slowly toward home, deep in thought. A light wind began to pick up, and she lifted her neckerchief to cover her hair. Crickets chirped in the grass along the street, and a turkey vulture patrolled the river's edge. The conditions of her employment were as she expected, but she hadn't thought about what would happen if she got married. Boyd hadn't proposed yet, but she was sure he would, sooner or later, and when he did, she wasn't sure she wanted to abandon teaching. Why was that a condition of employment? What difference did it make if she was married or not? And, why would she be paid less than a male teacher? It didn't seem fair.

\* \* \* \*

Boyd rose early and prepared a cold breakfast of leftover ham and biscuits, wrapped it in a sheet of newsprint and placed it on the porch bannister. He lit a small camp fire under an iron pot filled with river water and tossed in a handful of ground coffee diluted with chicory. He returned to the porch and waited for it to boil. Abe sauntered down the path and sat down, examining Boyd with sad eyes, thumping his tail occasionally. Large buckeye trees with brown, mottled bark dotted the river bank among the sycamore trees, their fruit just beginning to develop. Cool air flowed down the valley swirling the thin layer of fog rising from the warm water of the river, causing the trees' leaves to tremble. A soldier played revelry to wake the military encampment on the far side of town. A skein of wood ducks streaked down the river, a brilliantly decorated drake leading, their wings whistling. Their somber calls reverberated from the mountains–*ooeek, ooeek, ooeek, jeweep*.

Boyd was worried. This man, Sergeant, had proven himself to be extremely dangerous. He had abducted and nearly killed Lexus and more recently, Rachel, whose lacerations had yet to heal. Her eyes were still swollen and blackened, and there was no telling how long it would take her to recover. Emotionally, the scars might never completely heal. Boyd and Frank had agreed that the women should not be left unguarded. He worried about Lexus and her threat to kill the savage if she had the opportunity. He had no doubt she meant every word, but he wanted her nowhere near the man.

The pot began to boil and he lifted it off the campfire with a forked stick and set it on the porch. He poured a cup of the steaming drink and sat in the chair with his breakfast on his lap. The ham and biscuits were good, and he tossed a scrap to the dog that swallowed it in one gulp. He wadded the newspaper and tossed it on the fire, watching it crinkle and burst into flames, smoke swirling in the breeze.

He leaned back in his chair and thought about his father. He missed him, and he missed the sea—the tang of saltwater, pelicans skimming the waves in tight formation, seagulls squawking and bickering over scraps of fish, schools of bluefish as long as an oar flashing in the ocean swells, the squeak and groan of lines in a schooner's rigging—but he was growing to love these mountains too. He had heard that they were millions of years old, even older than the Rocky Mountains he'd read about. He didn't know about that, but they were intoxicating, drawing the eye to the far horizon with layer after layer of luxuriant green trees and tumbling streams. If Lexus wanted to remain here, he would desert the sea without regret. They could make this their home.

He closed the cabin door and walked across town, retrieved his horse, saddled him and rode toward Kingwood, suffering only a few stiff-legged bucks until the horse settled into a mile-eating trot. Boyd took the narrow road down the roaring river that bounded over rocks and swirled around boulders as large as houses. The locals called this part of the river "the narrows." It was an apt description. The mountains pinched down into a narrow shoot that was miles long, causing the water to increase in speed and ferocity. Boyd could only imagine what the river would be like in a flood. Leaves and debris hung from tree branches high above the present water level, attesting to severe fluctuations in water level. The trunks of sycamore and birch trees along the river were gashed and gouged by sheets of ice that sliced into them when spring rains broke the grasp of winter.

It was late morning before the sun's rays reached the bottom of the gorge, a pleasant light filtering through the trees. It was a pleasurable ride, and Boyd was thankful that the horse had fallen into a rapid walk rather than his earlier, bone-jarring trot. Clumps of rhododendron and mountain laurel crowded the road as it clung to the mountainside along the river. As the day warmed, Boyd stopped long enough to remove his jacket and tie it behind the saddle, then mounted and resumed the journey.

Without warning, the horse perked up its ears and shorted, testing the air. Boyd saw a flash of movement on the road ahead as a large black bear, followed by three half-grown cubs, stopped and looked curiously at him. One of the cubs rose onto its hind legs and sniffed the air, its black coat glistening. The larger bear swung its head from side to side, its nostrils dilating. Emitting a loud woof, it ran into the woods and up the mountainside with a speed that amazed Boyd. The cubs scrambled behind, climbing over fern-covered boulders, making an effort to keep up. The horse made one stiff-legged buck and then settled down. They resumed their journey.

Later in the morning, Boyd turned the horse from the main road up onto a narrow track that led along a roaring creek, gaining altitude rapidly. Toward the top of the mountain, he heard children laughing and giggling, followed by a loud splash as a naked boy with jet black hair plastered to his head jumped from a waterfall into the pool below. Two smaller boys, equally naked, sat hunched on a rock with their feet pulled up under them, rubbing their arms and pale bodies to warm themselves from the chill of the frigid water. They shouted to the boy in the pool, daring him to dive to the bottom and catch a fish with his hands. Boyd's horse snorted loudly, and their pale faces jerked toward him with startled looks of fright and guilt. They scattered into the bushes like a covey of quail flushed from a briar patch, leaving their clothes stacked on rocks along the creek.

Boyd laughed outright, remembering similar escapades when he was young and nudged the horse up the mountain He soon entered the town. Townsfolk walked along the streets, talked in small groups, and entered and exited the town's places of business. He tied the horse in front of the tavern and walked to the courthouse to find the judge.

Boyd climbed to the third floor. Court had just adjourned as he entered the large courtroom. Groups of men–lawyers, prosecutors, plaintiffs and defendants–filed out into the hallway. Boyd found the court clerk who immediately escorted him into the judge's chambers where a young, slim man with a shock of dark hair and a neatly trimmed beard was hanging his robe on a coat stand. The clerk introduced them and left them alone. The judge sat behind his desk and motioned for Boyd to take one of several wooden chairs arranged about the room.

"Now, Mr. Houston, what can I do for you?"

"Judge Hannah, I'm here on behalf of Frank Saunders who lives in Rowlesburg."

"Yes, I know Frank," the judge said. He settled into his chair and clasped his hands on his desk and looked at Boyd with interest. "How do you know him? I seem to detect an accent that isn't from around here."

"Well, it's a long story. I'm from South Carolina, and well, I escorted his niece, Lexus, from the southern part of the state to Rowlesburg after her parents died." He didn't feel like going through the long version of the story, so he moved on. "Mr. Saunders owns property up the river from Rowlesburg on Little Wolf Creek. It seems that someone is claiming they bought it from Frank, but he says that he didn't sign a deed or bill of sale."

"Oh, yes. I heard something about that from Ed in the county clerk's office. So, you're the one he swindled out of a dollar, huh?" The judge grinned at him. "Don't feel bad. You're not the first one to lose money to Ed. Just what is it that you want from me?"

"Frank had hoped that you could give him some advice as to how to proceed. He's filing suit, but doesn't even know who's behind it. The deed is filed under a business name." Boyd slid the suit papers across the desk, and the judge flipped through them quickly, asking a few questions.

"Okay, here's what he needs to do. Take these papers down to the circuit clerk and ask that they be filed. When the suit finally reaches my desk, I'll set a hearing date. The suit will be advertised in the local paper, and we'll see who shows up. I also advise Frank to hire a lawyer. There're several good ones in the county, but I can't make a recommendation. It'd be a conflict of interest, you know. He'll probably want to get notarized statements from the clerk's office about the missing documents or arrange for Ed to testify. I'd also get statements from Frank's neighbors about who owns what up there on Little Wolf Creek. The lawyer will know what to do, if he's any good at all. Hiring one from Rowlesburg might be a good idea since he'll know more about the community." The judge stood and extended his hand across the desk. "I'm pleased to meet you, Boyd. Give Frank and his missus my regards. I see my clerk wringing his hands; that means that I need to get back to court. So if you'll excuse me, I have a property line dispute to settle."

Boyd left the judge's chambers and walked to the sheriff's office. He found him sitting behind his desk reading a sheet of paper he held in his big hand. "Oh, there you are, Houston. I'm just going over the message Frank sent me. I've been really busy, but now I think I'll have some time to see what he wants done."

"That's why I'm here, Sheriff. Just to see what you think *can* be done."

"Let me get everything straight. Frank said someone jumped his daughter and beat her up. Is that right? You have any idea who it was?" he asked. "In cases like this, we usually go looking for a jealous boyfriend or a husband if that's the case."

"Rachel doesn't have a boyfriend as far as I know. I have a pretty good idea who it was from her description and from Lexus' experiences." He quickly told the sheriff about his belief that the Sergeant had followed them to Rowlesburg.

"That's quite a tale, young man. If I didn't know Frank Saunders, I'd suspect you of a prevarication. By the way, how is Rachel doing? Did the doctor get her patched up?"

"She's still in pretty bad shape. She can hardly walk, and the Doc's worried that she might be bleeding inside from the beating she took. She'll survive, but it will be a long while before she's back to normal."

"I don't know how to ask this other than to just spit it out. Did that depraved coward mess with her? If he did, he's in more trouble than he realizes. We don't stand for that kind of thing here. He'll be lucky if he isn't lynched," the sheriff said with a scowl on his face.

"No, she told Lexus that he didn't, but he ripped her clothes off her and groped her pretty bad. I don't want to go into detail, but he did some pretty bad stuff to her. I don't know if she'll ever get over that kind of rough treatment." Boyd's face grew dark thinking about it and about what the man had done to Lexus. If anyone needed killing, it was the Sergeant.

"I don't think I'll be able to get down to Rowlesburg for the next three or four days. I have to testify in court, and Judge Hannah will find me in contempt if I'm not there at his beck and call. Tell you what I'll do, though. I'll send my best deputy to see if he can locate this man, then I'll come as soon as I'm free. Tell Frank we'll not let this pass. And, give my best wishes to Miss Rachel."

\* \* \* \*

One warm morning, Lexus and Boyd walked through town to look at the train trestle. As they stood on the river's edge looking up at the enormous structure, one of the soldiers, a young captain assigned to command the men guarding the bridge, ambled over to them. He introduced himself saying that it would be his pleasure to answer any questions they might have about it.

"Mr. Albert Fink was one of three engineers who worked on this trestle. He came up with a through-truss design made of wood and iron. Before this was built, all other trestles were made entirely of wood. It takes less construction materials and is actually stronger to use his design. The B&O completed the railroad about ten years ago, and it's quite an engineering accomplishment. This section was the most difficult to construct."

"I can see why," Boyd said. "Everywhere I look, there's nothing but mountains, and this is a pretty big river. How did they ever do it?"

"It took a lot of work and engineering skill. The B&O had to build several viaducts and tunnels just within a few miles of here," the captain said. "Kingwood Tunnel, just west of here in Tunnelton, is the longest of its kind in North America. The Tray Run viaduct is four hundred and forty-five feet long and fifty-eight feet high, and the Buckeye Run viaduct is three hundred and fifty feet long and forty-six feet high. Mr. Fink designed them, too, using the same engineering methods as with the trestle." They could tell that the captain was proud of his knowledge about the railroad and the fact that he and his men had been given the assignment to guard it.

"Just how long is this trestle, Captain?" Boyd asked.

"Well, I reckon it's just long enough to reach from one side to the other," the captain said, lightheartedly. "All kidding aside, it's over three hundred feet long."

They laughed at the captain's witticism, and then Boyd said, "Why didn't the B&O build the railroad somewhere else? I mean, was it necessary to choose some of the most rugged terrain in the Appalachians as the route west? Surely they could have found an easier path."

"Yeah, they wanted to build it north of here in Pennsylvania, but their legislature vetoed the route. They didn't want the railroad competing with the National Road that runs through northern Maryland and over through Pennsylvania to Pittsburgh. Or, it would have been much easier to take the line down along the Cheat to the Monongahela River and on to Point Marion and thence to Wheeling. So, here we are. The railroad runs from

Cumberland through these mountains to Grafton and on west from there."

Boyd chuckled. "Isn't that the way it always happens? There's always someone who guards his own purse strings at the expense of everyone else. Has there ever been a train wreck on this section of track?"

"Oh, heavens yes. Back in fifty-three, a trestle over a side tributary collapsed and the train went over the mountain. Killed ten people and a lot of others were injured. Mr. Latrobe's face was red that day."

The captain went on to say that, along with the construction of the Northwestern Turnpike, the railroad had opened the area to commerce. "These mountains are really opening up to business. Take Fellowsville on the other side of Laurel Mountain, for example. They're on the pike, and stores and hotels sprung up along with a lot of other businesses. The Northwestern Hotel is one of the best on the pike. The stage stops there overnight, and they have corrals for the drover's herds. They were growing by leaps and bounds and probably would have become the biggest city in the county until the railroad cut into their business. In Rowlesburg, here, and across the mountain in Newburg, the railroad has triggered a lot of growth. But now, business has slowed down because of the war. They were really prospering before it started."

"How do you know so much about the railroad and this area?" Lexus asked.

The captain smiled and said, "I was born and raised in Preston County. I grew up in Mount Carmel, up east there on the mountain. I'm like a lot of the men in our detachment from the county; I volunteered, and I'm mighty proud to fight for our new state and the Union."

"Do you get to go home often? Mount Carmel is only a few miles from here, isn't it?"

"Oh yes," he said. "I get a furlough now and then and get to go home to see my folks and brothers and sisters. Lots of us are close enough to home to go visitin' from time to time. I suppose all of that will end when we get moved out of here."

They talked at length with the captain, enjoying the exchange and the warm weather. He pointed out various features of the trestle, and then offered to let them walk onto it. "Just don't say anything about me lettin' you do this. The colonel said we were to keep folks away, but I don't think it will hurt to let you take a quick look."

They walked along a narrow boardwalk on the side of the trestle, marveling at the huge iron and wooden beams that formed a support network for the tracks and looked down at the pier and abutments made of blue freestone. Lexus exclaimed at the weight and mass of it all, wondering aloud how the workers had ever moved the materials into place. Boyd looked at the roof that covered it all and asked the captain about the practice of covering bridges and trestles. He replied that it was built that way to protect the wooden beams from the elements.

The captain pulled out a heavy pocket watch and regarded its face solemnly. "It's about time for the train from Cumberland. We'd better get off before it comes. We'll all look like 'coons if we get caught on here with the smoke and all."

They thanked the captain for the tour and promised not to tell the colonel that he had allowed them on the bridge. He smiled and shook their hands and then returned to his men.

Boyd and Lexus walked back toward town and then made their way to the school house, perched on a knoll above the town. It was a small, rectangular building, painted white with a small belfry on its roof. It had a narrow porch on the front with a roof supported by posts. Lexus produced a key, given to her by Mr. Clawson, which opened the front door. They walked inside and were assailed by the odor of chalk and mildew, and a row of windows lit the room. She stood looking at the desks and bookshelves and smiled. She sat behind the teacher's desk and ran her hands over its smooth surface as Boyd watched quietly from a corner.

"I've always wanted to be a teacher," she whispered. "And now, I'm going to get the chance." She stood and wrote her name on the chalkboard–*Miss Saunders*. Then, she drew a small circle on the board six feet above the floor. "And, if you don't behave, Mr. Houston, you'll have to stand with your nose in this circle," she said, teasing. Boyd's eyebrows arched in surprise. "And I'll bet it won't be the first time."

Boyd chuckled and said, "You're right about that. I wasn't a bad student, but I wasn't completely innocent, either."

She looked around the room, noting the dunce's cap and stool which was stored beside the bookshelf and wrinkled her nose. She pulled first one book and then another from the shelves and paged through them, running her finger over the title on the front of each. She opened the door of a small storage closet and searched around inside, withdrawing a feather duster and broom. She began to tidy up the classroom and when she refused his offer to help, Boyd drifted outside and sat on the edge of the porch.

He heard Lexus humming inside, and the sound of the broom on the floor. A thin veil of dust drifted out the door. From his seat on the porch, he could see most of the town spread before him. People walked briskly, and an occasional team and wagon went by. True to the captain's prediction, the train made its appearance and crossed the trestle but moved through town without stopping, leaving a cloud of smoke hanging in the air. It soon disappeared up the tracks toward the viaducts.

Lexus sat on the porch next to Boyd and said, "I don't know how I'll ever keep the schoolroom clean. Dust and cinders from the locomotive is on everything. I suppose I'll have to sweep and clean just about every day."

"Won't the custodian do the cleaning?"

Lexus laughed and said, "Yes, in a way. Mr. Clawson said that not only would I be the schoolmarm, I'd be the custodian, too."

"Does that mean that you'll have to carry in the coal and make the fire each morning? And, carry in the drinking water, and …"

"Yes. I'll have to do it all, but some of the older children can help, and I'm already planning to ask some of the mothers to volunteer. We'll make do."

They sat together on the porch in the late morning sunshine, contented with being together. They relaxed as the small town went about its business, and the army camp buzzed with activity. Soldiers drilled in the field by their encampment, and they could see the cooks preparing the evening meal. Neat rows of tents spread away toward the river, and their sides flapped gently in the breeze. They could hear the beat of the smith's hammer and the occasional nicker of horses. Lexus sighed contentedly and then tilted her head against Boyd's shoulder.

* * * *

That night, Lexus lay on her bed with the bedclothes pulled up to her chin. Outside, she could hear the frogs down in the swamp along the river and an occasional, plaintive call from a night bird high on the mountain across the river. Her uncle's big black dog rattled its chain and she could hear him nosing his food bowl over the packed dirt around his doghouse. The house was quiet save for the rhythmic growl of her aunt's snoring down the hall. The pungent smell of smoke lingered in the house even though it had been repaired and cleaned thoroughly. She picked up the clock on the nightstand and looked at its face in the pale moonlight that filtered into the room. It was three o'clock in the morning. She rolled onto her side and pulled the blanket tightly around her even though the night was warm. She closed her eyes and tried to go back to sleep. *I shouldn't have drunk that big glass of milk before going to bed*, she thought. She covered her head and tried to ignore the growing pressure in her bladder. The clock ticked inexorably, and before long she knew it was inevitable–she'd have to make a trip to the outhouse.

She sat on the edge of the bed, slipped her feet into her slippers, and put on her robe. She debated lighting a lamp, but figured there was enough moonlight for her to find her way. The steps groaned in protest as she descended into the lower level of the house, made her way out the side door, and felt her way along the familiar path. The dog whined, rattled its chain, and beat its tail on the side of its doghouse. The door of the outhouse stood partially open, and as she stepped inside, a sudden flurry of wings startled her as a large bird flew by, brushing her hair with its wings. Her heart hammered in her throat. Some sort of owl looking for mice, she thought. Her heart settled as she completed her business. She hummed a nervous tune as she made her way back toward the house. With a rush, the Sergeant grabbed her from behind, clamped his hand over her mouth, and lifted her feet off the ground. She squirmed helplessly as he clinched her to his body, her eyes white in her pale face. She tried to scream but to no avail. She took in great lungsful of air through her nose and tried to bite him. He clamped down even harder, and she was afraid he'd cover her nose and close off her air. The dog went into a frenzy, flopping around at the end of its chain like a fish on a hook, snarling and barking.

"Gotcha, you little witch," he growled in her ear. "I've followed you all across the state, but I've finally caught up with you. You won't get away from me this time. I'm going to see you in your grave."

Lexus squirmed and scratched his hand, tried to pry it from her mouth, but he squeezed her tighter against his chest. He smelled of tobacco and whiskey, and a foul odor rose from his clothes. She reached back over her head and tried to find his eyes with her fingernails, but he dug his chin in her neck. He squeezed harder and shook her like a dog killing a snake, making her head spin. His powerful arms held her immobile as he began to drag her into the bushes. A light was lit in the house.

"Hold still, or I'll break your back, you hussy," he said with a hiss. As he carried her by a large tree, Lexus raised her feet onto its solid trunk and pushed with all her might. They tumbled backward into the weeds, and his hand slipped enough for her to sink her teeth into him. A gush of blood filled her mouth, but she hung on, thrashing her head from side to side, a horrible snarl in her throat.

"Yeowl," he screamed in her ear. "I'll kill you here and now!" He clubbed her on the side of her face with his fist, trying to break free of her, but she hung on. She clinched her teeth harder, finally taking a large chunk of meat from the side of his hand. She rolled away from him and started to crawl toward the house, but he caught her by the foot and dragged her toward him. He pinned her to the ground and kneed her in the stomach.

"You dirty witch. I'm going to cut your throat." His breath was hot on her cheek, and she thrashed her head from side to side, a guttural scream escaping from her bruised lips. The dog bared its teeth and growled as it lunged at the end of its chain trying to reach the Sergeant, foam from its mouth splashing over him and onto her hair.

"Here now, what's going on out there," Frank yelled from the porch. He was in his nightclothes and held a lamp in his hand. He began to run toward them. "Is that you Lexus? What's wrong?"

"Get back or I'll kill her," the Sergeant screamed. "I mean it. You stay back or I'll break her damned neck."

Frank stopped and gaped in astonishment. "Let her go! I say, let her go."

The Sergeant let out a maniacal laugh and dragged Lexus to her feet, holding her at arm's length by her hair, shaking her like a rag doll. Her knees were weak, and they shook uncontrollably. Blood streamed from his hand, and it flew in a shower as he cuffed her on the side of the head, sparking stars behind her eyes. She could feel the strength draining from her and knew that she was about done fighting. With her last ounce of strength, she twisted around, grabbed his shirt and pulled. He released his grip on her hair and with his good hand grasped her arm, twisting it painfully. She fell backward onto the ground and he tumbled on top of her. As they struggled, Lexus rolled his body just enough for the dog to grab his arm, sinking its teeth to the bone.

The Sergeant shrieked as the dog shook its head, its jaws like a vice. He clubbed it with his free hand and then grappled at his belt for his knife, but as he pulled it out, the dog shook him again and the blood-slick weapon slipped from his fingers. The Sergeant ripped his arm from the dog's mouth and rolled away. The dog lunged for him again but came up short on his chain. The Sergeant shouted and cursed as he fumbled around on the ground for a weapon. He found a large rock and raised it above his head to strike the dog just as Lexus unsnapped the chain from the dog's collar. The effect was immediate. The dog lunged into the Sergeant, latching its jaws onto the man's thigh, sending the rock flying. As they rolled in the dirt and bushes, the Sergeant bellowed and cursed grappling with the dog. Lexus scrambled to the rock he had dropped and approached the melee holding it above her head with both hands, blood streaming from her face and jaws, her eyes and hair wild. The Sergeant saw her coming, his eyes opening wide in horror.

"Get away from me," he screamed. The rock thudded inches from his head, and with the strength born of desperation, he pulled away from the dog and ran through the trees toward the river. The dog followed him, snapping at his heels.

Frank rushed to Lexus' side, swept her into his arms as her knees buckled and lowered her gently to the ground. Lexus looked up at him in the moonlight and said, with a tremor in her voice, "I tried to kill him. Oh, what have I become?" She pressed the tail of her filthy robe to her face with quaking hands and sobbed. The dog trotted back into the yard and sat in front of her as a rivulet of blood dripped from its muzzle.

\* \* \* \*

Lexus reclined on her bed with a bright coverlet drawn up over her as a thin morning light brightened the sky. A bruise darkened the side of her face, and scratches and contusions marred her features. Boyd sat on the edge of the bed, his face a study of concern. Frank leaned on the door casing as Martha fussed about.

"I'm so sorry you had to go through this again, Lexus," Boyd said. "I regret that I wasn't here to protect you."

Lexus frowned and said, "It's not your fault. I should have been more careful. Besides, I took care of myself."

Frank snorted, "Didn't look to me like she needed a lot of protecting, Boyd. I think that scoundrel came out on the short end of the stick. He was lucky to get away with his life. Between Lexus and Duke, he got about all he wanted. Did you see the blood on the ground out there? Most of it's his."

Boyd laughed and looked at Lexus with admiration. "Yes, I believe you're right, Frank. That man will think twice before he attacks her again. But, we'll have to be even more vigilant–he just might shoot her next time."

"I'm not afraid of him now. I'm not mindless enough to take chances, but I no longer fear the man the way I once did. I'm just disappointed that I didn't finish the job last night," Lexus said, a look of triumph on her face. "And, I'm glad Rachel is recovering. We'll both be all right."

Boyd said, "You get some rest now. I'll check in on you later."

"No, if y'all will step outside, I'm going to get dressed and go see how Rachel is getting along, and maybe help Aunt Martha prepare dinner."

Boyd's eyebrows rose, and then he turned and winked at Frank. "Seems like the Saunders women come from pretty good stock."

"Boyd Houston, I'll not have you talking about me as if I were a cow or something!" she said. "Now, scat."

Boyd and Frank clomped down the stairs and sat in the parlor. The voices of children at play drifted through the open windows. The odor of wood smoke from campfires in the Union encampment was a pleasant reminder of their presence as it floated on the morning breeze. A cow bawled for its calf in a field down near the river.

"What do you think, Boyd? Are those two young women going to be all right? That was a horrible thing that happened to them. Rachel is recovering, but she's quiet and isn't herself. Will she ever be the happy, vivacious young woman she was before this happened?"

"I suppose time will tell, but my best guess is yes, she'll recover. I'm concerned about both of them, and Lexus had only just begun to recover from what happened to her before. But, getting the best of the Sergeant has done her a world of good."

"I hope you're right," Frank said. "We're going to have to do something about that man, and soon. When you spoke to the sheriff, did he say when the deputy would get here to deal with that animal?"

Boyd told him about his conversation with the sheriff and that he was planning to send the deputy soon. "I talked to the judge, too, and filed your suit. He said he'd get the case on the docket as soon as he could." The two men discussed the pending suit and how they planned to proceed.

A loud knock on the front door interrupted them, and Frank went to see who it was. He opened the door to see a large young man standing on the porch. He wore dark trousers tucked into heavy work boots, and had a mop of unruly brown hair. He held a black, felt hat in front of him with both hands, and a heavy, brass badge was pinned to his shirt, causing the fabric to sag. A large revolver was tucked under his belt, and Frank could see the handle of a blackjack protruding from a hip pocket.

"You Frank Saunders?" he asked.

"Yes. I assume you're the deputy the sheriff promised to send."

"Yep. I'm Chief Deputy Benjamin Martenelli, but most people just call me Ben. Sheriff said your daughter had been attacked. He told me to come down here and sort things out. Arrest the feller if I find 'im."

Frank invited him in and introduced him to Boyd. "Deputy Martenelli, I'm a friend of the family and would like to help you any way I can," he said.

"Thanks. Mr. Saunders, tell me what happened to your daughter." Frank described the attack on Rachel, and what had happened to Lexus the night before. Boyd gave him a brief summary of Lexus' history with the attacker.

"How am I going to recognize this man?" Ben asked. "If I'm going to find him, I'll need a good description."

Frank laughed and said, "That won't be a problem, deputy. When he attacked and tried to abduct Lexus last night, he got more than he had counted on."

"What do you mean?" he asked.

"Lexus scratched him up some, bit a chunk out of his hand, and turned the dog lose on him. So, just look for a large man with a bandage on one hand and scratches on his face. Oh yes, he'll have dog bites all over him."

The deputy chuckled and shook his head. "That the same dog that's playing with those kids out front? He doesn't look like he'd harm a flea."

"Yes. Seems like ole Duke has a tiger inside him that we didn't know about."

"I guess any dog'll bite if presented with the right circumstances," the deputy said.

"Is there anything else you need, Deputy? We're anxious for this man to be found," Boyd said.

"Yes, one more thing. I need to talk to the two young women to see if there's anything they can add that will help me find him."

Frank stepped to the foot of the stairs and called for Rachel and Lexus to come down and talk to the deputy. He asked Martha to come too. They entered the parlor, and Rachel and Lexus sat side-by-side on the couch, their bruised faces turned toward him expectantly. Martha sat on a chair nearby.

Frank nodded toward the deputy and said, "This is Chief Deputy Martenelli. The sheriff asked him to come down here and see if he can find the Sergeant, and if he does, he'll arrest him. Do you feel up to talking to him?"

"Yes of course. I'll do whatever is necessary to catch that lout," Lexus said immediately.

"How about you, Rachel, you feel up to answering a few questions?"

"I...I don't know," Rachel said. "I suppose, as long as I don't ever have to see him again." She nervously tossed her black hair making her curls dance and twisted a strand with her fingers. "What do you want to know?"

The deputy turned toward the two men and said, "If you don't mind, gentlemen, I'd like to talk to these young women alone. Would you mind stepping out of the room for a few minutes? Won't take long. Mrs. Saunders, I'll ask you to stay, if you don't mind."

"Certainly," Frank said. "If it's all right with them. You don't mind, do you ?" Lexus and Rachel shook their heads, and the two men went outside to sit on the porch.

"He certainly seems to be competent, don't you think?" Frank asked.

"Yes. You can see why the sheriff made him the chief deputy. I don't think he's the country rube he pretends to be." A buggy carrying an elderly man and woman went by on the street in front of the house. The horse stepped along hurriedly, and Frank waved to them.

Frank said, "Why do you suppose he wanted to talk to them alone? I mean, what could they have to say to him that we couldn't hear?"

"Beats me, unless he thinks maybe you or I had something to do with what happened to them. I suppose he has to check out all possibilities, and maybe he thinks they'll be more comfortable telling him exactly what was done to them if we're not around."

They sat patiently on the newly painted porch, waiting for the interview to conclude. Frank leaned forward and placed his forearms on his legs with hands clasped and head bowed.

Boyd said, "I was just thinking how fortunate they were that they weren't killed. That man is a vicious killer. I don't know what either of us would do without them. We can't let him have another chance. As competent as this deputy seems, he'll require help finding him. What do you think about asking the army to give us a hand?"

"That's a good idea. I'll go talk to General Hill if the deputy hasn't found him within another day or too. It may take a group of men going door-to-door through town to find him. In the meanwhile one of us will have to stay close to Lexus and Rachel at all times."

They heard footsteps in the foyer, and the deputy motioned for them to come back inside. They all sat down again in the parlor, and Chief Deputy Martenelli briefly outlined his plan. He'd check all the boarding houses and bars to see if he could get a lead on where the Sergeant was. He said the army might have some idea where he was as well. "I'll keep you informed," he said as he stood. Hands were shaken all around, and he left the house for the center of town.

Rachel and Lexus watched out the window as the deputy walked confidently down the street. Lexus asked, "Do you suppose he'll be able to find that horrid man? Neither of us will be able to walk down the street without being afraid until they catch him."

"I don't know, but until they do, we'll have to be very careful." Rachel watched as the deputy disappeared from view, her brow creased with a frown.

# CHAPTER NINE

BOYD WALKED TO the center of town to retrieve the mare and wagon he and Lexus had used when they traveled up through the mountains only a few months ago. The mare nickered at him in recognition, and Boyd's horse thrashed around in its stall. The mare eagerly left the barn, impatient for exercise. He tossed the harness on her back and hitched her to the wagon. He climbed onto the wagon and returned to Frank's house where he found the family's horse and buggy tethered in front. Frank lifted a picnic basket onto the back seat and secured it there, as the three women waited patiently on the porch. It had been Martha's idea to go on a picnic as a break from the troubles that had befallen them. As far as Boyd could tell, it was working. The women talked and laughed with anticipation.

Boyd helped Lexus onto the wagon while the others climbed aboard the buggy. They left town following the road south past the army breastworks and on toward the turnpike where they turned west toward Laurel Mountain. They left the river behind and then started up Flag Run. The horses walked easily along, pulling the lightly loaded vehicles. Rachel, in the buggy, turned and waved to Lexus and Boyd. The valley closed in on them as they made their way along the small, rocky stream, and soon the road became steep and wound along the edge of the mountain as they gained elevation. The horses slowed and were soon covered with sweat. A series of switchbacks confronted them, one after another, as Lexus leaned over the side of the wagon to marvel at the drop-off down into the valley below. The horses were soon blowing, and Frank called a break to let them rest.

They sat along the road in the dappled shade of the forest, dipping glasses of lemonade from a large container that Martha had prepared. The mare shook its harness. The morning was bright, and a slight breeze drifted down along the mountain slopes.

"Daddy, tell Boyd and Lexus how this road was made. You know, about the Indians and all," Rachel said. Even though she enjoyed the retelling of a family story as would a child, she was far from being one.

Frank leaned back and assumed a professorial voice. "My grandparents used to tell me that this road was originally a buffalo trail. The buffalo are all gone now, but years ago, they were abundant here. Some places are named for them. Buffalo Creek is an example. From what I understand, Indians often used the trails to get from one place to another–mostly Mingo, Shawnee, Delaware, and even some Cherokee. There were others, too. Long ago, Mound Builders lived here, but they've been gone for centuries. Some of their burial mounds are still around, one just over the mountain on Little Sandy Creek, but they are often leveled to make working the fields easier. Others were dug up to see if anything of value was in them. They found some bones, 'n' clay pots, and other artifacts, but nothing much of value. I don't approve of digging into other folk's graves."

"Oh, Daddy! They were just heathens, so what does it matter? It's not like they were like us."

"No, Rachel, they weren't like us, but they still deserve the same respect that we give our graves," he said, admonishing her with a frown.

"Frank! Boyd and Lexus don't want to hear about all of this stuff," Martha said looking toward them. "He's always reading about such things. It almost bores me to death."

"No, no," Boyd said, "I'd like to hear more. Were there Indian wars here?"

"Only a few skirmishes," Frank said. "Just up the river, near St. George a man was killed by Indians, and down the river below town, at Drunkard's Bottom, some others were killed, but that was maybe a hundred years ago. There aren't any wild Indians left in the area, not like what you'd find out west."

"Tell them about Sand Camp Rock, Daddy. That's where we're going to have our picnic," Rachel said with enthusiasm.

"You'll see when we get there, but it's a really good place to eat our picnic lunch and relax for a while. There are places nearby where Indians carved images of birds, handprints, and animals on the rocks. Some of the carvings are almost worn away now, and all of them are covered with a crusty plant growth, ferns and lichens and such, so they're really hard to see. In other places along the ridges, there are said to be stacks of rocks that Indians left to commemorate graves. One legend has it that they left a rock on the stack to honor their ancestors each time they passed by. I don't know if that's so or not." They talked quietly, Frank continuing his lecture, and then they climbed back onto the wagons and resumed their trek.

Before long, they reached the summit where the land leveled off somewhat. There were a few houses grouped beside the road, and a large, log tavern stood under a cluster of trees. Pole corrals contained cattle and horses. Men worked swiftly to attach a fresh team to a brightly painted stagecoach as a cluster of travelers milled about, waiting to continue their journey.

They left the turnpike–following a faint trail through the forest–until they came to an extensive rock outcropping that clung to the mountain's backbone. They tied the horses, loosened their harnesses, and doled out a scoop of grain for each. Following an indistinct trail, they approached the impressive rock formation. A narrow opening, no wider than a man is tall, gave way to an enclosed room that was large enough to have contained both of the wagons and horses. Water dripped from the stone walls, echoing in the gloom, and bats, disturbed by their presence, dropped from cracks and crevices in the towering walls and fluttered about before flying away. Small animal bones littered the floor, and a variety of animal tracks marked the loose soil covering its surface. Boyd ran his hands over the walls, searching for symbols carved in the soft sandstone, but found none, and he used a stick to dig in the dirt hoping to find an arrowhead.

After exploring, they wandered back outside the stone enclosure and were grateful for the sunshine that warmed their backs and shoulders. The three women spread a tablecloth on a flat rock and set out silverware and food. The aroma of fried chicken made Boyd's stomach growl. They heaped their plates with food and sat on rocks and fallen logs as they ate. Frank told them more about the history of Laurel Mountain. The distinctive call of a large woodpecker sounded through the forest—*kuk, kuk, keekeekeekeekuk kuk*.

Lexus sat close to Boyd, touching his arm occasionally as if to assure herself that he was still there. Rachel sat beside her parents, her bruised eyes now purple-yellow, as she tried her best to put on a good front. They talked and laughed, appreciative of the distractions of the day.

When they had finished eating, Boyd and Lexus walked along the ridge-top, marveling at the mountains that sprawled to the horizon, their colors gradually changing from green-black to pale blue in the far distance. Just to the west, a spiral of smoke rose from a narrow valley, indicating the location of a mountain home. They walked along, enjoying each other's company and the solitude of the forest.

Lexus stopped to examine a mound of rocks partially covered by moss and ferns. "Do you suppose this was made by Indians?"

Boyd looked at it carefully, trying to imagine a group of ancient men and women stacking the rocks as a memorial to their lost ones, but he couldn't be sure. "I don't know, Lexus. It could be just a natural occurrence. There're rocks everywhere."

"Let's put a rock on top, just in case it's what we think it is," she said respectfully. They searched among the rocks scattered about to find just the right one and then lifted it onto the stack. They stepped back to see if they'd set it just right.

"What do you think? Did we do it right?" Boyd asked. Lexus liked that about him, that he'd respect the culture of others even if it was unlike his. She smiled.

"Yes, that'll do," she said. "Now, if their ancestors are buried here, they'll know we're thinking about them." She closed her eyes and said a silent prayer for the ancients.

They returned to Sand Camp Rock where they loaded the picnic basket onto the buggy, tightened the harnesses on the horses, made their way back to the pike and began the descent into the valley. Soon, they were back on Flag Run, and the horses picked up the pace. Near the river, they turned north toward town on the river road as a large wagon rumbled toward them. It was heavily loaded with boxes of supplies and burlap bags bulging with grain and was guarded by a detachment of soldiers. As they passed, the team of four large horses strained in their harnesses, grinding their bits with their teeth. Frank asked the soldiers where they were going, and a burly sergeant said that they were taking supplies to the detachment at the covered bridge. A fine veil of dust followed the wagon and settled on the leaves of the brush and trees along the road.

*  *  *  *

Former Sergeant Brown ached all over. The scratches on his hands were beginning to scab over, but his arm and leg throbbed where they were punctured with dog bites. He sipped bourbon from a grimy glass, and rubbed the back of his head, feeling the knot that had arisen there. He couldn't remember when that had happened. A bloody bandage was wrapped around his hand where that witch had taken a bite out of it. He was afraid the wound had gotten infected, and it hurt like a toothache. His eyes glowed with heat as he thought about her. He'd get her, take her into the woods, and when he got done with her, there'd be little left for the turkey vultures.

While he was trying to abduct her, she had set the dog on him, and he'd had to jump into the river to get away. Rage had filled him as he blundered about in the black water trying to escape the dog's snapping teeth. Surprisingly, it had quickly given up, and he was able to make his way back to his boarding house. Luckily, no one had seen him as he sneaked through the deserted town. He had torn rags into strips, poured whiskey on his bloody hand and bound it up. He had dabbed more on the scratches and tooth punctures, swearing vilely as the pain surged through him. He had fallen into bed in a drunken stupor and passed into a fitful sleep. He'd stayed out of sight for a couple of days allowing his wounds to heal. Luckily, most of the scratches were minor, except for those on his neck, which he had covered with a bandana. He'd have to keep his bandaged hand in his pocket to avoid being recognized.

Later, he sat at a corner table in the dark bar in the boarding house, hunched over a steaming bowl of beans. He sopped up some of the bean juice with a biscuit and crammed it in his mouth and eavesdropped on two men at a neighboring table. He could only hear sketches of what they were saying, but he got the gist of their conversation. The sheriff had sent a deputy to town who was going from bar to bar looking for him, and the deputy had asked about him at the hotel near the railroad tracks. He hunched down even lower and pulled his hat down to hide his face. He'd have to find another place to stay before the deputy came looking for him here, but one thing was sure—he wasn't leaving the area until he had satisfaction. That woman had bested him three times now, but he knew that her luck wouldn't hold.

He went back to his room and crammed his meager possession in a duffle bag, and started toward the door. He stopped, thinking. If he left without paying for the room, the boarding house keeper would tell the law, and they'd be on his trail in no time, so he left a handful of paper money on the bed. Maybe that would keep them off his back for a while. He managed to leave without being seen, walking swiftly down the street with his head and neck scrunched into his shoulders.

He entered the dry goods store by the back door, surprising Tingle. "What are you doing here? The whole town's looking for you," Tingle said.

"I know. I heard." He pulled the curtain aside from a window and looked outside. "I'm going to have to leave town, and I want my money now."

"What money? I don't owe you anything. As a matter of fact, get out of here right now! We're done."

"We're not going to have to go through this again, are we? I did what you wanted me to do. I caught Saunders the other night and told him to forget the lawsuit. He's so scared he won't dare go on with it. I told him to withdraw it, or I'd kill them all. I think I convinced him. So, you owe me my money, and I aim to have it."

Tingle's knees shook as he looked at the dangerous man who stood before him. He stooped, opened the safe, and withdrew a stack of bills. "Here, take the damned money and be gone," he said, shoving it toward the Sergeant. "Get out of town and don't come back."

The Sergeant thrust his chin out toward Tingle and laughed. "You don't tell me what to do. I tell you. You think this is enough to pay me off?" He shook the money at Tingle. "I want half of whatever that timber is worth, and I don't want paper money. I want gold."

"That wasn't our agreement. Besides, this is all I have. Take it or leave it," Tingle said with a tentative voice.

With a sudden move, the Sergeant violently shoved Tingle in the chest causing him to stagger backward into a small table. It upset sending papers and books flying. He flailed his arms trying to keep his balance, dragging a wooden filing cabinet down on top of himself as he slid to the floor. The drawers of the cabinet opened spilling files and papers onto the floor.

The Sergeant rummaged in the safe and stuffed his pockets with paper money. He turned toward Tingle, bouncing a cloth bag of tinkling coins on his palm, a big grin on his face. "I'll just take this as my share. I'm sure there's enough here to cover it. You can consider our partnership dissolved," he said as he turned and went out the door.

Tingle slowly got to his feet, righted a chair, and sat down heavily. He rearranged his clothes, smoothed them in place and pulled up a sleeve to examine a large, angry welt on his forearm where he'd scraped it on the edge of the desk. He hands shook as he adjusted his reading glasses, removed them, bent the arms back in shape, and stuck them back on his pale face.

The door in the store opened slowly and a balding clerk stuck his head in the office, his eyes huge. "Everything okay in here, Mr. Tingle? Looks like you've had a earthquake or somethin.'"

Outside, the Sergeant crept down the alley toward the street but hung back in the shadows long enough to see if anyone was coming. A horse, harnessed to a large farm wagon, stood with its head hung, its ears twitching to ward off the flies that circled it. A man, dressed in coveralls and a long-sleeved shirt, walked slowly down the street and entered the bank.

He stepped into the street and walked boldly toward the railroad tracks. He knew that he couldn't cross the trestle; it was guarded by the army, but by turning the other way, he'd be out of town and out of sight in no time.

"Hey you," a booming voice yelled from behind him. "Stop right there. Put your hands out where I can see 'em."

He stopped and slowly turned to see a large man with a star pinned to his shirt pointing a revolver at him. With the reflexes of a trained soldier, he drew his pistol from his belt and fired. A billow of white smoke filled the space between them. The Sergeant wasn't a particularly good shot, but as someone had said, he'd rather be lucky than good. The heavy ball from his pistol struck the deputy squarely in the chest.

\* \* \* \*

Dusk was settling as Lexus and Boyd sat together on Frank and Martha's porch, toeing the swing back and forth. The heavier, cool air that flowed down from the mountains around them was a pleasant reprive from the warm, muggy day they had just experienced. The wavering call of a screech owl sounded from the woods behind the house.

"Hear that, Boyd? Do you suppose that's the owl that was roosting in the outhouse? It gives me goose bumps. And, everyone says it's announcing a death. Do you believe that?" Lexus asked. "Do you believe that a bird can predict that someone is going to die?"

"I don't know. My mother said the same thing. There seems to be a lot of owls here in the mountains. The Indians that lived in the swamps in South Carolina placed great significance in them. They said they had great power. They also believed that ravens were omens of good fortune. They believed that if a raven perched near you, you'd have good luck. I'm not sure how one bird could be the carrier of death and another good fortune. Some other native people believe that one day an owl will call your name, telling you that you're about to die–that you'll be gone, over to the other side."

"You mentioned your mother. What was she like?"

"I can hardly remember her, but my earliest memory was of her holding me on her lap singing to me–a song about Galway Bay. She said I smelled like sunshine and dog. *She* smelled of shampoo and lilac soap. My *fathe*r smelled like fish, and the sea, and onions and garlic," he said smiling, "and once in a while whiskey, but I never knew him to smell of tobacco. I remember hearing my mother humming as she worked in the kitchen and as she pulled weeds in the vegetable garden behind our cottage. She kept a dozen or so chickens and one large red rooster that tried to flog me. It made going to the outhouse a challenge. I remember that she carried their chicken feed in her apron, and had a name for each one. When they saw her scatter the feed, they all came running. She sold extra eggs to the neighbors and kept the money in the pantry in a pint mason jar that was so old that it had turned blue–her egg money, she called it. She was kind to everyone, including our dog who she talked to when she thought no one was around. She went to church every Sunday and tried unsuccessfully to get my father to go with her. She took me, but I don't remember much about it, only that it seemed that the preacher was always shouting at everyone, and the service seemed to last forever. She always put some of her egg money in the collection plate, unlike old Mr. Shamus who pretended to make change but seemed to take out as much as he put in, and maybe more."

Boyd paused, looked away from Lexus into the gathering darkness and cleared his throat. Lexus sat quietly, willing him to continue. He never talked much about his past, and she didn't want him to stop.

"She believed in leprechauns and called them 'the wee ones.' When I'd get bored, she would tell me to go outside and look for them in the back yard, under the vegetable plants and bushes, and especially under overturned wooden buckets. I never found one, but it wasn't for lack of trying. She believed in heaven and that someday she'd get to see her dead parents again. Once, I asked her if dogs went to heaven. She said that they probably did, but only if they behaved. She liked to walk in the woods and gather flowers to put in her hair and on the kitchen table. In the spring, she picked greens that grew along the road and cooked them in a large iron pot over the fire in the fireplace and flavored them with a dash of salt and a piece of pork fat. On most mornings I would awake to the smell of baking biscuits and frying ham. My father delighted in saying that she was the world's champion biscuit baker, just to make her blush. We often had fish for supper–baked, or fried, or grilled over the fire, or in chowder, or salted in a big stone crock that she kept in the springhouse. When my father was due to return from the sea, she always waited on the widow's walk on the roof of the cottage, the wind whipping her skirts around her legs. She'd hold one hand flat above her eyes and the other on her hip, staring with a horrible dread at the horizon. When his boat finally came in, she'd take me by the hand and we'd walk down to the dock to greet him, and when the catch had been unloaded and the boat washed down, they'd walk back to our cottage together with me riding on his shoulders."

Boyd cleared his throat again and his voice softened to a whisper. "And then, one day she left us and never came back. My father tried to explain to me, a six year old boy, why he'd had to bury her in the cold ground, but I couldn't understand, and both of us were changed forever. I'll be thirty years old in a few years, and I think about her every day."

Lightning flickered in the narrow strip of sky between the towering mountains, and seconds later a low rumble of thunder sounded, making the hills tremble.

"Do *you* believe in heaven, Boyd? Do you believe that one day you'll get to see your mother and father again?"

He hesitated and then said, "It seems likely, Lexus. The people of almost every civilization have religious beliefs, and almost all of them believe in a life after this one. How could so many cultures, and all the people that inhabit them, be wrong? Some believe that heaven's up above in the clouds, and others that it's inside the earth, but no matter where they believe it is, *they believe.* Some Indians believe that when someone dies in a house or hogan, an evil spirit resides there forever, and it can never be lived in again. Others believe that if you die inside a house, a window must be opened to let your spirit out so that it can go free. So, it seems to me that after we've lived our lives, we must be more than just a pile of moldering bones in the ground."

"Oh Boyd, I pray so. That one day when our lives are over, we'll get to be together again and that we'll get to see those who have gone before us. Promise me, Boyd, that when I die, you'll be there to open the window to let my spirit go." They grew quiet again, there on the swing on the porch. "But, my, my, aren't we the serious ones? Let's talk about something else."

Boyd laughed and said, "Yes, we do seem to be a bit maudlin this evening. What else can we talk about? How about the weather? Think it'll rain?" Lexus playfully elbowed him on the arm.

They rocked quietly, and Boyd put his arm over her shoulders. They could hear Martha preparing supper in the kitchen, the rustle of Frank's newspaper in the parlor, and Rachel humming as she stitched a wedding sampler.

* * * *

At daybreak the next morning, Boyd was awakened by Abe scratching on his cabin door. He climbed out of his bed and invited him in, but he just walked back and forth on the porch and looked pitifully at Boyd. He got dressed, lit the campfire, and put the iron skillet on to heat. Abe watched intently as Boyd browned slices of bacon and then cracked half a dozen eggs into the sizzling grease. When they had cooked, he scraped half onto a plate for himself and gave the remainder to Abe who backed away from it when he burned his mouth. He tossed his head and approached more carefully and began eating, his lips curled back like a mule eating a cactus. Boyd sat on the steps to the porch eating lowly. Heavy clouds hung low over the valley casting a gloomy spell as the treetops swayed in the wind. He was forced back on the porch as a heavy rain began to fall. Small gray birds darted about close to the ground, and a flock of sparrows flew under the porch. It had rained during the night, the river was the color of weak coffee, and the water level had risen until only the tops of the water plants on the river's edge showed. Lightning flashed, and rain beat down on the cabin's roof.

Boyd watched rainwater pour off the porch roof, and the campfire sizzled and flickered as steam and smoke swirled away into the brush. He rummaged through his belongings, found his rain slicker and put it on. He plodded toward Frank's house, pulling his hat tightly on his head to keep the wind from blowing it away. The slicker was pressed against his body by the wind, and its tail flapped about as if it had a mind of its own. By the time he arrived, water was running down his neck. His boots and pant legs were soaked through. He pulled off the slicker, tossed it into a corner on the porch and slapped his hat against his leg sending a shower of rainwater onto the floor.

Frank stepped out on the porch and handed Boyd a steaming cup. "I thought you'd like to have some coffee that isn't cut with chicory. We're about out, but Martha insisted that we splurge this morning. She said something about warding off the chill of the rain."

Boyd accepted the cup and sat down on the swing, sipping the hot brew carefully. "Thanks. That really hits the spot."

"Looks like the rain has set in. Once it gets started, it seems like it doesn't want to stop. I hope we don't have a flood like the last one—the river got up in parts of town, and some folks had to stay with relatives and friends until it went down. It took a long time for the town to recover. I'm glad this house was built high enough above the river that we didn't have a problem."

As they sat talking, an army lieutenant rode toward them on a chestnut army horse. It plodded along as if it were tired, its head bobbing up and down. Rainwater pounded both horse and rider as the officer dismounted. The man was of medium height and sported a dark beard and mustache.

"Are you Frank Saunders?" he asked.

"Yes," Frank said, "and this is Boyd Houston,"

"I know who Houston is," he said, disapproval written on his face. "Do you know a man named Martenelli? He says he's the Chief Deputy for the county."

"Yes," Frank said. "What about him?"

"He's in our field hospital. He's been shot."

"Shot? How serious is it?"

"I don't know, but it's pretty bad. He was shot in the chest. I was told to come and find you, and take you back to the hospital, if you want to go. He's been askin' for you 'n' Houston."

"Yes, of course we'll go. Wait here until I get my raingear."

Boyd and Frank braved the rain and mud on foot as the lieutenant rode his horse beside them. They passed through pickets as they entered the encampment and soon arrived at the large tent that served as a hospital. Water ran in streams from the tent's roof.

"Go on in," the lieutenant said. "The sawbones is expectin' you." He turned the horse and rode away into the rain.

They stepped inside, and as their eyes adjusted to the gloom, they were assailed with the odor of vomit and disinfectant. A row of cots lined one wall, but only a few were occupied. The men sprawled on their bunks, suffering from a variety of accidental injuries and illnesses. A doctor dressed in a white coat spotted with blood and other unidentified fluids, extended his hand to them. The men introduced themselves, and then the doctor led them to a bed holding the deputy. His eyes were closed, and his chest was wrapped in a heavy bandage. A splotch of blood showed in its center. His chest rose and fell rhythmically as the acrid odor of antiseptic rose from him. A wooden stand beside his bed held a stack of clean, rolled bandages and a bedpan. A lower shelf contained an assortment of glass bottles filled with dark liquids, capped with glass stoppers and screw caps.

"Is he going to make it, Doc?" Boyd asked. They stood in a row beside the bed, peering down at the deputy as if they were looking at a corpse in a coffin.

"Honestly, I don't know. He's lost a lot of blood, but his heart and pulse are strong. He's a young man and that's on his side. I got the bullet out, but there was considerable damage done. It just missed his heart and major arteries. If infection doesn't set in, he may have a chance."

The deputy's eyelids fluttered open, and he looked at them, his brow creasing, his eyes darting about. He stirred, raising his knees under the woolen blanket that covered him. He licked his chapped lips and cleared his throat.

The doctor leaned over him and said, "Can you hear me, deputy?"

He moved his eyes toward the doctor and slowly nodded. He cleared his throat again and tried to speak, one hand waving uselessly over his chest.

"What's that?" the doctor asked. "I can't understand you."

He motioned the doctor to move closer. "I can hear you," he said weakly.

"Frank and Boyd are here to see you, just as you asked," the doctor said.

They leaned closer over the man and Boyd asked, "What happened, deputy? Who shot you? Was it the Sergeant?"

"Yes, I think so." His eyes closed for a moment, then reopened. "It was a big man with a bandaged hand. He limped a little, as if from a dog bite." The deputy moved about feebly and the doctor pulled the blanket up over his chest. "I yelled at him to stop, and he shot me before I knew what had happened. I don't remember anything after that."

"That's enough," the doctor said. "He has to rest now."

The deputy grasped Boyd's wrist. "You watch him. He's faster than a snake. I'm sorry..." His voice trailed off as he drifted off again.

They stepped away from the deputy's bed and the doctor said, "I'll send a messenger for you if anything changes, and the lieutenant's going to notify the sheriff. He'll probably want to come and see the deputy, and may God help that man if the sheriff finds him."

And may God help him if I find him, Boyd thought.

\* \* \* \*

Tingle paced about in his office. He was relieved the Sergeant was out of his hair. It had been a major mistake getting involved with him in the first place. What had he been thinking? Filing that false deed for the timber property hadn't been the brightest thing he'd ever done. How had he thought he'd get away with it? He was lucky that he hadn't put his name on the deed. They couldn't prove that he was involved, and coming up with a fake business called the Little Wolf Company had been a stroke of genius. He'd hired Jimmy, the clerk, to forge Saunders' signature, and since he was gone, that link to him was broken. The store's front door bell jangled, and muted voices and laughter filtered through the wall. He'd been surprised when the Saunders woman had applied for the job as teacher in the subscription school. She was a pretty little thing, and he wondered about her history with the Sergeant. Tingle knew that if the sheriff caught him, he'd rat him out in a heartbeat. He hoped that the man had left the county for good, but wouldn't be surprised if he showed up again asking for more money.

He sat behind his desk and looked at the ledger book again. His business was in dire straits since the Sergeant had stolen his money. Even though he had a modest savings in the bank, making payroll and buying inventory would be a problem. He sighed and leaned back in his chair, clasping his hands atop his head. He'd have to make a withdrawal from the bank and decided that he would no longer keep so much money in his safe, only enough for the minimum operation of the store. If the Sergeant returned, there'd be nothing to steal. If his store failed, he'd lose everything he'd worked for. What would he tell his wife and children?

He stood and paced back and forth in the small office again, studying about how he could shift money from one account to another to keep the store afloat until he could recoup some of his losses. Maybe he could survive this, but it would be close. He grimaced when he thought about telling his wife that she couldn't go shopping for a while. No more trips to Baltimore, no expensive furnishings for the house, no expensive food. She had grown accustomed to living a pretty good life and wouldn't give it up easily. He'd blame it all on the Sergeant; tell her he'd been robbed. But, one thing he knew for sure—when he broke the news to her, it wasn't going to be pretty.

Having convinced himself that he might be able to keep the store afloat, he shifted his attention back to the problem of the fake timber deed. Had he overlooked anything? Was there anything he had missed that connected him to it? He couldn't think of anything. He regretted that the clerk had been killed, but his death *did* sever any connection to him. Maybe he'd get lucky, and this would all blow over. When no one showed up to defend the suit against the timber sale that would be the end of it. Saunders would get his property back and would never know who was behind it all. He smiled to himself. Yes, that would work. He'd just stay out of sight until it all blew over. He'd have to figure another way to make money, but he knew one thing for sure—when the war was over, there'd be money to be made.

The bald clerk knocked on his office door and then entered. "Mr. Tingle? Mrs. Skaggs wants to know if she can put her purchases on her tab. You said last time that she couldn't charge anything more. She said she didn't have enough money to pay for it with her husband off fightin' in the war. What should I tell her?"

\* \* \* \*

The rainstorm lasted for days. The river had swollen over its banks, reaching heights even the old-timers couldn't remember being reached before. Broad sheets of dirty, brown water stood in the meadows and fields, and cattle stood knee deep, bawling mournfully. Mud, gravel and debris were carried from swollen streams and deposited across roads. Soldiers were deployed to clear them and to fill in gullies that had been washed out. They worked quietly in the steady downpour, their clothing sodden and hanging on their slender frames. The town's people bailed out their houses and dug ditches to divert the relenting streams of water that poured from the mountainsides. Businessmen worked frantically to move their wares to higher shelves in case the water flowed into their stores. A group of soldiers stood on the railroad bridge and watched the brown water flow swiftly by, marveling at the enormous trees and logs that tumbled in the flood. They pointed and laughed at the dead mule that was lodged in the network of beams under the bridge, and they could hear the roar of the river as it funneled into the narrows below town.

Lexus and Rachel stood on their back porch looking at the river, and pointing out various objects that floated by. They could see a large tree, its roots stripped of all soil, tumble end over end as it made its way downstream. The river thrummed with raw energy as dirty-brown waves broke over underwater obstructions. Ducks and Canada geese took shelter in side sloughs and at water's edge along the steep mountainsides. The two young women stood together, awestruck, their shoulders touching.

Rachel said, "Daddy told me about the deputy, Benjamin, being shot. Do you suppose the Army will allow me to go see him? He seemed like a pleasant young man."

"I don't know, Rachel. If Uncle Frank or Boyd goes with you, maybe they will. The pickets and the doctor should remember them. That could help. I understand he's gravely wounded." Since the attack, Rachel had been subdued and quiet. Lexus was pleased that she was showing cautious interest in the deputy.

"I don't know if I'll ever be able to trust a man again, but he seemed to be a nice person. And, after all, he was shot trying to help us."

Lexus smiled and said, "I'll talk to Boyd and see if he'll go with you."

Later that day, Boyd walked Rachel to the Army encampment and talked their way through the pickets and to the hospital tent. As they entered, Rachel wrinkled her nose at the odor. The doctor sat at a small folding desk in the corner, sharpening a wicked looking bone saw with a file. "I hope you're not planning to use that thing on me, Doc," Boyd said, joking.

The doctor turned to look at them. "Unfortunately, it's one of the tools of my trade. I've used it more times than I like to think about."

"Have you served in many battles?"

"Well, I've been transferred around a bit, so I was unfortunate enough to have been involved in some pretty nasty conflicts. This duty, here in the mountains, has been like a holiday. All I have to contend with is a few accidental gunshot wounds and a broken arm or leg now and then, but the most serious problem is disease. It seems like we lose as many or more men to sickness as in battle. And, once in a while I see a bunch of men suffering from eating bad food or from drinking bad whiskey."

"How's the deputy doing, Doc? Is he any better?"

"He's resting a little better now. He's in a lot of pain, so I gave him a little bit of laudanum to help him rest easier. I try to use it sparingly because you never know when we'll need it."

"Do you suppose we could see him? I'd like to see if he remembers anything else about being shot, and Rachel here would like to say hello. They met briefly a few days ago."

"I don't see why not. We've moved him over in the corner where it's a little quieter."

Rachel held back as they approached the bed, an apprehensive look in her eyes. When Boyd spoke to him, the deputy opened his eyes. "Hey, deputy. Are you feeling any better?" Boyd asked.

"Yeah, I'm a little woozy and it hurts like hell when I move around, but I 'spect I'll live," he said. He grimaced as he used his forearm to slowly push himself into a more comfortable position. "As much as anything, I'm embarrassed that he got the best of me." He closed his eyes and Boyd thought he'd drifted off again, and then he continued. "I've never seen anyone jerk a gun that fast."

"Is there anything you remember about him that would help me find him? We've got to get him put away before he hurts someone else."

The deputy took a long time before answering. "Not that I can think of. He looked like a lot of ruffians you see working around the railroad or hanging around the bars." He licked his dry lips, and the doctor lifted a glass of water to his mouth. He swallowed a few mouths full and then sunk back onto the pillow. "I'm sorry I let you down, Mr. Houston. When I'm a bit better, I'll have another go at him."

Boyd smiled and then said, "I understand the sheriff is planning to come here and lead the search for him."

The Deputy said, "I hope I'm well enough to see that matchup. It would be worth the price of admission."

Boyd motioned for Rachel to approach the bed. "Do you remember Miss Rachel here? She's Frank Saunders' daughter. She wanted to come along to see if you were improving."

Rachel moved next to the bed and smiled at the deputy. "Everyone's worried about you Deputy Martenelli. We're all so very proud of you for standing up to that horrible man." She picked at a corner of the blanket that covered him. "He's the one that beat me up and did horrible things to me. I wish you'd killed him so he couldn't hurt anyone else."

The deputy looked at her deep blue eyes and raven hair, and a little smile softened his features. "A man that would hurt a woman doesn't deserve to live." His eyes drooped and he spoke even more slowly. "I'll help all I can to get him."

They were silent for a moment, and then the deputy said in a rough whisper, "Won't you come back to see me, Miss Rachel? Maybe next time I'll be feelin' better."

"Yes. I'm come back tomorrow if I can. Will that be all right, Doctor?"

The doctor grinned and said, "I'm sure it would be good for him to have visitors. It'd probably be good for all of us."

Boyd leaned on a large post that supported the tent, crossed his arms over his chest, and smiled.

# CHAPTER TEN

SHERIFF ART PETROWSKI sat on a chair next to his chief deputy's bed in the hospital tent. He shuffled his muddy boots as he watched the wounded man's face as he slept. He didn't want to wake him but would need to talk to him soon. He needed to know what happened firsthand. Ben was a good deputy, his best, and he was surprised that the renegade had bested him so easily. Just the slightest hesitation made all the difference in the world when it came to a gun fight. Ben had a soft heart and would have been hesitant to fire. He supposed that was what had happened, but wouldn't know for sure until he had talked to him.

He left the hospital tent and walked back into town. He entered the hotel and went into the side room that he was using as an office. He was likely to be here for a few days and needed a center of operations. The hotel owner had graciously given him a room in which to work. He'd brought a couple of deputies with him, and they sat stiffly in the chairs arranged along the wall.

"He's asleep. I didn't want to wake him, so I'll have to talk to him later. In the meantime, we need to get a search organized for that renegade. I think it's unlikely that he's still in town, but we'll do a complete search just in case. The Army is willing to lend us a few men to help out," the sheriff said. He made some assignments to his men, and they left. He sat down behind his makeshift desk. There was a knock at the door, and he turned to see who it was.

"Mr. Houston. Come on in. You're just the man I need to see," the sheriff said.

"Yes, I heard that you wanted to talk to me, so I came on down. What can I do for you?"

The two men shook hands, and Boyd sat across the desk from the sheriff. After some polite conversation the sheriff said, "Tell me about this man, Sergeant Brown, who shot my deputy. What do you know about him, and how does he fit in with Miss Lexus?"

"I told you part of this before, but there's quite a history there. He was part of a bunch of renegade soldiers who were raiding the farms and businesses in the Greenbrier Valley. They'd steal whatever they could get their hands on and sell it to the army– they weren't particular which one. They were all deserters, and from what I heard, the Sergeant was the highest ranked, so he just naturally became their leader. There was a bunch of them, but over time, some of them were either killed or just drifted away. It turned out that he had some kind of infatuation with Lexus, and he abducted her and burned her house. Another man and I got her back from him, but he got away. Evidently, he followed us all the way here. If he gets his hands on Lexus, he'll kill her."

"I see. Just how did you get involved in all this?"

"Well, I knew Lexus some years back. She was afraid of the Sergeant and asked me to come help her. I was living in South Carolina. When I received her letter, I didn't know what to think since we hadn't exactly parted on friendly terms. But, she asked for my help, so I could hardly turn her down."

"What's your situation with her now? You plannin' to get married?"

Boyd paused and looked away from the sheriff for a moment. "I haven't asked her for her hand yet," he admitted. "But, it looks like we're headed that way."

"I don't mean to stick my nose in your business, Mr. Houston, but I'm just trying to fill in some blanks. It's a lot clearer now. At any rate, it's a certainty that we need to round him up. I don't take lightly to folks shooting my best deputy. The doctor said he'd survive, but it will take some time for him to get back on his feet. But, make no mistake, when I catch up with that renegade, I'm going to put him under the sod."

"How are you going to find him, Sheriff? Is there any way I can help?"

"Yes, you can help us search the town. If he's not here, we'll know to start looking elsewhere. There are a lot of ways he can get out of town. He could catch a train or steal a horse and just ride away. He could just walk to another town. Could be he's already gone."

Boyd walked outside with the sheriff. Several soldiers lounged on the front porch of the hotel. A sergeant identified himself and said they'd been assigned to help with the search.

"Here's how we're going to go about this," the sheriff said. "We'll start on the south end of the town, along the river road. We'll fan out and keep in a line and check each house along the way. This isn't a large town, so it shouldn't take too long. Knock on each door, and if there's someone home, ask them if they've seen the man. If the house is empty, check it as best you can. Keep in contact with the person on each side of you to keep in line. We won't have to worry about the Army encampment–they'll know if a stranger is among them. One other thing. This man is dangerous. He'll think nothing of back-shooting you. If you see him, yell for help. Don't take any chances."

The men began the sweep through town in a steady rain and picked up some help along the way. The residents of the town were anxious to get rid of the threat, too. They were especially angry about the Sergeant attacking women. They moved along

# INTO THE MOUNTAINS

rapidly, checking every home, barn, boarding house and hotel. One owner of a boarding house said the Sergeant had been staying there, but had left several days ago. The sweep concluded when they arrived at the lower end of town. They didn't find anything.

"Well now, it looks like the chicken has flown the coop. Or should I say the weasel?" the sheriff asked.

\* \* \* \*

Sergeant Brown sat on a rickety chair in the hunting cabin he'd commandeered. It was stuck on a bench on the side of the mountain, and was far enough out of town to make it unlikely that anyone would stumble onto him. Someone had cobbled the shack together from bits and pieces of leftover lumber and sawmill slabs. The roof was the only solid part of the building and had protected him from most of the rain and wind that had shook and banged for the last several days. He could hear the roar of the river far below in the canyon, and he was almost getting used to hearing the trains that labored up the grade from the town. There were only a few each day, and he was far enough away from the tracks that he'd not been seen.

He planned to hike to the depot in Tunnelton to catch a train out of this godforsaken valley and the sooner the better. It was only a few miles up the tracks. He had Tingle's money in his pocket and for the first time in his life felt like he wouldn't have to live from hand to mouth. He'd buy the best seat on the train and eat the best food. He'd buy some fancy clothes, get a good shave, and a haircut. No one would recognize him. He'd stay on the train until he was well away from here, then he'd buy a good horse. Why, he could go anywhere he wanted to.

But, first he had a score to settle. He'd been spying on Lexus at night. With the pouring rain, the nights were as dark as the inside of a black cat. He'd been able to get close to her house, but there was always someone around. Sooner or later, he'd be able to grab her. He'd get that other woman, too, if he had the chance. He leaned the chair back against the wall and looked out the door. Across the narrow hollow from where his shack sat, he could see the iron viaduct that spanned Tray Run. A square blockhouse squatted on the west end of the structure, and he could smell the smoke from the campfires of the pickets stationed there. Buckeye Run was spanned by a shorter viaduct closer to town. Occasionally, he could hear the soldiers' laughter filtering through the trees if the wind was just right. He'd have to circle around the viaducts on his way to Tunnelton. He didn't know how long that would take.

He thought about the deputy he'd shot. It had been a lucky shot, but he'd dropped like he'd been brained with a poleaxe. The Sergeant didn't know why the deputy hadn't fired, but he was glad he hadn't. It had been easy to slip away with all the excitement. He'd walked out of town following the tracks and was lucky to find the shack. It had rained for days on end, and he'd holed up except for spying on that woman.

He stepped out of the shack and looked up at the sky. The rain had slacked off a little, but he could tell that the storm wasn't over. It gave him good cover even if he got soaked, and so few people were out in the rain he had been able to move about unnoticed. He went back in the shack and looked in the bag of stolen food for something to eat. He'd make another trip into town to see if he could find that woman alone. He wouldn't take any chances with her this time—he'd shoot her if he got a chance.

\* \* \* \*

Boyd and the sheriff sat in the hotel office, their feet up on his desk, drinking coffee. One of the hotel cooks stuck her head in the door and asked them if they wanted some scones to eat with their coffee. "What kind of a law enforcement officer would I be if I turned down something to eat? Bring them on in here," the sheriff said. After the cook had left, they sat quietly, eating the scones and drinking the strong brew.

"What are you going to do now, Sheriff?" Boyd asked.

"We'll have to expand the search away from town. I'll send telegraph messages to points east and west along the railroad. I've already alerted the railroad bulls to keep an eye out for him in case he jumps a train. I'll send a deputy across Laurel Mountain to Fellowsville to let them know to keep an eye out, too. I suppose he could have gone east on the turnpike and on up to Mount Carmel, but he'd have to cross the covered bridge, and the soldiers there haven't seen him. Maybe he'll go south to St. George. There're some Confederates down that way, and if he's headed there, we may not ever catch him. It would be a bit touchy for my men if the Rebs caught them, even if they're not in the army. Everybody knows that Preston County's fiercely Union and was a strong supporter of our becoming a new state."

"Lexus and I came through St. George–stayed overnight there. We didn't see any Confederates then, but from what I hear, they come and go," Boyd said.

They were finishing their scones and coffee when one of the deputies knocked on the door jam, and then entered the office. "I got some bad news, Sheriff. A soldier came by and said one of their patrols was scouting down along the river below town. They found a body down in the bottom of a limestone pit. They didn't bring it back, figuring you'd want to take care of it. It looked to them like a civilian."

"That's about all I need, is another problem to take care of. Is the soldier still hanging around, deputy?"

"Yessire, Sheriff. He's out on the porch. You want to see him?"

"Yes, send him in. Oh, and deputy, go down to the livery and see if they'll loan us a horse and wagon."

"Sheriff," Boyd said, "I have a horse and wagon. I could go and get it."

"That'd be good, Houston. You go and get it, and I'll talk to the soldier."

An hour later, Boyd and the sheriff rode on the wagon seat, and the soldier rode in the bed, hanging on to the sides with both hands, complaining about the bouncing ride. They skirted the east side of the roaring river as rain dripped from the brims of their hats. Two deputies followed on their horses. They soon came to a limestone outcropping barely above the flood's edge where they found a shallow tunnel into the mountain and a pit where the remains of a man could be seen floating face-down in a puddle of water.

"Phew-eee," the soldier said, holding his nose, "smells like he's been in there for a spell. How're you goin' to get him out of there?"

"Seeing as how your sergeant loaned you to me, I thought we'd just drop you down there on the end of a rope, and you could just kinda toss him up here," the sheriff said.

"No sir, Sheriff. My sergeant told me not to fall for that. The only thing I'm to do is show where he is, and then my duty is done. I've smelled a dead body or two, but that one is plumb ripe. As a matter of fact, I'll just leave you now, and walk back to camp." The man jumped out of the back of the wagon and began walking swiftly back toward the encampment.

One of the deputies was appointed to scramble down into the pit and tie a rope around the corpse, and they soon had it pulled up on the ground. Rain fell on its decomposed face, washing away dirt and grime.

The men moved the body so they could get a good look it. Its head was crushed from a ferocious blow from behind.

"I'm not absolutely sure, fellers, but I believe this is Jimmy Smith from the county clerk's office. He's a bit decomposed, and he's been missing for weeks now. Just how do you reckon he found his way here?" the sheriff asked, muttering to himself.

"Sheriff, Jimmy was responsible for filing property sales. I think the Sergeant was mixed up in that land deed mess somehow. I think it was him who threatened Frank—said that if he followed up on the suit challenging the sale of his property, he'd kill him and all of his family. I don't know if he was the one who hatched the scheme to steal Frank's property or if he was working with someone else. Anyway, I'd bet the Sergeant killed him."

"Yes, that's most likely what happened, but we need to get him back to Kingwood so the coroner can take a look at 'im. He's the one to officially say what he died of. This is just one more reason we need to find that renegade. I'm looking forward to meeting him more all the time," the sheriff said.

* * * *

The Sergeant was getting nervous. He'd heard in town that the sheriff had found the clerk he'd knocked in the head. He'd thrown the body in a pit, but somehow the sheriff had found it. He'd also heard that he was being blamed for the killing. Just how did the sheriff connect him to the clerk? It didn't really matter–he'd have to get out of town for a while and let things cool down, but he wasn't ready to leave for good yet.

He waited for it to get dark and then he hiked through town and up the river road to the Northwestern Turnpike. He had a devil of a time getting around the barricade and all those soldiers, but he'd crept up the edge of the river, wading at times, and then sneaked through the brush until he was past them. There were soldiers everywhere, and he'd have to be careful they didn't catch him. The pike was deserted as he approached, but he was sure someone would come by soon enough. He knew that he couldn't go east to Mount Carmel because he'd have to cross the covered bridge, and it was guarded heavily. He wasn't anxious to try to cross the river since he couldn't swim, and it had been rising lately with all the rain they'd had.

He walked west on the pike until he came to the base of Laurel Mountain. He planned to go to Fellowsville and knew that it lay just over the mountain, ten miles or so. From what he'd heard, it was a busy place, and he'd be able to hide out there for a while. He could get a room in one of the hotels, and there were drovers moving along the pike often enough that no one would think twice about one more man just passing through. He started walking up the mountain switchbacks and was soon gasping for breath. He sat on a rock until his heartbeat slowed, and he could breathe without gasping. What he needed was for someone to give him a ride–it was well after midnight, and no one in his right mind would be out at this time of night. He moved a ways off the road and sat down against a large tree, pulled his rain slicker up over his head, crossed his arms over his chest and was soon sound asleep.

He awoke the next morning to an overcast sky and staggered to his feet. He was stiff and sore from sleeping on the hard ground, and his stomach growled. He was in a very bad mood. Here he was stuck in these awful mountains, the sheriff and half the Union Army after him, and that woman had bested him at every turn. He shook his head and rubbed his back. It was late in the morning before he heard the approach of a horse and rider. He brushed the leaves and twigs from his clothing and straightened his hat. The rider approached, and he stepped out into the road with a smile on his face.

"Howdy, there," the Sergeant said. "How are you this fine morning?"

The rider drew up, stopping some distance away. "Morning. You gave me a start there. Didn't expect anyone to be up here on the side of the mountain this time of day. You on foot?"

"Yeah, I'm on my way to Fellowsville. I don't have a horse and was hoping someone would come by and give me a ride."

"Well, I don't think my horse can carry two up over this mountain. You'll just have to wait until someone comes along with a wagon. Or, maybe the stagecoach will be along soon."

"No, I wasn't thinkin' that you'd give me a ride. That's a good lookin' horse you got there. You just passin' through, are you?"

The man looked the Sergeant over carefully. He didn't like what he saw. "I'm from Romney, on my way to Grafton. I've got business to do there."

"You come by this way often?" the Sergeant asked. "I'm not from around these parts, and I don't know much about the pike here. How far is it to Fellowsville?"

The man hesitated and then said, "No, this is my first time through the mountains. I'd heard how spectacular the scenery is, so I decided to ride rather than take the train. I usually just catch it and ride straight through. It's a long way through this way, and I don't believe I'll try it again. I'm not sure how much farther it is to Fellowsville, but it can't be more than ten or twelve miles. Maybe less." The man in the pike before him was asking a lot of questions and the rider didn't like it. He put his hand on the butt of the pistol under his belt.

"Oh, just hold on there mister. There's no reason to go pullin' a gun on a man. I'm harmless. I'm just on my way over the mountain and don't mean you any harm."

"No offense, but I don't know you from Adam. If you don't mind, I'll just be on my way. I wish you luck with finding a ride."

"No offense taken. A man can't be too careful in this day and time. You just go on now, and maybe we'll meet again somewhere down the road." The Sergeant stepped aside and waved the rider on.

As the horse and rider drew abreast, the Sergeant leapt toward him and grasped his coat front, pulling him to the ground. The horse shied and ran off a few yards and then stopped. The Sergeant struck the rider a savage blow with the butt of his gun, stunning him. The man rolled on the ground, groaning. Blood streamed from his nose and from a gaping cut on his cheek. The Sergeant stepped back and looked quickly up and down the pike, fearful someone would come along. He took the pistol from the rider's belt and riffled through his pockets, taking a leather wallet and some coins. He stuffed them in his pockets, dragged the stunned man across the road and pushed him over the edge of a cliff. The Sergeant could hear the body tumbling and crashing through the brush below, and then all was quiet.

The Sergeant smiled to himself. Good fortune had finally come his way. He caught up the horse's reins and calmed it by petting its neck and crooning to it. The horse moved away nervously, but soon calmed again. He cautiously mounted, and the horse began a miles-eating walk up the mountain. He was pleased with this turn of events. From what he gathered, the rider wasn't known here, nor was the horse. Drovers and stage drivers might forget a man's face, but they would always remember the horse he was riding. Just to be safe, he'd try to trade the horse as soon as he could. Maybe to someone off the pike who'd be less likely to be suspicious of him.

He spurred the horse gently to keep it moving along, and soon came to the top of the mountain where he saw a cluster of houses and a hotel. There was a large corral in the back that contained a herd of cattle that milled about, bawling. Two men stood along the corral, talking and waving their arms as they looked at the cows. He pulled his hat down and rode quickly by. The pike sloped steeply downward, twisting and turning along the mountain's side. There were a scattering of houses and farms along the pike, and he could see men working in the sodden fields. He laughed outright as he thought about the rider going over the cliff and the sound he made when he hit the ground. He would be long gone before he was found. He hummed an off-key tune as the miles fell away, and he was soon entering the bustling town. He stopped before a log hotel and dismounted. Yes, his luck had changed. He had a pocket full of money and with a couple of good meals and a few nights' rest, he'd be ready to go back to Rowlesburg and take care of some unfinished business. And then, and only then, he'd leave these dreadful mountains for good.

\* \* \* \*

The rider awoke in excruciating pain as the forest canopy dripped with rain. He had come to rest against a large tree, and his back and legs were twisted agonizingly. He raised a shaking hand to his cheek and felt the bloody flap that hung down, pushing it back in place. He touched his broken nose carefully, feeling the crushed bone. He pushed himself to his knees and tried to stand. His back screamed in pain, and his leg was sore and swollen. He looked around to find that he had come to rest on a steep, tree-covered slope. Each time he moved shale and rocks slid down the mountainside below him. He looked back up toward the cliff, wondering how he had ever survived the fall. All he could figure was that the steep, leaf-covered slope, on which he landed, had somehow lessened the impact. He quickly realized that there was no way he would be able to climb back up the cliff to the road; the only possible route was downward. He sat down and began to slide, feet first. He soon had a mass of rocks, shale and leaves pushed in front of him, and as the grade steepened, he lost control. With a great clatter, he fell onto the road of the switchback below just as a team and stagecoach started up the mountain. The fall knocked the wind from his lungs and he wallowed on the road like a beached whale.

The surprised driver pulled the coach to a stop, and men clambered out to help the wounded man. They questioned the rider as they helped him into the coach, exclaiming in dismay at his story. With great effort, the driver and his helper turned the coach and team and headed back down the pike. They turned onto the river road and soon deposited the rider with the soldiers at the blockade. The stagecoach returned to the pike and continued on its way.

Later that evening, Boyd and the Sheriff stood at the rider's bedside in the doctor's office. The man's face was a mass of cuts and bruises. His nose was flattened, and both eyes were blackened. His cheek revealed the tracks of stitches that the doctor had used to pull his torn flesh together. He moved about stiffly in his bed, complaining of a sprained back and a badly bruised leg.

"What did the man look like?" the sheriff asked. "You think you could identify him if we catch him?"

The rider groaned and said, "I'd know him anywhere. Big, rough looking man."

"Did he say where he was headed? Can you remember anything that might help us find him?"

"It's all a blur. I remember him asking about Fellowsville, but I got the opinion he wasn't telling me the truth anyway. He asked a lot of questions about where I was from and where I was going. I should have just ridden by him from the start, and not stopped to talk to him."

The sheriff said, "Do you think he was going up the mountain? Or, was he coming back down this way?"

"I can't say for sure why, but I think he was going up the mountain, at least that's what he said. That'd be toward Fellowsville, wouldn't it? I got the impression he was tired of walking up that steep mountain and was waiting for someone like me to come along."

"Okay, thanks. You've been a great help," the sheriff said.

Boyd stepped close to the bed and said, "One more thing. What kind of horse were you riding? Folks might be able to identify it."

The wounded man gave them a complete description of the horse and saddle. "He took my wallet and all of my money. How am I going to get home?"

The sheriff assured him that they'd see that he got on the stagecoach when he was well enough to travel. Boyd and the sheriff stepped outside the doctor's office and talked.

Boyd said, "I'm pretty sure that it was the Sergeant who did that." He nodded toward the doctor's office. "Maybe he's given up trying to get to Lexus and has decided to leave. We need to catch him before he gets away."

"I'm not so sure. I figure that if he wants to leave the area, he'll just jump on a passing train. Going off on foot doesn't sound like such a good idea."

"Well, no one said he was smart. If he was, he'd have never gotten himself in such a mess from the start."

"Oh, I suppose, but I've got a murder to take care of and don't have time to go chasing around the country. Tell you what. Why don't you and Frank ride over that way and see if you can find him. If it's the Sergeant, you come back here and get me. Don't take any chances with him."

"I'll be glad to do that, Sheriff, but Frank will have to stay here with Rachel and Lexus. We can't leave them by themselves."

"I guess you're right, but I don't think it's a good idea for you to go alone."

"I'll be careful. Besides, we're not sure it's the Sergeant."

Early the next morning, Boyd saddled his horse and rode out of town, and before noon, he sat on his horse looking at the town of Fellowsville spread out before him.

\* \* \* \*

Rachel sat on the corner of deputy Martenelli's bed, talking quietly to him as he reclined against a stack of pillows she'd brought from her house. His eyes were brighter, and he could move about without grimacing in pain. The doctor had said that so far there was no sign of infection in the wound, and that barring any unforeseen complications, he would survive.

As they talked, Ben told of his childhood growing up in Kingwood and going to school there at the Academy. They told each other stories about their schooling, laughing at the antics in which they'd engaged. They learned that they'd both attended an evening debate at Bonafield School near Tunnelton when they were younger, but had no memory of seeing each other. Rachel told him more about the attack she'd suffered at the hands of the renegade sergeant. He shifted in his bed, and his face became flushed with anger.

"I wish I'd shot him," he said. "I'm sorry I didn't. I hope the sheriff finds him and gives him what for."

"Oh Benjamin, I was so scared. He grabbed me and did terrible things to me, but it could have been worse." Her eyes dropped to the blanket that covered his body. "But, I won't let him take my future from me. What he did to me was terrible, but it's in the past. I'm going to forget it and get on with my life. The sheriff will find him and then this terrible ordeal will be all over."

"You're brave to say that." He paused, looking up at her. "I don't think I've ever held a hero's hand. Could I hold yours, Rachel?" She blushed and dropped her eyes again. He took her hand in his.

The doctor soon shooed her away so he could change Ben's dressings. She walked back to her house and was greeted by Lexus. After lunch, they sat in the parlor cutting long strips of cloth from sheets and winding them into rolls for bandages. They'd donate them to the Army's field hospital. They talked quietly of plans for the future and how they'd like their lives to be.

\* \* \* \*

The sheriff urged his horse up the road toward Kingwood. He was in a hurry, and Jimmy's killing had put him in a very bad mood. He wasn't sure if the renegade had killed him, but he just couldn't help thinking there was a connection with the attempt to steal Saunders' timber property. He was on the way to the courthouse to see if Ed knew anything more about what was going on. Maybe he was involved. No, he thought, he'd known Ed for a long time, and he didn't believe he would get tangled up in something like that. Would he?

He put his heels to his horse, and it broke into a canter. A short time later, he rode into town and dismounted in front of the courthouse. The street was a mess of mud and standing water. Only a few people were brave enough to slog through the streets, and a steady rain continued to beat down. He stomped the mud from his boots and went to his office. He hung up his wet hat and brushed the water from his shoulders. When will this rain ever stop? He used an old towel to wipe the water from his clothing, and then he walked down to the clerk's office on the first floor looking for Ed. He found him in his usual place behind the counter, sitting in an old swivel chair, swinging back and forth. "Hey Ed, I need to talk to you for a minute."

"Sure, Sheriff, come on back here to my parlor," he said, chuckling.

"I want you to put on your serious face for a minute, Ed." The sheriff's face was florid with anger. "We found Jimmy's body in a pit down at Rowlesburg. Somebody clubbed him to death."

"Oh, I'm sorry to hear that, Sheriff, but I'm not really surprised he's dead. I mean, he's been missing for weeks, and nobody heard a peep from him. Only something bad could have caused him to disappear like that. He wasn't one to run off and leave his job."

"Well, he's dead and I mean to find out who did it. What do you know about that missing deed for Frank Saunders' timber property? Do you suppose Jimmy was involved in that?"

Ed's face showed surprise, and he fussed with a stack of papers on his desk. He looked away from the sheriff and took a deep breath. "To tell you the truth, I sort of suspected something fishy was goin' on. Jimmy was usually pretty friendly, but lately he'd been a bit surly, and I saw him sneakin' around in the deed files on more than one occasion."

"What do you mean, sneaking around?"

"Just that, Sheriff. He'd go down there in the file room and just browse around like he didn't know what he was lookin' for."

"Do you have any idea what he might have been doing?" the sheriff asked, watching Ed's eyes closely.

Ed hesitated. "Well, maybe he was lookin' for a property that was suitable to be stole. That's all I can figure. But Jimmy didn't have the ambition to do anything that brazen. How would he get away with it?"

"It looks like someone tried it, and I think Jimmy was up to his eyeballs in it. It looks like somebody killed him to keep him quiet. You have any idea who that could be, Ed?" the sheriff asked.

Ed's color drained from his face, and he began fidgeting with a pencil. His eyes darted from one corner of the room to the other. "Well look here, Sheriff. You're not accusing me of killing him, are you? I didn't have anything to do with it."

"No, Ed, I don't believe you killed him, but from the look on your face, you must have been involved somehow," the sheriff said, not unkindly. "Why don't you just tell me what happened and get it off your chest?"

Ed squirmed on his chair. He said softly, "I didn't mean for anyone to get hurt. You know how I like to squeeze a dollar out of folks now and then? Well, sometimes folks will ask me to keep them informed about what goes on in the office here. You know, lawyers and such, and they slip me a dollar or two now and then. There's no harm in it, Sheriff. I help them out and they give me a little spending money in return."

"How long has this been going on, Ed?"

"Oh, I don't know. Couple of years anyway. I'm not going to lose my job, am I?"

"We'll have to see about that. Just what are you trying to tell me? Spit it out."

"Well, someone asked me to keep a lookout for anyone askin' about Frank Saunders' property. I didn't really know what was goin' on. All I knew was that Jimmy was acting funny. When Boyd Houston got to asking me about the deed, I sent the man a message letting him know. Honest, Sheriff, that's all I did. And, Jimmy was already missing by that time. Whatever happened to him isn't my fault."

"That remains to be seen, Ed. We'll have to let the judge decide that, but there's one question I want you to answer right now. Who did you send the message to? He's probably the one that killed Jimmy."

"I hardly know the man, Sheriff." Ed swallowed, making his Adams apple bob up and down, and he could barely speak. "It was Mr. Tingle that owns the dry goods store down there in Rowlesburg."

The sheriff got up to leave, then hesitated and said, "Let's just keep this conversation between the two of us, Ed. If I hear that you've warned Tingle that I'm coming for him, you'll have to answer to me. You got that?" The sheriff glared at him.

Ed's face turned red as he said, "Yes sir. I understand, Sheriff."

## INTO THE MOUNTAINS

\* \* \* \*

Boyd dismounted and led his horse to the side of the pike to allow a small herd of cattle to be driven past. The cows bawled as they plodded along toward Laurel Mountain, prodded by two men carrying walking sticks. The road was wet and muddy; the cows' legs and bellies were caked with thick layers of sticky muck. A steady drizzle of rain fell from the leaden sky. One of the drovers stopped long enough to talk to Boyd. They were driving the cattle to Rowlesburg where they would be slaughtered and fed to a hungry army.

"What you're seeing here is unusual. Most folks ship their stock on the railroad, but we can save a little bit on shipping costs by driving them to market ourselves," the drover said. "I reckon we're just about the last hold-outs. Before the railroad came through the county in fifty-one, there were thousands of cattle driven to market this way, an' there were hotels and holding pens all along the pike. Now, you'll only find one here and there that's still open. The stagecoach has just about petered out, too. Folks just naturally find it's faster and more comfortable to ride in a train car than in a bouncin' coach, but I reckon there's some local traffic left."

The drover told Boyd that Fellowsville was showing the results of being bypassed by the railroad. Traffic on the pike had been dwindling for the past decade. The towns along the tracks would prosper, and those along the pike would decline even further. Boyd turned their conversation to the Sergeant.

"I'm looking for a man that probably came through here. Did you see a lone man ride through sometime yesterday?" He described the Sergeant and his horse.

"No, we didn't. We started out just west of here and would have passed him sometime yesterday afternoon if he was goin' west. We stayed over in the hotel, but didn't see anybody of that description." The herd had passed them, and the other drover yelled that they needed to get to the top of the mountain by dark, so he'd better shake a leg. The drover trotted toward the herd to catch up.

Boyd rode into the town snuggled in a long valley at the confluence of two creeks. He saw a cluster of hotels and businesses arrayed along the pike, some of which were boarded up. A group of men toiled at tearing down a large building, stacking the lumber in neat rows. Tidy two-story houses lined the side streets, and he had to dodge pedestrian traffic as he approached a large hotel. He dismounted, tied the horse to a hitching post and walked into the false-fronted building.

A clerk, middle aged with a big smile on his face, greeted Boyd. "Afternoon. You looking for a room?" He gazed curiously at Boyd.

"No, I'm looking for some information. Maybe you can help me. A man was beaten and robbed and his horse stolen sometime yesterday, up on Laurel Mountain. I'm looking for the man who did it. The sheriff sent me here to see if I could find him. We think maybe he's coming this way." Boyd described the Sergeant and his horse.

"No, I haven't seen anyone like that. We don't have much business here anymore. Just a stagecoach now and then and a few drovers. I'd have seen him if he was staying here."

"Is there another hotel here that's still open?"

"Yeah, there's one other. It's down yonder along the crick, beside the pike. Mostly drovers there, a rough place, though. There's a tavern just beside it. Go on west on the pike. You can't miss it."

Boyd thanked the man for his help and then rode through the town until he came to the hotel. It was a two story log house with a broad porch across its front. A squat, board and batten building nearby had a roughly painted sign that proclaimed it to be a tavern. He guessed that the first place the Sergeant would visit was a place that served liquor, so he stepped inside and let his eyes adjust to the gloom. A boy, no older than ten or eleven, swept the floor with a broom that looked to be on its last leg. He had swept a pile of glass and dirt into a pile in the center of the room and was getting ready to scoop it into a box. A middle-aged man with a ruddy complexion stood behind a long wooden bar polishing glasses with a hand towel. They both looked up when Boyd entered.

"Afternoon," Boyd said pleasantly. "I'm looking for a man. He might have been in here last night."

"There were a lot of men in here last night, mister," the boy said.

"We don't usually give out that kind of information, especially to wives, old girlfriends, or the sheriff," the man said, grinning. "What goes on in here isn't any of their business, but who're you looking for, and what does he look like?"

Boyd told him about the assault and robbery. "He almost killed that man, and he took his money and horse. I'm trying to locate him so the sheriff can come and get him." He described the Sergeant and the horse.

"Oh, Lord yes, he was here last night! He got in a fight with Mike Johnson, he lives up on the mountain there, and they just about tore up the place. I've got a couple of busted chairs and a table out back to prove it. We're still cleaning up the mess. Johnny there is cleanin' up the last of it. I don't care if I never see him again. The drovers are rough enough without a man like that stirrin' up trouble." The man polished the glass vigorously and frowned.

"Do you have any idea where he went?"

"No, and I don't care as long as it isn't here." He thought for a moment and said, "He might have been stayin' in the hotel next door. He was drunker 'an a monkey when he left, staggering all over the place. I don't expect that he went very far. Yeah, I'd check the hotel."

"One more question. Where would he have left the horse? He wouldn't just tie it up somewhere."

"He could have left it in the corral out back. That's where the hotel owner keeps the drover's stock when they stay overnight. He makes a pretty good penny at it, too."

Boyd thanked the man and walked to the corral. It contained a small herd of cattle and a couple of mules. A horse stood to one side of the other animals eying him as he approached. It shuffled away from him to stand on the far side of the enclosure. Boyd guessed it was the rider's stolen horse. An expensive saddle and bridle had been tossed haphazardly onto the ground. Boyd nudged it with his toe noting that it was wet from the falling rain and grimy with mud.

Boyd walked to the hotel, stomping the mud from his boots before he entered. The hotel was laid out much as the other one had been, but with cruder craftsmanship. It had a dark foyer with a staircase leading to the second floor and a dining area to the side. A clerk stood behind a desk, sorting mail into cubicles attached to the wall behind him. He nodded at Boyd and put up the last of the mail.

"What can I do for you?" the clerk asked. He was a thin man with shaky hands and bloodshot eyes.

Boyd went through his story again, explaining why he was looking for the Sergeant. "He's a big, mean looking fellow, and he's dangerous. The sheriff wants him put away before he kills someone else."

"Yeah," the clerk said reluctantly. "He was over at the tavern last night. I saw him drinkin' in a corner like he didn't want anybody near him. He just sat there and glared at everybody. He was drinkin' like there was no tomorrow, but he seemed to have lots of money. When he got drunk enough, he got to talking to some other men and bought a round for the house."

"Were you there when he started the fight?" Boyd asked.

"No, I came on back here. I had to tend the desk until midnight. I heard he got in a big ruckus."

"Yeah, the tavern owner said he busted up the place and then left, drunk. Is he stayin' here?"

The clerk looked nervously at the stairs leading to the second floor. "Far as I know, he's sleeping it off up there right now. He's in the room at the back."

Boyd looked at the stairs and said, "Is there another way out? A back door or something?"

"No, but he could have climbed out the window and dropped onto the roof of the kitchen. It's only a few feet down to the ground from there. We had a drover did that once and he skipped out on the rent."

In the room above, the Sergeant awoke with a start. His head hurt like a toothache, and his mouth was dry and foul tasting. He ran his tongue over his teeth and rubbed his eyes. The bed sagged in the middle, and the old quilt the clerk had given him was wadded into a lump. He placed his feet on the floor carefully, trying not to move too quickly lest his head would burst. He heard a rumbling of voices downstairs and wondered what was going on. He pulled his boots on and crept down the short hallway to the top of the stairs. He could hear the clerk and a man talking. It didn't take long to figure out that they were talking about him. He squatted at the top of the stairs and could see the top of a man's head and part of his shoulder. Houston! He had little doubt he had been followed and now he would have to run for it. He'd kill the man if he got the chance, but not in town.

He walked quietly back to his room, hastily gathered his belongings and slid out the window. It was a short drop onto the roof below. He was soon on the ground and trotting toward the corral. It took him only a few moments to catch up the horse and toss the saddle on it. He spurred it ruthlessly back to the pike and turned toward the center of town. It was his muddled thought that he'd be able to hide in the town somewhere–he really didn't want to leave. He had a lot of drinking to do, and he was really angry that Houston was pushing him. Gobs of mud and dirt flew from the horse's hooves as he galloped along. People stopped to stare at him as he rode by.

A man came out of the hotel to see what the commotion was and then set up the alarm. "There he is," he shouted. "That's him. That's the man they're looking for. He's the one that robbed that man and took his horse." Other people started shouting and pointing. Reaching the forks of the creek in the middle of town, the Sergeant frantically turned north on a narrow road rather than continuing east and up Laurel Mountain the way he had arrived. He kicked the horse's flanks unmercifully, swearing revoltingly, a constant pounding in his aching head. The horse stretched its neck out and ran, its hooves digging into the soft mud. He clung to the saddle horn, twisting around to see if anyone was following him. He didn't see anyone.

Back inside the log hotel, Boyd had heard the drum of hoof beats as the Sergeant had fled. He ran out on the front porch just in time to see him disappear up the pike. He ran to catch up his horse, but it shied from him, and it took him precious minutes to calm it and climb aboard. The clerk stood on the porch and watched Boyd ride after the fleeing man. He shook his head and returned to the desk.

By the time Boyd reached the center of town, the Sergeant was gone, but people milled about talking loudly and gesturing excitedly. The hotel clerk yelled to him, "He went that way," pointing to the narrow road that led out of town.

"Where does that road go?" Boyd asked, shouting over the din.

"Tunnelton. It goes to Tunnelton, about six miles. He might be heading for the railroad."

Boyd yelled his thanks and spurred his horse up the road. He'd have to be careful, he thought. He had no doubt the Sergeant would shoot him from ambush, back-shoot him if he had a chance. He pulled the horse back into a trot, scanning the road ahead. He could see the deep imprints in the mud made by the horse the Sergeant was riding. Judging by the distance between the tracks, he was running the horse pretty hard. The narrow valley and hillsides were cleared of trees and a few cows grazed, raising their heads to stare at him as he passed. The road paralleled the creek for a ways, and then turned upward into the hills. As the road steepened, and he gained altitude, the forest pressed in, deepening the gloom of the rainy day. He moved cautiously along, scanning the road ahead. He tensed, thinking the Sergeant could be hidden behind any of the huge trees that lined the road. He watched his horse's ears carefully.

Just as he topped a ridge, Boyd felt the breeze of a bullet as it snapped by his head, followed immediately by the boom of a musket. He pulled his rifle from its scabbard as he tumbled from the horse and crouched behind a tree. The horse stood with reins dangling, its head up. Boyd peered cautiously around the tree and saw a white plume of gun smoke hanging in the air. Nothing stirred. This wasn't good. The Sergeant could run, or he could simply wait until he had a clear shot, or just as bad, shoot Boyd's horse and leave him on foot. Boyd had no way of knowing what he would do. He listened carefully for the sound of a running horse but heard nothing. He waited for a few minutes, and then carefully circled around through the trees until he came to the spot he figured the shot had come from. He found scuff marks in the wet leaves where the Sergeant had waited for him. Walking along, he saw tracks that showed that the Sergeant had led his horse for a ways, then mounted and rode rapidly away. Boyd trotted back to his horse and then moved along the road cautiously. He soon came to open fields and a scattering of houses along the road. A short, sandy-haired man leaned over a fence that paralleled the road, watching him approach.

"Did you see a man ride by here just now?" Boyd asked.

"Ayah, I did. He was in a big hurry."

"How long ago was that?"

"Not more 'an half an hour, I'd guess. Why are you asking?"

"He's wanted by the sheriff. If you see him again, I'd stay away from him if I were you. He'd just as soon shoot you in the head as look at you," Boyd said.

"Well, thanks for tellin' me. I've got a wife and a passel of kids to take care of."

"How far is it to town?"

"Not more 'an two mile, I reckon."

Boyd thanked the man and rode on. With cleared fields on both sides of the road, he could see well ahead and clucked his horse into a trot. Before long, he topped a rise and could see the town of Tunnelton before him. The hillsides bounding the town were practically denuded of trees, and a ventilator tower had been constructed on the hill above the tunnel. A remnant of dark smoke trailed from it. A secondary railroad bed snaked its way from the main tracks below, up and over the hill. To Boyd's untrained eye, it looked unused and was too steep for a locomotive to climb, but it must have worked, he guessed. A great trench had been dug as an approach-way to the mouth of the tunnel.

He rode into town and stopped at the train depot. The man inside told him that the train had left only minutes before and from Boyd's description of the Sergeant, said he had bought a ticket to Cumberland. Boyd asked if the Sergeant had taken his horse with him, but was told that they didn't carry civilian's horses. "If the army wants to ship horses, we have to order a special car for them. Anyhow, we hardly ever have a civilian askin' to take their horses with them on the train." He looked at Boyd as if the idea were ridiculous.

Boyd was discouraged. He talked to the man for a few more minutes. "You said that he bought a ticket to Cumberland. Is there anywhere he could get off between here and there?"

"Oh yes, he could get off anywhere the train stops."

"Where would that be? I mean, what stops does the train make?"

"Well, there's Rowlesburg, an' Cranberry, an' Oakland, an'…"

Boyd interrupted, "Do the trains always stop at Rowlesburg?"

"Well, no, it all depends. If the army has a shipment, or men to deploy, or somebody gets a big delivery or something like that, the train stops. Otherwise, it doesn't stop if it doesn't need to."

"One last question and I'll let you get back to work. When's the next train to Rowlesburg?"

The man chuckled. "I'm afraid you're out of luck. Won't be one until tomorrow morning. And, it might not stop on its way through. Just depends on what's on it."

Boyd stepped out the door and onto the narrow platform that crowded against the tracks. He remembered the day, weeks ago, that he and the two women had ridden the train on their way to Kingwood.

It appeared to him that he had just gone in a big circle, a wild goose chase. He had thought the Sergeant was on his way out of the county, but it looked like he was headed back to Rowlesburg. That meant that he needed to get back to warn Frank and the women that the Sergeant was likely back in town.

Boyd led his horse to the livery stable where he and the women had rented the hack when they were here before. As livery stables went, it wasn't much, just a pole corral and a small wooden office. There were several sturdy-looking mules watching his approach, and the only horse in the corral was the one the Sergeant had stolen.

A man came out of the office and asked Boyd what he needed. "If you're wantin' a hack, I don't have any. All rented out. There's a revival goin' on at the church an' some people have come in fer it. I'm all out," he said again.

"No, I don't need a hack. But, thank you kindly anyway," Boyd said. "Where'd you get that horse out there in the corral?"

The man's eyes grew large, and he fiddled with his chin whiskers, suddenly nervous. "Is that your horse? I saw him wandering around, and he came over to the trough and got a drink. I caught him and put him in with the mules. Is he yours, mister? Honest, I didn't steal him. He just came by on his own. I planned to get hold of the sheriff if someone didn't claim him."

"Don't worry, he's not mine, but I know who he belongs to." Boyd briefly told him about the beating and theft and that he was trying to catch up with the man who did it. The liveryman sighed with relief. Boyd told him to keep the horse, and he'd let the sheriff know where it was. Someone would pick it up sooner or later.

"I need to get back to Rowlesburg right away. Can I ride down along the tracks? It's only six miles or so, isn't it?"

"Yeah, but you can't get there from here. There are several narrow bridges on the railroad between here and there, and of course, there're the two viaducts. They have walk-ways along the side, but I've never heard of anyone ridin' a horse across them. No, I wouldn't try that, but you can go up over the hill and down through the woods. There isn't much of a road, just a trail, really. It's not a lot farther than by the railroad tracks."

The man gave Boyd directions and he was soon on his way. It was a hard pull up the hill to the top and his horse was soon winded. The sky opened, and a steady rain fell. It had been a long day of riding, and both horse and man were tired. Dusk was falling as he followed the faint roadway down through the trees, along a roaring stream. He was surprised when he came out on the road that led down the river from Rowlesburg and could see steam rising from the smoldering campfires of the army encampment.

He stopped on his way through town to tell the sheriff what had happened, disappointed that the Sergeant was likely back. Then, he rode to Frank's house and re-told his unhappy story. They agreed that they'd need to keep close watch over the women and hope that the sheriff would soon find the Sergeant and put him away. By the time Boyd had stabled his horse and found his way to his cabin, he was exhausted. He stripped off his sodden clothes and climbed unto bed, pulling the bedclothes over him. He could hear the river roaring and grinding through the valley, and rain beat down on the cabin's tin roof.

* * * *

Sheriff Petrowski and one of his deputies walked across the muddy street and stepped onto the boardwalk in front of the dry goods store. They looked up at the large sign over the entrance that proclaimed it to be owned by Mr. J. Martin Tingle. A bell jangled as the sheriff opened the door, and they stepped inside.

A thin, baldheaded man rushed forward, smiling broadly. "What can I do for you, Sheriff?" he asked. "We just got some nice boots in if you're interested."

The two lawmen looked around the store, noting the shelves stacked with expensive stock. A woman stood browsing through a rack of dresses. She moved closer to the men, eavesdropping, her curiosity piqued. It wasn't every day that the sheriff came to town. The deputy picked up an elaborately decorated kerosene lamp, running his finger over the embossed glass base. The glass chimney teetered dangerously in its holder.

"Careful there, Deputy. That's an expensive item. Came all the way from Baltimore on the train. I'm afraid if you break it, it's yours," the clerk said.

The deputy carefully returned the lamp to the shelf. He turned back to the front door and stood impassively, waiting for the sheriff to continue.

"I'm looking for Mr. Tingle. Is he here?" the sheriff asked. "I have some questions for him."

"Oh, he hasn't come in yet. He should be here just any time now. He's the boss, so he doesn't come in 'til later on. I come in at seven o'clock to open up. He doesn't come in 'til later," he said.

The sheriff turned to the woman, who had edged even closer to hear what they were saying, and said, "Excuse me, ma'am, but this is official business. If you don't mind, would you step outside so we can talk in private?"

"Well, I swear, Sheriff. I don't think I've ever been treated like this in my life. I wasn't listening to your conversation," she said with faked exasperation.

"Yes, ma'am, but we won't be but a few minutes." He escorted her to the door and closed it firmly behind her. He hung a sign in the window that indicated the store was closed.

"Look here, Sheriff. You can't come in here and close the store just any time you want to. Mr. Tingle will have my hide if we miss some business."

The deputy took a menacing step toward the clerk, and he scurried behind the counter. The deputy stepped back to the door and grinned at the sheriff.

"While we're waiting for Mr. Tingle to arrive, I have a couple of questions for you. Have you ever seen a big, tough man in here talking to him?" He described the Sergeant. "Maybe they were back in his office or something."

The clerk's face reddened. "I've seen a lot of people talking to Mr. Tingle. What's this all about, Sheriff?"

"Just answer the question, please," the sheriff said calmly.

"Well, yes. A time or two. He came in here actin' like he owned the place. First time, he bought some clothes and wanted a pair of boots, but we didn't have anything that would fit him." The clerk hesitated. "And then he was here a time or two, back in the office. One time, there seemed to be some kind of disagreement, some yelling and a scuffle. When I asked Mr. Tingle if everything was all right, he seemed really upset. That was after that man had left by the back door. Who is he, anyway? Is that the man you've been searching all over town for?"

"All you need to know is that he's involved in some pretty nasty business, and I'd like to talk to him. One more question. What do you know about Mr. Tingle buying some timber land up on Little Wolf Creek?"

"I don't know nothin' about that. Mr. Tingle doesn't tell me anything about his business. He keeps all of his records locked up in the safe in his office, and I've never heard him talk about anything like that. What's that about, Sheriff?" the clerk asked.

Mr. Tingle stormed into the store, slamming the door behind him. He turned and jerked the closed sign from the window and tossed it aside. "What's this all about?" He glared at the clerk.

The clerk said quickly, "It's not my fault, Mr. Tingle. The sheriff did it. He came in here and closed the store and ran off one of our best customers. I didn't have anything to do with it."

Tingle turned toward the sheriff, and said, "Is that right, Sheriff? Did you do that? Why would you cause an honest merchant to lose business?"

"Just calm down, Tingle. I need answers to some questions. We can do it right here in front of your employee, or we can do it in your office. What'll it be?"

"I don't have to answer any of your questions, Sheriff. What's this about anyway?"

The sheriff took him by the arm and led him to the office door. He pointed a sausage-like finger at the clerk and said, "Stay!" and then he nodded to the deputy who put the closed sign back in the window and stood beside the clerk. The clerk moved as far away from the deputy as he could, his face pale.

The sheriff had Tingle sit in the visitors' chair, and he sat behind the desk. "Look here, Sheriff, that's my chair and desk. You have no right to barge in here and…"

The Sheriff slammed his hand on the desk, making Tingle jump. "You're in big trouble, Tingle. I want some answers, and I want them right now. What do you know about Frank Saunders' property up on Little Wolf Creek?"

Tingle's face blanched. "What do you mean? I don't know anything about Frank's business. Why would I?"

"Did you pay Jimmy Smith to change Frank's deed in the courthouse? What do you know about that?"

"I don't know anything about any deed," Tingle said, blustering. "What are you gettin' at? Are you accusing me of killing Jimmy?"

"I didn't say anything about Jimmy's killing. Since you raised the issue, what do you know about that? He was murdered and thrown in a pit like he was a dead cow or something."

Tingle sat quietly, his head down. "I don't know anything about any of this, Sheriff," he said without conviction.

"How in the world did you get tangled up in a mess like this? Whatever possessed you to think you could get away with stealing a man's property, as if no one was going to find out what you did?" the sheriff asked. "And, how did you ever get involved with a murderer and woman-beater like the Sergeant?"

"I don't know anything about him."

"Your clerk said he was in your office, and more than once."

"Well, he might have been. I see a lot of people. I've had lots of people in my office, and I can't keep track of all of them."

"You know that we've chased him all over creation, trying to catch him, don't you?"

"Yes, of course. Everyone in town knows you're after him. What does that have to do with me?"

The sheriff changed the subject abruptly, "Did you pay Ed in the clerk's office for information?" He glowered at Tingle, thrusting his chin toward him.

Tingle laughed. "Just about everyone in the county has paid him for information at one time or another. What does that have to do with the price of tea in China?"

"Now, look here, Tingle, don't get smart with me," the sheriff said, standing to tower over the seated man. "You specifically asked Ed to tell you if anyone was nosing around the clerk's office askin' about Frank's deed. Looks to me like you knew a lot about that property. Ed said he'd testify to that in a court of law."

"Now Sheriff," Tingle said heatedly, "that doesn't mean that I knew about the Sergeant killing Jimmy."

"So, you do admit that you knew that it was the Sergeant that killed him, don't you?"

J. Martin Tingle sat mutely with his arms folded over his chest, staring into the distance. A nervous tic caused his eye to jump, and his face became even whiter. "I didn't mean for him to kill Jimmy," he said in a quiet voice. "I just wanted to scare him so he wouldn't tell what we had done."

The sheriff shook his head and said, "Stand up and turn around, Tingle. I'm gonna put the manacles on you."

Tingle's shoulders slumped, and then he stood and put his hands behind his back. "What am I going to tell my wife and kids?"

\* \* \* \*

Boyd and Lexus walked down to the center of town, looking in store windows, and Lexus greeted friends she had made since arriving in town. The rain had let up, but there were puddles and mud everywhere. Lexus took his arm as they strolled on the sidewalk. They could hear the roar of the river over the clamor of the town. A train's whistle sounded on Salt Lick Creek as it pulled up the grade to Cranberry. They relaxed on a bench in front of a store, enjoying the lull between rainstorms. A shaft of sunlight spilled through a break in the clouds and briefly lit the street with a feeble light. Lexus pulled Boyd's arm closer to her.

A man ran up the street shouting. "I saw him! I saw him! He was sneakin' back in town along the railroad tracks."

"Over here, man," Boyd shouted. "Who did you see?"

"That renegade the sheriff's been looking for. I saw him!"

"Just where was he? Where is he now?" Boyd asked, his voice rising with excitement.

"He saw me and turned around and started walking back up the tracks real fast-like. Up that way." He pointed up the tracks toward the viaducts.

"You stay here, Lexus. I'm going after him. Go get the sheriff," he ordered.

"I'm going with you! I want him captured as bad as you do," she said.

"No! I don't want you near him! Do as I say, and go tell the sheriff."

"You don't order me around, Boyd Houston! I'm going, too."

Boyd said to the man, "Go find the sheriff, and tell him what you told me. I don't have time to argue." He softened his tone and said to Lexus, "Please stay here. I'll find him, and the sheriff can help me capture him." He turned on his heel and began running toward the railroad tracks. People along the street pulled aside making way for him as he ran with his pistol in his hand. He turned onto the railroad bed, trying to adjust his pace with the spacing between ties, stumbling occasionally. His breath came in gasps as he ran, looking ahead, hoping for a glimpse of the Sergeant. He stumbled again and almost went down onto the rough ballast that supported the ties and rails. He righted himself and plowed on.

Far ahead, the Sergeant trotted along the tracks. Damn, he thought, that man in town had seen him. He'd heard him yelling his lungs out as he ran back into town. He'd been lucky before, not being seen, but the jig was up now. Half of the town would be on his tail in no time. Where could he go? The viaducts were just ahead, and the Army pickets there would stop him for sure. There wasn't another easy way to get across Tray Run. He could scramble down the ravine and up the other side, but they'd see him for sure, and besides, the stream was flooded and impossible to cross. It would be an easy shot for them. He picked up his pace, looking over his shoulder. Why was this happening to him now? He had a pocket full of money and could go anywhere he wanted, but he'd just had to make one last try for that damned woman. It was all her fault.

Boyd ran as fast as he could, keeping an eye on the tracks ahead. He remembered riding the train over this section, but couldn't remember exactly how far it was to the viaducts and the soldiers stationed there. But, it looked to him like the Sergeant was boxed in unless he left the tracks. If he did, it was going to be a long row to hoe. If he tried to go over the mountain, he'd be pinned against the cliffs, and if he dropped down to the river road, the soldiers would see him. Surely by now the sheriff was sending his deputies that way.

Boyd was deep in thought when a bullet whipped by his head, imbedding itself in a tree. The crack of the gun reached him, and he caught a glimpse of the Sergeant up ahead. Boyd dove aside, lying flat alongside the rails, and a second bullet sailed harmlessly over his head. He jumped to his feet and began a cautious approach along the brush that overhung the right-of-way. He figured that the Sergeant's pistol was good for five or six shots, depending if all the chambers were loaded, but then, he might have a second gun.

The Sergeant swore when his shots missed the man following him. It was Houston, he was pretty sure. He moved along cautiously, watching for pickets ahead, looking over his shoulder as he ran. He was tiring, and he breathed heavily, regretting sitting around too much, eating too much greasy food, and downing too many glasses of whisky. He came to the first viaduct, thankful that there were no pickets in sight. The small tributary below roared with whitewater as it plunged down the steep mountain. Some distance behind him he could hear his pursuer running in the gravel. He cautiously stepped onto the viaduct, hunching over as he made his way across, his shoulders tense, waiting for a bullet to strike him. On the other side, he paused behind some brush along the tracks, taking aim at the man who approached. He fired, causing dirt and cinders to fly near his feet.

Boyd jumped aside and stepped behind a large hemlock that clung to the mountainside. He could just see the Sergeant on the other side of the viaduct. It was a momentary standoff, one man on each side, neither daring to cross, and just then, the skies opened, and cold rain poured down upon them. Boyd put his pistol back under his belt and pulled his jacket closed as he tried to keep it dry.

"Is that you over there, Houston? I thought I'd killed you long ago. Had Hank drop you in Grapevine Cave. How'd you get out of that?" the Sergeant yelled.

"I remember you. You had someone else do your dirty work back then," Boyd yelled across the chasm. "It didn't work out very well then either."

The Sergeant laughed like a maniac as he yelled back, "Your woman is a sweet little thing. I had my way with her, you know. An' I'll live to have her again an' then I'll cut her damned throat. You just wait and see." He fired another shot at Boyd that caused bark to fly from the hemlock, and then he crept away toward the Tray Run viaduct. The rain poured from the leaden sky, and vapor rose from the mountainside, casting a ghostly pallor on the dripping forest.

Boyd held back for a few minutes, afraid to try to cross the viaduct least he be caught out in the open half way across. He yelled at the Sergeant again, trying to bait him into answering, but he didn't respond. He gritted his teeth and ran as fast as he could, heaving a great sigh of relief when he reached the other side. He followed boot tracks in the mud just filling with rainwater as he jogged up the tracks.

The Sergeant approached the end of Tray Run Viaduct carefully, noticing smoke rising from the blockhouse on the other side. With any luck, the guards were inside, out of the rain. Just as he was about to set foot onto the structure, he saw movement in the trees near the blockhouse. A picket shook the water from his hat and then hunched miserably under a piece of canvas he'd rigged between two trees. He had a clear view of the viaduct. "Damn," the Sergeant swore. He was boxed in. He couldn't get across the bridge, and he couldn't go back. Even if he got the best of Houston, there were sure to be others from town, hot on his trail including the sheriff and his deputies. He looked down into Tray Run gorge and what he saw was even more frightening than the torrent under the first viaduct. It was unbelievable how much water was pouring off the mountain. The flood raged over boulders and tore at the tree trunks that lined the stream before plunging from one waterfall to the next on its way downward. He hid behind a tree and waited for Houston to approach.

Boyd crept from one tree trunk to another, as he followed the footprints. The mist was getting so thick that he had difficulty seeing the railroad tracks ahead. He paused frequently to listen. The wind was picking up, and the rain fell in sheets, whipping away over the valley. The trees swayed and knocked together, groaning in the gale, their leaves flapping. Just ahead he could see the brighter opening over the gorge. He moved along, alert for the slightest movement. A bullet plucked at his jacket sleeve, and the sound of the shot and the smoke from the gun sailed away into the void. He saw the Sergeant standing on the near edge of the viaduct, his pistol extended for another shot. Boyd pulled his gun from his belt and fired, a muffled pop indicating his powder was wet. The ball struck well short of the mark. He pulled the trigger again, and the hammer fell on a wet cap making a sickening clack–the gun didn't fire.

The Sergeant cackled and laughed. "Yer done for, Houston. Yer powder is wet. You're mine." He walked slowly toward Boyd, his gun ready. "I'm going to take my time with you. I'm going to shoot you in the knees, then in the elbows, and then I'll put one between your eyes. Five for five. I'll teach you to fool with me."

The picket on the far side of the viaduct shouted at them, asking what was going on, but the two men ignored him.

Boyd lowered his head and with a roar, threw his useless gun and charged the Sergeant. The Sergeant fired, and the bullet struck Boyd in the shoulder, spinning him around. He fell heavily to the ground, blood leaking from the wound. As the Sergeant approached, Boyd tackled his knees, trying to drag him down. The Sergeant laughed and pistol-whipped him, stepping back as Boyd fell face-down in the mud. Boyd raised himself to all fours, spit blood onto the ground and tried to crawl toward the laughing man.

"Come on, big man. You want to try that again? Come on, let's see what you've got," the Sergeant taunted him. He kicked Boyd in the side, rolling him over onto his back. The Sergeant stood over him like the winner in a dog fight and pointed the pistol at his head. "Say goodbye to the world, Houston," the Sergeant said, and pulled back the hammer.

Lexus' bloodcurdling scream caused the Sergeant to whirl around just as she raised a wooden club into the air like a man splitting wood. She struck the Sergeant on the top of his head, causing the pistol to spin away. He fell to his knees then turned to face her. "Good God! Where'd you come from?"

Lexus circled the kneeling man cautiously, the club held over her shoulder like a baseball bat. "I'm going to kill you for what you did to me," she screamed. She approached and swung at him, but he caught the brunt of the attack on his forearms, protecting his head. He fell backward into the mud, crabbing away from her.

"You get away from me! Leave me alone," he shrieked. He shook his head trying to clear away the cobwebs.

Boyd stirred in the ditch beside the tracks, blood and mud covering his face and hair. He tried to stand, but fell onto his knees, his head down, one arm hanging uselessly at his side.

The Sergeant looked first at Boyd, and then Lexus. "Lemme go, an' I'll never bother you again. I'll just walk away 'n' you can take your feller to the doctor."

"I'm not about to let you go. I'm going to finish this here and now," she snarled. "I don't want you coming for me again some dark night." She charged the cringing man, striking him on the shoulder, sending him sprawling. She stepped in close to him and raised the club to strike again. The Sergeant lunged for her and grasped her ankle as she struck his back. He jerked her to the ground and crawled on top of her, pinning her arms cruelly. He flipped her onto her stomach and twisted her arms behind her back, grinding her into the cinders. Holding her crossed wrists with one hand and a knee in her back, he drew his knife from its sheath. He hooted in triumph, hitting the back of her head with the heel of the knife. She sagged into the mud, her eyes and nose filling.

Boyd struggled up from the ditch and grasped the Sergeant by the hair, his wound feeling as if a hot poker were stuck in him. He pulled the Sergeant off Lexus. The two men struggled and fought in the rain and mud. Boyd grabbed the man's jacket in a death grip, and the Sergeant stabbed at his arm with the knife. But Boyd didn't release his grasp on the man, drawing him closer. Lexus grabbed the club again and struck the Sergeant's wrist repeatedly until he dropped the knife. She frantically searched in the mud for it.

The Sergeant jumped to his feet and tumbled over the railroad embankment, desperate to get away, pulling Boyd down with him.

The pair slid down the steep bank toward the raging stream, and the Sergeant kicked at him, trying to free himself from Boyd's grasp. Lexus followed them screaming at Boyd to let him go, but he held on. The Sergeant grabbed at saplings and tree roots to stop their plunge toward Tray Run, but Boyd clutched at his clothing and used his weight to drag the frantic man down. Lexus grabbed at Boyd's jacket, lost her footing, and fell with them toward the swirling torrent. Two pickets arrived just in time to see them sliding down the steep embankment.

The three desperate people plunged into the raging water, locked in a lethal embrace. It sucked at their legs and arms and pulled their bloodied, clawing fingers from the rocks and trees along the stream. Lexus inhaled a lungful of water and rose above the surface to cough and gag, causing her to lose her grasp on Boyd. As the raging water swept the two men away, locked together, she felt Boyd's hand on her back, pushing her toward the shore. She dragged herself from the stream and scrambled along its bank just in time to see the two men, separated now, be swept over a cataract, their arms flailing weakly above their heads. She crawled down the steep gorge, brush and brambles tearing at her hands and face, blood running from her ruined fingers, down the mountainside along the stream toward the road that paralleled the river. She caught glimpses of the men tumbling from one waterfall to the next like rag dolls, the roar of the falling water deafening in her ears.

She arrived in time to see them carried across the flooded road and into the maul of the mud-gorged river full of trees, roots, dead animals and nail-studded lumber. She looked on in horror at the muddy torrent. The Sergeant was nowhere to be seen. Boyd rose from the muddy depths, and as the angry river carried him away, his hand raised toward the sky, and then he, too, was gone, into the narrows.

Lexus dropped to her knees, a mournful keening escaping from her lips. She rocked back in forth in the mud, her arms wrapped around her body, and an unspeakable agony ripped away her breath. Later, as dusk fell, the sheriff found her, still on her knees, rocking and weeping silently. Her eyes had a wild look, and her hair swirled in a sodden mass about her head. She shivered such that her teeth rattled.

\* \* \* \*

Lexus sat on the porch of Boyd's cabin with Abe at her feet. The river ran back within its banks, as ducks paddled across its placid current. Driftwood and trash rose in piles around trees and rocks, some as high as her head. Brilliant sunshine dappled the trees, highlighting their vivid fall colors. She lifted Boyd's satchel to her lap, dreading the task of going through his belongings. The sheriff had said that since he didn't have any relatives, she should be the one to do it. But, she put it aside and stroked Abe's ears. She wasn't ready yet.

She held out hope that Boyd had somehow survived the river. He was a strong man, and if anyone could do it, he could. She knew that he had been grievously wounded, but maybe someone had rescued him and nursed him back to health. It could be that he had survived the river and was making his way back to her. He'd come walking up the road, that silly grin on his face, wondering what was for supper. She placed her hands in her lap, noticing that her nails had almost regrown, and the scratches and bruises were gone. Oh, why hadn't she been able to save him?

She stepped from the porch and walked along the river, Abe by her side, somehow sharing the sorrow she bore. She marveled at the piles of sand and rocks that the flood had deposited, and at the patches of goldenrod and fall asters that bloomed in the aftermath. She sat on a rock, hugging her knees, remembering the first time she'd seen Boyd, so handsome and tall, limping a little from his wounds. She'd flirted with him shamelessly, but it hadn't worked out for them. And, then, he'd gone away, and she thought she'd never see him again.

She remembered Boyd holding her in the night, high in the mountains, as she dreamed and fought that appalling man who had attacked her. He had whispered to her, trying to make everything better. She remembered that summer day on Cannon Hill when they had shared their most intimate thoughts, and the day they had spent together on Laurel Mountain. Would her memories be enough to last a lifetime?

She remembered Rachel telling her just days ago, that when she'd first arrived with Boyd, she'd been jealous of Lexus for having a beau, and she had none. Rachel had cried when she'd said it, feeling guilty that now she had a beau and Lexus had none. Lexus had held her and smoothed her hair and told her everything was all right.

She returned to the porch and sat in the rocker. She took a big breath and lifted the satchel onto her lap again. She opened it slowly as if a snake might be inside and began removing his belongings one at a time. She withdrew the dog-eared letter she had sent him and opened it carefully. Her eyes misted over as she read it. Oh, why had she written it? If she'd trusted her first inclination and not mailed it, he'd be alive now. He'd be down in South Carolina somewhere on his fishing boat, living in the village by the sea. He had helped her simply because she had asked. She closed her eyes and took a deep breath, choking back the lump that had arisen in her throat.

There was an extra pair of pants and a couple of shirts, some socks, a shaving kit and a comb. She held the shirts to her face, breathing in his smell, remembering his warmth in her arms. She remembered the simple pleasure of walking in town with her arm in his, and the statement that made—she belonged with him. She remembered the thrill she felt when he touched the back of her hand with his fingertips. A simple touch, yet profound in its meaning.

Tucked in a side pocket of the satchel, she found a tintype of a handsome man in a fisherman's hat and a pretty woman with a little boy at her side. She found a locket of hair tied with a worn silver ribbon. She remembered him telling her about his mother, an honor to hear, a thing so personal and sad. She touched the image of the little boy with her fingertips.

In the bottom of the satchel, she found a money belt, heavy with coins. The profit from the sale of the cottage and boat, she thought. He'd told her about the sale on their way up through the mountains. She'd ask the sheriff to take care of that.

There were other items, but she replaced them all in the satchel and snapped it closed. She felt guilty looking at his personal belongings, thinking that any day now, he'd come back, and she'd have to explain why she'd been going through his things.

The river had taken Boyd, but she just knew that he'd survived. The sheriff and his deputies had searched the riverbanks for days— as far away as Dunkard's Bottom. They hadn't found him. Other people had died in the flood, as well as a soldier who had selflessly tried to rescue a friend who was being swept away. They had found some of their bodies, including the Sergeant's, but others, like Boyd, had gone missing. It was a dreadful thing. She felt as if she could *will* him to be alive, and as long as she believed, he'd not be dead.

As she rocked in Boyd's chair, the rattle of a wagon interrupted her musings as it pulled up beside the cabin. A tall man in a dark suit stepped down and came toward her. As he approached the porch, he removed his hat and smiled sadly. "You Miss Saunders?" he asked. "The sheriff said I'd find you here."

Lexus stood, the satchel dropping from her lap to the floor. "Yes, I'm Lexus Saunders. What can I do for you?"

The man hung his head and said, "I hate this. I hate that I might be bringing you some bad news. A body was found along the river way down about Albrightsville. No one seems to be able to identify him, so I brought him here. He's in the back of the wagon, wrapped in canvas. I put some ice on him to…er, you know. I don't know how to say this other than just come out with it. He's in pretty bad shape, his face mostly gone from his time in the river." The man's long face was lined with sadness. "I wonder if you'd be willing to look and see if you know him."

Lexus grasped the porch post, her face ashen. She swallowed the lump in her throat again that seemed to be a permanent part of her. "I...I don't know if I'd recognize him either."

"Yes ma'am, as I said, I really hate this, but I don't know what else to do. If you could step down here, it'd only take a minute. I'm really sorry to ask."

Lexus stumbled down the steps and approached the wagon. Her eyes glistened, as a raven lit in a nearby tree and called–*quark, quark, quark*. Lexus looked at the dark bird and wondered if it was truly a sign of good fortune. She steadied herself with a hand on the side of the wagon, and said, "Show me his right hand. If it's Boyd, there will be a rope scar."

The man pulled away the canvas, exposing the corpse's right hand. Lexus slumped to the ground, her knees giving way. The hand was without blemish. Her shoulders shook as she sobbed with relief. She raised her face to the sky and said a silent prayer of thanks. The raven bobbed its head and glided away through the trees.

# AFTERWORD

AN EARLY WINTER snow sifted down on the one room school house that sat on a rise overlooking the town. A sudden gust of wind rattled the windows and blew swirls of fine snow through cracks around their wooden frames. Lexus and her students had worked hard forcing strips of cloth into the cracks, using butter knives she had brought from home. Some of the cracks had been overlooked. Her students had made a game of it, laughing and chattering as they worked, and Lexus had used the time to get to know them better. They had talked and giggled, telling about their families and friends.

Now, she paused teaching long enough to shovel more coal into the glowing Burnside stove that stood at the back of the room. Soon, she'd have to put on her coat and make a trip to the coal bin behind the school. She shivered at the thought. The snow was piling up outside, and she planned to send the students home early. They had already missed one day of school because of the early storm, but she was worried about their safety.

As her students worked on their assignments, Lexus took time to tidy up the cloak room near the front door. She stooped to pick up a coat that had fallen from its peg and put it back in its place. She straightened a row of lunch buckets, arranging them neatly on their shelf. Some were fancy and store bought, but many parents had made-do with whatever they could find. Lard buckets were favorites. One student, a first-grader, often came to school without any lunch at all. I'll have to organize the students' mothers to provide hot lunches for *all* of the children when I have a few spare moments, she thought. She added it to a long wish list she had compiled. It got longer with each day.

The morning went by quickly, as it always did. Lexus taught the younger children their arithmetic lessons, while the older children read an assignment in their primers. Later, the older children helped the others with their practice problems and then read them a story. The older students loved helping the younger ones, swelling with pride when they were looked up to as if they were teachers. Lexus circulated around the room giving special attention to those who tended to lag behind. She was proud of the progress they were making.

They stopped work for lunch, and after gulping down their food, the older children put on their coats and hats and went outside to play fox and goose in the snow. Lexus stayed inside and played games with the younger ones. Soon, the children outside grew cold and came trooping back into the classroom. They held their gloved hands to the stove and watched the steam rise from them—the smell of wet clothing spread throughout the room. They hung up their coats and left a pile of wet boots for Lexus to straighten. Their cheeks were red with the cold, and their wet socks sagged around their ankles.

She herded the children back to their seats and got them settled. Lexus sat on the edge of her desk and read to them from a novella written by Charles Dickens, a new author. It was called *A Christmas Carol* and had been written only a few years ago. Lexus felt fortunate that Uncle Frank had bought the book for her birthday, having it shipped on the train from Baltimore. She was planning to make the story into a play to be performed for the students' parents. She was expected to have a Christmas party for the community, and the play would be the main feature.

A few of the older students nodded knowingly as she read. Some had books and newspapers at home, but most did not. The younger students sat with rapt attention. Big eyes followed her every word and gesture. For a change, they were as quiet as mice. Soon, one first grade boy, sitting near the stove, began to nod off. Lexus encouraged him to get a drink of water and move to another seat farther away from the heat. When she reached a good place to stop for the day, she put the book aside amid groans and complaints from her audience. They would resume the story tomorrow.

The students cheered when Lexus told them that the school day would be cut short, and they could go home early. They crowded to the cloak room, struggling to get their coats and hats, jostling each other good naturedly. They sat on the floor and pulled on their boots and soon were dressed for the walk home. The older children helped the younger ones and took them by their hands to make their way through the snow and into town. Lexus stood on the porch and watched them until they were out of sight.

She pulled her shawl closely around her shoulders and shivered. A raven flew out of the swirling snow and lit in the schoolyard, searching for scraps of food left by the children. It walked through the snow, occasionally springing into the air as if frightened by something on the ground, only to walk on as if nothing had happened. Its mate landed beside it, their black feathers glistening against the white snow.

She returned to the classroom, closed the door against the chill air and began cleaning the room. When she had finished, she sat behind her desk, took out a pad and pen and began work on the next day's lessons. She worked diligently until the plans were done. She put them aside and straightened the books and papers on her desk. She put on her coat, carried the coal scuttle to the coal bin behind the school building and filled it. Back inside, she banked the stove so they'd have a warm fire the next day, tamping the coal down with the back of the shovel. She looked around the classroom, checked that all was in order and stepped outside onto the porch, locking the door behind her. The wind had fallen, and snow fell in a silent curtain around her. It clung to the hemlocks and oaks, weighing down their branches. The air was perfectly calm, and the town was silent. Lexus marveled at the beauty of the winter day and caught a few of the large flakes with her hands.

As she raised her face to the snow, she heard the muffled plod of hooves. A horse and snow-covered rider materialized from the gloom. He slumped in the saddle, clutching the saddle horn with both hands. The horse stopped, its nostrils steaming in the cold air. Boyd slid from the saddle and stood unsteadily before her, his face as pale as an invalid's.

"Oh!" Lexus whispered, "I knew you'd come. Welcome home."